Barbara at her Best

The Army Cadets

C.R. Cummings

Also By
CHRISTOPHER CUMMINGS

The Green Idol of Kanaka Creek

Ross River Fever

Train to Kuranda

The Mudskipper Cup

Davey Jones's Locker

Below Bartle Frere

Airship Over Atherton

Cockatoo

The Cadet Corporal

Stannary Hills

Coast of Cape York

Kylie and the Kelly Gang

Behind Mt. Baldy

The Cadet Sergeant Major

Cooktown Christmas

Secret in the Clouds

The Word of God

The Cadet Under-Officer

Through the Devil's Eye

The Smiley People

*Barbara at her Best

Barbara at her Best

The Army Cadets

C.R. Cummings

DoctorZed
Publishing
www.doctorzed.com

Published 2018 by DoctorZed Publishing

DoctorZed Publishing books may be ordered through booksellers or by contacting:

DoctorZed Publishing
10 Vista Ave
Skye, South Australia 5072
www.doctorzed.com

ISBN: 978-0-6483421-9-9 (hc)
ISBN: 978-0-6483421-8-2 (sc)
ISBN: 978-0-9873452-5-7 (ebk)

National Library of Australia Cataloguing-in-Publication entry

Author: Cummings, C. R., author.
Title: Barbara at her best / Christopher Cummings.
ISBN: 9780648342199 (hardcover)
Series: Cummings, C. R. The army cadets.
Target Audience: For young adults.
Subjects: Adventure stories, Australian.
Military cadets--Queensland--Fiction.

Cover image © Scott Zarcinas

Printed in Australia, UK & USA

DoctorZed Publishing rev. date: 28/06/2018

Dedication

This book, while a work of fiction, is respectfully dedicated to all those members of Australia's armed services who have lost their lives while training to defend this wonderful country.

And especially to the 15 members of the Special Air Service Regiment and the 3 army air crew from 5th Aviation Regiment who lost their lives in the tragic crash of two Blackhawk helicopters on the High Range Training Area west of Townsville on the 12th of June 1996.

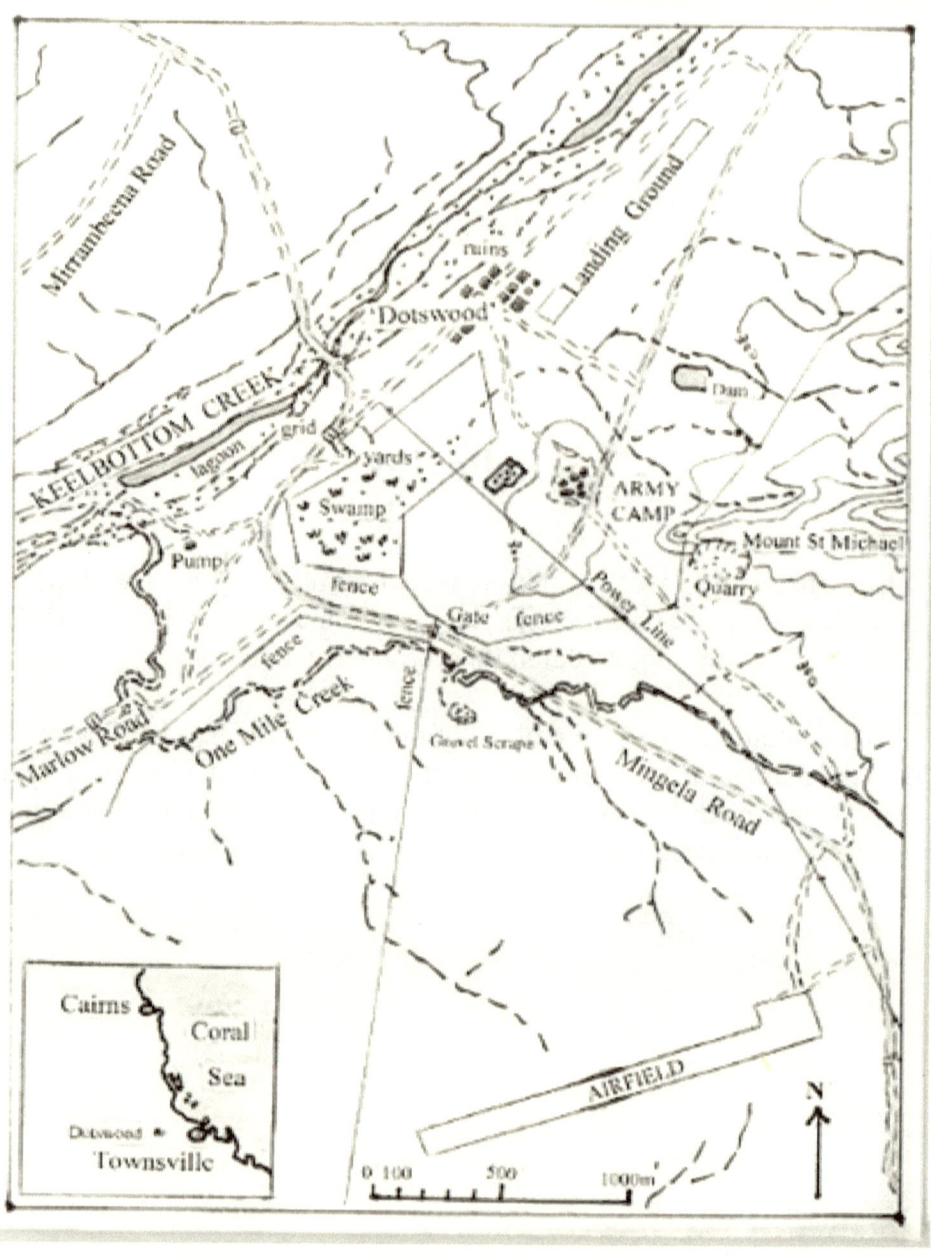

Chapter 1

NIGHT NAVEX

North Queensland, Australia
1st October
Hot
Dry
Sunset at Dotswood, Townsville Field Training Area
Day 3 of the Army Cadet's annual camp

Cadet Under-Officer Barbara Brassington, 17 years old, commander of Number 4 Platoon, the senior platoon in her cadet company, stood up and looked around. With her were her platoon sergeant, Cadet Sgt Dan Russell, and the Company Quartermaster Sergeant, Sgt Tracey Rowley. A hundred metres to her left-front, clearly visible through the open savannah woodland, was the old wooden bridge over One Mile Creek. Two figures could be seen seated there: her friend CUO Fiona Davies, commander of 3 Platoon, and Fiona's sergeant, Sgt Dave Blockey. Both groups had small UHF radios and were acting as Check Points for a Night Navigation Exercise.

The exercise involved twenty-five small groups from two cadet units: Barbara's own unit from Cairns and 130 Army Cadet Unit from Townsville. Each group of five or six cadets was led by a corporal and had to navigate by map and compass from check point to check point. In all there were twelve check points, each staffed by two or three older cadets or by adult staff. Each patrol was to follow a different route with six legs to it, to cover approximately two kilometres. Thus, the patrols were to zig-zag from check point to check point, often crossing each others' paths. The whole exercise was in dry, fairly open country.

The nearest adults to Barbara's group were two Officers of Cadets; a male and a female, both lieutenants. They sat in a Land Rover about two hundred and fifty metres to her right front, out on the Mingela Road. The Mingela Road was a gravel road that ran roughly East-West across her front. The small bridge was on a rough vehicle track that ran from the small gravel scrape where Barbara was to the road. The safety vehicle where the Officers of Cadets waited was parked near a dip where the Mingela Road crossed One Mile Creek. Between Barbara and One Mile Creek was a gentle down slope covered with a scattering of ironbarks and a carpet of sun-dried, knee-high grass. The creek itself was nothing but a dry, dusty gully with steep sides.

The nearest town is forty kilometres away along the gravel road. It is the tiny settlement of Mingela: a pub, railway siding and a few houses. Thirty-five kilometres the other way the gravel road joins a bitumen road that runs inland from the coast to the dry interior of North Queensland. A hundred kilometres to the East along that bitumen road is the sea and the city of Townsville. But Dotswood is in the 'Inland': hot, dry, savannah woodland; mostly flat, the creeks dry for most of the year. The only high ground visible was the two-hundred-metre bulk of Mount St Michael. Barbara could see it through the trees and knew it was about a kilometre and a half away. To her it looked very rugged: a bare covering of scattered trees and with numerous rocks poking up through the sparse blanket of brown grass.

The whole area is part of a vast army training area, a huge expanse of bush called the Townsville Field Training Area: an area the size of a European country but without any towns and with only that one bitumen road crossing it. All the remainder is dry Australian bush: flat plains and ranges of rugged hills crossed by a few rough vehicle tracks. There are no permanent inhabitants within thirty-five kilometres, and these only a few 'Rangers' based at 'Range Control'.

Dotswood: a harsh, forbidding place which Barbara did not particularly like. All her previous annual camps had been beside the Bunyip River, seventy kilometres to the southwest. She liked the Bunyip River. The river bed in particular was very pleasant: green grass, shade, flowing water. Here at Dotswood it was just dry grass seared by the blazing sun. Even the trees seemed to droop with the heat.

She took off her hat and wiped perspiration from her face. As she did the last rays of the sun gleamed on her short red hair, making it shine like burnished copper. Tracey looked up from stirring a cup of coffee. Glancing at Barbara she said, "You are badly sunburnt Barbara."

Barbara nodded and fanned herself. "I know. This is the hottest camp we have ever had."

"We are a week or two later than usual," Tracey replied.

That was true. Normally the camp was in the last week of September, but a combination of circumstances had led to the school holidays being a week later in the year. The cadet camp was in the first week of the school holidays. As all the cadets were High School students who only did cadets for a few hours each week, with weekend camps, this was important. October was well into the 'Dry', that season of high temperatures and no rain that extended through until December in this part of Northern Australia.

Barbara was a '4th Year' and she had now reached the highest rank possible for a cadet. She was very proud of that. Being an army cadet was an important part of her life. She knew it had given her purpose, direction and self-confidence at a critical time. Now she wanted to give something back and was very keen to help the younger cadets.

The three cadets had walked to their Check Point only half an hour earlier and their OC, Major Conkey, had just left them after checking they were in the right place. Barbara did not resent him checking as she knew from hard experience that nothing caused more trouble on a night Navex than a Check Point in the wrong place. She had no desire to spend half the night searching the bush for lost patrols. This was even more so in this area, which seemed to have an unusual number of snakes. These were mostly 'Browns' of various types and obviously poisonous. The previous day Barbara had almost stepped on one and she shuddered at the memory of that half-metre of tail slithering into a tuft of grass.

Still fanning herself Barbara turned to look at the Gravel Scrape. This was only a shallow depression about fifty metres long by thirty wide. The gravel had been scooped out some years before, leaving a shallow depression about three or four metres deep, exposing yellowish clayey soil. The back edge was a crumbled 'cut'. Beyond it was a low, rocky rise covered with a thicket of prickly bushes and gnarled and stunted little trees.

Making a face to show her opinion of the place Barbara sat down again and resumed sipping the cup of cordial she had opted to have after eating her canned meal. As she did the last of the sunlight went. While she and the others packed their cooking gear in their basic webbing twilight set in. Barbara breathed a sigh of relief. She had endured quite enough sun for one day.

"Isn't it quiet?" Tracey commented.

Sgt Russell answered. "Very. This is a funny place. There are hardly any birds."

Barbara hadn't noticed that but, in the two days they had been there, she had noted there were almost no animals. "I haven't seen a single wallaby or emu," she said.

"I saw a wallaby at the rifle range," Sgt Russell offered.

They all laughed at that. On the first day they had travelled the three hundred and fifty kilometers from Cairns to Townsville and done a range shoot with the Steyr rifle at the Mt Stuart Range. During the shoot a wallaby had nonchalantly hopped out of the surrounding bush and across the mowed clearing of the rifle range. The cadets had not been allowed to fire but it drew the sarcastic comment that the soldiers must be rotten shots if that was what the local wildlife thought of their marksmanship!

Darkness set in, still and warm but with the temperature dropping noticeably. *Semi-desert climate: hot days; cool nights,* Barbara thought, remembering a Geography lesson by Major Conkey, who in his normal life was also one of her teachers.

At last 1900 hours came around and the exercise began. They were informed by radio that the first patrols were now on their way. Even so it was a kilometre from where the companies were camped astride the road to the army camp and it took over an hour before the first group arrived. They came from the Bridge, and could be heard before they could be seen, as they stumbled over logs, washouts and rock in the grass.

It was 4 Section from their unit, led by Cpl Sharon Morrow. She was a competent navigator and was able to quickly plot the next position given to her by Barbara as a Grid Reference. With a cadet holding a torch to light up her map Sharon quickly ruled a line and used her protractor to calculate the Grid Bearing. On her notebook she rapidly and correctly converted it to a Magnetic Bearing (In North Queensland by subtracting the Magnetic Variation). Satisfied that the bearing was correct (they were heading for a gate near the base of Mount St Michael) Barbara allowed the patrol to leave.

By then the next patrol was arriving. That patrol had crossed One Mile Creek halfway between the Dip and the Bridge, with a lot of grumbling and noise. Its commander was Cpl Halyday leading 10 Section from Barbara's own platoon.

"Bloody hell!" Halyday cried, "That creek is a bugger to cross! The sides are bloody vertical."

Barbara agreed. She had looked at the creek in daylight. It was only five metres wide, its banks lined with a tangle of long grass and rubber vine, but the sides were two or three metres of steep, eroded, bare clay. During the safety briefing the cadets had been warned to go slow and use their torches if they needed to but Cpl Halyday admitted it was the thought of snakes lurking in the long grass, more than the effort of climbing down and up, that had caused him concern.

His patrol had come from a power pole near the army camp and were to go to the Bridge for their next leg so that was easy. Even so Barbara made him work out the bearing correctly. As the aim of the exercise was to train the cadets to use the compass at night it was set by Cadet Nolan, who then led the way off northwards.

No sooner had they departed than another patrol arrived, this time from the safety vehicle at the Dip. It was 1 Section of 130 ACU led by Cpl Kim Auckland. They were on their third leg as well and were going well. Barbara knew most of the 130 ACU corporals as they had been on their promotion course at the Bunyip River Army Camp at the same time as she had been doing her CUOs Course the previous December. For just a moment Barbara dwelt on that experience and then shuddered. It had led to a gruelling ordeal where she had been kidnapped, almost raped, escaped and marched alone and naked cross-country for 30 kilometres through similar country.

After Cpl Auckland's patrol had departed there was a lull for twenty minutes. Sgt Russell wanted to brew a coffee on his hexamine stove, but Barbara vetoed this.

"No fires," she replied. "That makes it too easy for the navigators. Then they don't need skill. They just walk to the light."

Three patrols all arrived from different directions just before 2030 hours. They were all from 130 ACU: 3 Section led by Cpl Candy Dickson, 4 Section led by Cpl Shane Brady, and 5 Section led by Cpl Warren. Barbara liked Warren, who was a cheerful, intelligent Kiwi; but she disliked both of the others. Candy Dickson she disliked because of the rumours about her behaviour on the promotion course.

Shane Brady had an entirely different effect on Barbara. He was a ruggedly handsome lad with dark curly hair, two years younger than her.

What bothered her was the way he looked at her. Barbara had very long, shapely legs and a pair of very prominent breasts, about which she was quite self-conscious. Now he seemed to keep glancing at them while he worked on his calculations.

Barbara felt uneasy and glanced down to check that her top button was done up. Satisfied that it was she sat in a hunched posture to make her body less noticeable. Brady finished his sums and showed them to Barbara, giving her a challenging smile as he did. She could only return a wry face and tell him to get going.

But he did not make her feel like a sex object the way the next corporal's leering gaze did. He was Cpl Steiner from 130 ACU. After he had gone she whispered to Tracey, "I don't like him. I hate the way he runs his eyes over you as though he is mentally undressing you."

"He's a creep!" Tracey agreed.

"What did you say?" Sgt Russell asked.

"Nothing Dan. Just girl talk," Tracey replied.

"Humpff!" Sgt Russell grunted.

His response, so full of a sense of unspoken male superiority, nettled Barbara but she actually liked Dan. If he had been in any way openly sexist or objectionable she would not have chosen him to be her platoon sergeant. But there were times when she intensely disliked males. Having been several times subjected to sexual assaults and attempted rapes had not helped her like them.

Silence settled, broken only by the chattering of the radio. Several messages gave Barbara spurts of malicious pleasure. The patrol led by Cpl Milikin of 130ACU was apparently lost. *Good!* she thought. In her mind Milikin was another objectionable male who was always ogling the girls and making hints, but one who was too cunning to ever provide evidence that could be placed before the officers.

Tracey checked the Control Sheet for the exercise. "Only three more patrols to go through our Check Point," she commented.

"Who are they?" Sgt Russell asked.

"Our Two Section and Five Section, and One Thirty's Eleven Section," Tracey replied.

"Grey and Woodhouse," Barbara added, naming the section commanders. "They should be alright, but we will be their last Check Point."

"What time is it?" Tracey asked.

Barbara checked her watch. "Twenty-one ten. Only twenty minutes to 'cut-off' time." She stood up and stretched. Now she was feeling tired and drained and was looking forward to bed. She bent and extracted a waterbottle from her webbing, had a big drink, then replaced it. Then she realized she needed to do a pee.

Taking out her torch she said, "I'm just going to the toilet."

"Don't get bitten on the bum by a snake," Sgt Russell replied with a chuckle.

"You can bite yours!" Barbara retorted, but with a laugh. What was really bothering her was the thought of being caught with her pants down by one of the patrols. With that in mind she headed off across the gentle slope to her right, moving away from the likely tracks of any patrols which might be coming from either the Dip or the Bridge.

Using her torch to ensure she did not step in a hole or on a snake Barbara walked slowly to the eastern end of the Gravel Scrape, then on for another fifty paces across the gentle slope. This was through the knee-high grass. In doing so she crossed a couple of small washouts and an animal pad. Several times she stumbled on small rocks or logs in the grass. Satisfied she was far enough away from the others for modesty's sake Barbara found a patch of bare ground and switched her torch off. For a minute she stood and listened, to detect any approaching patrols. Hearing none she undid her trousers and pulled them down.

As she squatted there she heard Sgt Russell suddenly gasp and cry, "What's that?"

Barbara was facing towards the road and her eye had already detected an unusual flicker low in the sky to the east. Now she saw it rapidly grow in size and brilliance. *What on earth is it?* she wondered. Her initial thought was that it was an aircraft.

To her horror the rapidly approaching light suddenly blossomed into an explosion. A sudden flare billowed pink, almost instantly followed by a massive, vivid flash.

"It's exploded!" she cried in horror.

As she squatted there, frozen by fright and uncertainty, she saw the object begin to shred bright points of light. These went arcing off in all directions, a rain of burning debris she realised. Then it dawned on her that the fiery particles were still travelling towards the area at incredible speed, as was the main object, which was now streaming bluish flames. Even as this realisation came to her so did a worse one: the whole blazing mass appeared to be hurtling directly towards her!

"I'm going to die!" she thought, or yelled. But she was quite unable to move.

Chapter 2

BUSHFIRE

Barbara half-rose to her feet, pulling up her knickers as she did. Then she froze in sheer terror as the blazing object continued to speed directly towards her. As it did, her numbed mind noted that the main object was rotating in a twisting, corkscrewing motion, tossing off flaming particles in all directions. Then her mind was able to calculate the trajectory of the main mass and she decided it would not hit her at all. All of this happened in a few seconds, so fast was the thing travelling.

To her immense relief, she watched the blazing mass dip towards the dark bulk of Mount St Michael, the smaller pieces now mostly glowing dimly red but still streaking in all directions. Before her astonished eyes, the main flaming ball vanished below the skyline. A moment later, there was an enormous flash, which lit up the bush brighter than day.

On the far side of Mount St Michael there was another large explosion. A vivid flash lit up the whole area. This was succeeded by a volcanic shower of sparks and what looked like white-hot cinders. Only then did sound start to register. Then Barbara's mind understood what her eyes had been seeing: the original glowing fragments were still hurtling apparently directly towards her at fantastic speed. Worse still, the blazing debris flung up on the other side of Mount St Michael was now showering in her direction in a massive cloud of flaming particles.

Before Barbara's mind could even scream at her to duck the first of the glowing objects arrived, and arrived with mind-numbing speed and shock. Even as she dived flat something struck the large gum tree near her with an ear-splitting crack. Leaves and splinters showered on her and she found herself choking for breath as she was engulfed in a shock wave of dust. Out of the corner of her eye she glimpsed something glowing white hot and about the size of a twenty-litre drum strike the ground at the base of the shattered tree, throwing up a terrifying spray of leaves and splinters as it did.

Overhead whizzed something large which crashed into the trees behind the Gravel Scrape with an ear-splitting crash. Waves of sound battered at Barbara and she closed her eyes and gritted her teeth while cowering on the ground, her arms over her head. Other objects whirred viciously past, some striking other trees with savage force. Branches were lopped off and showers of leaves rained down.

A particularly vicious thud close to her jerked Barbara's eyes open. She found herself staring at a glowing piece of metal which had embedded itself in the trunk of a nearby tree. The metal was so hot it was a bright, cherry red. More things thudded and crashed down all over the slope behind her and she cringed in fear. Dust and grit whipped up by the shock waves got in her eyes, causing her to blink and weep.

Screams of fright penetrated Barbara's consciousness. *Tracey!* she thought in rising panic. Fearing that Tracey had been struck Barbara risked lifting her head. Blinking tears to try to clear her vision she looked around. Dust and smoke now obscured everything, but she realised the screams were coming from the direction of One Mile Creek rather than from the Gravel Scrape.

Definitely female screams, but of fear, not pain. Barbara's first thought was that it might be Fiona and her breath caught in her throat. Then she decided that the sounds were coming from more to her right, not from the Bridge. *A patrol,* she decided.

That got her moving. The waves of shock and sound were receding and the rain of falling objects seemed to have ended. In their place were thick clouds of dust and smoke and the swirl of leaves. Flames began to flicker in a dozen places. The big tree near Barbara was smouldering and she saw that the object which had smashed into it was deeply embedded in the shattered trunk and was now glowing cherry-red. Smoke was billowing from the splintered bark and the tree was making cracking and sizzling noises. Even as Barbara watched small flames began to flicker from the broken timber.

Barbara remained flat for a few more seconds until she was reasonably certain that no more blazing objects were coming down. Glancing up she saw that the stars were obscured by clouds of smoke. Her eyes began to water. Coughing and sneezing she struggled to her feet, half stunned by the shock and uncertainty. Her trousers nearly tripped her, so she hastily pulled them up and did them up. Remembering her torch, she pulled it out of her pocket and clicked it on, then began to make her way back towards where she thought the Gravel Scrape was.

So stunned was she by the whole event that she was disoriented. It was when she heard Tracey call out in a frightened voice that she realised she was off course, heading too far to the right. Barbara called back and hurried across to where she had left the other two. They were hard to find because of the clouds of smoke. Flames were now spreading across the slope as the dry grass took fire. Through watering eyes Barbara saw dark shapes moving.

"Tracey! Is that you?"

"Yes! Here! Oh, thank God! I thought you had been killed Barbara," Tracey cried. Her voice trembled, and she was clearly on the edge of hysteria.

Sgt Russell swore and then said, "Bloody Hell! What was that?"

"I don't know. An aircraft of some sort I think," Barbara replied as she thankfully joined the others.

"Too fast. More like a meteorite," Tracey suggested.

"No. It was made of metal," Barbara answered. Then she shook her head and tried to make her ears work. She found her senses spinning and there was a buzzing in her ears which made it hard to hear. As she looked around through stinging eyes she saw flames in almost every direction. She also heard a girl's voice calling.

Tracey shook her head and rubbed at her ears. "Maybe it was an Air Force jet on exercises," she suggested.

"Never mind what it was!" Barbara snapped. "We need to get out of here. Where is the radio?"

"Here," Sgt Russell replied. He handed it to her, then sneezed and shook his head vigorously.

Barbara held the radio up to her ear, but it sounded as though every call sign was trying to talk at once. She tried twice to call but was cut out each time. The person she really wanted to contact was Fiona but, because her check point was so close to two others, hers had not been issued with a radio. Shaking her head both with annoyance and to clear it Barbara said, "Get your webbing on and let's try to get to the road."

"Which way is that?" Tracey asked, the fear clear in her voice and on her face. Barbara realised that the flames were now lighting things up but that the smoke was blinding them and obscuring details. She gabbed her own webbing and then decided that trying to cross a hundred metres of now blazing grassland was not a smart move. It was the first bushfire she had ever been caught in and she was appalled both by the size of the flames and by the speed at which they were spreading. What really frightened her was when the leaves on a tree canopy suddenly exploded with a loud 'whoof!' into a huge fireball. The heat was intense and she cringed back from it.

"Into the middle of the Gravel Scrape. Lie down and try to cover your face with a wet cloth," she ordered.

The three cadets turned and hurried back into the shallow depression. By then all were coughing and their eyes were streaming with tears. Barbara was shaking so much she could hardly function. She admitted to herself that she was really scared.

It is the smoke and lack of oxygen that kills, she told herself, remembering something she had read.

As she lay down in the middle of the bare clay the thicket of scrub along the back of the Gravel Scrape seemed to erupt in a wall of flame. The heat was so intense that it seemed to sear at her eyeballs and she gasped in fear and in an attempt to breathe.

I hope I haven't made a tragic mistake, she thought anxiously. By then she was panting as though she had run a race and her heart was hammering frantically.

Ignoring her own advice, Barbara lay flat and gazed at the roaring scrub in fascinated horror. Clouds of smoke enveloped them, and she had to close her eyes and was wracked by spasms of coughing. But she found it unendurable not to be able to see so she ignored the stinging pain and kept looking.

Then she heard the girl's voice screaming again. *Someone is in trouble,* she thought. *Oh my God! I hope that isn't Fiona!*

Her conscience and sense of duty alike goaded her to act. Raising herself to her hands and knees she peered into the smoke and flames. It took a conscious effort of will but she forced herself to be calm and to study the situation. Only then did it become clearer to her. The smoke was drifting by but was mostly rising above where they lay. The fire in the thicket behind the Gravel Scrape was still raging but appeared to be slowly moving away or dying down. In front of her the grass was on fire in a dozen places. The pattern of the flames now became apparent to her.

It was not just one huge fire at all. Half a dozen fires were burning, each slowly spreading outwards, their progress marked by wavering but very clear lines of flame. Between the fires were areas of darkness where the grass had either not yet caught fire or had already been burnt. Better still very few of the tree canopies seemed to be catching fire. Best of all there was almost no wind, so that the fires were only spreading slowly. Even so the flames were leaping two or three metres into the air and the heat near them was shrivelling.

Barbara stood up and sucked in a deep breath so as to shout. That was a mistake as she immediately began to cough. Taking more care she tried again, then yelled at the top of her voice, "Fiona! Fiona!"

There were distant shouts, coming from two directions. Barbara yelled again and this time she distinctly heard a girl's voice call.

"Barbara! Is that you?"

"Yes. Are you alright?"

"Yes."

Another bout of coughing silenced Barbara, but she felt enormously relieved. *Fiona is safe!*

Then Barbara spotted movement. Out in a patch of darkness to her right-front there were pale blobs that she realised were faces.

Cadets! And trying to avoid the flames, she noted.

She saw they were on her side of One Mile Creek and it instantly dawned on her that they must not try to go towards the road as the long grass along the creek would incinerate them if it caught fire while they were crossing.

I must act, she told herself.

"Stay here," she commanded Tracey and Sgt Russell. "And try to tell HQ we are safe," she added.

Then she ran forward. Tracey called something, but Barbara ignored her, her mind concentrated on picking a safe path through the flames. That turned out to be easier than she had at first thought. Only once did she have to jump over a line of small flames which were licking at clumps of grass on a bare patch that marked an old vehicle track. The smoke was the real problem, causing her to gasp and cough and her eyes to water.

It took her only two anxious minutes to cover the hundred paces to the cadet patrol. As she reached them Barbara saw that they were carrying someone on an improvised stretcher. The face of the patrol leader was briefly illuminated by a flaring bush and Barbara almost snorted with a mixture of annoyance and relief.

Bloody Chloe Cummings! she thought, seeing the girl's face split into a grin.

Chloe was a corporal in 130 and was famous for her alleged misbehaviour. Two years earlier she and her friend Jane had been kidnapped by smugglers during a cadet exercise at Flying Fish Point and Barbara had been part of the search party that had met up with them as they were pursued by the kidnappers. Both had been stark naked. Apparently, they had escaped and then swum a crocodile infested swamp in the night. The stories about that escape were legends among the cadets and included rumours of rape and murder. Barbara had marvelled that Chloe had not been chucked out of the cadets there and then. But she had been denied promotion for nearly two years.

Most teenagers would have given up and dropped out, Barbara mused. But now here she was, a corporal, and obviously handling a fairly desperate situation with coolness and skill.

Chloe grinned at Barbara, her blonde hair gleaming in the firelight. "Hi Barbara, I mean CUO Brassington. Boy, are we glad to see you!"

"What's the matter?" Barbara asked, indicating the person on the stretcher.

"Only a sprained ankle," Chloe answered. "He got scared and tried to run and tripped in a gully."

"I'll buy that!" Barbara added with grim humour, memories of her own terror returning. She coughed and looked around. They were close to the bank of One Mile Creek, but the flames were now spreading along it and cutting off any chance of reaching the road. That confirmed her earlier estimate. "This way," she said. "Up to the Gravel Scrape."

"Oooh good! That's our next Check Point," Chloe replied.

"I think the Navex is over," Barbara replied sarcastically as she moved to help hold the stretcher. She now saw that it was made only from two broomsticks stuck through webbing. At that she nodded her approval. All the 130ACU NCOs carried a broom handle and she had seen them practising making an improvised stretcher with them as part of a snake bite drill: one minute and thirty seconds to get the patient treated and moving on the stretcher. Now she was glad of that training as it had obviously helped this team to keep their heads during the crisis.

There were five of them, so they were able to keep walking. First, they hurried away from a line of advancing flames, then made their way across a patch of smoking ground and along behind another line of fire. A short rest allowed them all to get their breath and for Barbara to plan the next stage. She saw that the fire was dying out up to her left along the eastern end of the Gravel Scrape and that the fires in the thicket were dying down to reddish flames and clouds of thick smoke. Luckily this was rolling slowly away from them.

"Hands on... Prepare to lift... Lift!" she ordered.

The stretcher was hoisted up to hip height and they hurried on, angling upslope. A minute later they were on the lip of the Gravel Scrape and thirty seconds later Tracey and Sgt Russell were helping them. The stretcher was lowered to the bare clay and the cadets all flopped down, coughing and gasping with relief.

"I got through to HQ," Sgt Russell reported. "They said move out to the Front Gate if we could do it safely."

The Front Gate was at the junction of the Mingela Road and the road in to the army camp. It was three hundred metres to the left, beyond the Bridge. Barbara wiped her streaming eyes and studied the fire. A drink from a waterbottle and then the rinsing of her eyes helped. She saw that the grass along the creek was now flaring and spreading.

"Not yet. We are safe here," she said. "We will wait a few minutes." That took an effort to decide as she was now worrying about Fiona.

I hope she really is alright! she fretted.

Since she had helped rescue Fiona and her father from the religious fanatics near Kuranda the previous June the two girls had become very close. Barbara felt an instinctive urge to try to reach her friend but reasoned that her duty was to keep the cadets under her command safe. So she sat and stared into the drifting smoke and wished she could contact Fiona on the radio.

As realisation that they were not in fact in imminent peril of being burnt to death sank in the cadets began to chatter about the incident.

Chloe shook her head and even laughed. "I nearly bloody wet myself," she said. "I never saw whatever it was until it was about to lob in. Talk about a fright!"

"What was it do you think?" asked a cadet.

None of them knew and the various theories about crashing jet fighters and meteorites were bandied around. Barbara did not join in. Instead she made sure Sgt Russell reported to HQ that Chloe's section was safe with them and then had another big drink and lay back. Only then did the real shock start to hit and she was glad it was getting darker as she began to tremble uncontrollably. Suddenly the tears were real and she found herself sweating and shivering at the same time. She was glad it was dark so that the others could not see.

Ten minutes went by. The flames in the thicket still crackled but by now only a few logs and stumps were burning. Most of the area was just smouldering darkness. The moon came up, almost completely obscured by the smoke. The whole area between the Gravel Scrape and the Mingela Road was now mostly in darkness because the grass had all been burnt but very few of the trees or logs had caught fire. Only one large tree off to the right was burning fiercely but that appeared to be all. Wisps of smoke streamed up from dozens of small sticks and logs that were alight.

The sound of a vehicle attracted Barbara's attention and she sat up and saw the headlights of a Land Rover heading west along the Mingela Road from near the Dip. The vehicle stopped out near the Bridge and began to toot its horn. "That will be Lieutenant Hamilton calling us in," she said. She struggled to her feet, surprised at how stiff and sore she felt.

"Get up! Webbing on. Can you walk?" This to the cadet with the sprained ankle. "No? Ok, stay on the stretcher. Right you others, gather around. Hands on... Prepare to lift…"

Chloe's voice suddenly cut across her command. "Kingsly! Grab the broomstick in the middle as well as at the end or it will snap."

Barbara grunted with annoyance but then looked to check that all had a firm grip, and in the right places. "Lift!"

The group set off along the trace of the vehicle track down to the Bridge. With three cadets either side of the stretcher and one to relieve it was no great effort and they did not lower it until they reached the end of the Bridge. Here Barbara had them put it down and walked forward to check on the condition of the Bridge. She was worried that it might have caught fire and been weakened. However, a glance showed that it had not been affected at all. The Bridge had been constructed using thick logs and was designed to stand up to the weight of loaded tip trucks, so she had no qualms at ordering the others to pick up the stretcher and to follow her across.

On the other side she found a group of people including Lieutenant Hamilton, the unit QM, Lieutenant Standish, one of the lady teachers, and Fiona. Fiona hurried over and hugged Barbara. "Oh Barb, thank heavens you are safe! I was so worried," she cried.

"Me too. Anyone hurt?" Barbara asked her, giving her friend another squeeze as she did.

Fiona shook her head as she eased herself away. "Not really. One cadet in a section out on the road got hit by a splinter from a tree, and I got a small burn, but that was all."

At the mention of being hit by a splinter Barbara shuddered, remembering the vicious shower of broken timber around her. She said, "Is the cadet alright?"

"It was only a small piece, stuck in his cheek. Mrs Standish has fixed him up," Fiona replied.

"What about your burn?"

"Oh, it's nothing," Fiona replied, flapping her left hand to show which one it was.

Barbara seized her hand. "Show me," she said. She switched on her torch and critically examined the side of Fiona's hand. A small blister and reddish area was visible but that was all. "Does it hurt?" Barbara asked.

Fiona shook her head. "Stings a bit, that's all."

Barbara almost lifted the hand to her mouth and the expression 'kiss it better' was on the tip of her tongue. Instead she gave her friend another squeeze and then released her. "You were lucky then," she said.

"Not as lucky as you. When that huge red thing crashed into the trees up there I was sure you were all dead," Fiona said.

"Huge red thing?" Barbara queried.

Sgt Russell gave a nervous laugh and cried, "Huge! It looked as big as a bloody bus! That was the thing that lobbed into the trees behind us."

Barbara dimly remembered seeing something flash overhead. She shook her head. "All I saw were a couple of smaller things come down near me."

She was about to add that she had been caught with her pants down but held her tongue, then shuddered and almost broke into tears again. It had been a truly terrifying moment.

"What was it do you think sir?" Sgt Russell asked Lt Hamilton.

The OOC shook his head. "Don't know. Not an aircraft, that is for sure. It was going far too fast. It might have been some sort of guided missile."

"Guided missile!" Sgt Russell cried incredulously. "Who would aim a guided missile at this dump? It's the middle of bloody nowhere!"

"Maybe. Now stop talking, collect all your gear and get up to the gate so we can do a head count," Lt Hamilton ordered.

Still carrying the stretcher, the cadets and officers made their way out to where the Land Rover was parked. The injured cadet was helped in. Chloe's section then retrieved their webbing and broomsticks and set off walking along the road with Barbara and the others. The Land Rover started up and drove past them to the Front Gate. It was only two hundred metres along the dusty road. As the cadets marched along Barbara noted that all of the grass on the left of the road was now burnt off or smouldering but that there appeared to be no fires at all on the right of the road.

That's good, she thought. That was where most of the cadets on the exercise had been and was also where their camp was.

At the Front Gate was another Land Rover. In this one was Lt Hamilton's brother, a captain but in 130 ACU. He told them to keep marching and to get back to camp as quickly as they could. There was no problem with that. It was just a dusty uphill slog along a gravel road with bush on both sides. It was only 600 metres and they covered it in 8 minutes. At the top of the long, gentle hill they found several vehicles parked and many figures milling around. Torches flashed and voices shouted orders.

Both unit OCs were in personal command, adding their voices to that of their CSMs. Barbara saw what she expected: Cairns was being seated in section lines in a cleared area off the road on the right and 130 ACU was doing the same on the left of the road. She reported to Major Conkey and sent Sgt Russell to help the CSM to seat and count the cadets.

After reporting to the OC, Barbara and Fiona moved to the rear to join the other CUOs and HQ sergeants. As she did a figure pushed his way through the throng and gripped her elbow. It was her boyfriend Roger Dunning. Roger was also a CUO and was commander of 2 Platoon. He was the same age and in her class at school, a solid, usually cheerful boy of 17.

"Are you Ok Barbara?" he asked.

Barbara put her hand on his and squeezed. "Yes, thanks Roger. I got a bit of a fright, that's all."

"Did any of that stuff come down near you?"

"One lump hit a tree right next to me," Barbara answered. "And a few other bits came down fairly close."

At that Roger stepped closer and hugged her. "Then thank God you are safe!" he muttered.

Barbara was glad it was dark and that they were at the back. Even though everyone in the unit, including the officers, knew that she and Roger were an 'item', fraternisation was severely frowned on. It was a rule she strongly agreed with, so she just gave him a strong hug back, then eased herself free. Roger understood at once and stepped away. That was one of the things she liked about him. He was very sensitive, and very quick to catch on. He was also very moral.

Barbara had another big drink, draining her second waterbottle. From a third waterbottle she used some water to wash her face and to rinse her eyes. These were still smarting as smoke was still drifting by. As she stood there she was able to look around. From where they were camped the electric lights at the army camp four hundred metres further along were just visible through the trees. So was the bulk of Mount St Michael. One glance at it caused her to suck her breath in in shock. Half the mountain looked to be aflame. Long lines of fire were working their way up the rugged slopes. Thick masses of smoke were billowing off, to drift overhead, shielding the moon and making it appear dimly as a pale, brownish ball.

That looks serious, Barbara thought, shocked at the extent of the fires.

Then her eyes detected more areas of light which were glowing and flickering against the base of the smoke clouds in the distance. Some were obviously extensive fires and they seemed to be spread over a huge area of bush away to the eastwards.

We might be in real trouble here, she thought.

Chapter 3

MIXED EMOTIONS

The system both cadet units used to check that they had all their cadets safe at the end of an exercise was to seat each section in line behind its corporal, with all the sections side by side in numerical order. That way the company fitted into a small area for briefings and also allowed the platoon sergeants to do a head count or mark their roll. In this case Major Conkey insisted that the rolls actually be marked, even though the platoon sergeants had reported that all sections were present and accounted for.

While this was being done a Land Rover arrived from the direction of the army camp and, in its headlights, Barbara saw Major Ross, the army staff officer responsible for running the camp, get out and go over to Major Conkey. Major Wickham, OC of 130 ACU, joined them and the three had a short conference over to one side. After a few minutes they separated. Major Conkey called for platoon commanders.

The four Cadet Under-Officers: Lofty Ward (1 Platoon), Roger (2 Platoon), Fiona, and Barbara moved to where the OC waited. The other adult officers also joined them, as did Cadet Warrant Officer Pat Sheehan, the Company Sergeant Major.

Major Conkey turned to him. "Well CSM, what is the situation?"

"All present Sir," CSM Sheehan answered.

Major Conkey nodded. "Good. That is a relief. Now, we aren't sure what happened, beyond knowing that something crashed and set fire to the bush. It is the fire we are concerned with." He paused and gestured towards the blazing slopes of Mount St Michael. "That fire is not only going up the mountain, it is also coming our way across the flat. We have just been ordered to move. So get your platoons packed up and moving. Take your platoons to the army camp. Make it fast. I want this area empty of cadets and their personal gear in fifteen minutes."

Lt Hamilton at once protested. "But sir, we can't pack up the CP and HQ stores in that time."

"Then we leave them to burn," Major Conkey replied grimly. "All

I am concerned with is keeping the cadets safe. Now get packed up and moving as quickly as you can. Once the company is all there we will worry about saving any gear that might be left behind. Now move!"

Goaded by the spur of flames visibly spreading towards them only half a kilometre away they did not argue. Barbara called her platoon to follow her in single file and hurried them back towards where they were camped. She was anxious but not deeply worried. She knew that, if the worst came to the worst, they could just leave their gear and run across to the other side of the gravel road to where 130 ACU was camped. Having walked all over the area on a day Navex she also knew that there was another gravel road between the area of bush they were camped in and the fire burning across the flat.

There were a couple of minutes of confusion and calling out before the platoons dispersed to their own areas. Barbara led her people at a fast walk to their own bivouac. The company had no tents. Instead they had set up Shelters Individual, 'hutchies' in the jargon of the cadets. These were merely sheets of camouflaged plastic tied between two trees by slip knots. In some cases they had clipped two shelters together. The corners were pegged down or tied to other trees or bushes. As all their gear was already packed (A unit Standing Operating Procedure, particularly with bedding, so that snakes could not slip into the sleeping bags) it was the work of only minutes to pull down the shelters, fold them and stuff them into the top of packs. A quick check with torches was done by Barbara and her NCOs to ensure nothing was left lying around.

Within five minutes the platoon had their packs and webbing on and was starting to line up in single file. By then smoke was rolling through in thick, choking clouds and Barbara became quite anxious again. Her emotions were further tested when Cadet Selfridge began to call out in fear and then Cpl Walsh shouted for his section to run.

I don't want a panic, Barbara thought, both pride and common sense helping her.

Barbara shone her torch at the figures hurrying through the darkness, dust and smoke. "Stop that running! Slow down and calm down!" she ordered sharply.

Her own heart was hammering but the last thing she wanted was a panicked stampede. To her relief the cadets came to a stumbling, shuffling halt.

"Now corporals, keep your sections together and quiet," she commanded.

Satisfied that nothing was left behind she moved to the front of the line and then waited till Sgt Russell had walked forward counting them to check no-one was missing. Only when he had assured her that all cadets were present did she lead off. They walked quickly in single file back to the gravel road, coming on to it near where the officers were hastily loading gear into vehicles. Major Conkey was there and waved them to keep moving.

Barbara turned right on the gravel road and was pleased to note that hers was the first platoon moving. Now she was no longer worried. The situation was just unpleasant and uncomfortable. The smoke made her eyes water and she found herself wracked by coughing. Moving at a steady walk she marched the platoon to the army camp. As she did she continually glanced to her right-front to check on the progress of the flames. By the time she reached the army camp the first flames were close to the edge of the camp and were reaching the other gravel road that ran off southeast—the 'Back Road'.

There was no danger of the 'camp' being burnt. It was surrounded by a gravel ring road and car park and there was no long grass inside that; only short, green grass, concrete slabs (for tents to be set up on) and the few permanent buildings (HQ, showers, toilets, kitchen and so on). As well the four cadet units actually camped there: Broadsound, Mackay, Sarina and Mount Isa, were all awake and lined up along the edge of the camp with fire beaters, knapsack sprays and rakes.

On reaching the unused concrete slabs that the company had allocated for their use during meals and showers Barbara had the platoon drop their packs and kitbags in three neat rows. Then she ordered the cadets to sit. Only after she was sure all her cadets were present and safe did she feel free to look around. The first thing she noted was 3 Platoon following close on the heels of her own people. Another platoon was hurrying in out of the smoke and darkness behind them, but they went on past to sit on another set of concrete slabs.

130 ACU, she noted. Then she saw Chloe's blonde hair and knew it was their rivals, the 'other' 4 Platoon. A Land Rover arrived and was parked and three of the officers got out. One was Capt Maclaren, the unit 2ic.

Barbara went over to him. "Is there anything you want us to do sir?"

"Not at the moment. Just keep your people together and watch for any cadets with breathing difficulties," Capt Maclaren replied.

Barbara knew that a couple of her cadets were prone to asthma attacks, so she nodded and went back to study their faces and to ask how they felt. A quick inspection showed the platoon to be excited but apparently in good health.

1 Platoon and 2 Platoon came in, with HQ on their heels, then the second Land Rover. Major Conkey was with them and Barbara now acted. She went over to him and reported her platoon all safe. Once the other platoon commanders had done likewise she pointed out to the southeast along the gravel road, nicknamed the Back Road, that ran directly towards the main airfield. She had been watching the progress of the fires and had noted that the flames were moving fairly slowly and that they tended to flare up, then die down, depending on the amount of fuel.

"Sir, if we are quick we could stop the fire crossing the Back Road. That will save any HQ gear left behind and also keep that area of bush unburnt."

Major Conkey turned to look and pulled at his chin thoughtfully. "We have all the gear, but you might be right."

Roger pointed to the back wall of the HQ building. "There are all those fire beaters and rakes there, sir. We could use them."

Major Conkey nodded, then said, "Alright, but only CUOs and corporals. The CSM and sergeants are to stay here to control the cadets. Mel (this to Capt Maclaren), you stay here."

With that Major Conkey led the way across to the wall. By the time Barbara had collected her corporals and ordered her cadets to stay put (much to their annoyance) he was hurrying off towards the road junction at the edge of camp, fire beater in hand. Barbara also grabbed a fire beater and set off after him. The other CUOs and corporals grabbed fire beaters or fire rakes, except Lofty and Dave Blockey, who opted for knapsack sprays.

As she hurried across to the road junction through the smoke Barbara had to dodge a long line of 130 ACU cadets, all laden with packs and kitbags. They were evacuating their bivouac area as well, even though they had two roads between their bivouac and the fire. But Barbara did not think that unreasonable.

The last thing we need is a burnt cadet, she thought.

Just near the southeast corner of the camp was a road junction. The main Camp Road ran past as the eastern boundary of the camp. This continued North East through the bush to the far end of the old homestead airstrip, left over from the days when 'Dotswood' was a cattle station. Barbara had never been along that road or seen the airstrip, only knew it from the map. Due East of the junction and five hundred metres away was the base of Mount St Michael. The hill began as a stony ridge that ran up past a fenced-off quarry and on up to a rocky summit. The whole ridge was now ringed and dotted by flames, and half-hidden by smoke. The Back Road to the 'East Gate' ran southeast between the base of Mount St Michael and the patch of bush where the cadets had been bivouacked. The Back Road was a gravel road four metres wide and easy to follow, even in the smoke and darkness.

Major Conkey spaced the cadets out along the road for about four hundred metres, working in pairs. As he did he reminded them that safety was paramount and that they were not to leave the road or take any risks. "We do not want a cadet hurt," he cautioned them.

Barbara naturally teamed up with Roger. They then stood on the side of the road away from the advancing flames and prepared to deal with any sparks or flying cinders. Several times Barbara's heart leapt into her mouth when clumps of grass flared into pillars of flames but in fact it turned out to be a tame assignment. There was almost no wind and only once did any sparks drift across the road to start a fire on their side. This was quickly put out by Lofty and his sergeant, Wendy Werribee.

The only really worrying thing was the wildlife. Several wallabies bounded by, as well as several small rodent-like marsupials which Roger suggested were Bilbies. Barbara doubted this as she thought Bilbies were only found way out in the far west of southern Queensland, in the true desert country. What did frighten her were the slithering shadows of two snakes which slipped across the road to escape the advancing fire.

As the fire reached the road it quickly consumed the available fuel and then began to die out. Within a few minutes all that remained were a few glowing tufts and a couple of burning sticks. The cadets walked along the edge of the scorched ground to beat these out, but Barbara found it so unpleasant that she quickly gave it up as pointless. All they seemed to be really doing was stirring up an irritating cloud of ash.

The real danger was of sparks drifting across the road to set the dry grass alight, but Barbara saw no signs of this happening. The breeze was not strong enough and both she and Roger were vigilant. From time to time she looked affectionately at Roger, admiring him. He was not particularly handsome, with a rather plain face and a slightly chubby build, but she still liked him a lot.

He is a really nice person, she thought. She knew from hard experience that she could trust her life to him.

Major Conkey called them in just before 2215 hours and they walked back along the road to the lights of camp. Here they found the unit preparing to bivouac on and around the concrete slabs for the night. By then Barbara was feeling badly dehydrated and exhausted. She placed her fire beater handy to her gear and went to get a big drink. Lt Hamilton helped by handing them each a can of cold softdrink.

"Well done people," Major Conkey said as he returned from reporting to Major Ross. "We can bed down and get what sleep we can and the situation will be reviewed in the morning."

"What do you mean by reviewed Sir?" Roger asked.

"If these fires keep up we may have to cancel all training. We might even have to be evacuated back to Townsville."

"Oh sir!" Lofty said incredulously.

Major Conkey just shook his head and pointed off to the North East. The camp was built on a low, flat 'hill', giving a view over quite a spread of country. As far as Barbara could see there was the glow of fires or their loom, reflecting off the smoke clouds above them.

"Do we know what it was that crashed yet Sir?" Roger asked.

Major Conkey shook his head. "No. Not an aircraft anyway."

"Thank God for that!" Roger said feelingly. That caused a spurt of sympathy in Barbara. She knew that the previous year Roger, with some of his friends, had witnessed a fatal plane crash on Black Mountain, north of Cairns[1].

Major Conkey ended any further discussion by ordering them off to bed. Barbara then asked, "Can we have a shower Sir?"

"The fire fighters only, not the whole unit," Major Conkey answered.

That satisfied Barbara. She went back to her platoon and made sure they were settling down. They were sleeping in a long row, side by

---

[1] Read *The Secret in the Clouds* by C. R. Cummings.

side on the small patch of lawn. Sgt Russell reported all in bed and all well. Barbara thanked him for his steadiness and efforts and they quietly discussed the event, being joined by CSM Sheehan as he did his 'Lights Out' rounds. Their opinion was that it would be a real shame if the camp was cancelled, as it was only the third night.

Barbara left them and went to her gear. After digging out her towel, clean clothes and toilet gear from her kitbag, she made her way to the shower block allocated to females. Here she met a female lieutenant from Mackay who questioned her as to why she was there. Satisfied with the explanation the lieutenant allowed her in. There were several other girls inside.

It was a typical army shower block, a long row of twelve open-fronted cubicles, each with a shower in it. A plastic curtain hung across the front of each cubicle but there was nowhere in it to place clothes. That meant the girls had to either undress in full view of the others, or go into a cubicle with its wet floor to take their clothes off, move out to place their clothes on the long bench seat outside and then walk the couple of paces back to the cubicle.

Barbara did not mind her friends seeing her nude, but she was very conscious that other people might be embarrassed by the situation. She wasn't but, to her own shame, she was very aware of being interested in seeing the other girl's bodies. As both Fiona and Wendy were there as well she did not know where to look.

If she could have Barbara would have used the very end cubicle but Wendy was in that one and Fiona in the next. So Barbara sat down and took off her boots, then slipped on rubber thongs (to protect her feet from getting tinea) and moved into the cubicle. Here she undressed then wrapped her towel around herself and hurried out to dump the clothes on the bench before hurrying back into the shower cubicle. As she did she glimpsed Fiona's back as she stood in her shower.

Gosh Fiona has a nice shape, she thought, noting the lovely curve of hip and the long smooth thighs.

Ashamed of having such thoughts Barbara hastily looked away and hurried into her own cubicle. Here she took off her towel and turned to hang it over the beam at the front. As she did Wendy came out of the next cubicle and put down her towel, then reached down to pick up her clothes. Once again Barbara could not help seeing. Wendy had her back to her but the image vividly reminded her of the time she had soaped Wendy's back while they had swum nude in Surprise Creek near Kuranda the previous June.

Barbara noted Wendy's large, flabby buttocks. Then she shook her head at the sight of Wendy's boobs. These hung down and quivered as she moved.

Heavens they are big! Barbara thought. *Poor Wendy!*

Barbara knew that Wendy was very self-conscious about them and hated being called by her school nickname of 'Wobbles'.

Shaking her head at her own wicked thoughts and weakness Barbara looked away and turned on the taps to adjust the temperature. The water was bliss. For several minutes she just stood and enjoyed the cool sensation of water on her skin. But her relaxation was interrupted by laughter and giggling, and she glanced out to see a naked blonde.

Bloody Chloe! Barbara thought.

Chloe loved being nude and did not seem to care who saw her, or where she stripped off. Now she and her friend Jane were both there.

Chloe waved to Barbara and brazenly ran her eyes up her body. "Gee Barbara, I mean CUO Brassington, you look lovely. The boys must go crazy over you."

Barbara went as red as her hair. "Chloe! Behave," she chided, before turning back into her cubicle. Chloe and Jane both went into the next cubicle to scrub each others backs. That both scandalised Barbara and aroused strong emotions, not least of which was jealousy.

I wouldn't mind someone rubbing my back and massaging me at the moment, she thought.

That got her thinking about her boyfriend Roger. *He is really kind and gentle,* she thought, but that gave her twinges of guilt as she sensed that he did not really set her on fire the way she secretly craved. They had never had sex, only indulged in some passionate 'petting'. Indeed Barbara, even though she was nearly eighteen, was a still a virgin.

Thinking about this, and about boys, got her all mixed up. She really cared about Roger and valued the friendship but suspected that she was not being honest with herself about the relationship.

He is a really nice boy. He is caring and brave and loyal and hard-working, and...

And she wasn't sure if that was what she wanted, or even if she preferred females to males. It was all very disturbing. Over the years she had suffered some horrible experiences with males and that made her quite unsure if she liked them at all.

The female officer hurried them along by calling out from the door, ordering them to get out and to go to bed. That led to more titillating embarrassment as Chloe stepped out of her cubicle at the same time as Barbara. But while Barbara immediately wrapped her towel around her Chloe used hers to dry her back, arching her body and thrusting out her very prominent boobs as she did. As Chloe towelled her back her breasts wobbled and quivered. Barbara felt a surge of what she knew was excitement, if not desire, and she made herself look away.

Heavens! Chloe has the best figure I have ever seen, she thought.

That made her feel sad because of the stories about Chloe and boys. It made her seem cheap and tarty, yet she also came across as reliable and very capable. It worried Barbara that, despite feelings of scandalised disgust, she could still experience frank admiration for Chloe. Despite everything, Barbara had to admit that she liked her as a person.

For modesty's sake Barbara took her bra and shirt back into the cubicle and put them on, then came out again to finish dressing. Not so Chloe. She stood there nude and dressed in full view of everyone. Barbara tried not to look, but still got an eyeful and could only blush and avert her eyes.

To her annoyance Barbara found she was feeling quite aroused and she bit her lip. *Am I really like that? Do I prefer women to men?* she worried.

It was a very thoughtful girl who walked back to the company area with Fiona. The two girls talked quietly for a while, before moving to their respective platoons to sleep.

As she unrolled her bedding Barbara saw that Lt Standish was awake, sitting on a folding chair, and that two of the HQ NCOs were also awake, obviously the piquet. Satisfied that they were all as safe as possible Barbara lay back and closed her eyes. The last thing she saw were the flames licking at the summit of Mount St Michael and she sleepily wondered what had caused the fires.

Chapter 4

ARROGANT, IGNORANT!

That was the main topic of conversation as soon as the cadets were awake next morning. The consensus was that it was either a guided missile that went wrong, or a satellite that had crashed. It was Major Conkey who ended the speculation when he said good morning to the CUOs while the company was having their morning 'Check Parade'. This only involved the CSM, sergeants and all the cadets but Major Conkey insisted that the officers also be out of bed and visible. To ensure this he made it a rule that they come and talk to him. That also allowed him to pass on any new information and instructions.

"I've just been listening to the six o'clock news on the radio," he said. "It was a French military satellite. The French were trying to bring it down in their Pacific territories, but something went wrong and it got out of control and has crashed here. We are world news."

"Pacific territories?" Lofty queried.

Both Barbara and Major Conkey looked at Lofty in surprise. Major Conkey then explained: "The French own quite a number of islands out in the Pacific Ocean. The main one is New Caledonia, which is a big island out from Rockhampton. They also own Tahiti and hundreds of smaller islands."

Fiona nodded and added, "They also own those islands where they used to test nuclear weapons, the Tuamotos." Her voice carried clear disapproval.

"They own some in the Indian Ocean too," Roger said.

Lofty looked suitably chastened. "So what is this about a satellite?"

Major Conkey answered, "Well, it is apparently one of those spy satellites that takes photos from space. It was running low on fuel or something so the French tried to bring it back down, presumably to retrieve the more valuable parts of it. Obviously, something went wrong."

He gestured to the blackened and still smouldering country across the road and up the slopes of Mount St Michael.

Barbara was mildly interested but really wanted to know what was to happen to them. "Sir, do you know if the camp is going to be allowed to go ahead?"

"Not yet. Major Ross is finding out now. There is still a significant fire hazard."

This time he pointed off to the North East again. In daylight the fires were no longer visible, but a massive pall of brownish smoke covered half the horizon. The light breeze was causing this to drift off westwards, so the camp area was relatively clear at that moment but columns of thick smoke from more fires could be seen climbing into a clear blue sky to both the South and South West.

There was no real argument when faced with such obvious evidence. All Barbara could do was hope. This was the last camp she would attend as a platoon commander and she badly wanted to have an opportunity to actually lead her platoon in the field.

By then the CSM had completed the Check Parade and sent the platoons back to where their gear lay on the concrete slabs. He reported to Major Conkey that all were present and then sat down to mark the roll book.

Breakfast was next. This was tinned food heated in mess tins over hexamine stoves. Barbara sat with her platoon and passed on what Major Conkey had said.

"French military satellite eh?" Cpl Walsh said. "I hope it didn't have nuclear warheads in it."

Lance Corporal Farley jeered. "Oh, get real Walshy! Nuclear warheads!"

"They do!" Cpl Walsh retorted. "Some satellites have guided missiles in them and can launch nuclear strikes."

"They do not!" Farley sneered.

"Do so! I read it," Cpl Walsh replied heatedly.

Cpl Halyday laughed. "I didn't know you could read," he cut in.

"He can't! He just looks at the pictures," Cadet Selfridge said with a laugh.

"Bite your bum!" Cpl Walsh cried angrily. "I did read it."

Farley sneered. "What, in a science fiction comic?" he retorted.

Barbara swallowed the mouthful of braised steak and onions she had been chewing and said, "Drop the argument! Talk about something else."

It spoke volumes for her leadership and strength of character that the teenage boys obeyed. Instead they began discussing a Check Point run by 130 ACU that they believed had been in the wrong place the night before.

At 0730 the platoon commanders were called over to Major Conkey. He waited till all were there, then said, "Good news so far. We're to stay here for the present, but not to do any field training until further notice."

"No field training! But sir!" Lofty protested.

"Those are the orders. I don't like it either. Now, we will be sensible about that. This morning is only lessons by section commanders and so on anyway and they can be done just around the camp," Major Conkey replied.

Barbara looked around the camp and was not impressed. *That won't be too bad while it is still relatively cool,* she thought, *but it will be scorching hot by mid-morning.*

Already she could picture the shimmering heat haze that would develop later. She said, "It is going to be very hot sir, with no shade. Could we train just in the edge of the scrub there, next to the car park?"

She indicated the thin, dry scrub: knee high dry grass and a scattering of spindly trees and spiky bushes which covered the ground just across the other side of the gravel car park facing the RAP and HQ.

Major Conkey considered this, then said, "I will ask HQ, but I suspect that area will be snavelled by One Thirty. Their camp was just in there and it is on their side of the road." With that he told them to return to their platoons to inspect them while he went back to HQ.

The upshot was permission to train beside the road on the same side of the road as their evacuated bivouac site. It wasn't ideal, but it was certainly better than trying to share the camp area with five other units. They had to leave their packs and kitbags on the concrete slabs but as they were told they had to cook there (in case a hexamine stove set fire to the grass) that did not matter. HQ Section was detailed to guard the gear while the platoons filed off along the road to near their old area.

Company parade was held along the road. As soon as it was over the platoons moved into the edge of the sparse scrub to start training. This was in the area bounded by the Camp Road, Back Road and a powerline clearing along which the powerline ran roughly North—South, crossing the Camp Road one hundred metres from their old campsite. The powerline then ran on southwards through the scrub for two kilometres to the New Airfield.

The first lesson was revision on making improvised stretchers. For this the unit borrowed broomsticks from 130ACU. The stretchers were made using the broomsticks and webbing. Barbara had Sgt Russell teach this lesson while she and the other CUOs sat in the meagre shade of some straggly small trees with the OOCs to plan the activities for the next day.

Barbara studied the photocopied map enlargement she was handed and then asked, "Sir, are we going to send out any patrols to keep an eye on St Michael's Cadet Unit?"

Major Conkey shook his head. "I wasn't planning to. They and One Thirty can continue their private feud if they wish, but I don't think they are worth taking on in a field exercise."

"They are a mob of undisciplined cowboys," Lt Hamilton offered.

Major Conkey replied, "It is their lack of military method and skill that I am concerned with. Anyway, I believe they are concentrated at the New Airfield at the moment and we are not to do field training until further orders remember."

"Yes sir," Barbara replied. But she was unable to hide the disappointment in her voice.

Major Conkey smiled and said, "Do your people want some action?"

"Yes sir. And they get very jealous that One Thirty ACU always seem to be doing exciting field exercises."

"We don't do too badly," Major Conkey replied. "Besides, we had plenty of real action at annual camp last year."

That got them all talking and agreeing. That camp had been beside the Bunyip River and 4 Platoon had become involved in a deadly week of hide and seek with a gang of crooks. Roger had been 4 Platoon sergeant and had been intimately involved, even to firing live ammunition at the crooks. Barbara had also shot one, breaking his leg, when she had escaped to warn the army.[2]

Major Conkey added, "I don't want that sort of trouble this annual camp. The parents won't let their children join if we keep getting involved in things like that."

"What about exercises against other units sir, like the raid we did on the Bunyip River Rail Bridge a few yeas ago?" Lofty asked.

Barbara had been a 'First Year' cadet then and vividly remembered that exercise. She nodded in enthusiastic agreement. Major Conkey

---

[2] Read *The Cadet Under-Officer* by C. R. Cummings.

grinned and said, "We are doing an exercise, if we are allowed to and are not moved out of the area. In two nights time. Now get on with this planning."

The CUOs turned back to their note taking and map work. As they did the peculiar vibrating sound of a helicopter's rotors came to them. Next the growl of aero engines came from the East and they glimpsed an army Blackhawk skimming close past the burnt-out slopes of Mount St Michael. The helicopter flew on to the West then circled southwards. Five minutes later, just as Barbara and Fiona were walking back to their platoons, it re-appeared, coming northwards along the line of the Back Road. The machine came to a hover near the army camp, its rotor wash sending up a cloud of dust, soot and ash. Then it landed, and the engines were switched off.

Seeing army helicopters in the Training Area was not unusual so Barbara gave it no more thought. She collected her platoon and settled them in what shade she could find to revise them at map reading: Grid References, measuring distance, and so on.

While she was doing this, she heard a man call out loudly, "All you kids get out here on the road, now!"

Barbara looked towards the sound of the voice and saw a man in army uniform standing on the road. He shouted again, and her cadets looked at her.

Barbara shook her head. "Just a minute," she said to her platoon as several cadets went to get up. "Wait till Major Conkey tells us to move."

The man shouted again, his voice angry and impatient. "I told you bloody kids to get out here, now get moving!"

Some cadets in other platoons began to move and Barbara saw Lofty stand up, looking puzzled and anxious. Then she heard Major Conkey's voice. "Cairns, stay put till you get my orders."

The man, a warrant officer Barbara could now see, looked towards Major Conkey and yelled at him, "Hey you, are you in charge here? Get all these kids together."

Barbara looked around, nettled by both the interruption and by the tone of voice. She saw Major Conkey walk into view, his usually cheerful face clouding with irritation. "Are you speaking to me?" he asked.

The warrant officer nodded. "Yes, I am! Get all these kids up to the camp, at once!"

"And who are you?" Major Conkey asked. He spoke softly but Barbara, knowing him well, could tell he was deeply offended and angry.

"Warrant Officer Gately, now do what I say and get them moving!" replied the warrant officer.

"And who am I?" Major Conkey asked in a mild tone.

"One of the people running the cadets I suppose."

"I am Major Conkey, and I am the OC of this unit. If you want them to move, then please ask me."

"Major? Are you a real army officer?" the warrant officer snapped back, his voice changing slightly with uncertainty.

"Real army? I thought there was only one Australian Army," Major Conkey replied, making a sly dig at the regular army's usual derogatory attitude towards reservists. Barbara knew that Major Conkey had been a reserve officer when he was younger, had even been a regular soldier who had seen active service fighting in the Makassang Campaign, but now he was retired.

"So, are you an officer?" the warrant officer queried.

"I am a major AAC," Major Conkey replied, his face now tinged with anger. Barbara watched with a mixture of anger and pleasure as the confrontation developed.

The warrant officer scowled. "You know what I mean," he retorted, his voice barely civil. "Now get these kids moving mister."

"I am only an Officer of Cadets now," Major Conkey replied with icy calm, "But I am either an officer appointed for this purpose by the army, in which case you will call me 'major'; or I am a civilian voluntarily giving my time to assist the army, in which case you will call me 'Mister Conkey' or 'sir'. But in any case, you can be civil."

The warrant officer went very red and looked quite angry, but he managed to reply in a more respectful voice. "Yes, well, so get these kids moving."

"Is there a safety or medical emergency?" Major Conkey asked.

The warrant officer hesitated and then said, "Yes... er... well, no. But we want them up at the camp quickly."

Major Conkey stepped closer. "Are you a professional soldier?" he asked, his jaw clenched.

"Yes," replied the warrant officer, drawing himself up and looking down his nose.

Seeing the man's body language caused Barbara to bristle with resentment. *You arrogant bastard!* she thought.

"Then act like one!" snapped Major Conkey. "We are trying to teach the cadets the correct military procedures and etiquette. In this unit we use the military chain of command, so don't you cut across my lines of authority without a good reason. I am the one legally responsible for these cadets, not you."

Barbara saw the warrant officer's face mottle with anger as the rebuke sank home. He opened his mouth several times and Barbara thought he was going to shout at Major Conkey. With an obvious effort he mastered his emotions and gestured. "Colonel Green wants all these kids at the camp," he said.

Still no 'sir', Barbara noted with growing irritation. She now thoroughly disliked the warrant officer.

Major Conkey stared hard at the warrant officer. "You could have explained that before," he replied. Then he turned his back on him and called into the scrub, "Platoon commanders! Bring your platoons out onto the road, now!"

"Up you get Four Platoon," Barbara ordered. She led them out to the edge of the road.

As the platoons began filing out the warrant officer again shouted, "Get them lined up on the road!"

Major Conkey stepped over beside him and hissed angrily, "Stop cutting across my line of authority! We are doing what you asked."

Again, Barbara thought the warrant officer might make some retort but he held his tongue, merely giving Major Conkey an insolent glance. Barbara was now almost enjoying the struggle of wills, feeling that Major Conkey was getting the better of it.

Suddenly there was the growl of motors and the warrant officer looked down the road, then shouted, "You kids get off the road!"

Barbara could not help herself. By then she was close to the man. Cheekily she called, "But you said get on the road."

The warrant officer spun round and glared at her. "Don't you get cheeky with me girlie! Now get off the road! There are trucks coming."

"I'm not a girlie!" she snapped back. "I'm a Cadet Under-Officer."

Major Conkey stepped over quickly. "That will do! CUO Brassington, get your platoon off the road." He then turned to the warrant officer and

Barbara heard him hiss, "And they are cadets, not kids. Try to present a positive image of the army to them. Then they might be your future recruits."

Barbara felt a malicious spurt of pleasure at that, then turned and ordered her cadets to move well back. A convoy of army vehicles came into view: several Land Rovers with radio antennae; then a dozen trucks. The trucks were carrying soldiers. These stared down at the cadets. Most of their faces were friendly but it seemed to Barbara that a few were sneering, with an air of contemptuous superiority. That rankled but she could only shrug philosophically.

The vehicles ground past, churning up a thick cloud of powdery dust in the process. Luckily most of this drifted across onto 130ACU, who were also starting to form up on the other side of the road. The vehicles went on to the army camp, then along the continuation of the Camp Road which ran to the far end of the Old Airstrip.

"Regular troops from Lavarack Barracks, come to search for the satellite," went the rumour. Barbara had no reason to disbelieve this but had to smile at Cpl Halyday's sarcastic comment of, "Good luck to them! I wonder if they know it's in a million pieces and scattered across half of Australia?"

It seems that they did because as soon as the company was all seated on the concrete slabs at the camp the warrant officer called out wanting to know if any of them had seen any of the pieces land. Because she already disliked him, and because he again called them kids, she felt like just sitting there, but then she saw Sgt Russell put his hand up, while looking at her. Reluctantly she put up her hand.

Major Conkey called, "All you people who saw bits of the satellite land move over here."

Barbara joined the small group, which included Fiona and Sgt Blockey. While they waited the helicopter started up and took off, its rotor wash engulfing them in an irritating cloud of ash and dust. That annoyed Barbara even more and she coughed and spat to try to clear the gritty feeling from her teeth. Then another Blackhawk came clattering in to land. It unloaded a dozen people and lifted off. Among the people were both civilians and higher-ranking officers.

They walked past to the HQ building and a long, boring wait for the cadets ensued. They quickly became restless sitting in the sun with nothing to do. *We could have kept on training,* Barbara thought. *They could have just asked for the people they wanted.*

Major Conkey obviously thought the same thing as he sent orders for the training to resume, but to be done on or near the slabs. This was less than ideal but was better than nothing.

After about three quarters of an hour the dozen or so who had seen objects land were called to move over outside the HQ building. Among them was Chloe and Barbara was amused, but concerned, to watch her begin flirting with a young regular soldier who stood at the door controlling entry. Major Conkey, Major Wickham and Lt Standish joined them and Chloe immediately became less forward.

An army officer appeared at the door and said, "Alright, bring the first one in."

Major Conkey immediately beckoned to Barbara. She walked over to the door with him, feeling unreasonably anxious. As she did the young soldier looked her up and down with an appraising look that irritated her. Just inside the door she had to stop as Major Conkey was asked to wait. Beside the door was a table with two regular soldiers sitting at it. One had a radio and the other was doing paperwork. Both looked at her and once again Barbara noted their gaze run over her body. She experienced the surge of resentment and annoyance she always felt when she saw that male look of leering, accompanied by the knowing smirks.

Her attention was then diverted by raised voices in argument. She glanced past Major Conkey and saw a red-faced and chubby civilian arguing with Major Ross and a lieutenant colonel she had never seen before.

"Is this satellite dangerous?" Major Ross asked.

Barbara saw a momentary hesitation on the civilian's face. Then he answered, "No."

He's lying! she thought. That got her even more anxious. How could the crashed satellite be dangerous? The reason that immediately sprang to mind was radiation. *If it was a nuclear satellite it could be radio active,* she thought, remembering Cpl Walsh's claims.

"It had better not be," Major Ross replied firmly. "Because if it is I will get all these cadets out of the area at once."

The lieutenant colonel looked annoyed. "It might be a good idea if you did. We don't need a lot of snotty-nosed kids getting in the way and causing trouble. You could clear them out of the area as soon as we have questioned them," he snapped.

Oh, you ignorant bastard! Barbara thought.

At that moment the lieutenant colonel looked and saw Barbara. He scowled and said, "What are you doing in here? You can wait outside girlie."

At that Barbara bristled. Before Major Conkey could speak she retorted, "I'm not a girlie SIR. I am a Cadet Under-Officer. And I was told to come in here by your people." With that she spun on her heel and stormed back out through the doorway.

"Wait! Come back here you!" called the lieutenant colonel.

Barbara stopped on the porch, her chest heaving with fury. "Bloody ignorant, arrogant...!" she muttered.

Chapter 5

IRRITATED

"Barbara!" Major Conkey called. He had followed her out of the room.

"Sir?" Barbara replied. She was feeling tired, irritated and now angry and was in no mood to be insulted.

"Come back inside please."

"Yes sir, but that man can be civil to me," she answered, making sure her voice was loud enough to be heard inside.

She followed Major Conkey and Lt Standish back in. As she did she saw the lieutenant colonel give her an angry glare. Before he could speak Major Conkey saluted, then went over and introduced himself. Lt Standish did the same and the awkward moment passed. Barbara, considering herself to be a subordinate 'under command', remained where she was and did not salute.

It was the chubby, red-faced civilian who spoke to Barbara. "My name is Beecher," he said. "Who are you?"

"Cadet Under-Officer Barbara Brassington," she replied, disliking the man instantly. Words like 'smarmy' and 'oily' flitted across her mind.

He gave what she considered to be a crocodile smile and then went on, "We heard that you saw some pieces of our satellite land last night."

"Yours? I heard it was French," Barbara replied. She was further nettled by the way the man's eyes kept flicking to her bosom.

"Er... Yes. I meant ours in that we have been given the job of finding it," Mr Beecher replied, giving another ingratiating smile.

"Did the French ask you to do that?" Barbara asked.

At that the lieutenant colonel said, "Don't you worry your pretty little head about such matters. This is government business little girl."

As he spoke the lieutenant colonel's eyes flicked down to Barbara's bosom. She felt a surge of resentment at the leering gaze and this added to the sense of insult in his comment.

You patronizing bastard! she thought. But she kept her face neutral and looked Mr Beecher in the eye. "Well, did they?" she said.

Beecher looked back at her and compressed his lips. "No. The Australian government."

"Are you going to give it back to the French?" Barbara asked. She didn't quite know why she was so blunt but something about the men irritated her.

Again, a momentary hesitation. The men seemed taken aback by the question. Mr Beecher exchanged a glance with the lieutenant colonel.

They don't plan to, Barbara deduced.

"Of course," Mr Beecher replied.

"Good. Thou shalt not steal sayeth the Lord," Barbara quoted.

A peculiar look crossed Mr Beecher's face and the lieutenant colonel looked angry again. Mr Beecher gave another false smile and said, "And the French will be asked to help pay for the clean up and restoring the environment."

"What is there to clean up?" Barbara asked. "Are they going to water the bush to make the grass grow again?" she added sarcastically.

At that the lieutenant colonel exploded angrily. "Enough of this silly nonsense! Did you see the thing land or not girl?"

Barbara eyed him coldly, then replied quietly. "I did, and if you speak to me in a civil way I might show you." She felt overawed by the man's high rank but equally his manner seemed to drive her to be defiant.

At that the lieutenant colonel spluttered with rage. "How... how dare you!" he snapped. "This is a matter of national security, not some sort of a game."

"How is our national security involved?" challenged Barbara. "I thought France was a friend and ally?"

"They are," Mr Beecher spoke, gesturing to the lieutenant colonel to keep out of the conversation. "We are just helping them."

Like hell! Barbara thought. *You just want it for yourself.* But she did not say this. Instead she stood there waiting.

Mr Beecher smiled again. "So, can you show us?" he asked.

"Yes. I can take you straight to the pieces of debris I saw," she said.

"Good. Can you show us on the map where you think the wreckage you saw is?" Mr Beecher asked. He held out a copy of the army 1:50 000 scale map. Barbara quickly pointed to the place and Mr Beecher made a pencil mark. He then said, "Good. Now please wait outside while we speak to the others?"

Barbara nodded, then saluted, though more towards Major Conkey than the lieutenant colonel, earning a venomous scowl from him. Then she turned on her heel and left the room. Outside she found she was trembling and had to suck in several deep breaths to steady herself. This resulted in a bout of coughing as the air was full of smoke and dust again.

Fiona joined her. "What happened Barbara? You look a bit peeved," she commented.

Barbara gave her a wry smile but did not answer. Just at that moment she did not trust herself to speak. Luckily Fiona was called in next, so she was able to slowly calm down. By the time Fiona came back out she felt better.

"We will be going to have a look soon," Fiona said.

The others were called in one at a time. Barbara sat herself against the wall in the shade to one side and closed her eyes. They felt sore and gritty and she wondered why she was feeling so irritable.

After a few more minutes the adults came out of the HQ, following Chloe, who was the last to be questioned. Chloe gave Barbara an impish smile and adjusted the hat she had acquired from somewhere so that it sat at a jaunty angle on her blonde hair.

Barbara could not help giving her a wry smile. "That hat is too small for you Chloe. You make sure you have some sun cream on," she said. That allowed her to avoid looking at Beecher or the lieutenant colonel. The group was told by Major Ross to get into two Land Rovers parked at the front of the building.

Major Conkey then asked the lieutenant colonel, "Sir, are they going to be walking around the bush?"

"Yes, if they are to show us where these pieces landed," the lieutenant colonel replied.

Major Conkey turned to the cadets and said, "Go and get your webbing cadets. Bring mine please CUO Brassington."

The lieutenant colonel frowned. "Is that necessary? We are in a hurry," he queried in an irritated voice.

"For safety," Major Conkey insisted.

Barbara heard the lieutenant colonel say, "It is just wasting time," but by then she was walking away. As quickly as she could she collected Major Conkey's webbing and then got her own. On returning to the HQ she hung back and made sure she wasn't in the same vehicle as Beecher or the lieutenant colonel. She climbed into the back of the other vehicle and sat next to Chloe, with Fiona opposite her and Sgt Russell on her other side. A third Land Rover with the warrant officer and some army signallers in it pulled out and followed them.

The vehicles drove down to the Front Gate and turned left on the Mingela Road. At Major Conkey's direction they pulled off to park just past a small dip. This was close to the Bridge. Everyone climbed out and Barbara stood looking at the smoking wasteland that was the area she had been in the night before. Most of the grass was now ash but a few tufts survived, particularly along the bank of One Mile Creek. Wisps of smoke rose from logs and a few shattered trees. A couple of trees were still burning. The flames were all but invisible in the daylight and there was very little smoke.

Beecher eyed the burnt off area with distaste, then said, "Well, who saw what?"

Fiona at once pointed. "We were over there at the bridge and a big piece went overhead to land somewhere back there."

"I saw that," Chloe agreed. "But I was further along to the left, just on the far side of the creek."

"We saw it too," Sgt Russell agreed. "It landed up behind the Gravel Scrape."

"What Gravel Scrape?" the lieutenant colonel asked. He had been studying the army 1:50 000 scale map.

"That one," Sgt Russell said, pointing across the blackened slope.

To Barbara the yellowish colour of the scrape was really obvious, but the lieutenant colonel had trouble seeing it.

He then looked at his map again. "This bridge and that gravel scrape aren't on this map."

"Try this enlargement," Major Conkey said, handing him a photocopied map that the unit had prepared for the activity.

The lieutenant colonel looked at it and Major Conkey indicated their position. The lieutenant colonel frowned and asked, "Is this accurate? It looks hand drawn."

Major Conkey nodded. "I drew it. It is more accurate than the real map," he assured him. "It includes things that have changed since the other map was made."

The lieutenant colonel looked sceptical and that annoyed Barbara.

You ignorant bugger! she thought, knowing that Major Conkey was a trained cartographer as well as being a senior Geography teacher.

The lieutenant colonel told the warrant officer to take a compass bearing and they began walking across to the bridge. Barbara handed Major Conkey his webbing, then swung on her own and followed. She was then granted some amusement as she watched Mr Beecher trying to keep his good leather shoes and grey suit trousers from getting dirty.

As they came up to the Gravel Scrape Barbara at last spoke up. She had been looking over to her left and now her eyes had found what they sought. "There is a piece over there, sticking out of a tree."

"Is it far?" Beecher asked.

"No, only about fifty metres," Barbara replied. "You can see it from here."

They turned left and walked across the powdery ash and hot sand. As they got closer to the place Barbara noted that the tree the piece was stuck in was scorched but that the jagged piece of metal was still there. Then she was irritated even more. The warrant officer said, "How did you know there is a piece here?"

"I was here last night," Barbara replied.

"Are you sure?"

That did annoy Barbara. "Yes, I am sure. I am a Cadet Under-Officer. I am a good navigator and have a lot of experience at walking around the bush at night," she replied hotly.

To her further irritation the warrant officer looked doubtful and all but rolled his eyes. Luckily the group reached the piece at that moment and her statement was supported. The piece was a jagged flat section of grey metal about the size of a dinner plate. Its edges were sharp and had a look of white crystalline matter along them.

Sgt Russel moved closer to look at it. The lieutenant colonel held out his arm. "Don't touch that boy," he said.

"Why not sir?" Sgt Russel asked.

"Er... It might be hot," the lieutenant colonel replied.

It did not look at all hot to Barbara. *It's had all night to cool down,* she thought. Then another idea came to her.

"Is it radio active?" she asked.

The lieutenant colonel looked irritated and shook his head, but Mr Beecher nodded and said, "Yes, it might be."

There was a moment of tense silence. Then Major Conkey frowned and said, "We were assured it was safe or I would not have allowed the cadets to come here."

"Oh it is!" the lieutenant colonel at once said.

Mr Beecher made a face and nodded, then added, "We are here, aren't we?"

Major Conkey looked unhappy but did not object. "I hope it is safe," he replied.

Mr Beecher looked around at the burnt bush then turned to Barbara. "What were you doing here in the middle of nowhere?" he asked. He mopped his red face with a handkerchief and looked quite unhappy.

"I was at a check point for a night navigation exercise," Barbara replied.

"What, here?" the lieutenant colonel asked. He looked around in obvious disbelief.

That annoyed Barbara. "No. At the Gravel Scrape with Sgt Russell and Sgt Rowley," she answered.

"So, what were you doing here?" the lieutenant colonel queried.

Barbara hadn't wanted to explain that and now she blushed and hesitated.

"Well?" insisted the lieutenant colonel. "Were you lost?"

"No. I came away from the others to answer a call of nature," Barbara answered, blushing with embarrassment.

At that the warrant officer snickered. "I'll bet you wet yourself when this thing came down!" he commented, leering at her as he did.

Barbara nearly had but she was too offended to answer. She had been about to tell them about the bigger piece that had struck and shattered the big tree near where they were standing but now she compressed her lips. Her hand, which had been raised to point, she now lowered to her side. The irrational thought that they could find the thing themselves caused her to feel peevishly ashamed. Then she shook her head and turned her back on it. Inside she boiled with embarrassed anger.

The lieutenant colonel did not seem to notice. He glanced at the piece or metal stuck in the tree near them and shrugged then asked them to move back to the gravel scrape. The warrant officer called forward two soldiers who were carrying a roll of bright yellow plastic tape. They took a photo and began taping off the area.

While they did this Barbara looked for the shattered tree and could not find it. Then she realised that its trunk had been completely splintered and then burnt away. The tree had been a Ghost Gum. Some of the larger branches had been smashed off and still lay on the ground and Barbara could see that the inside was rotten and all but hollow.

The trunk must have been similar, she mused, noting a large hole full of smoking ash which indicated that the fire had burned the stump and was still burning underground as it consumed the roots. There was no sign of the big metal object, so she just shrugged and followed the others back towards the Gravel Scrape.

But her conscience got the better of her. Swallowing her pride she changed her mind. *I'd better do the right thing,* she told herself.

Pointing towards the hole she said, "Another bit landed here. It struck that tree."

The lieutenant colonel looked back and frowned then said, "I can't see anything."

The warrant officer walked closer to the smouldering hole and scanned the ground. Then he shook his head. "Nothing here. Are you sure you didn't get such a fright that you imagined it?" he commented.

"No!" Barbara replied, stung by the man's attitude. She was about to explain how the object had struck the tree trunk and punched in when the warrant officer turned his back on her. That really annoyed her, so she closed her mouth.

The lieutenant colonel looked sceptical then asked, "Did anyone actually see any other pieces land?"

Sgt Russel pointed to the west. "I saw a big piece go overhead and thought I heard it land somewhere over there."

"You didn't actually see it land?" the warrant officer queried.

Sgt Russel shook his head. "No sir."

The lieutenant colonel looked hot and irritated. He shrugged and said, "I suppose we had better have a look."

From the Gravel Scrape the group walked South West up into the charred and smoking remains of the thicket. By then the full force of the tropical sun was making itself felt and it was very hot. Barbara licked her lips and was glad she had brought her webbing. She had a big drink and was not impressed to note that the 'professional' soldiers had not brought their own webbing. To her the whole area was now unpleasant and the smoke further irritated her already sore eyes. She rinsed them, but they still stung. By this time, she just wanted to go back to camp. Any desire to help the men find the pieces was gone.

For half an hour they plodded around the burnt-out bush, working their way steadily further and further away from the Gravel Scrape. As they searched the smouldering wasteland Barbara kept track of their movements by both map and compass. She noted Major Conkey doing the same.

The lieutenant colonel and Mr Beecher became visibly hot and annoyed and began to question whether the cadets had actually seen anything, further annoying Barbara. She vividly remembered the large object flashing overhead.

It was Sgt Russell who pointed to a tree which had a large branch smashed off. The broken bough lay on the ground, charred but obviously freshly fallen. That gave them a line and Fiona spotted another broken and splintered tree another fifty metres further on. The group walked to this and then saw more trees with signs of impact damage. A hundred paces further on they came to the piece of wreckage. It was made of the same grey metal, charred and twisted and looking like a curved sheet from the outside of a large drum.

After the wreckage had been photographed and then taped off Mr Beecher looked dissatisfied. "Well, this isn't it," he muttered.

"Do you mean it isn't from the satellite?" Major Conkey asked.

"Oh yes! It is from that for sure. It just isn't... well... isn't the bit we are looking for," Mr Beecher replied. He fanned himself and looked even hotter and more bothered.

The lieutenant colonel, who even to Barbara's inexperienced eyes, was plainly a 'desk soldier', also looked flushed and far from happy. Out of petty spite Barbara took out a waterbottle and had a big drink in front of him. She had the pleasure of seeing him lick his lips, but he did not ask for a drink. Instead he asked, "Are you kids sure you didn't see any other pieces of debris come in this direction?"

It was that 'kids' that did it. Barbara just looked away and made no answer. She felt bad about it but couldn't seem to help herself. Fiona and Sgt Russell both shook their heads and Chloe made a face and wrinkled her nose up.

Major Conkey was the first to speak. "I told you that the thing exploded in the air way back to the East and the main part of it struck the other side of Mount St Michael. Only a few pieces landed over this way."

"I saw a couple of small pieces go over high up," Fiona added. "They must have landed a long way west of here."

The lieutenant colonel looked irritated. "We have the troops from Lavarack searching the other side of Mount St Michael" he said.

"You will have to search all the areas that have been burnt-out," Major Conkey suggested. Then he went on, "Well, if you are finished here, I would like to get these cadets back to the camp."

The lieutenant colonel looked at Mr Beecher who reluctantly nodded. The group began walking back towards the road. As they did Barbara noted that all of the soldiers were now looking very hot and dry. She felt a bit sorry for the young soldiers who were under orders but had no sympathy at all for the warrant officer or the lieutenant colonel. She was further annoyed when they began to question the direction they were walking.

Major Conkey, who had his compass in his hand, was also visibly irritated. "This is the way we came," he snapped. "There are our boot prints."

That obviously peeved the warrant officer who had earlier been told to navigate. When, after another hundred metres, Major Conkey began deviating to the left away from the line of boot prints he questioned this. "The footprints go that way," the warrant officer said.

"Well you can follow them if you like," Major Conkey retorted. "But I am going to walk a straight line."

There was a moment's silent struggle of wills and then the party split into two groups. The lieutenant colonel, warrant officer, Mr Beecher and the soldiers went along the boot prints while the cadets, led by Major Conkey, went left on a compass bearing. The result did nothing to improve relations. The cadet group were almost at the Bridge before the army group appeared at the back of the Gravel Scrape, a full hundred metres behind them.

When they reached the parked vehicles the cadets all had a big drink while they waited. Barbara looked at the approaching group of hot and annoyed people and thought, *Serves you right, you arrogant...* It was obvious to her that the regular army people held the cadets, even the adult officers, in contempt. *They think we don't know anything!*

The cadets were all told to get back into the vehicles and were then driven back up to the camp. On arrival they dismounted and were told to go back to the company. As they walked away Barbara overheard the lieutenant colonel say to Mr Beecher, "Do we clear all these cadets out of the area?"

She did not hear Beecher's reply, but it was certainly a worry. *My annual camp as a CUO might be over,* she thought sadly.

Chapter 6

REDEPLOY

Barbara walked back to where the cadets were having lunch seated on the concrete slabs. The day was blazing hot and there was no shade at all. Barbara was not impressed with the organization that had caused this but could only complain to Major Conkey. He also looked irritated and hot, and agreed, "I've spoken to Major Ross about it, but he says we stay at the camp until we get the all-clear."

"Do you think we might have to pack up and leave sir?"

"It is a distinct possibility Barbara, but don't say anything to the troops yet."

"Yes sir."

Barbara joined her platoon and settled to eating her lunch. That was difficult as she had no appetite. The walk in the heat, combined with having drunk so much water, meant she did not feel hungry. Knowing that drinking too much could be harmful as it washed out all the body salts she forced herself to eat.

Must replace my electrolytes, she told herself. She then made herself drink some more: cold orange cordial this time. *I need a bit of sugar as well as more salt,* she thought.

After lunch, training was resumed at the camp itself. Major Conkey quickly briefed the platoon commanders. While he gave a theory lesson on 'Types of Patrols' to the whole company, the platoon commanders went and set up two 'Observation' courses in the scrub on the far edge of the car park. These were simple activities. The first one involved twenty-five items being placed in clear view of a particular spot, and all within twenty-five paces of it. The cadets were to be called there one at a time from a waiting area and given two minutes to see if they could spot them all. They would then move on to a second waiting area. The second course also involved twenty-five items but this time they were laid out along the edge of the bush and the cadets had to walk along one at a time with either a CUO or sergeant and were to point out all the things they saw.

Barbara and Fiona chose to organize the stationary course and soon had it done. When they were finished they walked back to where Major Conkey was briefing the company in the meagre shade along the side of a building. When he was finished his lecture the CUOs took their own platoons to the first waiting area and began. The two platoon sergeants acted as controllers at the two waiting areas.

Normally Barbara really enjoyed these activities but now she was feeling worn out and upset. She knew in her heart she had been petty and was feeling guilty about not pointing out the other piece of wreckage. Finally, Fiona asked her what the matter was.

Barbara shrugged then looked down. "I just feel bad," she admitted. "There was another piece of wreckage that I saw last night but I didn't show those horrible men exactly where it was."

"Why not?" Fiona asked.

"They just made me so angry with their patronising, sneering superiority," Barbara replied.

"They were certainly arrogant," Fiona agreed.

Sgt Russell walked over and waited till Barbara finished. She turned to him, "Yes, Sgt Russell?"

"All finished, ma'am," he replied.

Barbara was surprised. The time had gone faster than she had expected. "Good. OK, take the platoon over to where CUO Dunning is running the other Observation Course," she instructed.

Sgt Russell left to do this. When Fiona had finished with the last cadet from her platoon the two friends stood in the sparse shade of a small tree and discussed the unpleasant events of the morning.

Barbara sighed. "I was seriously thinking of joining the army as a career," she admitted, "But if those two are typical, then I'm not sure I want to."

"They would be hard to put up with day after day, that is for sure," Fiona agreed.

The arrival of the two platoons from the other course ended their conversation. Their sergeants were briefed and the platoons seated in the first waiting area. Then the process began again. This went on for another hour until all had been through the 'stand'. By then Barbara had a headache and was feeling distinctly dehydrated. She found it a real relief to go to the toilet and to wash her face and have a big drink.

As she walked back from the toilet Barbara saw another dozen army trucks go driving past. They were also loaded with more regular army troops and headed off towards the eastern end of Mount St Michael.

Major Conkey had the company seated in the shade of the same building, the strip of shade at least now being big enough to accommodate everyone as the afternoon sun sank lower. Lt Hamilton gave a lesson on 'Patrol Preparation'.

Barbara sat at the back, half her mind an anxious worry about the camp being cancelled. What was particularly bothering her was the thought that the big inter-unit field exercise planned for the next afternoon and evening might now be cancelled. The lessons on patrolling were in preparation for that and she had been training her own platoon for months to be ready for it. It was to be the 'big event' of the camp.

It will be a real downer if it doesn't happen, she thought.

An army Light Observation helicopter went buzzing past and began to fly up and down over the country to the southeast. A Blackhawk could be occasionally seen in the distance. More vehicles drove in, mostly Land Rovers with radios on them. The HQ area became congested and there was a real bustle of troops coming and going.

Two more Blackhawks came in to land on the burnt-out flat across the road. Barbara was intrigued to note that four officers in two different styles of foreign camouflage uniforms were among the people who got out. She was even more interested to note the lieutenant colonel go over and salute one. As they walked past towards the HQ she saw that the man who had been saluted had a single silver star pinned to his collar.

An American brigadier general! This satellite must be a bigger deal than I thought, she pondered.

Another wave of guilt crept over her and she contemplated going to the HQ to tell them about the other piece of wreckage. She was distracted from this by the Blackhawks taking off and then by Major Conkey finishing his lesson and calling the platoon commanders.

"Have dinner," he said, "and get organized for the night training."

"Are we still having a lantern stalk sir?" Fiona asked.

Major Conkey nodded. "That is the plan. I am going to check with Major Ross now."

Barbara joined her platoon on the concrete slab allocated to it. By now the afternoon sun was well down in the west but its rays still had enough strength to bite and she began to wish it would just hurry up and go down. By now it was shining through the vast pall of smoke off to the West and it looked like a giant red ball. Barbara decided that the effect was weird as everything was bathed in an eerie reddish-orange glow.

Sgt Russell and the section 2ics returned with the rations and these were issued. Still feeling devoid of appetite Barbara sat and made an effort to eat. To her intense relief the sun finally set, vanishing slowly but leaving the whole western sky one massive sheet or red and gold.

While Barbara was standing staring at this Major Conkey came over and told her that the lantern stalk was definitely still on and that she was to have her platoon ready by 1900 hours. As it was already 1835 this got her moving.

After telling Sgt Russell and the corporals to get the troops ready on time Barbara packed away her mess gear, then hurried to the ablution block to brush her teeth. Next, she refilled her waterbottles, and then made her way back to the company area.

By 1855 her platoon was seated in section lines with the remainder of the company. The lantern stalk was being conducted by Capt Hamilton from 130ACU, the brother of Lt Hamilton. He had 130ACU seated beside the Cairns unit, then called the CUOs and sergeants of both units to join him. They were to be the 'defenders' for the lantern stalk and while he led them away to be briefed and placed in position Major Conkey gave a lesson to both units on 'Sounds at Night'. Barbara went with the other CUOs.

Now that the sun had set she felt a bit better but still had a headache and really just wanted to lie down. The group walked west down the Camp Road towards the Front Gate. As they did they twice had to get off the road to allow vehicles to drive past. Even though the vehicles drove slowly they still stirred up clouds of fine dust which caused Barbara to cough and sneeze. When added to the irritation from the drifting smoke which still pervaded the area it made her eyes sore and caused her to cough and feel nauseous.

Away from the lights of the camp it was still quite light as the moon was coming up and was almost full. Fiona laughed and pointed back at it, saying, "Going to be hard for anyone to hide on a night like this!"

Barbara had to agree and smiled. During her cadet career she had done a dozen lantern stalks and usually enjoyed the challenge.

Being one of the guards isn't nearly as much fun, she decided.

Down near the Front Gate they halted and Barbara saw that Major Wickham was there, briefing two sections. One of the section commanders was Chloe and Barbara overheard her getting some final instructions. From that she learnt that Chloe's section were not taking part in the lantern stalk but was deploying as a sentry post to watch the Mingela Road near the One Mile Creek Dip. The other section was to go to the gate on the Back Road. Their task was to provide early warning in case St Michael's Cadet Unit tried to sneak in some raiding parties. Chloe gave a cheery assurance that she was ready and then led her section away.

Lucky thing! Barbara thought, wishing she was leading a raid rather than doing a lantern stalk.

Capt Hamilton then briefed the defenders and deployed them in three lines across the hillside. Each line was a hundred metres apart, the last one being a hundred paces from the lantern, which was hung in a tree. The left flank of each line was at the road. The defenders were in pairs and all had torches. The area selected, on the north of the road down from 130's bivouac, had not been burnt-out but had only a sparse cover of grass and dead leaves. The ground sloped gently down for five hundred metres to the fence line along the Mingela Road. Barbara made sure that she was teamed up with Fiona.

The two friends were placed at the left of the line, covering the last fifty metres to the Camp Road. Lofty and Roger were the next pair to their right. Behind them, near the lantern, were some of the adult officers and Lt Hamilton parked his Land Rover beside the road to act as safety vehicle.

At about 2000 hours the two companies of cadets came trampling past down the road. As they passed they stirred up a cloud of dust which set Barbara coughing again. She took out her waterbottle and had a big drink, then rinsed her eyes.

"I don't like this training area," she said. "I much prefer the Bunyip River area."

Fiona agreed, and the two girls discussed previous camps, particularly the one the year before when the gang of crooks had taken most of the company hostage while they searched for 4 Platoon and a girl with a briefcase full of incriminating documents. That was when Barbara had knocked one of the gang down, then run off. She had escaped, but still shuddered at the memory. Twice crooks had fired at her, and she had shot one of them in the leg.

It was all very character building, she mused.

Next, she shuddered at the memory of the unasked for sequels, almost equally as deadly: when she had been abducted by the two pig hunters during her CUOs Course in December; and when Berzinski had stalked and pursued her in March at Mt Mulligan. Almost as harrowing and traumatic had been the court appearances.

Compared to those sorts of experiences a lantern stalk was very tame stuff and she went through this one almost in a daze. Fiona helped, and Barbara was glad she had such a good friend. She was also glad that Fiona was such a true friend. After rescuing Fiona from the religious fanatics near Kuranda the previous June the two girls had been almost inseparable. It was partly this closeness that led to the rumours about Barbara being a lesbian, and which fuelled her own doubts and confusion.

The aim of the lantern stalk was to develop the individual fieldcraft skills of the cadets, and to build up their self-confidence. To that end, if they did the right thing, it was possible for them to creep past the lines of defenders to reach the lantern. This was both the objective and a navigation aid. All Barbara and Fiona had to do was walk backwards and forwards along a fifty-metre track, trying to detect cadets sneaking past.

The whole event had become a bit of a chore to Barbara until after about an hour Fiona suddenly gripped her arm. "What's that noise?" she asked.

Barbara had also heard the sound and had already tensed. She swung her head from side to side trying to locate the source of a very deep vibrating sound. Suddenly it came to her. "An aircraft!" she said.

Even as she spoke the noise rose dramatically in volume and the aircraft flew overhead. Barbara flinched and ducked. It was very big machine, and very low. Fiona, open mouthed with surprise, pointed up then said, "There it is!"

Barbara got a fleeting glimpse of a large black object. It crossed over their heads, travelling west and moving at what must have been several hundred kilometres per hour. "No lights," she commented. "The pilots must be using night vision equipment."

"What is it?" Fiona wondered aloud.

Nearby came CUO Sharon Whalley's voice. "A Hercules transport."

"How do you know?" Fiona queried.

"Because we see them all the time," Sharon replied. "The landing approach for Garbutt RAAF Base goes right over our school."

"But you can't see it," Barbara said.

"Doesn't matter," Sharon replied. "I can tell the engine noise."

"What's it doing now?" Fiona asked.

The girls stood and stared westwards into the moonlit sky. Because of the bright moonlight there were very few stars visible, just a sort of greyish background. The Hercules was now quite invisible to them.

"Turning back, I think," Barbara suggested. The Hercules might be too common for the Heatley cadets to bother about, but she rarely saw military aircraft in Cairns and now watched with considerable interest.

The engine noises changed, with a distinct drop in revs. Then the sound came ever lower and further to the south. Fiona again pointed. "There it is. I think it's going to land at the New Airfield."

Barbara saw a tiny black shape above the tree tops. Then the aircraft was down and all she could hear were its engines roaring as reverse thrust was applied. "No lights alright. They've landed. I hope those noddies from St Michael's weren't doing an exercise out on the airstrip."

Neither girl had visited St. Michael's camp, but they knew the unit was camped beside the New Airfield. Both had commented on how odd it was that they always seemed to isolate themselves from the other units. Barbara knew that 130ACU frequently sent secret recon patrols to observe them and remembered that Chloe and her section were even now out beside the Mingela Road somewhere guarding against a surprise raid.

An attempt by some cadets to sneak past distracted the two girls for a few minutes. Then their interest was again focused on the aircraft as a swelling roar indicated it was taking off. They did not see it, but the sound went off to the southeast, vanishing behind Mount St Michael. The girls listened for a few more minutes but they heard nothing more so refocused on the lantern stalk.

Barbara found it a real relief when the exercise ended an hour later. By then the air had cooled down somewhat but was still pungent with the reek of smoke. All the cadets were called in to the lantern and seated in section lines so that the respective CSMs could check that nobody was missing, a basic precaution to ensure no cadet was left lying injured out in the bush.

While they were doing this Barbara again heard the sound of aircraft engines. This time the plane was very high up and travelling from North to South. She saw no sign of it at all but could tell from the engine note that it was also a Hercules transport.

Major Wickham and Major Conkey had both joined the exercise after attending a co-ord conference. Barbara saw Major Wickham point up and heard him say, "I wonder if that is the same plane that landed earlier?"

Major Conkey answered, "I wonder if it is going to land again! Apparently, that really gave St Michael's a fright."

Major Wickham chuckled. "Yes, Cpl Cummings reported that she heard some cries of alarm."

"Major Ross isn't very happy about it," Major Conkey added. "He said he was told by Range Control that there were no air movements in this area at night during the camp period."

"Might be something to do with this crashed satellite?" suggested Major Wickham.

The two majors then moved out of earshot, so Barbara was unable to glean any more information. It did interest her to learn that Chloe's patrol was close enough to St Michael's camp to hear people cry out. *I wish my platoon could do that,* she thought. She knew that 130ACU and St Michaels had a long running feud which soured relations between the two units.

After the roll check was completed they all trooped back to camp in a long line. This again stirred up the dust and got people coughing, sneezing and wheezing. Back at camp the cadets were dismissed and the canteen opened. Major Conkey called over the platoon commanders and CSM for a final briefing before bed.

"Good news so far," he said. "We are allowed to go ahead with our field exercise tomorrow. So, at zero eight hundred we will redeploy from here. One Thirty will also be moving and is on our flank. I will give detailed orders tomorrow morning but have your platoons packed and ready to move by zero seven fifty."

To Barbara that was great news and her morale lifted appreciably. She went off happily to sit with Roger and have a drink of 'Fanta'. Even though they were boyfriend and girlfriend they did not seek any privacy. Instead they sat under a light at the end of the row of slabs. There was no way Barbara would condone any fraternisation or deceit and one of the reasons she had chosen Roger as her friend was because he also had high integrity and a strong moral character.

After chatting for a while Roger said, "You seem a bit down Barbara. What's the matter?"

Barbara shrugged and gestured towards the now blackened silhouette of Mount St Michael. "I feel a bit guilty because I didn't show those army people a piece of that wreckage."

"Why not?"

That put Barbara on a spot. Now that she thought about it she felt quite ashamed of herself; at the pettiness of her reactions. She tried to explain but then gave up. Roger just laughed and said, "Don't fret about it. You can tell them tomorrow."

"Yes," Barbara agreed while secretly doubting if she could pluck up the courage to admit why she had not done it earlier. To end the conversation she said, "Now, bed for me."

After cleaning her teeth, going to the toilet and washing her face yet again, Barbara took herself to where the platoon lay in a row on the ground. She found her pack, noted that the security piquet was on duty, then unrolled her bedding and slid into it. As she did she saw a patrol of camouflaged cadets come walking into camp along the Camp Road. It was Chloe's section returning and she saw Barbara and gave a cheerful wave as she went by.

Lucky devils! Barbara thought. She lay back and thought about leading patrols to prove that hers was a good platoon. Within ten minutes she was fast asleep.

* * * *

Barbara awoke to a world of cool stillness. For a few minutes she lay in her sleeping bag and relished the pleasure of waking to the Australian bush. From where she lay Mount St Michael was outlined by the pink glow of the dawn. The only irritation came from the odour of burnt grass. That reminded her of the events of the previous two days and she wrinkled her nose and made a wry smile. Then she sat up and began her 'morning routine'.

By 0815 she stood at the head of a line of 17 cadets, her pack newly hoisted onto her back. Major Conkey and CSM Sheehan walked past and her UHF radio crackled, ordering them to move. Major Conkey had explained to the platoon commanders that he was leading them to their new bivouac site via a circuitous route which would cross the ground the field exercise would be on. As they were the 'defenders' this was judged to be fair.

"It will give the corporals a good idea of the ground," he explained.

The company moved in one long line. Initially they walked back along the Camp Road to their old bivouac site five hundred paces away. From there Major Conkey deviated to the left, leading the line on a compass bearing into the bush. As always Barbara was impressed to see a long line of cadets marching into the field. To her it all looked very military. The cadets were also excited. It was not only a change but they were looking forward to the field exercise.

After walking through the dry scrub for about three hundred metres Major Conkey halted the line at a small clump of dwarf pines on top of a distinct change of slope. He called in the platoon commanders and pointed to the bare sand under the small trees.

"That is where company HQ will be tonight," he said. He then led the way down a gentle but rock-studded slope for another 100 metres. At the base of the slope they came to a vehicle track and the camp boundary fence. After crawling under the fence, the company walked into a thicket of twisted and stunted trees growing in knee-high dry grass. From being able to see hundreds of metres visibility dropped to about fifty. Several steep-sided little washouts were crossed.

As he jumped one Cpl Halyday snorted. "That was the bastard we fell into the other night," he grumbled.

"You should watch where you are walking," Barbara commented.

"We were, but then that bloody satellite came crashing down and we were so busy gaping up at it I forgot to look," Cpl Halyday replied.

Sgt Blockey, the platoon sergeant of 3 Platoon who was walking just in front of Barbara, called softly back over his shoulder, "Serves you bloody well right then!"

The route Major Conkey followed brought them out onto the Mingela Road near the One Mile Creek Dip. Capt Maclaren was waiting there with a safety vehicle. To Barbara's concern Major Conkey then led the way across to One Mile Creek. One at a time the company slid down into the narrow, dry creek bed, then clambered up the other side. From there they angled across the burnt-out slope towards the Gravel Scrape.

This is going to take us right past that tree which was hit by that other piece of wreckage, Barbara thought.

Her guilt got her scanning the ground ahead. She was now thinking she would show Major Conkey as they went past. And she would have, she realized later, if only Cadet Lawler hadn't called out he was feeling sick. For the next ten minutes she was distracted by checking his well-being and by getting Cpl Halyday to take Lawler's pack, and by her making sure he had a big drink (He just hadn't drunk enough).

By then they were passing the Gravel Scrape. Barbara looked back and was able to spot the still smoking hole where the tree had once stood but she just shrugged and kept on walking.

I will tell him when we arrive, she decided.

Their route led on across the burnt-out country past the Gravel Scrape. There was another fence to roll under, an unpleasant experience in the heat and ash. Then they had to weave their way through another much larger thicket, burnt-out this time, for another half-kilometre. On the west side of the thicket they again came to One Mile Creek. The creek twisted and turned far more than the map indicated and had steep, eroded sides which were awkward to cross except at a few places.

After finding a place to cross they walked across another three hundred metres of scorched and blackened country. This was burnt-out savannah woodland. Off to their right a hundred metres away was the Mingela Road, glimpsed through gaps in the stunted vegetation. Several army vehicles drove past towards the camp and Barbara watched them. She was sure the soldiers in them had no idea the cadets were there. After crossing some small gullies, the company crawled under another fence and came out on a dirt side road. This was one of the roads which formed 'The Triangle', an area bounded by three roads.

A check of the map informed Barbara that this road was the Marlow Road. It appeared to her to be largely disused. It led South West in a straight line from the point where it left the Mingela Road.

Waiting beside the road were 130ACU. They had walked down through the scrub where the lantern stalk had been held, then along the other side of the Mingela Road between the road and the Swamp Paddock fence, then crossed to join them. The Cairns company sat down on their packs to have a drink while the two OCs conferred beside the safety vehicles. It was 0900 by then and the heat was already quite overpowering.

Then it was on again, trudging northwest across the Triangle. The country was almost completely flat and covered with unburnt savannah woodland. The trees were numerous but mostly small and spindly and the grass was very patchy. In places the grass was thick and knee-high but in others it barely hid the sand. Four hundred paces brought the company to another vehicle track. This road was the third side of the Triangle and was merely two dusty wheel ruts.

Major Conkey and CSM Sheehan stood there waiting. The CSM directed the platoons to sit in section lines and Major Conkey indicated to Capt Maclaren and Lt Hamilton where to park their Land Rovers under the trees. The company had arrived at the new bivouac site.

Chapter 7

ODD CHARACTERS

Major Conkey called the platoon commanders and CSM to him. He then led them around, pointing out the area allocated to each platoon. While they walked around the area Barbara noted that 130ACU was bivouacking a hundred metres further along the track to the east, near the junction with the Mingela Road.

The company was to deploy in a defensive circle. The area allocated to 4 Platoon was in the quadrant through which they had walked in, the southeast. 4 Platoon had to extend around to the vehicle track on the western end of the bivouac area. On their left was 2 Platoon. Across the track on 4 Platoon's right was 3 Platoon which covered the northwestern quadrant. 1 Platoon had the northeast corner.

Having determined boundaries, and also indicated the direction for boys and girls to go when latrines were dug, Major Conkey said, "Show your platoons their area and get them started setting up. Then I want you back for a company O Group." He looked at his watch then said, "Be here by ten hundred. Tell your people no move before fourteen hundred. Now off you go."

Barbara took her platoon to their area. It was only a hundred paces. Once there she pointed out the platoon boundaries and section areas, then selected two suitable trees on the inside of the area. "This is where platoon HQ will be. Those are my hutchie trees," she said. "Now get set up. Be ready for a platoon O Group by eleven hundred. No move before fourteen hundred, so have lunch at twelve."

The platoon split into sections and then into pairs and individuals. Within minutes shelters were being extracted from packs. Barbara took out her own shelter and stared up at the clear blue sky.

Bit pointless really, she thought wryly. Rain would be very welcome but there wasn't the slightest chance of that. *At least the hutchies will give some shade,* she thought.

By the time of the Coy O Group Barbara had her own shelter up and had placed her pack under it. She now walked across to where the

O Group was assembling. The platoon commanders and CSM from 130 also joined them, as well as most of their officers. Barbara knew that Major Conkey and Major Wickham were very good friends, so it was no surprise when Major Conkey began giving orders to both units. They were to work side by side, Cairns on the right and 130 on the left.

To begin with Major Conkey seated the platoon commanders in the layout they would be exercising in. Then he made sure they all had a fresh copy of the map enlargement. Major Conkey then said, "The first thing I want you all to be clear about is the main aim of this exercise. It is to provide small group leadership opportunities. It is not, I repeat NOT, to try to prove which cadet unit is the best."

CUO Glenn from 130ACU at once interrupted. "We all know who that is. We are!"

Major Wickham instantly rebuked him. "That will do CUO Glenn! We are among friends."

"Sorry sir."

Major Conkey gave a thin smile and resumed giving his orders. "So, keep in mind that I have designed this exercise so that both sides have opportunities and that it is not set up as a win-lose situation. If the leaders do the right thing they will get plenty of experience. We are the defenders, but I have so arranged it that the attackers have a good chance of achieving their aim by infiltrating our defences."

He then went on to explain the topography, confirming what Barbara had suspected; that they were to do the exercise over the ground they had been camping and training on. The exercise area extended from a line between the army camp and the base of Mount St Michael (both of which were out-of-bounds), westwards to the Gravel Scrape area. The northern boundary was a fence that ran from the army camp westwards to a cattle grid on the Mingela Road just this side of the Front Gate in the camp fence. This fence then continued on southwards to the New Airfield. Barbara remembered crawling under it just after they had left the Gravel Scrape on the march that morning. The southern boundary was the fence across the base of Mount St Michael, and then an easting. Major Conkey explained that the area they had originally planned to use for the exercise, off to the southeast a few kilometres away, was all burnt-out and was now off-limits because the army was searching it for the pieces of crashed satellite.

To her own delight Barbara learned that her platoon was to operate right out in front on their own. She was to advance and set up her HQ on the lowest knoll of Mount St Michael. This was a low rocky ridge just north of the fence which surrounded the quarry. From there she was to send out section patrols to cover the low ground across to the camp. Later they were to withdraw to Coy HQ and be the reserve. During the last phase they were to remain after the company had withdrawn and were to operate alone.

As she realised just how much she would be exercising independently Barbara's excitement mounted, as did a vague feeling of apprehension. She knew it was a great vote of confidence in her ability.

I hope I am good enough, she worried.

The 'attackers' aim was to try to infiltrate undetected from the army camp to the Gravel Scrape. To make this difficult the defenders were to deploy in four lines of patrols and section posts. Later on the forward lines were to be pulled back close to the Gravel Scrape. 130ACU's 4 Platoon was given the task of guarding the Front Gate, Bridge and Gravel Scrape, and of patrolling along the Mingela Road to the Dip. The 'front line' of static posts was to be along the Power Line.

Major Conkey kept talking for nearly 45 minutes, covering all the detail about timings, routes, boundaries, action on contact, action if lost, the administrative details, and 'Command and Signals'. At the conclusion he asked them each a question, then asked them if they had any questions. By the time they finished, Barbara had a very clear idea of what was planned and was looking forward to the event.

This enthusiasm she transmitted to her platoon when she gave them their orders at 1100. She could tell by the looks, comments, and flashing eyes that the cadets were really keen to get going. It also took her nearly three quarters of an hour to pass on the orders, suitably amended. Then she set them to work preparing.

4 Platoon was to have four handheld radios and Barbara took the corporals over to HQ to get issued with them. To her great satisfaction they were also issued with the only four headsets the unit owned. This meant they could talk, and more importantly receive, without the noise of the radio alerting any members of the opposing units who might be close.

By then it was 1220 hours and the others were busy eating. It was so hot that Barbara did not really feel like food, but she made herself eat.

To ensure there was no danger of a grass fire the platoon had to cook on the vehicle track, a process twice interrupted by Land Rovers going out to get water or to collect stores. Major Conkey also went to liaise with the other units to ensure that their orders matched his as far as the outline plan.

Barbara then felt an urgent need to go to the toilet. A quick check showed that the work party digging the girl's latrine were not yet finished.

Blast! Where can I go? she wondered, biting her lip in vexation. To find a suitable spot she began walking west along the vehicle track. Just past the last hutchies she noted what appeared to be a small fold in the ground off to her right. To reach it she had to walk through the dry grass and that she did gingerly, wary of possible snakes. After walking a hundred paces she saw with some surprise that what she had taken for a small gully was in fact a sizeable creek line, dropping down a fifty-metre-wide slope to a steep-sided, sandy bottom which was mostly hidden by a wall of head-high grass.

One Mile Creek, she realised, remembering from the map how the creek swung back to the northeast after the Marlow Road crossed it.

By now she was in quite a state of urgency, so she hurried down over the crest and out of sight of the camp. Here she paused. She could see along the sloping sides of the creek for at least one or two hundred metres each way and she looked to check that no boys were in sight. For a few seconds her modesty got her to contemplate pushing down through the long grass, but it looked so thick and unattractive that she shook her head and stopped where she was. There were clumps of bush dotted along both banks of the creek line and a few washouts where people could have hidden but she could see no-one.

After another look around she undid her trousers and pulled them down, then squatted to do her pee. As she did she felt very exposed and uneasy and that hurried her to finish. Feeling relieved in both senses she dressed and hurried back up the slope and across the flat to the camp.

By 1330 the platoon was busy 'camming up'. Camouflage paint was added to faces and scrim to the webbing and shoulders. Even better, the whole platoon was issued with old US army helmet liners. These were fibreglass and quite light and strong. With a scrim net over them they looked really military. Barbara was particularly pleased as it set her platoon apart and she could sense their pride. To this were added green cloth slides which were worn on the shoulder straps as identifying marks. 130ACU had yellow ones and the opposing units were to have pink or red.

By the time the platoon was lined up with camouflaged helmets, faces and webbing they looked really good. That they were conscious of this was obvious by their high morale. As they prepared to move out Barbara cautioned them on this.

"Don't you lot get big heads about how good you are and then get humiliated by not doing things properly. Those other units all want to win and they all want to bring us and One Thirty down a peg," she said.

"Pity we aren't doing an exercise against those show ponies from St Michael's," Cpl Halyday replied.

"That is One Thirty's battle," Barbara replied. "We will stay out of it. Now, all section commanders, do a radio check."

As soon as that was done Barbara reported to Major Conkey. When he saw her, he nodded with approval and then came back with her and took several photos of 4 Platoon. That pleased Barbara too. Normally she disliked putting on camouflage cream but this time it seemed to really put her in the mood. *War paint,* she decided.

Major Conkey pointed south and said, "Off you go CUO Brassington. Keep well spread out and make sure you check for any OPs that might be hiding along the way."

"Yes sir. OK Cpl Halyday, start moving," Barbara said.

"What about our camp ma'am? Who is going to guard that?" Cpl Walsh queried.

"Nobody. Both sides have agreed that the respective camps are out-of-bounds. You were told that in orders. Don't you listen?" Barbara replied.

She walked to the front of the platoon and then stood as Cpl Halyday led his section of six past. As they moved they spread out into an 'Arrowhead' formation, the scout fifty paces ahead of Halyday and the wings fifty metres back on each flank. When that section was fifty paces away Barbara began following. Sgt Russell walked with her. With them came Cpl Tracey Batt, a medic from Coy HQ. She carried a First Aid kit. Behind platoon HQ, well out on either flank, came the other two sections, each moving in a well-spaced single file.

The first three hundred metres was easy. They just walked southeast on a compass bearing, crossing the Marlow Road a hundred paces along from where they had crossed it earlier. The other side of the road was an abrupt transition. The grass ended and the burnt-out area began. The ground was just bare sand and ash, with the occasional smoking log and singed tuft of grass. The heat of the afternoon was scorching, and Barbara began to worry about heat exhaustion and what to do if they had a casualty.

Rolling under the fence beyond the Marlow Road really brought home to her just how hot it was. The sand seemed to burn her hands as she went down. It was a relief to stand up. She watched the platoon rolling under one at a time as they came up to the fence and experienced a surge of pride. The platoon was moving well and really looked like soldiers. Back behind her she saw the flicker of movement which indicated that the remainder of the company were following in her footsteps. 4 Platoon were the point platoon, the vanguard, and Barbara was very conscious that it was her duty to prevent the company being ambushed.

To that end she signalled Cpl Walsh to move his section further out to the right and to change into 'Arrowhead' so as to cover more ground. By then the first section had reached the bank of One Mile Creek and was searching for places to safely cross. Barbara had anticipated a few difficulties but was quite surprised to see just how hard the dry creek was to cross when she reached the top of the bank. Along that section the creek was ten metres wide at the top of the banks but a second, lower level was only 3 metres wide and just as deep, with vertical sides. Most of it was quite unclimbable for cadets and they had to scout along to find washouts and gullies to climb down and then often found they had to walk along the bottom of the creek for ten or twenty metres to find a place where they could climb out again. Down in the bottom the heat was stifling. The air felt superheated and there was absolutely no breeze.

It was hardly any better up on the far side. The route led into the large burnt-out thicket of twisted little trees and spiky bushes. Visibility dropped to between twenty and fifty metres and the heat seemed to radiate up from the scorched ground in shimmering waves. Wisps of smoke caught at Barbara's throat making her cough.

To cover the ground better Barbara halted Cpl Halyday's section and moved Cpl Walsh's up beside it on the right into a 'Two-up' platoon formation. Cpl Wallis's section she closed behind her. This took a deal of gesticulating with field signals as she was loath to use the radio, suspecting that the opposing cadet units would be listening on their frequency.

Beyond One Mile Creek the route changed to head more to the east. The vegetation remained 'close' and difficult to walk a straight line through. It was also hard to retain control as the section commanders were hidden from view most of the time.

Thus, it came as a surprise to Barbara to find that Cpl Halyday had halted his section. He came hurrying back through the thick scrub, his face a flush of heat and anxiety. Barbara raised an inquiring eyebrow.

Cpl Halyday pointed and said softly, "There is an enemy patrol just ahead of us in some gullies."

"You are sure?"

"Yes ma'am. They are wearing a sort of dark green camouflage uniform," Cpl Halyday reported. As Halyday was a 4th Year cadet and one of the famous 4 Platoon who had battled the crooks the previous year Barbara had great faith in him. She nodded and signalled to the others to halt, then moved quickly forward behind him.

From behind a bush she studied the ground ahead. A maze of small gullies crossed their front, leading left down towards One Mile Creek. The vegetation was relatively dense and included large trees, thorn bushes and the gnarled little trees. Just visible in the gully were four camouflaged figures. Barbara at once saw that what Halyday had said was correct—they were wearing some sort of dark green and brown camouflage uniform. They also had dark green webbing and packs. One had a radio on his back and an earpiece.

Suddenly two of the camouflaged people rose to a crouch to peer off through the bush towards Barbara's right. Two facts at once clashed in her brain. The first, annoyingly, was that she could hear movement and knew it must be Walsh's section. *They didn't get the signal to stop,* she thought. Reluctantly she broke radio silence and called, trying to keep her voice to a whisper.

Even as she did the second fact registered in Barbara's brain: the people she was looking at were adult males, and they were carrying guns!

Those are real soldiers, she thought, more with curiosity than alarm. Then she became concerned. *Uh oh! I hope we haven't crossed into some army unit's exercise area by mistake!*

She knew that the various sectors of the training area were booked by different units for use during particular periods of time and she was also aware that there were co-ord conferences to ensure that units did not interfere with each other's training by blundering about in someone else's territory.

While she was trying to puzzle out what to do Barbara gained contact with Walsh's section and told him to stop. Even so this took time and she glimpsed the end people of the section off to her right. The soldiers ahead of her could obviously also see them as they went down low, picked up packs, and began moving off to the left at a crouch.

As they did Barbara got a very clear view of them and was able to watch the leader's face. She also saw the weapons they held and noted they were not Australian Army F88 Steyrs.

They look like Enfield SA80s, she decided.

Suddenly the situation changed. One of the soldiers spotted Cadet Stewart. The man dived flat, dropping his very bulky looking pack as he did. His weapon came into his shoulder and he aimed at Stewart.

Cadet Stewart called out, "Bang! Bang! Gotcha!"

The soldier swore and looked over the top of his sights, then swore again. He turned and called to the man who was obviously the patrol leader. At that moment the leader looked in Barbara's direction and she saw his eyes widen as he spotted her. His weapon was whipped up to aim at her, even as he dived for cover. The speed of the man's reaction quite stunned Barbara and a shiver of fear ran through her. There was something about the way the weapon was being handled that chilled her.

Cadet Stewart again changed the situation. He stood up and moved forward, calling down at the men in the gully, "Hands up! We caught ya!"

Barbara saw the rifle barrels swivel to aim at Stewart, then heard a man snarl, in a very British accent, "Ah bleedin' hell! Friggin' cadets!"

The leader of the soldiers now stood up, lowering his rifle as he did. He snapped at Cadet Stewart, "Shut up kid! Six Section, packs on."

Barbara now stood up and hurried forward, not wishing Cadet Stewart to cause any trouble with the army. As she did the weapons swung to point at her and she experienced a most peculiar feeling of unease.

Before Barbara could speak the leader of the soldiers turned and snapped at her, "What are you bloody kids doing here?"

English, she thought, then replied, "An exercise. Our whole company is coming this way. And we aren't kids, we are cadets." She wasn't sure if she should have given away that information but something about the men's demeanour made her want to hint to them that her platoon was not alone.

The Englishman bit his lip and looked at her. That gave her a good chance to study him. She found herself quite thrilled to see that he was actually ruggedly handsome under his camouflage paint.

About mid-twenties, and a lieutenant, she decided, noting the badges of rank on the front of the man's shirt.

He looked annoyed and snapped at her, "Cadets eh? Well get out of here, and don't tell anyone you have seen us."

That irritated Barbara. She pursed her lips and stared back. "Who are you?" she asked.

"Never mind girlie. Just get going," the English officer snapped back, gesturing with his weapon as he did.

"I'm a Cadet Under-Officer thank you, and you can explain the situation to my major," Barbara replied frostily. She pressed the switch of her radio and began to call Major Conkey.

"Don't do that!" snapped the English officer. He then swore under his breath and wiped sweat from his mouth. A solid, tough looking sergeant joined him and scowled at Barbara. The English officer then shook his head in apparent disgust and turned to his men. "Packs on chaps. Let's get out of here."

As the English troops swung on their very bulky packs the officer turned back to Barbara. "Look Miss, we are the enemy for an exercise against your chaps. We'd appreciate it if you didn't report seeing us."

"What are you doing in our area?" Barbara challenged. Now that she had radio contact with Major Conkey she felt more confident.

"We aren't in our own exercise area yet," the English officer replied. "We were only dropped in last night and are still moving to it."

"Dropped in? Do you mean parachuted? Did that Hercules we heard last night drop you?" Barbara asked.

The English officer made a wry face but did not answer. The stony looks on the faces of his men told Barbara that she was right. He then said, in a placating voice, "Where do you think we are?"

Barbara had to smile at that. She could see a GPS hooked on the man's webbing. She gestured to it then pulled out her map. As she unfolded this he moved over beside her and she experienced a quite feminine thrill at how muscular he was, and at the depth and sparkle in his grey eyes. He unfolded the standard army 1:50 000 scale map and peered at her photocopy. Barbara pointed to where she thought they were.

The English officer studied her map with interest, then grunted and nodded. For a moment their eyes met and Barbara was quite astonished at the way her heart leapt.

He is very handsome, she thought.

"Thanks. That's what I thought," he said, in a voice whose timbre seemed to resonate through her body. "Well, we will be off. Please don't say you saw us."

With that he signalled and he and his men set off, hurrying south along the small gully at a speed that astonished Barbara. It was almost a loping run, yet the soldiers appeared to do it effortlessly.

How can they trot like that with all that gear! she marvelled.

Cpl Halyday thought the same. "Bloody hell! Running with full packs, and in this heat!"

"Who were they ma'am?" asked Sgt Russell as he moved forward.

"Not sure. British paratroopers or commandos I'd say," Barbara replied.

A minute later Major Conkey arrived, hot and perspiring. By then the British troops had vanished from view. Barbara explained what had happened to Major Conkey, quite ignoring the English officer's request not to tell.

Major Conkey looked thoughtful then said, "We weren't told about any exercise in this sector. I know we are in the right area. Never mind, I will check with Major Ross, now keep moving. We don't want to fall behind time."

Barbara got her platoon moving again, relieved the incident was over. She knew they were now going to do a daylight rehearsal for their night exercise and was conscious that the minutes were ticking away.

Their track took them across the gullies and on across the burnt-out country. It was so hot and unpleasant that Barbara felt quite nauseous.

What terrible country, she thought. *It is bad enough to have to exercise across it. I'd hate to have to battle across it for real.*

As she got down to roll under the fence that led south to the western end of the New Airfield she had a mental image of crawling on the hot sand and ash under fire. It was so unpleasant she just shook her head.

From time to time she carefully scanned the bush off to their right, in the direction in which the British troops had gone but she saw no sign of them. Much of her attention was taken up by controlling the movements of her two forward sections and by navigating. Once past the fence they swung half-left and went east, heading for the 'rear' of the Gravel Scrape. Barbara now knew exactly where she was, recognising the country they had walked through the previous day while looking for the large piece of satellite.

I must tell Major Conkey about that other piece of wreckage, she thought as the Gravel Scrape came into view.

After passing the Gravel Scrape to the right she deployed her sections to secure the area: Cpl Halyday facing towards the Bridge, Cpl Walsh towards the Dip and Cpl Wallis towards the rear. The remainder of the company then filed in, to be seated in section lines down in the shallow depression of the Gravel Scrape.

It was 1515 by then and Major Conkey called on the radio to Capt Maclaren. While they waited for the safety vehicle the platoon commanders were called in. Major Conkey walked them down to the Bridge and then along the near bank of One Mile Creek to the right to show them where they were to withdraw to later that night.

"One Thirty's Four Platoon will be securing this area and you have to pass back through them to the Gravel Scrape," he explained.

As they walked across the burnt-out slope back towards the Gravel Scrape Barbara called to Major Conkey and pointed up to their left.

"Yes Barbara?"

"Sir, I saw some more wreckage from that satellite land up there," she replied.

"Was it very big?"

Barbara used her hands to indicate how big she thought the object was. "About the size of a jerry can sir, about half a metre long I guess," she said.

Major Conkey nodded. "Good. I will tell the army people about it," he replied.

"Do you want me to show where it is? It is just up there near that other bit of wreckage," Barbara asked, pointing to the taped-off tree on the burnt-out slope.

Major Conkey shook his head. "No. Show me later. We are behind time now so let's keep moving. I will report it when I go to HQ this afternoon."

Barbara shrugged and trudged on, aware that she was dehydrating and feeling quite light headed. Back at the Gravel Scrape she found that Capt Maclaren had arrived with a Land Rover. Jerry cans of water had been unloaded. 4 Platoon was called in first to refill. Sgt Russell called a section at a time and when they were all done Barbara refilled her waterbottles and had a big drink.

As soon as all members of the platoon had done the same Barbara checked with Major Conkey and he told her to get going. She at once signalled to the corporals and they got their sections up and moving. Each section was to follow a different route, checking for enemy 'OPs' as they went. 4 Platoon was still the advance guard and the sections were to sweep ahead of the company.

It was 1545 by then and Barbara was conscious that the heat had at last begun to ease slightly. She and her Pl HQ followed Cpl Wallis's section down to the Bridge and across it. As they reached the flat grassy area between the Bridge and the road they met cadets coming the other way from their left. After an initial fluster they were identified as being from 130ACU by their yellow flashes. On meeting they were revealed to be CUO Karen Harvey's 4 Platoon. They were arriving to guard the Bridge and Gravel Scrape.

Barbara gave Karen, whom she really liked and admired, a friendly smile and comment. Next, she gave Chloe a wry grin when she made a smart remark about getting caught by the enemy.

"We have already caught one lot," Barbara replied, "Real soldiers. A bunch of Pommie commandos. They were over there beyond the Gravel Scrape, so keep your eyes peeled."

Karen nodded. "Thanks, we will," she replied.

The two groups passed each other, and Barbara continued on towards the Mingela Road. This was only another hundred paces. By the time she reached it Cpl Wallis's section had already crossed and was rolling under the fence beyond. As Barbara came out to the edge of the road she looked both ways then stopped as a vehicle suddenly appeared from out of the Dip.

It was a civilian car and was travelling quite fast towards her. For safety sake Barbara waited. To her surprise the car came to a skidding stop in front of her. Dust from its progress then enveloped her, causing her to cough. Through watering and slitted eyes Barbara noted that there were two men in the car, both civilians. One climbed out, waving the dust away and coughing.

"I am ver sorry," the man said in a distinct foreign accent. He then moved closer and peered at the blue 'cadet' flashes on Barbara's sleeve. "Kadet?" he queried with a harsh emphasis on the initial letter. "Not soldati?"

Barbara shook her head. "Only cadets," she replied. *Another odd character,* she thought, adding 'foreigner' and 'Slavonic' to her mental description. The man was tall, thin-faced and fair-haired. A cigarette appeared to be stuck to his bottom lip.

The man gave her an ingratiating smile. "Can you please to tell us where we are?" he asked.

As he said this Barbara saw that there was a military map open on the seat of the car. She gestured to it and the man pulled it out. She pointed to where they were.

The man gave another false smile. "Ver many thanks. I tourist. Ve not sure ver ve are," he said. Then he looked around and said, "What you do here?"

"Exercise," Barbara replied unhelpfully, not liking the man.

The man smiled and shrugged, then gestured to the burnt-out country. "The grass, it burns?"

Not liking the man Barbara replied, "Yes. You should not smoke. It is bad for your health and also starts bushfires. Now, we must get on. Goodbye."

Chapter 8

NIGHT EXERCISE

Barbara led Sgt Russell and Cpl Batt across the dusty road and into the dry grass beyond. After pushing through it for ten metres they came to a barbed wire fence. This was expected.

The fence around the army camp area, she told herself.

Along both sides of the fence there was a clear lane with vehicle tracks and Barbara was able to see along it almost all the way to the gate on the Back Road. The bulk of Mount St Michael showed up clearly.

She rolled under the fence and then stood to wait for the other two. As she did she noted that the two foreigners were standing beside their car studying the map.

Sgt Russell stood up and dusted himself, then gestured to the pair. "Who do you reckon those jokers are ma'am?" he asked.

"Dunno. Foreigners of some sort," Barbara replied.

"Probably bloody Russian spies looking for that bloody satellite," Sgt Russell said.

Barbara laughed but actually thought the idea quite possible. It also reminded her she had not shown the OC the other piece of wreckage. Shrugging and telling herself to remind him she turned and started walking up the long gentle slope towards their first bivouac area. A hundred metres ahead she could see Cpl Wallis's section.

As she made her way cautiously through the long grass in the blazing afternoon heat Barbara kept blinking sweat from her eyes. She had several drinks as she walked, having to hold her waterbottle in one hand and the radio in the other when HQ called. "Spider" was all they said. Barbara nodded and looked around with keen expectation. That meant that the 'opposing force' had an Observation Post somewhere that was observing and reporting the movement of her platoon. She knew that the unit Intelligence Section was monitoring the other unit's frequencies so must be hearing the opposing force OP's reports to their own HQ.

Looking around she studied the various clumps of bushes, then smiled. Cpl Walsh's section was moving up the slope a hundred metres out on her left, near the Camp Road. She quickly called Cpl Walsh on the radio. "Search those clumps of thorn bush just on your right," she ordered.

While they did this Barbara stopped her HQ in the shade of a tree and watched. Then she heard yells and voices calling: "Bang! Bang! Gotcha!" and she smiled. Even before Cpl Walsh radioed his report she could see what had happened. His section had flushed an opposing force OP out of a thorn bush. *That OP would have been put there to watch the Front Gate,'* she decided. There was a short and heated argument about who won the 'battle' but as Walsh had seven and the OP only four that was soon settled.

Cpl Walsh radioed, "Sunray, what do I do with the prisoners? Over."

"One Zero, take their names and send them back to their own base camp to start again, over," Barbara replied.

She saw the instructions passed and waited till both her own section and the captured OP were moving before continuing on. Cpl Walsh then radioed to report that the OP was led by Cpl Keating from Sarina. As the Coy HQ was monitoring her net she did not bother to pass any of this back. Indeed, she could now see a long line of cadets crossing the Mingela Road behind her.

"Here comes the remainder of the company," she said. "We had better get a move on."

The group set off up the slope again. Cpl Walsh and the Sarina OP paralleled them through the bush. Barbara knew the area so well she did not bother to navigate. Five minutes later she was walking through the area where her platoon had been camped in their first bivouac. The place looked dusty and deserted but very familiar.

Now Barbara angled off to the right, heading down the gentle slope towards the gate on the Back Road. This course led her through waist high long grass in the area where she had nearly trodden on the snake and she became quite anxious and went as slow as she dared, without shaming herself in front of her cadets. The group crossed the Power Line clearing and went straight on across a gentle upslope until they reached the Back Road. Beyond this was the burnt-out area that extended all the way to the top of Mount St Michael. As she reached the edge of the bare and blackened flat Barbara saw ahead of her both Cpl Halyday's and Cpl Wallis's sections.

From her orders Barbara knew that Major Conkey expected her move to be observed and reported by the opposing units so she just shrugged again and kept on walking across the Back Road and onto the bare, open country. Up to her left Cpl Walsh's section also came into view, angling in to join her.

We are some sort of decoys I suppose, she mused.

As the two leading sections began climbing the base of the small knoll outside the southern boundary fence Barbara began to fret.

I hope they remember my orders not to go right to the top.

She did not want them to 'skyline' themselves. As the tiny figures moved closer and closer to the crest she fingered the pressle switch of her radio, ready to halt them. However, they did stop and go to ground just back from the crest. Only two cadets crawled right to the very top and they vanished from view among rocks.

The knoll was not high but in places it was steep, and Barbara found she was puffing and perspiring as she went up. When she placed a hand on a rock to steady herself she discovered it was unpleasantly hot. She quickly removed her hand and paused to get her balance and to recover her breath. After wiping sweat off her face she looked left and noted that she could clearly see the buildings at Camp Macaliney. The tents of the rival units were just hidden by the rise but another 'Spider' call from HQ warned her that her platoon was being observed from somewhere.

Just below the crest Barbara motioned Sgt Russell and Cpl Batt to stop. Then she crept up to join Cpl Halyday and Cpl Wallis among the rocks on the top. Crawling on the rocky, burnt-off slope was another unpleasant experience. Ash and soot covered everything, and she noted that her hands and uniform were now filthy.

Cpl Halyday pointed to the north and smiled. "Lot's of movement in the enemy camp."

Barbara found a sheltered position and peered around a tree trunk. Now she could clearly see the tents and shelters of the Sarina, Mount Isa and Mackay cadet units. There were dozens of people moving about and a few were looking in their direction, but she could not discern any pattern to the movement.

"We've certainly got their interest," she commented, smiling to hide her apprehension.

She knew that her platoon was now three hundred metres out in front of the company 'front line', which comprised six section posts in the grass just back from the Back Road. By looking that way, she could see these sections moving into position.

At least we are covering their move, she thought.

Cpl Walsh's section joined them, and she deployed them to cover the rear. Cpl Walsh then joined her on top. Barbara pointed to the open flat area between the base of the ridge and the tents at the camp. "Study that dry claypan area where the helicopters were landing," she said. "That is where you will be patrolling when it gets dark."

The section commanders did so. Suddenly Cpl Halyday pointed to the east. "Look at all those troops! Are they moving to try to outflank us do you think ma'am?"

Barbara's gaze followed his pointing finger, to scan the bush along the northern slopes of Mount St Michael. To her amazement she saw a long line of troops moving in her direction. Then she shook her head.

"No. They are the regular troops who are looking for that satellite."

That gave her a twinge of guilt. Then she worried about whether the advancing line would come all the way up to the end of the ridge. More movement got her focusing in the distance and she saw several small parties searching up gullies and in rocky outcrops. There was even a Land Rover halfway up the ridge, she noted. Away to the northeast two helicopters could just be seen moving slowly above the smoking tree tops. However, these were so far away she could not hear them.

This satellite must be important, she thought unhappily. *I'd better remind the OC to report my sighting in case the bit I saw is what they are looking for.* The thought of all these troops wasting their time searching now bothered her a lot.

At that moment the radio crackled into life and the codeword to withdraw was sent. Barbara acknowledged. She gestured to the corporals to move down off the crest. Once they had done so she made them take out their compasses and she checked that they had the correct magnetic bearing set for the night withdrawal. Once that was done she told them to start their sections moving.

These moved to her command: first Cpl Walsh's section, then Cpl Wallis', next Pl HQ and last of all Cpl Halyday's. During this move the sections spread out and had a fifty-metre gap between them. During the night move they would move in a long, single file. As she picked her way back down the rocky slope Barbara saw with surprise that it was now 1645.

Where did the time go! she wondered. She did not enjoy that walk back across the burnt-out flat as they were walking almost directly into the setting sun and she was feeling sunburnt and dehydrated. *I wish the damned thing would just go down!* she thought irritably.

Their route led them into the grass across the Back Road. Here they passed Cpl O'Grady's section of 2 Platoon. Barbara made a point of stopping for a moment to talk to him to remind him that her platoon would be moving back again later that night, this being only a rehearsal. A hundred paces further back she found Roger and his platoon sergeant sitting in the bushes near the Power Line clearing. That was the 2PL RV. She gave Roger a smile and he grinned back.

Then it was back across the slope through the long grass to where Major Conkey waited with Coy HQ. Here the platoon was redeployed in a long-extended line facing back towards the army camp. The platoon was now the company reserve. Even as they deployed Major Conkey gave the codewords for the forward platoons to move back. He staggered these by a few minutes so they did not all arrive at once. By then the sun was getting low but the air was still very hot and dry.

The 'First Year' platoons came hurrying back in single file, to be met by CSM Sheehan. He lined them out in single file facing down the slope to the southwest, where they sat and waited. As soon as the last platoon came in Major Conkey got them all up and moving, leaving 4 Platoon as 'rearguard'.

Watching the remainder of the company hurry off towards the rear gave Barbara a mix of emotions. She was glad and proud to be holding the post of honour, but also quite anxious lest she somehow fail in the duty. Once the remainder of the company were out of sight she checked that the corporals had their compasses ready and then sent them off to practise the night patrols they were to do.

These were simple triangles that scoured the whole area for two hundred and fifty metres out. She only allowed them the one practice because it was already 1720 and she knew they had to return to the Ridge by 1830. As the sections returned to her she had them deployed facing out and made each one position a sentry. Once she was sure the area was secure she ordered them to eat.

All the while Barbara was very conscious of being out on her own. She knew that the remainder of the company had walked back to the Gravel Scrape where they were to have tea and do their final preparations. It gave her a peculiar sense of being important and she determined to keep the area free of any enemy who might cheat (Their recon patrols and OPs were supposed to withdraw to the main camp for tea and not come forward until Last Light).

By 1815 they had eaten and the whole platoon was seated in what cover there was, ready to move. As the last few minutes ticked down Barbara felt her stomach tightening up and she wondered how it must feel for soldiers who were waiting to go into a real battle.

I hope I never find out, she told herself.

Then the time to move came up and she stood up, adjusted her webbing and signalled the sections to move. The exercise had begun!

Walking forward through the bush was a pleasantly exciting experience for Barbara. Now she was out on her own! And it was already appreciably cooler. The tree tops and upper slopes of Mount St Michael were all tinged a ruddy pink by the last rays of the sun. By the time they platoon crossed the Power Line Clearing this had faded and a duller greyness took over. A couple of minutes later the platoon reached the Back Road and the burnt-out flat.

Ahead of them stretched those hundreds of metres of open, burnt-out country. Only a slight rise hid her move from the tents at the army camp and Barbara was able to see the buildings as she signalled to Cpl Halyday to continue on. He grimaced, shrugged and then led his section on out into the open. To Barbara it felt all wrong to be just walking across such bare, open ground but she knew it was part of the OC's plan, so she went ahead.

If they still have an OP watching this area they will know for sure we are up on the knoll, she told herself. She began to mentally prepare herself for sudden disasters and dramas. However, nothing happened and they reached the rise without any trouble. A few minutes later the platoon were crouched in all-round defence just below the crest. By then twilight was setting in and the lights of the camp twinkled clearly in the smoky air. Voices could be heard at the camp yelling for cadets to get somewhere.

Cpl Walsh jerked a thumb towards the camp and grinned. "Sounds like they still haven't got themselves organized over there."

"Let's hope not," Barbara replied. "Now don't get cocky and get caught out. You keep a good lookout up that ridge."

A check of Barbara's watch told her it was 1900 hours. "Time to go Ten Section," she said. Inside she tensed. This was it! Her platoon was to scatter across the flat on patrol leaving only her HQ on the knoll, and herself depending on her corporals when the action began.

Cpl Halyday nodded and signalled to his section. They rose and began clambering down along the end of the ridge in the direction of the camp. Barbara adjusted her headset as Cpl Halyday did a radio check. After replying she moved right up onto the crest, judging it was too dark by then for her to be seen from the camp.

Ten minutes later Cpl Wallis and her section were sent on their way. By then Barbara estimated that Cpl Halyday's section should have been over near the army camp. This was confirmed by the sound of shouts and yells of "Bang! Bang!"

Cpl Halyday called up, audibly chuckling, to report he had bumped the enemy all seated at a briefing in front of their tents. He reported that he was now on the second leg of the rectangular compass course the patrols were to follow. All patrols were to follow the same course to avoid clashing with each other.

At 1950 Cpl Walsh's section was also sent on its way. As they vanished in the darkness Barbara felt quite lonely and helpless, in a frustrated sort of way.

All up to the section commanders now, she thought.

As this was one of the primary aims of the exercise: to provide small-group leadership opportunities, she could not complain. She and her companions now seated themselves to face in all directions, ready to defend the patrol base.

Just on 2000 there was another clash out on the flat. This time it was Cpl Wallis reporting she had run into a platoon of Mount Isa cadets who were heading towards the 'front Line'. Barbara acknowledged but did not relay this, hoping that Coy HQ was actually monitoring the calls. From time to time she heard brief code words over the radio, which indicated that the First-Year platoons were in position. She consoled herself by remembering that all three of her corporals had been in the famous 4 Platoon battle the previous year.

They have actually been shot at, and fired back, she thought. Knowing they had coped with being under fire helped her relax. *Taking on a few cadets who aren't as well trained as them should be kid stuff after that,* she reasoned.

Then Cpl Wallis called again and reported she was in contact near the tents. As she spoke yelling broke out much closer to the hill and it was obvious that Cpl Walsh had run into something. He reported that a platoon from Sarina was heading straight for the hill. That got Barbara all anxious. She called up Cpl Halyday. "Ten, this is One Four. What is your ETA? Over," she asked.

Cpl Halyday answered at once, a chuckle in his voice. "Just coming up to you now, One Four, over."

His section had gone off to the east and then south until they reached the vehicle track along the fence that ran across the lower slopes of Mount St Michael. Now they were returning on a westerly heading. As the sounds of voices and boots on rocks could be heard lower down the spur to the north Barbara began to fret and she and Sgt Russell and Cpl Batt all faced that way.

In the end it was almost a tie. Cpl Halyday brought his section in just as Barbara challenged the approaching OPFOR patrol. A fierce little mock battle broke out with Halyday lining out to almost flank the attackers, who paused, unsure of just how strong a position it was. Then Cpl Walsh attacked the enemy from their rear, on his own initiative. That did it. The Sarina platoon withdrew and regrouped at the base of the ridge.

Barbara told Cpl Walsh to go on with his patrol. Then she moved Cpl Halyday's section to the western slope but by the time she had done that the sounds indicated that the Sarina platoon was now heading for the 'Front Line'. Radio warnings were sent and then calls from 4 Section and 6 told her that her assumption was correct. A series of small mock battles erupted along the 'front'.

At 2030 Cpl Wallis' section returned and Barbara sent them to the bottom of the slope at the rear ready for the withdrawal that she was now expecting to be ordered. Sounds of contacts with the 1 Platoon posts made her sure this would not be long coming. A radio message from 3 Platoon reporting its sections in contact made her even more certain.

By then the moon was right up and the whole area was bathed in an eerie light. Cpl Walsh's section was clearly visible as a line of dark silhouettes as they made their way up the slope from the east to rejoin.

Next Coy HQ reported a contact. Barbara could just hear the yelling. *That means that an enemy patrol has penetrated our outpost line. The OC must pull us back now,* she reasoned.

She was right. The codeword to withdraw came within the next minute. It was well timed as Cpl Walsh's section was just returning. Barbara was able to get Cpl Halyday's section up and moving so that all Walsh had to do was tack on the end and follow.

The value of the day rehearsal now became evident. The platoon pulled back across the burnt-out flat and arrived at 4 Section within four minutes and only a few paces off course. Barbara gave Roger a wave as she passed 2 Platoon HQ and she saw his teeth flash in the moonlight. Then another enemy patrol bumped 6 Section and Barbara began to become anxious that her platoon might be urgently needed back at Coy HQ.

She hurried them on. And they were needed, arriving just in time to counter attack into the left flank of a Sarina platoon that was coming in from the north. There were a few hectic minutes and Barbara had to yell her loudest to regain control. The corporals were not listening to either her, or their radios. Major Conkey helped, placing Cpl Halyday's section on the left flank of HQ and then getting her to swing the remainder of the platoon around to do a flank attack. This sent the Sarina cadets running off into the darkness.

Unfortunately, this was in the direction of the Gravel Scrape. By then Major Conkey was angry and began calling Sarina on the radio to remind them that their people were supposed to be moving in section patrols, not platoons. Barbara re-orged her platoon with Halyday's section facing north, Wallis's facing east and Walsh's facing south. She found she was sweating and panting for breath but really enjoying herself.

Another contact with 2 Section and then one with 7 Section convinced Major Conkey to begin Phase 2. He radioed the codeword to pull back the First-Year platoons. The CSM and two members of HQ came to stand near Barbara. The HQ cadets were to act as guides for the First-Year platoons. The platoons arrived soon after, 1 Platoon first, then 2 and finally 3. In the bright moonlight there was no need for challenging with passwords as their identity was clear. As each platoon arrived a guide led them past to where they were to wait in a long single file, seated in the grass on the downslope.

As 3 Platoon came into view Major Conkey walked over and stood next to Barbara. "OK CUO Brassington, you are on your own now," he said.

Barbara grinned and said, "Yes sir." She found she was actually looking forward to being left as the rearguard.

Major Conkey and the CSM walked away. There was a stir in the grass as the waiting 'First Year' platoons stood up. Within a minute they were moving. 3 Platoon just tacked on the rear without stopping. Two minutes later Barbara could not hear the company at all. It had vanished down the slope. By then she had called in her corporals.

"OK, we are on our own. Out you go," she said to Cpl Wallis and Cpl Halyday. "Make sure you are back in ten minutes."

The two section commanders moved away and soon after that Barbara saw the dark shapes of their cadets heading away into the night. She was keeping Cpl Walsh's section with her while the other two patrolled out on either side. Now that she knew her platoon was the only 'friendly' force left east of the Mingela Road Barbara felt quite tense and excited, but this soon passed. There was action back near the Gravel Scrape and Bridge but none of her sections met any patrols from other units.

The two sections both returned within a few minutes of each other. Cpl Walsh's section was sent off, being replaced by Halyday's. Cpl Wallis's was sent out again. Barbara stood and peered into the darkness, hoping there would be some action. But all remained quiet.

Sgt Russell fidgeted then muttered, "Plane."

Barbara had heard the aircraft. It was a big, multi-engine type and was very high up. *Jet?* she wondered. It sounded like it. She scanned the sky but saw no sign of the aircraft. But it got her thinking about the British commandos they had encountered that afternoon. *He is good looking, that lieutenant,* she mused.

A vehicle went down the camp road to the Front Gate and then south along the Mingela Road. There was another noisy outburst of action back near the Bridge and then a clash near the Front Gate but still no action for her own people. Then Major Conkey radioed with the signal to move to the RV at the Front Gate. Feeling quite disappointed Barbara acknowledged, then passed the codeword on to her own sections.

They came back to rejoin her and she lined the platoon up. Sgt Russell did a head count then reported to her. Still hoping for a contact Barbara sent Cpl Walsh's section on ahead in arrowhead. Then she followed. The platoon walked down the gentle grassy slope towards the Front Gate.

Well before they reached the Front Gate Barbara could hear talking and laughter from other groups there. When she got there a couple of minutes later she found two safety vehicles there, plus a cluster of OOCs, and hundreds of cadets. These included her own unit and nearby a group of Sarina cadets. 130ACU was also waiting, seated in a long line.

Barbara reported to Major Conkey and was told to lead the way back to the bivouac area, and to make sure the two units weren't ambushed on the way.

"I don't trust that St Michael's mob," Major Wickham added. "So, you go first and I'll have my 4 Platoon come as rearguard."

Major Conkey concurred with that so Barbara set off along the road towards the Triangle. As she did she spread her platoon out, warning the corporals to have scouts well ahead. Every hundred paces she had the lead section stop and move into the scrub on either flank to check for ambushes. They then joined on at the rear of the platoon and another section took over as point. It was good practice but led to no action. There were no skulking enemy and the platoon arrived back at their bivouac area without incident, Barbara leading them through the bush of the Triangle on a compass bearing.

Chapter 9

SNICKERS

On reaching the bivouac area Barbara deployed the platoon in three widely spaced section posts to secure the area. When Major Conkey arrived he had the remainder of the company seated in section lines. 4 Platoon was then called in and seated as well. CSM Sheehan had the sergeants mark their roll books while he counted heads to ensure no-one had been left behind. Then Sgt Henning and Cpl Hodgins collected all the radios. Once that was done Major Conkey spoke to the company. He praised their discipline, teamwork and radio procedure. It was obvious to Barbara that he was proud of the company and that when he said he was pleased he wasn't just saying it.

We have done well, she told herself.

Major Conkey then looked at his watch and told them they could have another half-hour before bed, and that the canteen would open. He then added, "All CUOs and CSM to report to me in fifteen minutes time. That is all, dismiss!"

Feeling pleasantly tired but happy Barbara walked back in the darkness to her shelter where she took off her webbing and helmet. She then devoted a few minutes to washing and cleaning the camouflage cream off her face. Feeling much fresher she joined the queue to buy a softdrink. By then she was feeling relaxed and happy. Both her own performance and that of her platoon had pleased her.

The cadets were mostly in high spirits, believing that the unit had done well on the exercise. That made Barbara feel good too. A strong sense of achievement caused a sensation of satisfaction to glow deep inside. She purchased her softdrink and made her way to join the other CUOs at Major Conkey's shelter. Roger was there and he moved aside to make room for her. She gave him a friendly smile and sat down.

Major Conkey had been chatting to the other Officers of Cadets and Barbara was further cheered to hear him laughing. He obviously thought the unit had done well and told them so when he joined them a few minutes later. It was usual for the CUOs and CSM to have a briefing after the cadets had all been put to bed but this time they had it before 'lights out'.

There were three events planned for the next day: a Leadership Evaluation Exercise in the morning, an Orienteering Exercise in the afternoon, then a 'Free' night. At the mention of that Barbara experienced a twinge of sadness. That meant the camp was almost over, and so was her year as a platoon commander.

Once the details had been passed on Barbara remained to talk to Roger and the other CUOs while CSM Sheehan went off to get the company to bed. Roger's main interest seemed to be what skit the CUOs and sergeants could put on to entertain the troops the following night. Usually Barbara really enjoyed 'Campfire Concerts' but this time she felt sad. Feeling quite withdrawn she said goodnight to the others and took herself off to see Major Conkey.

He was talking to the other OOCs near the parked vehicles. "Yes Barbara?"

"Have you told Headquarters about the wreckage I saw, sir?"

"Yes. I mentioned it when I went to HQ during the exercise," he said.

That made Barbara feel relieved. "Do they want me to show them where it is sir?" she asked.

Major Conkey paused and then said, "Er... yes. They said they would follow it up."

That answer sounded a bit odd to Barbara, but she was already feeling anxious enough about being in trouble over it that she said no more about it. After chatting for a few minutes, she took herself off to bed. As usual she just took off her boots and slept in her uniform.

She slept well, not waking till the company was called out on check parade at 0600. After pulling on her boots and picking up her hat she walked over to say hello to Major Conkey and the other CUOs. Sometimes he had new information or orders but this morning he just chatted cheerfully and dismissed them as soon as the check parade was completed. Barbara returned to her platoon area and gathered Sergeant Russell and the corporals and passed on the orders for the day. Then she went to her own hutchie. Knowing that they were to move again that day she quickly rolled up her bedding and packed, leaving only her shelter standing. This was all done by the time the platoon was called out for breakfast.

Breakfast was a barbeque with bacon, fried eggs, toast, cereal and fruit juice. It wasn't Barbara's favourite food, but she sat with her platoon and ate it anyway. As she ate she noted that there wasn't a cloud in the sky and knew it was going to be another very hot day.

After breakfast the CUOs, CSM and sergeants were all called over to where the OOCs were seated. Major Conkey then briefed them for the Leadership Evaluation Exercise. This was set up as a series of 8 'stands' along a route. At each stand were two or three of the OOCs, CUOs or sergeants as the Directing Staff or DS. The remainder of the unit was then grouped in sections of seven and moved to a start point. Each stand was out of sight of the next so that the cadets had no warning of what was to happen further along. To make it fair the corporals were all removed from their sections and grouped into two sections. Likewise, the Lance Corporals made up two sections. That way the ordinary cadets did not have to compete against people of higher rank, only their own peers.

The exercise had its own story: that the section was a raiding party on its own behind enemy lines. They had attacked an enemy HQ and captured some secret documents. However, in the battle the section commander and section 2ic had both gone missing. This meant that the section had to find its own leaders and make its way to the sea, where a submarine would pick them up. The aroused enemy was hunting for them.

To her own satisfaction Barbara was given the 'Sentry at the Bridge' stand. The route started from a waiting area where the Marlow Road crossed One Mile Creek. It then went along the bed of the creek (The story being that they had no map—the missing corporal had that—so the section had to follow the creek).

The first stand was an armed enemy who called on them to surrender and then dived for cover and opened fire. This was among the sharp bends of the creek down in a one hundred-metre-wide depression. The stand was staffed by CUO Ward, Sgt Werribee and Sgt Henning. A hundred paces and several bends down the creek was 'The Prisoner'. Here Lt Hamilton was to hide and step out at the last moment with his hands up. The section had to quickly decide what to do with him. Another hundred paces down the creek, at a point where it opened out a bit to make a small clearing, was 'The body and the sniper'. Roger was in charge of this one, with Sgt Ashburton and Sgt Russell taking turns at being the sniper or the body. To tempt the cadets a very obvious map was placed with the body. Another couple of hundred paces, at the point where an old fence crossed the deep gully, was 'The minefield', staffed by Fiona and Sgt Blockey.

Barbara was next, at the point where One Mile Creek joined the dry flood channel of Keelbottom Creek. A vehicle track came down the bank at this point and went on across the bed of the main stream. On a low rise a hundred metres away were two stands: First Aid with Lt Standish and 'Blinded in the Minefield' with Sgt Rowley. From there the course went down to the main channel of Keelbottom Creek at the western end of the lagoon. The last stand was at this point. It was 'Someone must stay', a secret ballot to vote one of the cadets out of the section. Because of the sensitive nature of this two OOCs were the DS: Capt Maclaren and Lt McEwen.

Major Conkey next gave out copies of Personal Qualities Reports. These were a key tool in selecting who went on the promotion courses in December. Each CUO was to fill one out on every member of their platoon. The platoon sergeant was to fill one out on every person of lesser rank in the platoon. Likewise, each Section Commander was to fill one out on each member of their section. The CQMS was to do one for all lance corporals and the CSM on all NCOs and for any cadets who had come to his notice. Thus, each cadet had at least 3 or 4 reports by different people. Using the marks Major Conkey could add the results together and rank order the unit.

Barbara knew that this was how the 'Best Cadet' and 'Best Corporal' were selected as prize winners at the annual Passing-Out Parade in November and she thought it a very fair system. She also approved of the method of selecting people for promotion because it removed most of the bias and accusations of favouritism and bribery that got bandied around by some of the ones not selected.

Having briefed the staff Major Conkey told the CSM to assemble the company for their briefing and told the DS to move to their stands and get set up. The DS collected webbing, radios and stores and set off in groups. Barbara went with Lt Standish and Sgt Rowley and helped carry the stretcher and First Aid Kit. They made their way through a hundred metres of dry bush and across a small, dry claypan. Already the temperature was rising to uncomfortable levels and Barbara broke into a sweat. The group walked past a small pump house (for water to Camp

Macaliney) and then through a gate in the fence along the top of the main creek bank. From there they followed the vehicle track down over the top of the bank.

As they walked down the steep bank the faint breeze was cut off and Barbara shook her head at the stifling heat down in the low ground. As they reached the bottom of the ten-metre slope Barbara heard Sgt Rowley cry out in horror. She stopped and looked, wondering what it was that had frightened her. 'It' turned out to be two snakes. One was in the process of swallowing the other. The larger snake was fully two metres long, an olive-brown coloured thing that was plainly of a deadly variety. The snake saw them but was unable to move and could only lie in the middle of the track and keep on slowly gulping down its meal. Barbara watched in sick fascination.

That horrible thing must live here somewhere, she thought.

It made her go cold with fear thinking of all the times she had run through long grass or crawled along during fieldcraft exercises. Because snakes were 'protected' by law the trio could only stand and watch. Sgt Rowley was all for killing it, claiming self-defence, but Lt Standish refused to allow her to go anywhere near it.

"That is when you are liable to get bitten," she said. "So stay away from it."

At last the snake finished its cannibalistic meal and then slowly slithered off into the long grass beside the track. As this was quite close to where the cadets would later be walking past Barbara was told to keep a careful watch and to detour them around the spot. She was then left alone as the other two walked on to their stand. Selecting an open spot in the shade of a tree up on the slope of the bank between the vehicle track and bed of One Mile Creek Barbara sat down, but not before she had a very careful look for more snakes.

Then she had trouble relaxing. Every rustle in the leaves or grass had her staring anxiously at the place in case it was another snake. Even though she could see Lt Standish and Sgt Rowley up on the 'island' beyond the overgrown flood channel she felt quite isolated and alone. Even when Lt Hamilton drove down to the bed of Keelbottom Creek with the safety vehicle carrying Capt Maclaren and Lt McEwen she still felt alone.

Despite being in the shade Barbara found it hot and she was glad that most of the exercises were discussions rather than actions. She knew it must be so hot that the regulations would only allow them to do short physical activities.

Becoming bored she cautiously made her way down to the bed of One Mile Creek. At this point it was dry, white sand about three metres wide. The banks sloped steeply up for about five metres then levelled slowly out. The sides of the creek were covered in a thick growth of long, dry grass. Ten metres upstream the creek the bed curved to the right. Barbara walked around this, thankful that the shade made it relatively cool. As she did she kept a cautious eye on the long grass which grew close on either side. Her imagination pictured a snake suddenly striking at her from its cover.

Twenty-five metres further on, at the point where the fence and a rough vehicle track crossed the creek, were Fiona and Sgt Blockey. They had planted a pretend minefield using empty softdrink cans. Only a few of the cans were partly visible but the impression was suitable for the cadets. A rope strung across the creek ten metres further up the creek bed marked the other fence of the minefield.

Barbara sat and talked to them for the next half-hour. Among the topics they discussed were who should be promoted and the crashed satellite. By this time Barbara was feeling quite guilty about that so she told them about the large piece she had seen. Then she made her way back to her stand and sat down to wait. While she waited she started filling out the Personal Qualities Reports on the members of her platoon.

After about another half-hour Major Conkey appeared. By then he had briefed the company and set the first section moving. He was in the process of walking along the course to check that all the stands were in the right place. Red in the face and hot he greeted Barbara with a cheery smile and then walked on towards the place where an animal pad left the creek to go up onto the vehicle track. As this was close to where the snake had last been seen Barbara at once called out to warn him.

She walked down to where Major Conkey was carefully hitting at the long grass with his staff and explained the two snakes. Major Conkey nodded and kept on hitting the grass.

"I'll just move the slimy reptile along," he said.

It was then that Barbara remembered the big piece of debris. Feeling awkward because she had not shown the exact spot to him earlier she now licked her lips and spoke up. "Sir, do you remember yesterday when we were at the Gravel Scrape and I mentioned another piece of that satellite that crashed? I should show you where it is. It is quite a big piece of wreckage."

"I did tell Warrant Officer Gately," Major Conkey replied, but he kept his eyes focused on the long grass as he thrashed at it.

"Does he want me to show him where it is?"

Major Conkey stopped thrashing the long grass and looked at her. "He did not seem very interested. In fact, he suggested that he did not believe you."

"Didn't believe me!" Barbara answered, quite flabbergasted by the statement. "Why not?" she demanded to know.

"Because he said you gave them a bit of run around and weren't very co-operative the first time we looked," Major Conkey replied. He looked quite uncomfortable to Barbara and she suspected he was not telling her the whole story.

"Well, I did see it and I would like to tell them again sir," she said.

"Yes, alright. Where exactly is it?"

"About fifty metres south of the Gravel Scrape, about twenty paces from the first bit of wreckage they marked," Barbara answered.

"Alright. I will tell the army people when I go to the camp co-ord conference at ten," he replied.

Having checked that Barbara was ready Major Conkey walked on along the vehicle track across the dry flood channel to where Lt Standish and Sgt Rowley waited. From there he vanished over the rise in the direction of the main channel of Keelbottom Creek. A few minutes after that the first section reached Barbara and she set to work. They were all corporals and had most of the answers from doing similar exercises the previous year. Their rivalry was intense, fuelled by the fact that out of sixteen only eight of them would be promoted to sergeant. Barbara listened and tried to mark her report impartially, despite having some strong likes and dislikes.

Major Conkey came walking back just as that group was moved on and when the second section reached her. He stood and listened for a few minutes, then went on up the bank, puffing and sweating in the heat. "Off to the co-ord conference," he grumbled. "Back in an hour or so."

From then on Barbara was very busy. She had to keep checking her watch to push the sections through, one every fifteen minutes. That allowed a couple of minutes to seat them, take names, then read them the problem. After that they were allowed a strict five minutes to discuss the problem and present their solution. She then gave them the 'DS Solution' and sent them on their way. It became tiring and a little boring, but she tried conscientiously to concentrate, knowing that both individual cadet's careers and the good of the unit might depend on her judgements.

Ten o'clock went by and the flow of sections continued. By then Barbara was feeling tired and dehydrated. She kept drinking, but it seemed to sweat out of her just as fast. The cadets were also feeling the heat and she told several to have a big drink. Flies and ants both annoyed her, and she realised she had forgotten about the snake. The glare and heat combined to give her a headache and she became quite irritable.

Just after eleven Major Conkey returned, walking along the bed of One Mile Creek again. He had CUO Ward, Sgt Henning and Wendy Werribee with him. Their presence told Barbara that all of the sections had passed the first stand and that the whole exercise was now running down. They stood to one side and listened till she finished with the group she was assessing. Then Major Conkey said, "Barbara, hand over to Lofty and Sgt Henning. You are to come with me to HQ. The army people want you to show them where this piece of satellite wreckage is. Sgt Werribee, you come with us."

That irritated Barbara and for a moment she regretted having mentioned it. Then she shrugged and stood up, collecting her webbing and passing the exercise paperwork over to Lofty. Her bundle of half-completed Personal Qualities Reports she stuffed into her map pocket. She knew that Wendy had been asked so that Major Conkey did not compromise either her reputation, or his own, by being alone together.

The three walked up the vehicle track up the creek bank, through the gate and back across the flat to the bivouac site. Once there they climbed into a Land Rover and drove back to the camp. This only took a few minutes. Major Conkey parked the vehicle in front of the HQ building and told Barbara to wait outside till he called her in.

Barbara climbed out of the vehicle and walked over to stand on the shade of the small porch. While she waited she talked to Wendy and looked around, noting that there were at least a dozen army vehicles parked in front of HQ, and that there were now several large tents on the concrete slabs. Regular soldiers could be seen walking around the camp or sitting at the tents. In the distance she could see the Sarina Cadet Unit lining up near their tents. After a couple of minutes, Wendy excused herself and went off to the toilet.

A man looked through the door at her and then went back inside. *That was that horrible warrant officer,* Barbara thought.

She walked away from the door and into the shade at the car park side of the building. As she did, she heard the warrant officer's voice coming through the windows. "Yes, that's her," he said.

Another voice replied, "Bit of a temperamental drama queen if you ask me," said another voice.

"She's a very good, very capable cadet under-officer," Major Conkey said in reply.

"How do we know she isn't just making it up to get attention," the second voice asked.

Barbara experienced a horrible qualm. *They are talking about me!* she thought.

Major Conkey again spoke in her defence. "If she said that she saw it then she did."

At that moment Barbara saw a man's head through the window. The man wasn't looking at her but rather than be thought an eaves-dropper she moved quickly across to the shade of the RAP ten paces away. Inside she boiled at the injustice of not being believed. The insult hurt and made her feel very annoyed.

Two very grubby and sweaty male soldiers walked over from the kitchen area. As they approached her Barbara was aware of their eyes scanning her and that both irritated and pleased her. She was used to males looking her over but did not always enjoy it. And this time it was too obviously an ogle, not an appreciative glance. One of the men, a corporal in his mid-twenties, met her eye and grinned. To Barbara it came across as a leer and she felt annoyed and looked away. The two soldiers walked past her and into the HQ building.

As they went through the door one of them muttered to the other, "Lovely big tits. I'd like to get my hands on them."

The other chuckled and said something which Barbara did not hear but which made his mate turn and leer at her. Both sniggered and then the door closed. Barbara was even more annoyed now.

He deliberately said that loudly so I could hear it, she thought.

She knew that breached the army's policy on harassment and was annoyed that the adults did not set a better example. But the comment also got her looking anxiously down at her breasts.

Oh! she sighed, *They are too big!* Even in the shapeless camouflage uniform they were still very obvious. *I wish they didn't stick out so much,* she thought unhappily.

The door opened and Major Conkey came out. "The colonel isn't there. Just wait here Barbara while I go and look for him. They said he was over at Mackay Cadet Unit."

Major Conkey walked away, leaving Barbara alone on the porch. By now she was feeling hot and tired and she wished there was a chair or stool she could sit on. As she stood wondering if anyone would mind if she sat on the concrete she heard more male voices from just inside the screen door.

One said, "Come and look Frank. It's really good stuff."

The other, presumably Frank, replied, "OK. Is that her outside?"

That got Barbara's attention and she turned to look, just as the other man replied, "I think so. I'll just check."

The screen door swung open and a soldier looked out. As the man stared at Barbara their eyes met and she thought he looked guilty or embarrassed. Then a knowing smirk crossed the soldier's face and he closed the door and turned away. She heard him say, "That's her." Then he snickered and she glimpsed the two men walk off across the room towards the far end.

A distinct feeling of uneasiness and annoyance swept through Barbara. *What was that all about?* she wondered.

That the men had been discussing her was obvious and the snickers made her sure it was some sort of disgusting conversation about sex. That got her even more upset and annoyed.

At that moment a young regular army captain, a very fit looking, handsome man in his late twenties, walked across from the next building. He looked at Barbara and smiled.

"Are you the girl who saw the satellite wreckage?" he asked.

Barbara came to attention. "Yes sir."

The captain nodded. "Good. Come in and show me on the map where it is."

He led the way in through the screen door. Inside he stopped and muttered with annoyance as his eyes swept over the deserted chairs. Barbara saw that the tables set up for telephones and radios had no-one sitting at them. The building was divided into two large rooms by a sheet metal wall. A doorway led through to the next room. Two soldiers were visible through the doorway. They were seated at tables and had their backs to her. Over on the right-hand end wall next to the dividing door was a large map of the area. The plastic overlay was now marked with red and blue shading, presumably showing the areas already covered and those still to be searched.

As Barbara and the captain walked across the room towards the map a telephone began to ring. The captain muttered with annoyance, then detoured across and picked it up. "Captain Green," he said.

Barbara stopped, unsure if she should go to the map or not. Captain Green saw this and gestured to the map while he began talking to the person on the other end of the phone.

Barbara walked over to the map and began to study it, noting that the area around the Gravel Scrape was now marked as having been searched. As she looked she heard male voices cry out from just inside the next room.

"Oh yes! Oh, very good Charlie! That really got her!"

"Play it again Jack," cried another.

There were loud snickers that both aroused Barbara's curiosity and made her stomach turn over with distaste. She glanced through the door beside her, noting a group of six or seven male soldiers, all watching a computer screen. The screen flickered and she glimpsed a girl's face on the screen. For a moment she thought it might be one of those X-rated pornographic videos. She had only ever glimpsed one for a few minutes and been horrified and disgusted. Now she felt a surge of intense embarrassment.

Knowing that the men were not aware she was there caused an instant desire to flee before they discovered her presence. She was about to turn away and leave when her eye focused on the face of the girl on the TV screen. Barbara gaped.

That girl looks like me! she thought in astonishment.

She was so surprised she paused and looked again. Now she saw that the video had been taken in the bush and that the girl was wearing

Australian Army camouflage uniform. Then the face of the girl on the screen came clear again as she turned her head to look around. This time there was no doubt. Barbara found herself staring in amazement at a picture of herself.

That is me! she thought, quite astounded. *When was that taken?* she wondered.

She did not remember seeing any video cameras during the camp. As these thoughts raced through her mind she saw the girl on the screen turn to face away and then start undoing her clothing.

What on earth am I doing? Where was I? Barbara puzzled.

Before her astonished and embarrassed gaze Barbara saw herself turn her back to the camera then pull down her trousers and then her knickers. As she watched with growing dismay the men began to snicker and call out rude comments.

Dismay turned to horror as Barbara watched herself squat down and begin to do a pee. The men all snickered and made disgusting comments, and these grew to cheers as the cameraman focused so that her buttocks filled the screen and came into sharp relief. Barbara was so horrified she gasped, even as shame began to scorch through her. Now she recognized the place.

That was when I went down to the bank of One Mile Creek yesterday, she remembered.

At that moment one of the soldiers glanced over his shoulder.

Chapter 10

OUTRAGE

As the soldier glanced over his shoulder his eyes widened and his facial expression changed to a look of guilt. He nudged his neighbour, who also looked over his shoulder. Barbara was outraged. Frozen by emotion she stood there, flaming with shame and embarrassment. Half of her instincts were to flee, to escape from the shameful situation. But now there was anger too, fuelled by the outrage, and growing by the second.

"Turn that off!" she cried.

At that, all of the men looked at her, some astonished, others embarrassed or ashamed. Nobody moved to switch the computer off, so Barbara walked into the room, barely aware of what she was doing.

"Turn it off!" she screamed.

The men all straightened up and stepped aside as she stormed into their midst. On the table beside the computer she saw a small video camera. The camera was connected to the computer by a cable. She reached down and picked up the camera. Holding it with shaking hands she tried to work out how to switch it off.

One of the men called angrily: "That's mine. Take your hands off it!" He reached over and grabbed Barbara's wrist.

"Let go of me!" Barbara grated.

"Give me back my camera," the man said, twisting her wrist as he did.

The man was strong and it hurt but Barbara was furiously angry by now. Being grabbed only added to her sense of outrage. "Take your hands off me!" she shouted.

From behind her a man's voice snapped, "What the devil is going on here?"

Barbara glanced over her shoulder and saw that the handsome captain had come into the room. Close behind him were Major Conkey and lieutenant colonel.

By now Barbara's emotions were seething to such and extent she could hardly speak. She pointed at the men and cried, "These crude animals are watching a disgusting video of me!"

"Watching a what?" Captain Green queried.

"They... someone..." Barbara gestured to the man holding her arm, "Took a video of me when I went to the toilet yesterday. I want it."

"It's my camera," the soldier holding her said.

"Let me go or I'll have you charged with assault!" Barbara shouted. She was so inflamed that the whole world appeared to be tinged crimson.

"Let her go!" Major Conkey snarled, "Or I will have you charged as well!"

The soldier immediately released Barbara. She had fleeting impressions of his face: anger, embarrassment, fear. She held up the camera, jerking the cord as she did. "I want the memory card or tape or whatever; and I want an apology!"

The lieutenant colonel now stepped forward. "What memory card? What on earth is going on?" he demanded to know. Behind him Barbara saw the warrant officer she disliked also appear.

The soldier gestured at Barbara. "This bitc... er... girl just burst in here and started shouting at us!"

That outraged Barbara even more. "You were looking at..."

"Be quiet!" snapped the lieutenant colonel. He frowned at Barbara, then at the soldier, who was now standing to attention but looking truculent and concerned. Barbara was pleased to note that most of his friends now looked worried and a few had the good grace to appear ashamed. A couple had begun edging towards the door.

"Well? Looking at what?" the lieutenant colonel demanded to know.

"A video recording sir," the soldier replied. "Part of one we took while on patrol yesterday."

"What is on it?" the lieutenant colonel asked.

"Me going to the toilet!" Barbara cried. She was now bristling with indignation and dislike. She was also very aware of her femaleness in a room full of males. That made her feel uneasy and ashamed.

The soldier retorted: "Well, you just came along and dropped your dacks in front of us!"

"I didn't know you were there!" Barbara snapped back. "If you'd been decent you would have called out, and if you'd been a gentleman you wouldn't have watched!"

"We couldn't help seeing," the man said, now blushing deep red.

"Even so, you didn't have to take a video, you disgusting pervert!" Barbara snapped.

The lieutenant colonel held up his hands. "That will do! No name calling. Let me see this video."

"No!" Barbara cried.

The lieutenant colonel frowned and said, "I'm in charge here girlie."

"I don't care!" Barbara cried. "You aren't going to see it."

She hugged the camera to her, aware that it was still playing but that the picture was of some military camp, not of her.

"Listen girlie, I'm an officer and I'm giving you an order," the lieutenant colonel snapped.

A wash of impressions and fears flooded through Barbara. She had cherished a desire to join the army as a career and she sensed this could harm such an ambition. But her pride was badly hurt and she felt instinctively it was all wrong. She shook her head.

"You might be sir, but I don't want to be humiliated and embarrassed by people looking at it. If you look at this, I will make an official complaint. In fact, I will make one anyway against these... these..."

At that the soldier next to her snarled, "You bitch! You do and..."

Capt Green cut him off. "Shut it Cpl Gates! If you value your stripes, and if you want to stay in the regiment, you get yourself under control."

Gates did so, but with obvious bad grace.

Barbara could see that her threat of an official complaint had caused the lieutenant colonel real concern. He frowned and tried not to glower at her. She pressed her advantage. "I want the memory chip or tape out of this so I can destroy it."

Corporal Gates looked at the lieutenant colonel, his face wooden. "But sir, it has restricted military information on it." He flicked a hostile glance at Barbara.

"Rubbish!" Barbara snapped. "You have just been here on an exercise. Anyway, you can watch it being destroyed so you are sure any military secrets..." she said with a sarcastic sneer, "don't get compromised."

Major Conkey now stepped in. "Give me the memory card and I will destroy it while CUO Brassington watches."

The lieutenant colonel looked doubtful. "Oh, I think we might need it for any investigation," he said.

Before Barbara could speak Major Conkey said, "There will be one if we don't settle this quickly. I will refer it to Canberra."

Barbara nodded. "And I will complain to the Minster," she added. She was now seething with outrage and very determined. She sensed that she might be compromising any chance of a military career but was now determined to protect her own dignity.

The lieutenant colonel frowned but was clearly worried by the threat. "You should work through the army chain of command," he said huffily.

Again, as Barbara opened her mouth to indicate what she thought of that Major Conkey beat her to it. "We aren't army. We are army cadets and as you people seem to delight in pointing out, we are civilians, so we have every right. So please order this soldier to hand over the card or whatever it is. You can watch while we destroy it. Sorry to make such an issue of this Colonel Nevison, but the welfare and reputation of one of my cadets is involved."

The lieutenant colonel, Nevison, frowned again and tried to hide his anger. Then he gave a curt nod. "Yes. Do that Major. Corporal, give the major the card," he ordered.

Barbara reluctantly handed the video camera to Cpl Gates. He met her eyes for a second, but she held his stare. Unable to prolong the battle of wills for fear of the officers Cpl Gates stopped the machine and opened a panel in the side. He took out a small memory card which he held out to Major Conkey.

Major Conkey looked at Barbara. "Is that alright CUO Brassington?"

"Yes sir," Barbara replied, nodding. Inside she felt relief and also a flush of gratitude. If there was one man on earth she liked, admired and trusted it was Major Conkey.

Major Conkey took the card. By this time Barbara was starting to shake with nervous reaction and she just wanted to get out of the room. She stepped forward, causing Capt Green and another soldier to step hastily aside. Major Conkey turned to follow. Wanting to run and hide but managing to hold her pace to a rapid stride Barbara went through the door into the HQ, all her senses tingling.

As Barbara marched across the next room Capt Green called from the doorway behind her, "Wait! What about showing us where you saw this piece of wreckage"

Now Barbara really saw red. She halted and halfturned to look back.

"I did!" she said, pointing at Lt Col Nevison. "I showed him. You can find it for yourself now!"

As she turned to go Lt Col Nevison called out, "Stop girlie! This is a matter of national security."

"Rubbish!" Barbara cried. "It is a matter of national security for France maybe, but you just want to steal their secrets."

"But... How dare you!" Lt Col Nevison began.

"But nothing!" Barbara cried. "You can chuck me out of cadets if you like; and you can stick your satellite..." She paused, aware she had been about to lapse into obscenity. "And I want a written official apology, or I write a complaint to the Minister of Defence."

With that she spun on her heel and hurried to the front door. By then she was on the edge of losing control and knew it. Tears were prickling in her eyes and she was breathing so fast and deep that she was almost hyperventilating. She knocked the screen door open and hurried out, then turned towards the vehicle. By then the tears had started and she could hardly see through the blur. When she reached the vehicle, she hurried around to the far side out of sight, then stopped and began sobbing.

She heard boots crunch on the gravel behind her and glanced back to see Major Conkey. That increased her distress and she felt deeply ashamed of herself. He stopped and said, "Take a minute or two to recover Barbara then get in the vehicle. Don't worry, I have the memory card and I think you acted within your rights. I will just try to smooth down a few ruffled feathers back in there. I will show them the area you indicated to me and that should be sufficient."

Barbara could only sniffle and nod. She heard Major Conkey's footsteps retreat and then slumped against the side of the vehicle and burst into tears again. For several minutes she stood there, shaking with shame and anger. Slowly the tears dried up and she calmed down. All the while the incident replayed itself in her mind: the humiliating images of her every intimate detail!

Having regained control, she wiped her face and then moved to sit in the passenger seat. Anxiety now began to grow; niggling little fears that she would be in trouble for back-answering an army colonel, or that she might be breaking some sort of national security laws. That got her miserable again and she shivered and sobbed a few times.

While she was waiting Wendy returned. That put Barbara in a

dilemma. She badly wanted to talk to Wendy about the incident or to some other female anyway, but she did not want rumours and gossip spreading through the unit. Imagining the snickers, sly looks and behind-the-hand comments that would result made her feel sick. So she resolved to say nothing and tried to act calm and relaxed. It only took Wendy a few minutes to realise that Barbara was upset but after a tentative query, she thankfully left her alone.

After about ten minutes Major Conkey returned. He walked over and got into the driver's seat without a word, started the engine and reversed out. Only when he had the vehicle moving back along the Camp Road did he speak.

"They are not happy," he said, "But they are also very worried. That captain, Capt Green, was really angry with his men, and Lt Col Nevison is very concerned and has just given those soldiers a real tongue lashing and threatened them with being charged."

Barbara nodded and sniffed. She managed to ask, "Am I in trouble sir?" She was hotly aware that Wendy was sitting behind her and would be 'all ears'.

Major Conkey looked at her in surprise. "You! No. Why should you be?"

"Because I was rude to the colonel and did not call him sir and defied him," Barbara replied.

Major Conkey snorted. "Huh! Don't worry about that. You were in the right and they knew it."

Barbara was doubtful, so she replied, "I was so humiliated—outraged—when I saw those men snickering at the pictures on the computer."

"So you acted. Good for you!" Major Conkey said. "Don't worry about it. Nothing will happen to you. They are much more worried that you are going to make an official complaint to Canberra, believe me."

That put Barbara on a spot. She had said she would but in her heart she did not really want to. "That will cause a lot of trouble won't it sir?"

"Yes, it will. There will be a high level official investigation; and the whole incident will have to be described to senior officers," Major Conkey agreed. "But if you feel you must, then do it."

Barbara made a wry face. "I rather think they might have been punished enough," she said, remembering their embarrassed faces and knowing that their officers were really angry with them. She was aware that Wendy was listening to all of this and it made her blush, then feel relieved, when Major Conkey turned and said to Wendy, "Barbara suffered an unpleasant bit of harassment back there. I am asking you not to say anything to the other cadets please Sgt Werribee."

"Of course, sir," Wendy replied, shooting Barbara a sympathetic but inquisitive look.

By then they had driven past their first campsite and were heading down the slope towards the Front Gate. Barbara gave Wendy a smile and said, "Thanks Wendy." Then she turned back to Major Conkey and said, "I think I will drop it. That will be best."

Major Conkey replied. "I agree. So don't worry about being in trouble. The colonel was more annoyed at you not showing them where the wreckage was."

"Oh him!" Barbara sniffed, curling her lip. "I did show him, but he is so arrogant he didn't listen. He can find it himself."

"I did show him on the map the area you indicated, but you can show me where again," Major Conkey answered. As he said this he steered the Land Rover through the Front Gate and turned left on the Mingela Road.

Barbara had expected that and as they came out of the first small dip she gestured towards the Gravel Scrape. "The big piece of satellite is over there near that piece stuck in the tree that I showed you," she said.

She had expected Major Conkey to turn off to go along the track across the Bridge so was surprised when he kept on driving along the road. "Where are we going sir?" she queried.

"To see St Michaels to see their OC and to find a fire to burn this memory card in," Major Conkey replied.

That got Barbara anxious. "What about the card sir? Is it really important, I mean in a military way?"

"I doubt it," Major Conkey replied. "The patrol just took pictures of parts of their exercise and you just happened to be in the wrong place at the wrong time."

"What were they doing sir?"

"They didn't explain," Major Conkey said, "but they are SAS and were obviously doing some sort of patrol."

Special Air Service! Barbara thought in awe. *And I shouted at them!* She, like most army cadets, had been inculcated by the media with an almost mystical respect for the members of the elite Special Air Service Regiment. "They must be doing the same exercise as those British Commandos," she suggested.

"Probably," Major Conkey replied. By then they had driven past the Gravel Scrape and were approaching the Dip where the Mingela Road crossed One Mile Creek. Major Conkey slowed the vehicle down to go through the Dip, then kept the speed to a crawl while he studied the ground on the right of the road. This was the burnt-out area beyond the place where Barbara had been when the satellite crashed and she saw it was a maze of small gullies amid a thicket of twisted and gnarled trees and bushes.

Major Conkey brought the Land Rover to a stop and pointed. "There. That should do us."

Barbara saw the smouldering trunk of a large tree. It was about twenty metres from the road and lying across some of the smaller gullies amid a blackened wasteland. A thick trail of whitish ash showed where a part of the trunk and some of the branches had already been consumed. A wisp of smoke was rising from the end of the trunk. Wendy was told to stay with the vehicle. Barbara climbed out and followed Major Conkey off the road.

As they scrambled across the first gully, a steep-sided thing a metre wide and the same deep, she was surprised at how broken this small area of country was. The map did not indicate anything like it and she had been within a hundred paces of it several times and not noticed it. She and Major Conkey made their way into the thicket and across another small gully to the smoking log. Barbara noted that all of the country away to her front and left appeared to be burnt off.

"It looks like a lot of country got burnt-out," she commented.

"Most of it all the way to the New Airfield," Major Conkey agreed.

They stopped at the end of the log and Barbara saw that the tree had been mostly hollow and full of termite dust. This was smouldering and she could see shimmering waves of heat rising. As she got close she could feel the heat on her skin. Major Conkey took the memory card out of his pocket and broke it open. It took an effort to snap the plastic and he grunted with annoyance as he did. Then he placed it down onto the white ash where the smoke was emanating from.

Barbara watched with satisfaction and relief as the brown plastic began to curl and blacken. After a few seconds it burst into flames. It took another minute or so for the whole thing to melt and flare up. Barbara stood watching the bluish-greenish flames consume the melted plastic, her emotions in turmoil.

As the last of the card was reduced to an unrecognizable black chunk she asked, "Sir, why would they carry a video camera on patrol?"

"For Real Time Surveillance," Major Conkey replied. "They can link it to a small computer or a mobile phone and can relay the images via satellite back to their base."

Barbara was amazed. "Satellites are important aren't they sir?" she said.

"Yes, they are," Major Conkey replied. "They are now the key to many military situations. Whoever has the best satellite system controls the Intelligence gathering and communications. Whoever dominates Space and Cyberspace has the military power in the world."

Barbara nodded and felt guilty at not having shown Lt Col Nevison the other wreckage. But she also now had another, more immediate and embarrassing problem; she had an insistent desire to do a pee! She bit her lip and hesitated. Major Conkey turned to go back to the vehicle and that forced her to speak. "Sir, you just go back. I need to do something."

Major Conkey stopped and looked back. He raised his eyebrows, then grinned, making her blush. "You'd better check there isn't another patrol lurking nearby first," he said.

"Oh sir!" Barbara cried, blushing even more.

Major Conkey laughed. "Sorry! Just kidding. I will go across the road for the same reason. I will meet you at the vehicle."

He walked off, leaving Barbara to look anxiously around. Her rational mind told her that it was unlikely that there would be another SAS patrol in the vicinity but that did little to ease her concern.

Those British commandos might be in this area. They went towards the New Airfield, she thought.

With them in mind she carefully scanned the surrounding bush. As she looked around she was struck by just how much cover there was in this particular area. There were at least four parallel gullies and dozens of logs and anthills. As well as them the remaining trees of the thicket were dense enough to limit visibility.

For modesty Barbara made her way across to the next gully and looked into it. It was about a metre deep and the same wide and had a sandy bottom. The course of the gully wriggled down the gentle slope with sharp bends every ten metres or so. Just to be sure she was not being observed at close range Barbara walked to the next bend and looked down. Satisfied no-one would see her in there she clambered down and then eyed the holes in the vertical banks, fear of snakes now pushing worries about Special Forces 'Peeping Toms' from her mind. She looked over the top and glimpsed Major Conkey out near the road and heading away from her. Satisfied she was safe she dropped her trousers and did a pee.

By the time she was finished she was sweating. Down in the small gully it was stifling. The sun's rays seemed to beat down vertically and then get magnified. She stood up and pulled up her trousers. As she began to button them up she heard a vehicle approaching along the road from the direction of the New Airfield. From where she was to the road was about thirty metres away and the intervening thicket made it hard to get more than glimpses but she did see a cream coloured civilian car come to a standstill near the Land Rover.

Having adjusted her clothing Barbara wended her way back through the thicket and across the other gullies to the road. Here she found Major Conkey talking to two civilians. They were both dressed in white shirts and brown slacks and had a distinctly 'Middle Eastern' look about them: black hair and moustaches, swarthy complexions, dark brown eyes.

As Barbara made her way across the ditch beside the road one of the men looked at her. He had a huge, hooked nose and she saw his eyes widen, first in what she thought was alarm, then with surprise as he noted her gender.

Major Conkey was showing them where on the map they were. As Barbara joined them the man with the huge, hooked nose gestured to the burnt-out country and said, "There has been a fire?"

Major Conkey nodded. "Yes. A satellite crashed and set fire to the bush," he explained.

"Ah yes. We heard about that," the man said.

Barbara noted that he spoke with a pronounced accent. She was so sweaty she took off her cloth hat and wiped her face with it. As she did she saw the man's eyes flick to her hair and then widen in surprise. Then they narrowed in a way she recognized, and which annoyed her: a male noting her appearance. It always peeved her, even though she knew that many people found her copper coloured hair very attractive.

In her annoyance Barbara stared hard at the man and asked, "Where are you from?"

The man looked taken aback at being spoken to. He then smiled and turned to face Major Conkey. "We come from Sydney," he said.

His arrogant male attitude of ignoring a female irritated Barbara even more so she said, "You aren't Australians. What country do you come from?"

The man glanced at her and smiled, but Barbara could tell he was annoyed. He did not answer but said to Major Conkey, "Thank you for showing us the way. We must keep going."

With that he and his companion walked back to their car and got in. As they drove off Major Conkey raised a quizzical eyebrow and asked, "You were a bit rude Barbara. What was that all about?"

"I just hate the way the men from those Middle Eastern cultures treat women like dirt; as though we are of no importance and don't really exist except as their possessions or slaves," she replied.

"He didn't like it when you asked where he came from," Major Conkey said, looking at the trail of dust left by the departing car.

"Probably another spy looking for the satellite; from Iran or one of those Arab countries," Barbara muttered crossly.

"Another spy?" Major Conkey asked with a humorous chuckle as he moved to open the door of the Land Rover.

"Yeah. There were two characters who looked and sounded like Russian spies here yesterday," Barbara replied, pointing back along the road to where they had crossed it during the day exercise. She walked around to get into the passenger seat.

Major Conkey laughed. "You are imagining things," he said as he started the engine.

"Maybe, but those two characters didn't look like tourists, and they certainly aren't local bushies," Barbara replied. She was getting tired of the satellite and hearing about it irritated her.

Major Conkey did not turn the Land Rover but drove on along the road. "Just going to talk to the OC of St Michael's for a minute," he explained.

A kilometre further along they came to the junction of the Back

Road. This came in on their left. Just opposite the junction a dirt track went up the gentle slope to the right and Major Conkey turned off along it. Only parts of this area had been burnt-out, large patches of dry grass remaining among the scatter of straggly ironbarks.

Near the top of the slope the track turned left and they came out onto the parking apron for the New Airfield. Major Conkey stopped at the edge of the actual landing strip and looked carefully both ways, then drove across the very end of the strip. Out of the right-hand window Barbara saw the airstrip stretching away into the distance and was amazed. From the map she knew it was over a kilometre long, but it was something else to actually see it; a huge clearing a hundred metres wide stretching off through the bush along the gently undulating crest of a wide ridge top.

Among the trees on the other side of the airstrip were a scatter of tents and lines of hutchies: the bivouac area of St Michael's College Cadet Unit. Barbara did not have any friends in that unit, so she just sat in the Land Rover with Wendy while Major Conkey got out and talked to their OC for a few minutes. While Barbara waited she noted that the country for many kilometres around appeared to have been burnt off, only the small area around the actual bivouac was still unburnt. She and Wendy discussed the fire and the previous night's exercise.

When he returned a few minutes later Major Conkey said, "Right, now back to the unit for lunch."

Chapter 11

SADNESS

On arrival back at the company bivouac area they found that lunch was almost over. The last sections had just returned from the Leadership Evaluation Ex. Further along the back track of the Triangle Barbara could see 130ACU also moving in for lunch. They had been doing their 'Treasure Hunt'. Because the two units often worked together Barbara knew that 130 would use the same Leadership Evaluation Exercise that afternoon, along One Mile Creek and down to the bed of Keelbottom Creek. As she climbed out of the vehicle Barbara caught Wendy's eye.

"Wendy, please don't say anything about that incident, or the thing we just burnt," she said.

Wendy nodded. "I won't. I promise."

Barbara smiled and felt like hugging her. *She is a good friend really,* she thought, remembering how Wendy had never given up or complained when they had been battling with the religious fanatics in the jungle near Kuranda back in June.[3]

After collecting her mess gear Barbara joined the queue. She still felt upset and did not really feel hungry but knew she had to act normally. To her relief nobody asked where she had been. She was able to join her platoon in the shade of the straggly ironbarks and could pretend she was happy and well.

It was so hot by the time lunch was over that CSM Sheehan came around and told them that Major Conkey had ordered them all to lie down and rest till 1500. Barbara saw it was only 1300 and felt even more relieved. She was actually feeling quite drained and down. So she washed up, packed her mess gear away then unrolled her bedding in the shade of her hutchie.

Even lying in the shade wasn't much relief as there was no breeze and she found she was sweating and dehydrating just resting. Her main problem, apart from how she felt herself, was getting Sgt Russell to keep the platoon in the shade and resting.

[3] *Barbara and the Smiley People* by C. R. Cummings.

No sooner had she settled down than a group of a dozen CUOs and sergeants from 130ACU arrived. Major Conkey led them away to set up the Leadership Course. Barbara sat up to wave to the ones she knew and noted with surprise that Chloe was with them and was wearing a brassard with sergeant stripes on it.

What's Chloe doing wearing sergeant's stripes, Barbara wondered. Resolving to ask later she settled back under her hutchie.

For the first hour Barbara worked on filling out her platoon's Personal Qualities Reports. It was not a task she enjoyed, mostly because she knew her recommendations would cause disappointment. She had no hesitation in recommending that Dan Russell be sent on the Cadet Under-Officers Course, but with the three corporals it was harder.

Debbie Wallis will make an adequate sergeant, she decided, *but only in HQ, or in a junior platoon. She is a bit too nice and too gentle.* Cpl Walsh, she knew, would make a good platoon sergeant for 4 Platoon and said so. *But not Cpl Halyday,* she reluctantly decided. Halyday was now in his 4th year as a cadet, had joined the same year as her, but had spent two years as a cadet before making lance corporal.

It was his inability to read and do maths to a sufficient standard that was his failing. As a soldier he was very good: excellent fieldcraft, good at drill and weapon handling, satisfactory at First Aid but barely adequate at things like encoding and decoding in signals and hopeless at working out bearings for navigation. Knowing that he badly wanted to be a sergeant just made the decision not to recommend him all the more painful. But Barbara knew it was her duty to make sure the people who were put in charge were capable and safe.

A sergeant who can't navigate or write orders is a safety liability, she thought, then regretfully wrote 'Not recommended for promotion' on the form.

She knew her opinion, while not the only one Major Conkey would consider, would carry a lot of weight. Writing those words saddened her and made her aware she was not a hard person, and certainly not a ruthless one. That got her thinking once more about whether the army would be the right career for her. Unable to decide she settled to completing the reports. When that was done she had a big drink and lay back, aware she was still tense and upset from the morning's incident.

While Barbara lay there trying to relax she felt a sense of sadness slowly creep over her and deepen. She knew that the event after lunch, the 'Treasure Hunt', was the last exercise of the annual camp, and it did not require her to act a platoon commander.

I have done my last platoon leadership activity, she thought.

It dawned on her that, if she was unable to join the army and become and officer, then the camp might be the last time she ever acted in such a role in her whole life. That idea grew and had quite a profound effect on her.

How sad, she thought.

In her own estimation she was a good leader. She knew she had really enjoyed cadets and had relished the challenge and emotional rewards of being a platoon commander.

Now it might be all over, she told herself.

There was only one more day of camp and that was just administration and travel. After camp she would be a cadet for another month, until the annual Passing-Out Parade in early November—and that could be it.

Part of what was bothering her was the indecision about her future. At the end of November, she would also graduate from High School and she still had not decided what career she wanted to do. Now her feelings about trying to join the regular army crystalized. She knew that her opinion was being adversely influenced by the recent encounters with regulars and she tried not to let it sour her thoughts.

But I don't think I am suited for the regular army, she told herself.

But what else to do? She knew she had a good brain and felt sure she would get good enough marks to be able to enter university and to do virtually any course she wanted to. The dilemma was choosing the right thing to study.

Something that helps other people, she told herself, *and I can do my military service part-time in the General Reserve—or maybe stay with cadets?*

The decision had still not been made by 1430 when the remainder of 130ACU came walking past in a long line of sweating cadets. Their passing stirred up the dust and drew many ribald comments and grumbles. As the last of them went by Major Conkey sent runners from HQ to assemble the Coy O Group. Barbara collected her reports and webbing and walked over to join the other CUOs. The completed reports she handed to Major Conkey, who thanked her.

As Barbara sat down Roger gave her a concerned look and she managed a smile in reply, not wanting to tell him about the video, or her clash with the lieutenant colonel. That gave her a jolt too as it dawned on her that maybe Roger was not the man for her either.

If I don't feel like unburdening myself to him, is he the right one? she wondered unhappily. She really liked Roger and did not want to hurt his feelings.

Major Conkey briefed them on what was to happen that afternoon and evening then sent them back to their platoons. The troops would be doing the orienteering exercise in basic webbing. Their packs and kitbags were to be moved by Land Rover to the First Campsite. The temperature was still sweltering hot but Major Conkey got them moving. The other OOCs were all busy by then, either setting up the 'Treasure Hunt' course or pre-positioning water along the route.

Barbara briefed Sgt Russell and the section commanders and they at once got the platoon up and hard at work. Shelters were dropped and packed, bedding rolled up, latrines filled in and the area 'emu-bobbed' of litter. Packs and kitbags were then lugged over and dumped in a dusty line beside the vehicle track.

"Time we were gone from this area anyway," Sgt Russell commented, indicating the extensive area that had been dry grass two days earlier, but which was now mostly bare earth and fine, powdery dust.

The company was then seated in section lines for the Treasure Hunt briefing. The Treasure Hunt was an orienteering exercise, but it was run as a race between sections and was a good test of section leadership and teamwork. The results counted for the 'Section Competition' as to which were the best junior and senior sections in the company. The course was a secret, each leg being marked by a sign in code. Eleven different coding systems were used and each section had a sergeant or CUO from another platoon attached as DS to make sure they decoded properly and that they did not cheat. Barbara was allocated to Cpl Holly Jensen's Number 3 Section. She was happy with that, considering Holly to have great potential.

She should make sergeant or even CUO, she mused.

It took Major Conkey half an hour to brief the troops on how the exercise ran, and on its 'story' (A bushranger named Captain Flashlight had held up stage coaches back in the gold rushes during the 1880s. At that time the main road from Charters Towers to Townsville had been the one they were camped astride. It ran on southwest beside Keelbottom Creek to the Burdekin River. Captain Flashlight had hidden his gold and left the clues in code. He was caught and hanged and only recently was his dairy, which contained the coded clues, discovered). The first clue was then read out and the exercise began. By then it was nearly 1600 hours and the fierce heat had eased a bit.

For the next two and a half-hours Barbara walked, hurried or waited while 3 Section struggled to decode the clues and to navigate. Never once did they lead but they were always up in the top four or five. The course went first to One Mile Creek where the 'minefield' had been. From there they hurried to the Lagoon in Keelbottom Creek. On the way they passed close to where the snake had vanished but the cadets either did not know or had forgotten about it and Barbara was at the rear and they ignored her warning.

Barbara had never been to the Lagoon and found it interesting but not very attractive. The waterhole was about twenty-five metres wide and extended off to the right out of sight. Both banks were steep and ten metres high, covered with a thick matt of tall grass and bushes, and studded with a line of large paperbarks which cast a welcome shade. The water was stagnant and looked green and scummy. It did not appear to be very deep. Down in the hollow the air was stifling. Barbara was glad when they climbed up out of the creek bed on the next leg.

This took them on a compass bearing southeast across the dry 'island' and flood channel and up to a cattle grid on the Mingela Road. At the cattle grid Barbara could just see the buildings of the deserted 'Dotswood' Station homestead. Because she enjoyed exploring historical places she would have liked to go there but she knew the area was 'Out of Bounds' so could only shrug and refocus on the Treasure Hunt.

Maybe one day? she thought.

The next leg took them back west along the Mingela Road to the eastern road junction of the Triangle. From there they were directed to the southern junction of the Triangle. By then the sun was well down to the west but the air was still and dust laden, the heat seeming to hang and cling. The next leg was a compass bearing to where three fences met at the edge of the Swamp Paddock and the Camp MacAliney Paddock.

The clue there was so hard to decode that it held them up for twenty minutes, allowing Barbara a chance to sit down and rest. While she waited the sun sank even lower and was almost gone from them before the section moved on. This was on a compass bearing to a jerry can in the middle of the area where they had done the night lantern stalk. The leg after that took them down to the Front Gate. By the time they left there the sun was only glowing on the tree tops and Barbara saw Major Conkey looking anxiously at his watch while he talked to Lt Hamilton at the safety vehicle.

The leg after the Front Gate took them to the Bridge. As they hurried across to it in the growing twilight Barbara realised she was becoming quite tense.

I'll bet we go to the Gravel Scrape, she thought.

Then she felt guilty about the wreckage of the satellite as there was no sign that the army had searched the area again.

They did go to the Gravel Scrape, hurrying across the blackened wasteland in a race against the failing light. As they did Barbara kept looking over to where she thought the wreckage was but saw no sign of any digging or similar work. But when she became guilty and considered going to tell the army she remembered the humiliation and shame and shook her head.

No, it belongs to the French. They should have it, she reasoned.

Luckily the clue at the Gravel Scrape was an easy one and they had it decoded in three minutes. By then the sunlight was still glowing on the distant slopes of Mount St Michael, but twilight was setting in and Barbara expected Major Conkey to call the exercise off. But a call on her radio told her to carry on. So she set the section moving. The route took them east and they passed within about fifty paces of where she thought the wreckage was. As she walked past the area Barbara studied the remains of the burnt tree trunk and saw that it was now only a streak of white ash and a hole full of soot. For a moment she was tempted to detour so she could mark the spot to make it easier for the army to find but Cpl Jensen kept urging her section to hurry, so Barbara just shrugged and kept walking.

The leg went to the Dip where One Mile Creek crossed the Mingela Road. Here they found Capt Maclaren with another safety vehicle and he told them to keep going for another half-hour.

That leg was a compass bearing to a post on the power line near the

Back Road Gate. Barbara was a bit uneasy about it but Cpl Jensen was keen to continue. "There are only three sections ahead of us Ma'am," she pleaded. "We are in with a chance."

So they set off, striding through the waist high grass and thicket of small, twisted trees. The narrow, deep gully was negotiated with some difficulty as by then it was almost dark. Fear of snakes and worry about accidents made Barbara anxious but she allowed them to keep going. She was relieved when they came to the vehicle track and fence which was the boundary of the camp paddock. This was the area where they had come down the slope during the night exercise the night before so was familiar territory to them all. They rolled under the fence and strode on, passing a hundred paces to the south of the low rise where Coy HQ (and later 4 Platoon) had been located the previous night.

They reached the power pole at 1845 to find Lt Hamilton there with his Land Rover. He told them to go north along the powerline clearing to the Camp Road, then left back to their first campsite. Barbara knew this area so well that navigation was not a problem. The group just plodded along. By then Barbara had a tongue that felt dry and puffed up and she knew she was dehydrated. The last of the red sunset faded as they made their way up the gentle slope.

On reaching the Camp Road the group turned left and trudged the hundred metres to the First Campsite. As they reached the parked vehicles Barbara noted a long line of cadets carrying packs marching off the road into the scrub on the north side of the road. At first she thought they were the company but then realized it was 130ACU. They had also returned from the Triangle to their first camp site.

Back at the First Campsite Barbara found most of the company already seated in section lines. It was fully dark by then and the moon was not up, but she could see them clearly enough in the starlight. She learned that only two more sections had been allowed to continue on from the Dip after Cpl Jensen's. The others had been sent to the camp along the road. There was a wait of twenty minutes till those two sections came plodding in. Then CSM Sheehan did a roll check before reporting all present to Major Conkey.

The results were then announced. Cpl Jensen's section came in 4th (2nd of the Junior Sections, beaten by Cpl Grey's 2 Section). Major Conkey congratulated the winners and then briefed the company on the evening's activities. As he did a wave of sadness swept over Barbara. *My last exercise as a cadet platoon commander is over,* she told herself. Anxiety about the future gnawed at her, quite spoiling her mood.

The first task, on being told to 'carry on', was to collect their packs and kitbags from beside the road. There were ten minutes of milling and confusion while people located their gear. They then moved to the same area they had occupied previously and set up their hutchies. Barbara insisted that everyone use exactly the same trees as before, to prevent any disputes.

Once the camp was re-established they were called out to a barbeque tea. This was done by platoons. The cooks were Lt Hamilton, Lt Standish and HQ. The cadets were now in a festive mood with a lot of laughing and joking. There was also a fair amount of subtle tension as male and female cadets who had 'discovered' each other during the camp tried to make a pass. This was always a problem on camps. 'Frat Night' was the cadet nickname for the last night and it meant that the staff and leaders had to be particularly vigilant to make sure nothing improper occurred.

And not only the lower ranks, Barbara thought wryly as Roger came to stand close beside her.

There was not much tension in her case, and nobody seemed to take any particular notice. In the eyes of most people she and Roger were boyfriend and girlfriend and therefore hardly worthy of note.

Like being married I suppose, Barbara mused. *No thrill or scandal then, even if you do the same things.*

Not that she had any concern about Roger trying to get her to do the wrong thing. He was so damned honourable it was sometimes irksome.

I need a hug at the moment, Barbara thought. She was aware she was feeling somewhat melancholy.

But at least the food was good. The aroma of grilling steak and onions aroused a good appetite in her and she was able to eat two hamburgers. The CUOs sat in a group with a couple of the sergeants and the CSM while they ate.

Fiona made the comment that they would be able to sit at a table the next day and that had the effect of deepening Barbara's depressed mood.

The camp is almost over. We will be home tomorrow. It will all be finished, she thought sadly.

After the meal the platoons were sent to have a shower. They went in the same order as they had been rostered to eat in, so 4 Platoon was second. Barbara did not really want to go near the army camp but knew it would be difficult to make an excuse. She had to lead her platoon and supervise in the girl's ablutions. Reluctantly she gathered her towel, toilet bag, thongs and a change of clothes, then had Sgt Russell line the platoon up.

The troops were in very high spirits by then, despite the announcement that there would be no campfire ('Total fire ban,' had been the reason, which drew some sarcastic comments). Capt Maclaren gave Barbara the nod and she led her people off along the road to the camp. They walked in single file beside the road, stirring up quite a cloud of dust as they walked. Along the way they passed cadets from 3 Platoon coming back and also groups from 130ACU.

As the platoon approached the bright lights of the camp Barbara was amazed at how tense she had become. She realized she was hyperventilating and forced herself to slow her breathing. However, she could not control her thoughts so easily and she had alternating images of her humiliation and embarrassment at the HQ that morning, and surges of guilt at not showing the army where the wreckage was.

The feeling of guilt increased as she walked past the rows of tents that were now erected on the concrete slabs and saw the regular soldiers there. Her feelings rapidly changed to resentment and anger when one of the soldiers yelled angrily, "Stop stirring up the bloody dust you snotty-nosed little shits!"

Barbara had been about to hand over to Sgt Russell so she could go to the HQ to tell them where the wreckage was, but a sharp stab of anger made her scowl and keep walking.

Well you can find it yourselves! she thought, angry at them, then angry at herself for being so petty.

It all just left her feeling sad..

Chapter 12

HOME

A shower did a lot to cheer Barbara up. So did the behaviour of Chloe and Jane. Some of the girls from 130ACU were also there. As Barbara finished her shower Chloe and Jane came in with another girl. The girl was crying and Chloe went to the end cubicle and quite deliberately asked the girl using it to hurry up. She then stood and shielded the crying girl and Jane as they sat on the bench.

Barbara was at once concerned, noting that none of the female officers was at that moment inside. She grabbed her towel and wrapped it around her then went to over to them. "Is everything alright Chloe?" she asked.

Chloe met her gaze and gave a faint shake of the head. "Mmmm. No, not really. Kym here is just a bit upset and we are going to look after her."

"Does she need to see a medic?" Barbara asked, looking past Chloe.

Chloe smiled. "No, nor an OOC. It's nothing serious. She is just a bit upset because of a bitch fight over a boy. She will be OK. Janie and I will look after her."

Barbara realized she must have looked doubtful because Chloe huffed with annoyance, then said, "Really, it is alright."

"If you say so," Barbara replied. "Just as long as you aren't teaching her your old tricks."

Chloe's indignation showed clear on her face. "Oh, I like that!" she cried.

Then she grinned and ran her eyes very obviously up Barbara's legs and across her towel-wrapped form to where her bosom was bulging out of the top. Her face dimpled into a cheeky grin and she added, "Anyway, who are you to talk at the moment?"

Barbara blushed but had to grin in return. "You know what I mean," she replied.

Chloe laughed. "Don't you worry Barb... I mean CUO Brassington. I have turned over a new leaf. I aim to get promoted again at the end of this year," she said.

That reminded Barbara, and she said, "I see you are wearing a brassard with three stripes on it. What is that all about?"

Chloe shrugged but smiled. "I have been promoted to acting sergeant," she replied.

"What for?" Barbara asked, then wished she hadn't as she realized her actions were prying and bad-mannered.

Again, Chloe shrugged and Barbara noted Jane frown and give Chloe a worried glance. Chloe shrugged again and said, "One of our sergeants got... er... got moved out of a platoon," she explained.

Noting the sensitiveness of the answer Barbara hesitated. *There has obviously been a problem in One Thirty,* she decided.

Not wanting to pry into another unit's affairs, despite her inquisitiveness, she replied, "So you are acting as a platoon sergeant then?"

Chloe nodded. "Three Platoon," she replied.

"Good for you!" Barbara said. "So your chances of being a substantive sergeant are good. I hope you make it. And you too Jane."

Chloe smiled and nodded. "I hope so, and one day I will be a CUO, just like you."

"Oh good!" Barbara replied, unable to keep a tinge of sarcasm out of her tone. Despite that she was impressed. This changed to blushing pleasure when Chloe added, "I think you are just the greatest role model. I want to be just like you."

"Oh! Oh, thank you," Barbara stammered. She felt sure that the praise was genuine, and she was touched. To cover her confusion, she turned to dressing. That was awkward too as she felt very self-conscious with the other girls there. To hide herself she pulled on her shirt first, then took off the towel and pulled on her knickers and trousers. The tactic was successful except that it meant she had not put on her bra. For a moment she hesitated and considered going to one of the toilet cubicles to do this. Then she smiled and the impish idea that it was Frat Night crossed her mind.

I won't bother, she thought. *Nobody will notice.*

She did not articulate the thought but for a few seconds it flickered across her mind that a bit of physical play would be nice. Then she shook her head.

Roger wouldn't. Not at camp anyway. That got her wondering if he would at any other time. He was very proper and the complete gentleman, even in private. A niggling doubt crossed her mind. *Is he really the man for me?*

By then Chloe was tossing off clothing without a care in the world so Barbara quickly left, rather than get an eyeful and have her own doubts aroused. She set off back along the Camp Road. At once she began to reconsider the bra as the front of her shirt wobbled quite alarmingly with her motion. To hide it she held her towel and dirty clothing in front of her.

On the way she met Major Carroll, OC of Sarina. She thought he was one of the nicest men she had ever met. Not wanting to appear rude she stopped and chatted to him for a few minutes. While she did she was acutely self-conscious and was careful to keep her bosom covered.

When she continued on, Barbara noted that a large group of people were sitting between the kitchen and the HQ watching a movie. It was a war movie and the audience appeared to be mostly soldiers, so she stayed well away and thankfully walked off into the darkness.

A few minutes later she was back at the company bivouac. Here she packed her washing and toilet gear. Then she stood in the darkness and thought about her bra. There were a few cadets around but it was quiet dark. She knew she could probably take off her shirt and put the bra and shirt on without any chance of being seen.

Chloe wouldn't hesitate, she thought. Then she smiled and felt the delicious sense of daring. *No, I will leave it off.*

So she walked around looking for her friends, enjoying the sensation as she did. She soon found Fiona, Lofty and Roger. They were sitting near Coy HQ and were drinking softdrink. The canteen was operating by lantern light and Roger at once sprang up and went to get Barbara a drink. "You don't have to!" she expostulated, but he ignored that.

It was a very relaxed gathering. From time to time others joined or left. The conversation flowed and so did the jokes. Despite that they were mostly fairly quiet.

The others must feel how I do, Barbara thought. *Tired out.*

She decided it was the heat which had done it, sucking the energy out of them.

Wendy joined them and sat close beside Lofty but nobody commented. It had been unit rumour for years that Lofty and Wendy had been more then just friends. Seeing Wendy snuggle against Lofty, her bosom pressing against his arm, caused Barbara a spurt of jealousy. The thought that Wendy would probably enjoy a bit of physical passion soon caused Barbara to sigh in frustration.

It would be nice if Roger at least tried something, she thought. *But I doubt if he will.*

And she was right. Roger was the perfect gentleman and did not even hint at any thing, much less try it. By bedtime Barbara was tingling with suppressed desire and was ashamed of herself for being so weak. Then, after Roger had said a cheery goodnight and walked off towards his platoon, she stood and stared at the rising moon and sighed. "Oh, a bit of romance would be nice!"

Despite her tiredness Barbara slept poorly. She woke a dozen times and kept changing position, fidgeting in an attempt to get comfortable. As the first hint of dawn lightened the sky she got up and looked around. All was quiet and she noted that it was only just after 0500. With nearly an hour to Check Parade she lay down and tried to go back to sleep. That plan was defeated by an insistent urge to go to the toilet.

Resigning herself to staying awake Barbara dressed properly and then set off for the toilet. Apart from two HQ cadets on piquet there was no-one else awake and Barbara made sure she walked as quietly as she could while she passed 1 Platoon. As she approached the buildings of the army camp she admitted to herself she was feeling both tense and guilty.

I hope no-one is awake, she thought.

She continued on until the buildings came into sight. As she walked past the side of the camp she kept glancing anxiously at the HQ building.

I should go over and show them where I saw that bit of wreckage, she thought.

But she didn't, rationalizing that Major Conkey had shown them the general area. Feeling ashamed of her own pettiness and weakness she walked on to the toilet.

Afterwards she hurried back out of the camp, hoping that none of the people moving about the kitchen were army people who might recognize her. Back at the company bivouac she lay down again but could only rest. As she watched the daylight strengthen behind Mount St Michael she wondered if she really loved Roger—or if he really loved her. She also thought hard and anxiously about her future. It was all very stressful, and she sighed a few times.

After 0600 the routine of the camp drove most of these gloomy thoughts out of her mind. The company was going home that day and most of the cadets were in a happy mood. They were scheduled to leave straight after breakfast so there was a lot to be done. As soon as Major Conkey finished briefing the officers Barbara returned to her hutchie and pulled it down. As she folded the plastic shelter she felt a stab of genuine regret.

"I might never sleep under a hutchie again," she told herself. That idea set the tone for her that day. She packed her bedding and then got the platoon organized. Breakfast followed: fresh rations from the camp kitchen. These were collected by Lt Hamilton in hot boxes and the food was doled out by the CQ and a work party from HQ. 4 Platoon was the third group to go through the mess parade and by then their bivouac area was cleared and they sat on their packs near the road.

After washing up and packing away her mess gear Barbara cleaned her teeth. She used water from a canteen rather than walking to the camp. Now that it was time to go she just wanted to get away from the place.

But it wasn't that simple. By 0730 two large motor coaches had parked beside the road and the company was packed and ready to go. Their bivouac area was clear of litter and was now just looking forlorn and dusty. Major Conkey then ordered the CSM to parade the company. While they were lined up Barbara joined the other CUOs at the front.

Several people in uniform arrived from the army camp. For a moment Barbara felt a stab of concern, thinking they were coming to question her again. But it was only Major Ross and his regular army warrant officer from Cadet HQ, plus another warrant officer. Major Conkey took over the parade from the CSM. While they were still at attention he ordered, "Open order march!" He then posted the officers in front of their platoons. That done he handed over to Major Ross.

Major Ross gave them all an official warning that the area was an army firing range and that it was... "an offence, both civil and military, to remove any ammunition or range produce from the range." It was something Barbara had heard a dozen times during her cadet career but his time it seemed to strike a chill of anxiety into her, even though she knew she did not have any such items on her.

After the warning the cadets were given a minute to declare anything they may have 'accidentally' picked up. Then Major Ross and the two warrant officers went along the ranks and asked each person if they had anything. When Major Ross came over to Barbara she broke into a sweat and felt extraordinarily guilty. When he gave her a hard and not very friendly look she felt even more anxious. It took her an effort to reply without a quaver that she did not have any ammunition or range produce in her possession, sir!

Major Ross gave her another hard look and for a moment she thought he was going to ask her about the wreckage, or perhaps reprimand her for her insubordinate language to the colonel the day before. However, he just grunted and turned away.

Major Ross then handed back to Major Conkey who fell the officers out and told the CSM to load the gear onto the two coaches. While this was being done Barbara noted that most of 130ACU were standing watching from the other side of the road. After passing her kitbag, pack and webbing in to the bottom of the coach she turned and walked across to where they stood.

"Goodbye you lot!" she said, the emotion now welling up to half-choke her.

It was Chloe who came forward and hugged her. "You take care CUO Brassington, and good luck," she said.

"And good luck to you, Sergeant Chloe," Barbara sniffled in reply, tears now streaming out as the awareness of ending overcame her. Chloe squeezed her tight and that felt both very good and very comforting to Barbara. She hugged her back and then moved to say goodbye to others she knew, shaking hands with one hand and wiping away tears with the other.

It was a tired and relieved Barbara who filed onto the coach at the end of her platoon a few minutes later. 4 Platoon shared the coach with 3 so Barbara sat next to Fiona on the left-hand side. There was then a delay of five minutes while the CSM and Lt Standish, the OOC who had marked the Bus Roll, did a double check of numbers to ensure no-one was missing. During the wait Barbara began to fret with impatience.

"Oh, I wish we would get going," she muttered to Fiona.

Fiona nodded. "It is a hot, dusty dump. I hope I never come her again," she commented.

"Me too!" Barbara agreed.

To Barbara's relief the door closed and the coach began to move.

She settled back in her seat, glad of the air-conditioning as the day was already heating up. As the coach rolled down past their First Camp towards the Front Gate she looked out the window and experienced a mixture of regret and anxiety.

I didn't really enjoy the camp as much as I had hoped, she thought.

As they passed 130ACU Barbara waved and was pleased to see a dusty Chloe, still sporting her sergeant's stripes, waving and grinning.

And I wish her well too, she thought.

As the coach turned right onto the Mingela Road at the Front Gate Barbara glanced left towards the Bridge and Gravel Scrape and experienced another wave of guilt. The more she thought about it the more she was sure the thing she had seen strike the tree was quite a large and solid piece of wreckage. *I should have shown them,* she told herself. But then she rationalized that she had. She remembered standing next to the smoking hole and pointing to it, then being embarrassed by crude suggestions about wetting herself. With that came hotter waves of indignation and shame at the crude video.

No, I won't tell them. They don't deserve it. Besides, it belongs to France, not Australia.

Fiona nudged her. "You are looking very pensive Barbara," she said.

Barbara nodded. "Yes, just feeling guilty I didn't show the army the piece of wreckage from that satellite."

"I thought you did?"

"So did I, but they did not seem to take much notice at the time."

"What did it look like?" Fiona queried.

Barbara described the glowing object but found to her dismay that she was now having trouble remembering exactly what it looked like. She then told Fiona what Major Conkey had said about space weapons and world power.

Fiona sniffed and shook her head. "Sounds like the sort of thing the world might be better off without."

Barbara agreed but then shrugged. "If the French built it they undoubtedly have the plans and can make another one."

Fiona nodded and agreed. "They probably want it back so that no-one else can just copy it," she suggested.

By then the coach was passing the burnt-out thicket and Barbara experienced a spurt of strong pride at how good her platoon had looked and how well they had patrolled across that bit of ground. As the coach went past the Triangle she sighed.

They are a good platoon—but now it is all over, she thought.

A minute later the coach crossed the cattle grid and then passed the turn-off to the derelict 'Dotswood' homestead before the road dipped down across the small bridge on Keelbottom Creek.

As the coach ground up the dusty slope on the other side of the creek Barbara thought, *We are leaving the Dotswood Exercise Area now. I hope I never see the place again!*

For the next twenty minutes the coach bumped along the gravel road northwards, frequently slowing to cross small dips and washouts. It then turned right along the main Herveys Range Road and headed towards Townsville. The road changed to a wide bitumen highway which wound through a range of low hills. During all this time they travelled through empty, dry bush, much of it burnt-out. There was not a single building and they only passed one civilian vehicle travelling in the other direction.

Ten kilometres further along the road recrossed Keelbottom Creek on a new concrete bridge. There were then several more kilometres of empty savannah woodland before they came to the first buildings, the 'Range Control' complex for the Townsville Field Training Area. As the wheels of the coach hummed along the road, Barbara sat back and sighed with relief. Somehow it felt better to be out of the army training area.

Fifteen kilometres of good bitumen road, mostly through more uninhabited bush, had them at the scattered settlement of Herveys Range. By then Barbara was feeling tired and wanted to sleep. She was awake and interested while they traversed Thorntons Gap and then wound their way down the face of the escarpment to the coastal plain, but after that she dozed off.

When she was shaken awake by Fiona she found they were at Cardwell, a small town beside the sea halfway back to Cairns. Barbara was surprised to see it was 1130. They had covered nearly two hundred kilometres while she was asleep.

There was a half-hour break during which Barbara went to the toilet, then to the shop. After filling up on a milkshake and a hamburger she stood outside and looked at the sea, finding it a pleasant change from the desolation of Dostwood.

The next three hours of driving were also a definite change as the

Bruce Highway to Cairns ran through the 'Wet Tropics' region: lush green vegetation, jungle on the mountains, fields of sugar cane, rivers with water in them...

As they got closer to Cairns Barbara became both restless and emotional, remembering the unhappy times in Year 9 when she had twice run away from home. It was during that period of misery she had joined cadets and found a group of good friends and people who cared about her. Barbara had discovered her mother was having an affair with another man and it had almost driven her to suicide. Finally, her mother had left and Barbara had stayed with her father.

It was he who was waiting for her at the school when the coach pulled in just before 3 pm. Seeing him caused a lump to block Barbara's throat and she was hard put not to burst into tears.

Poor old Dad! she thought. *He still misses Mum and loves her.*

She sighed and once again wished the 'if only' which she knew her father also secretly shared. Then she sighed again, knowing it was probably not to be. Feeling quite emotional she climbed off the coach to collect her gear.

But there was no instant dismissal. There was administration to do: issues to return to the Q Store, gear to check and clean, paperwork to complete. Only when all of that was satisfactorily done did Major Conkey tell the CSM to line them all up for the dismissal parade. He then thanked them all for their good behaviour, told them the dates for the next parades and next bivouac (the Section Competition weekend), then dismissed them.

As Barbara and her father made their way towards the car outside the gate she was surprised to see a TV crew and a couple of reporters. She was even more surprised when several of the cadets being spoken to by the reporters turned to point at her. The reporters came hurrying over.

Seeing them approach caused Barbara's heart to beat with anxiety. She had a sinking feeling she knew what they were going to ask about. She was right. They wanted to know all about the crashed satellite.

A young man pushed in between her and her father, his eyes raking over her body as he demanded she tell him the story.

"Ask the army," she snapped.

"But we were told you saw the thing land," said the man, thrusting a recorder close to her face.

That did annoy her. She pushed the recorder aside and said, "Excuse me. I am going home."

Her father then stepped between her and the man and angrily told him to back off. "Act like a gentleman!" he snapped. "Now please get out of our way."

The reporter was forced to step aside. Barbara tossed her gear in the back of the car and climbed in. Her father climbed in, ignoring the reporter's pleas for a story. As quickly as he safely could her father started the car and drove off.

"Sorry about that Bub. Was that all about that French satellite?"

"Yes," Barbara huffed. "I hope I never hear about the stupid thing again. Please just take me home Dad."

Chapter 13

ANNOYED

To Barbara's annoyance, her period of rest at home was very brief. She had only one evening and night before events began to intrude. The upsets began as soon as she woke up the next morning and went through to the kitchen to have a drink. Her father was sitting at the table having his breakfast, reading the newspaper while he did.

As she walked in he held this up to show her and said, "You are in the paper Bubs."

The headline instantly told Barbara the problem. NUCLEAR SPY SATELLITE CRASHES INTO LOCAL ARMY CADET'S CAMP it read. "Terrifying near miss causes alarm" read a sub-title.

"Oh, what a stupid headline!" Barbara cried. "It makes it sound like it was our fault. I am sick of hearing about that satellite," she added, moving to the fridge to get herself a glass of cold orange juice.

"This article mentions you by name," her father added. "I'm not very happy about that. I wish you hadn't told them anything."

"I didn't," Barbara replied, feeling both interested and annoyed. "Not to the newspaper people anyway."

"I wonder who did tell them then?" her father said.

As she walked over to sit at the table Barbara wondered the same thing. Was it Major Conkey or one of the officers? She shook her head.

No. They wouldn't mention details like the ones I can read here, she thought. For a few seconds she puzzled over who it might have been. *Was it one of my friends I mentioned the wreckage to?* she wondered. Both Wendy's and Fiona's names flitted across her mind as she focused to read the small print.

And there was her name. It was both a shock and a thrill to see it in print. Cadet Commander Barbara Brassington it said.

Huh! They couldn't even get my rank right, she thought irritably.

The article gave an exaggerated and lurid description of flaming wreckage showering down around the cadets. For an instant Barbara relived those terrifying seconds and in her mind's eye she quite clearly saw the glowing chunk of wreckage embedded in the splintered tree trunk.

So hot it was pink and white, she remembered.

Her father spoke gently. "Was it really like that?" he asked.

"Well... not really. I mean one big bit landed a few metres from me but none of the other kids had anything land close to them at all, as far as I know," Barbara replied.

Her father frowned. "They say they can't find several important parts of the satellite that should have survived the crash. Did they ask you?"

"Yes, they did, and we took them to the area and showed them, the army that is," Barbara answered. She then blushed at the humiliating memory of the SAS video.

Her father nodded. "Oh well, I wish the world didn't have things like that in it."

"I hope I never hear of the thing again," Barbara replied, then realised she had spoken more forcefully than she had intended as her father looked at her and raised a quizzical eyebrow. Rather than respond Barbara went to the cupboard and began preparing her breakfast cereal.

As it was now the school holidays Barbara remained at home for the remainder of the day. Her father went off to work and she set about cleaning her boots and webbing and washing the dirty uniforms. That done she lay on her bed and alternately dozed and read. Only then did she realise just how much the camp had tired her out. She was glad of the chance to relax.

While resting on her bed during the afternoon Barbara was aware of a growing feeling of excitement. That evening there was to be an informal unit dinner and after it she and Roger would have the chance to be alone. The emotions Barbara now experienced were a growing sense of desire, a sort of tingling and tightening that she had only been aware of for the last few months. She did not want to admit it to herself but instinctively knew she was experiencing an urge for love, and not just romance but physical affection... and maybe more?

Thinking about that made her squirm with both aroused passion and doubt.

Do I want that? she wondered. Sex was something she was having trouble coming to grips with, but she knew she was capable of being aroused. *Maybe Roger will want to do something?* she thought.

If he did, she decided, she would let him. *I might even encourage him.*

But he didn't. There were more than forty cadets and five adult staff at the dinner which was held at a local Pizza Hut. To begin with they met out the front and stood in groups talking. Roger greeted her brightly enough and took her hand but when she snuggled against him he seemed to shy away and be a bit distant.

As they stood waiting to go in Fiona joined them and said, "I see you got your name in the paper Barb."

Barbara experienced a spurt of annoyance. "Yes, and Dad wasn't very happy about it. He wanted to know who spoke to the reporters and told them."

Fiona shook her head. "Not me."

Wendy, who was snuggled up to Lofty, had been listening. She now bit her lip and said, "That might have been me. Sorry."

Barbara was peeved but instantly forgave her friend. "It's alright Wendy. No harm done."

At that moment CSM Sheehan, who was organizing the dinner, came out and told them to move in. They filed in and Barbara thrust the satellite and the news article from her mind, concentrating on the feel of Roger's hand and wondering if he was noticing that she was pressed against him as they were jostled.

During the meal they sat together, and Roger was friendly and witty and kept her laughing, but she sensed that the charm was for everyone, not especially for her. That caused a tiny amount of disappointment but not nearly as much as his saying he would like to join the others when they voted to go to the movies. Barbara had been hoping they might go somewhere to be together and found it difficult to keep her annoyance out of her voice.

The movies always offered possibilities and Barbara deliberately pushed them, holding Roger's hand and leaning over to press against him. On both sides and in front she could see couples snuggling and even kissing but Roger just seemed to smile and focus his attention on the movie.

But still hope lingered. *Maybe after the movies?* she thought.

No luck. Roger muttered he was tired and just drove her home in the car he had borrowed from his mother. At her front door he did at last give her a kiss but it was only a friendly peck, not the red-blooded pash she was now yearning for. As he drove away Barbara stood and squirmed with irritation and unfulfilled desire.

Oh drat! Barbara sighed, giving herself a frustrated hug. Then came the niggling doubts: was there something wrong with her? *Am I too ugly? Am I too forward? Do I have bad breath, or a pushy personality?*

None of that made sense as she had been told too often she was attractive, desirable and beautiful. *If Chloe thinks I am beautiful then I am,* she told herself.

That brought other doubts: was she really a lesbian? Her mind flooded with images of naked Chloe and she knew such thoughts aroused her. Or was it Roger?

Is there something about him? she wondered.

There were there those persistent rumours about him being gay. It was all very unsettling and worrying and left her feeling anxious and slightly depressed. She was also concerned to note that she had been in the mood to allow things to be done to her that she had so far never had happen.

Maybe it is just the phase of life I am going through? she thought.

That thought led to others dealing with her future and again she agonized over what to do with her life and over her sexuality and her philosophy of life.

It was a thoroughly confused, frustrated and unhappy girl that slid into her bed twenty minutes later. For a while she lay, worrying and wondering, until sleep finally claimed her.

The next day was Saturday—the middle of the holidays. Barbara had no fixed plans for the next week, but she woke up realizing she had a lot of vague dreams and hopes about it being somehow romantic. Now she became anxious that it might all just be boring and that her misty hopes might all come to nothing.

The usual morning routine brushed most of these thoughts aside and then she went shopping with Fiona and Wendy and that kept her cheerful and happy for most of the morning—until Lofty arrived. He at once embraced Wendy and gave her a long, passionate kiss. Wendy rubbed herself against him and Barbara could clearly see that Lofty was responding and enjoying it.

Towards the end of the kiss, Lofty slid his hand up Wendy's side and cupped her left breast. Barbara noted this with mildly scandalized interest, but it was done so naturally that she did not take offence.

Fiona also noted it and looked shocked. "Lofty!" she cried.

Lofty looked up and raised his eyebrows, clearly not sure what she wanted. Fiona looked at his hand and he went red and hastily pulled it away.

"Oops! Sorry. Just habit," he admitted. Then he realized what he had said and started to stammer excuses.

Wendy opened her mouth and also cried "Lofty!" but then she blushed and giggled.

Barbara could only smile at their embarrassment and secretly wish she was enjoying the same attentions. Later, when they were seated at a table outside a cafe and Lofty had gone in to get them drinks Wendy said, "Sorry about that. We didn't mean to embarrass you."

"Is it a habit?" Barbara teased.

Wendy went very red but nodded and giggled. "He is a naughty boy sometimes, but I don't mind. I enjoy it."

Fiona looked shocked. "Wendy!" she gasped, but Barbara could only agree. There were times now when she felt a distinct need to have her body caressed and loved. She smiled and said, "From what I hear you two have been doing that for years."

Wendy nodded to confirm this. "Ever since I was a First-Year cadet. We... we get a bit ashamed of breaking our promise to Major Conkey but... but... I... well, you know, we both sort of need it. And it doesn't do any harm. It just feels nice."

"Lofty obviously enjoys it," Barbara commented. She found she was quite unable to stop glancing at Wendy's very full bosom. Having felt it several times in the past she could only go hot and red and again wonder about her own sexuality.

Wendy also went very red and giggled again. "Mmm. He gets really horny," she replied.

Fiona looked anxious. "Wendy! You don't do anything more do you?"

Wendy made no reply but blushed even redder, confirming Barbara's suspicions that she and Lofty had been lovers for some time. Luckily the conversation was ended by Lofty coming back out with four milkshakes. All the girls went silent and he looked quizzically around.

"What are you lot talking about?" he asked.

They all blushed and Wendy said, "Never you mind. Secret women's business. Is that mine?" She took the offered milkshake. As he sat down Lofty grinned at Wendy, causing Barbara a distinct stab of jealousy. He had obviously arranged to meet her.

Why didn't Roger arrange to meet me? Barbara wondered. That thought re-occurred twenty minutes later when Lofty and Wendy wandered off together.

Roger had arranged to meet her that evening and they went to a party together. It was a 'school friends' party and she knew most of the people there. It offered many possibilities for her and Roger to be alone, but he did not seem inclined to take them and she did not like to make hints that were too blatant. That some of the others were making the most of things was very obvious, with couples continually going off outside and even into some of the bedrooms. A few just pashed openly in the lounge room. Fiona was one of these. Wendy and Lofty went outside twice, for long periods, and when they returned Barbara noted with what she admitted was jealousy that Wendy appeared to be glowing with satisfied pleasure.

Once again Roger did not get passionate, just took her home and gave her a friendly kiss. Barbara went to bed with very frustrated and dissatisfied emotions, her whole body on edge. All she could do was sigh and wonder how she could tell Roger what she really wanted, without seeming to come across as a tart.

Then, just as she was drifting off to sleep, another, even more unsettling thought crossed her mind. *If he is the right man for me he should know what I want and not have to be told.*

Sunday was no help. Barbara did not see Roger at all. In the morning he went to church and in the afternoon he went with his mother to visit an aunty in Atherton. She spent the day moping around at home, helping her father with household chores and reading or watching TV. She did not want to visit her friends in case her unhappiness showed. As she lay in bed that night she thought things over and came to a decision.

I am going to be more pro-active here, and arrange things so that the situations are right. Then Roger might take the hint, she told herself.

She began to map out a program of activities that would involve them both and place them in romantic settings where they might be alone.

So she got on the phone and set up a Monday afternoon meeting at the swimming pool. That gave her something to look forward to and she was able to spend Monday morning happily doing a history assignment that was due the week they went back to school.

But before that she suffered a rude shock and an annoying incident. Being Monday, her father had gone off to work, leaving her at home on her own. She was in a bit of a mood, so she had not dressed after her morning shower. Instead she had remained nude, enjoying the pleasant feeling of naughtiness and the relaxed freedom. Thus, when the front doorbell chimed at about 1100 she experienced a mild thrill and scampered naked to her room, where she snatched up the first items of clothing that came to hand: a cotton T-shirt and a silk wrap. Thinking that it would only be one of her friends, or perhaps a door-to-door salesman, she did not bother to put on a bra. Having pulled the T-shirt over her head she walked to the front door, adjusting the silk wrap around her hips as a skirt while she did.

The moment she opened the door and saw the two men in suits standing at the top of the steps she knew she had miscalculated. Her first thought was that they were religious people: Mormons or Seventh Day Adventists, or something like that. Her second thought corrected that to policemen. The two men were in their thirties and looked quite serious, even though they both smiled.

Hotly aware that she had made a mistake in not dressing fully she half-hid behind the door frame and asked, "Yes?"

Both men held up leather wallets containing some sort of identity card. The older of the two said, "Mr Cavendish, Commonwealth Security Service. Are you Miss Barbara Brassington?"

Barbara nodded, uncomfortably conscious of their male gaze. "Yes."

"May we come in?"

That request made Barbara acutely conscious, both of the fact that she was a girl alone and of not wearing very much. She hesitated and wanted to say no. To give herself time to think she looked at the other man and said, "Can I see your ID again please?"

The man smiled and nodded, then handed her his ID card. Mr Cyril Blaketon it read. Barbara had never seen such a card so could not tell if it was genuine or not, but it certainly looked authentic. Reluctantly she handed the card back and nodded, then turned to lead the men inside. Gesturing to the sofa she seated herself carefully on the edge of an armchair, taking care to keep her legs together. She felt particularly vulnerable.

"What do you want?" she asked.

"We are here to ask you for any information about the French Satellite," Mr Cavendish replied.

Barbara had suspected that, but she was still irritated. She was already angry at herself for not dressing properly and that was fuelled by her irritation and by the way the men were eyeing her front. "I've told the army people," she snapped.

"We understand that there was a small misunderstanding and that you had other information," Mr Cavendish said.

That nettled Barbara too. Through her mind raced the humiliating images of the SAS video, and of the put-downs and superior airs of the army people she had dealt with. She shook her head. "I showed the army people where I saw things land. If they were too ignorant or inefficient to note that, then I can't be held responsible."

"That's not what they say," Mr Cavendish replied, his voice a little firmer.

"They would, wouldn't they?" Barbara retorted. "They wouldn't want to admit they had mucked things up and been incompetent."

Mr Cavendish half-closed his eyes and his mouth settled into a firmer line. "I have been told you refused to co-operate."

"After they had insulted me, yes," Barbara replied. She was feeling distinctly nervous now and more than a little scared.

Commonwealth Security Service, she thought anxiously. *Who are they and what sort of power do they have?* Images from dozens of spy movies crowded her brain.

Mr Cavendish smiled. "I am asking you to co-operate with us," he said.

"I showed that lieutenant colonel everything. We walked there, and I pointed to where I saw things come down," Barbara replied.

"He says you were very unhelpful and obstructive and refused to help."

At that Barbara's anger flared. "Only because of the embarrassment they caused me," she answered. She did not want to detail the shameful episodes and comments.

"You'd better explain," Mr Cavendish replied.

"I'd rather not. It was humiliating, and I don't want to be embarrassed even more," Barbara answered. By now her heart was beating fast and she was feeling quite anxious.

"I insist," Mr Cavendish said.

Reluctantly Barbara described the incident of the video. As she talked she saw a frown develop on Mr Cavendish's face and he several times exchanged annoyed glances with Mr Blaketon. It was obvious to Barbara that the incident had not been mentioned.

When she finished Mr Cavendish said, "Yes, well, I'm sorry about that. But I still would like you to show us where the pieces of the satellite landed."

Barbara was already feeling hot and ashamed and now she felt insulted. "I did!" she snapped. "I told you I took the army people there and pointed to where the pieces landed. They even taped some of the area off."

"There was a suggestion that you had given misleading locations," Mr Cavendish suggested.

Barbara's annoyance flared into anger. "Oh, what an insult! I did not!"

Mr Cavendish looked momentarily irritated and then said, "Colonel Nevison also said that you would not help because you were supporting the French."

"Oh, that's not true!" Barbara cried. "He's twisting my words. I asked if they were going to give it back to the French and they gave me the impression they would not and that they only wanted it for themselves. Besides, I don't know any French people."

"By they you mean Australia of course," Mr Cavendish commented.

"Yes, I suppose so."

"This is a national security issue," Mr Cavendish said.

By now Barbara was feeling more than anxious. Fear had begun to seep in. She realised she was breathing rapidly, causing her bosom to rise and fall. The men's eyes moved in time with it and that nettled her too. "How?" she asked.

"We can't say," Mr Cavendish answered, giving a thin smile. "It is a secret. That's why we have been sent to ask you."

Barbara felt foolish at that but still did not believe them. She bit her lip and shook her head. "I have nothing more to add," she said.

"Are you refusing to help us?" Mr Cavendish asked. He spoke softly but to Barbara it held more than a hint of menace.

"No," she replied, now feeling distinctly scared. "But I can't see what else I can do. I told the army people. I also took them there. And I showed Major Conkey. Ask him."

"We have. However, he was only able to indicate a general area to search," Mr Cavendish answered.

"Well go back and ask those army people. I showed them exactly where to look. We were within twenty paces of the thing," Barbara answered. She now had another anxiety. The wrap had started to slip and she had to grip at it to stop it falling undone.

Mr Cavendish looked unhappy. "So you won't help us further?"

That did annoy Barbara. "I just told you all I know!" she cried. "Now please leave." She stood up, gripping the wrap tightly at her waist.

To her relief both men stood. Mr Cavendish walked to the door, then turned and said, "You will probably be hearing from us again."

Barbara said nothing. She just felt annoyed and unhappy. As the two men went down the front steps she slammed the door angrily and felt both scared and upset.

"Stupid men!" she muttered, meaning Lt Col Nevison and the warrant officer. "I showed them exactly where." But then she began to doubt. Had she? She remembered pointing to the burnt tree and had pointed it out to others as well.

Or did I only think I had? she wondered, trying to remember exactly what she had done or said.

Then she shook her head with annoyance. "Stupid satellite! I hope I never hear about it again!" But inside her lurked a suspicion that the men would indeed be back.

Oh, I hope not! Now, let me worry about my love life. That is more important, she told herself.

Chapter 14

UNEASY SUSPICIONS

For quite a while after the two Commonwealth Security men had gone Barbara sat deep in thought. She knew she was being petty and stubborn but still considered her original stand justified.

If the satellite belongs to France, and if France is not an enemy, then Australia has no right to it; and if Australia is France's friend then they should not try deceit or theft, she reasoned.

"Anyway, I've shown the dopey buggers where the pieces landed. If they can't organize an efficient search of that small area, then it serves them right if they don't find it!" she muttered.

She stood up and shrugged with annoyance, then became aware that her silk wrap had slipped off. That made her smile and she gently slid her hands down over her body. A wicked idea crossed her mind and she gave a mischievous grin.

Next time I will let if fall off "accidentally" and that will take their mind off satellites, she thought.

"Now, to the pool," she muttered. She quickly changed into her dark green, one-piece bathers, after hesitating over her bikini. Over the top she pulled on the T-shirt and a pair of tight, short shorts. After collecting her sunglasses, towel and a few other items she closed the house up. Making her way downstairs she checked her bicycle, then mounted it and set off.

As she pedalled along the quiet, tree-lined street Barbara noticed a white car parked in front of the next-door neighbour's house. There were two men sitting in it but neither looked at her. *I wonder who is visiting the Jessups?* she thought.

Two houses further along a white van was parked out the front of another house. It looked like a delivery van, so she ignored it. Pedalling along in the sunshine raised her spirits, as did the thought that she was heading to meet her friends, and in particular Roger. It took her about twenty minutes to ride to the swimming pool at North Cairns. It was a ride she had often done before and usually enjoyed but this time she was aware that she was irritated, although whether this was a residue from the visit by the security men or because Roger had not offered to pick her up in his car she was not sure.

At the pool Barbara secured her bike then went in. As she passed through the entrance she looked eagerly around, hoping to see Roger and her friends. Almost at once she saw waving arms and smiling faces, but Roger's was not one of them. Fiona, Dan Russell, Lofty and Wendy all sat or lay on towels on the lawn over beside a garden bed near the deep end of the pool.

Barbara walked over and joined them, then spread her towel and peeled off down to her bathers and sat down. As she tugged the T-shirt up over her bosom she felt a twinge of coyness, increased by awareness that several males were watching. As she sat and neatly folded her clothes she glanced towards the pool and noted two young men in their twenties who were obviously watching her.

Males! she thought, partly exasperated and partly pleased.

At that moment two people heaved themselves up out of the pool and came walking towards them, their faces grinning a welcome. One was a youth of her own age and the other a busty girl a year younger. Barbara at once recognized them and returned the smiles.

Willy and Marjorie, she thought.

Willy Williams had been in her class for five years and for much of that time he had openly admired Barbara. From an annoying crush it had now developed into a strong friendship, helped by the fact that Willy had fallen in love with Marjorie. Willy was also a Cadet Under-Officer, but in the Air Force Cadets. He and Marjorie were famous around the school for kissing and cuddling at every opportunity.

Just thinking about them doing that made Barbara blush. She was uncomfortably conscious that she found the idea very arousing. Her eyes ran over Marjorie's body and she shook her head but smiled. Marjorie wore only a quite skimpy bikini, the bottom almost a G-string and the top just two tiny triangles of cloth secured loosely by strings. She was a well rounded sixteen-year-old and had boobs almost as big as Wendy's, and of the same type, soft and bouncy, and so big they bulged out of the bikini top at all sides.

Willy and Marjorie stopped near them and looked down, arms around each other. Willy met Barbara's eyes and asked,

"Hi gang! How was your camp?"

"Good," Barbara replied, "except for the heat and the dust."

"Where did you go?" Willy asked.

Lofty answered that. "A place called Dotswood, about a hundred 'Ks' west of Townsville."

"Never heard of it," Willy replied. He and Marjorie both sat down. Willy then irritated her further by saying, "So tell us about the French spy satellite."

Barbara did not want to talk about it but the others were more than happy to provide graphic details. Several times they looked to Barbara to provide confirmation of their tale and she nodded and agreed.

Willy turned to her. "Sounds like you had a close shave Barbara," he commented.

"I did. Haven't you two just been to an air cadet camp as well?" she replied, wanting to change the subject.

"Yes, we have, at Garbutt in Townsville," Willy answered. "We just had our GST Camp. I did a lot of flying, got my unrestricted licence, and Marj. did her Senior GST."

Barbara knew that Willy now had his pilot's licence, but the Air Cadet jargon puzzled her. "GST?" she queried.

"General Service Training," Willy answered. He then went on to describe the Air Cadet system of training by year levels, so very different from the training pattern of the army cadets.

Lofty listened to all this with a look of mild annoyance on his face. He then asked, "What are you doing for the rest of the holidays?"

Marjorie answered that. "Just seeing more of each other!" Then she giggled and hugged Willy.

Lofty laughed and said, "I didn't think there was any more you hadn't seen!"

Marjorie poked her tongue and then giggled again. Willy went very red but hugged her in return. "We have been very good this camp," he said. "Anyway, I am going to get a chance to fly some vintage and replica aircraft. That millionaire we helped find the plane wrecks two years ago, Mr Jemmerling,[4] owns a Spitfire replica and also a replica of the Red Baron's Triplane. He is going to let me fly both and I hope to fly one at the air show in Mareeba in three weeks time."

"I didn't know there was going to be an air show," Lofty said.

---

[4] Read *Coasts of Cape York* by C.R. Cummings

Marjorie nodded enthusiastically. "There is. It will be great. There are going to be at least a dozen vintage or replica planes there: the Spitfire, a Mustang, three Harvards, a couple of Winjeels, a Dakota, a Hudson and a few other types like Tiger Moths."

"Even a replica of a World War Two Japanese Zero," Willy added.

"And some Chinese Nanchangs from North Queensland Warbirds," Marjorie said.

"Sounds good," Lofty commented.

"It will be," Willy replied. "You must all make an effort to come and watch." With that he looked at Barbara and raised an eyebrow.

"If I'm not tied up with something else I might try," Barbara conceded, secretly glad of Willy's adoration but wishing he would focus completely on Marjorie.

The conversation stayed firmly on aeroplanes for the next few minutes. While they talked Barbara made herself comfortable and noted with a pang of jealousy how Lofty had his arm around Wendy's waist. It was resting snugly under her bosom and both seemed to be happy and relaxed.

I wish Roger would join us, Barbara thought.

Lofty gestured towards the water. "What about a swim?" he suggested.

"We've just had one," Willy replied.

"Well we haven't! Come on gang," Lofty called. He stood up and hauled Wendy to her feet, hugged her, then walked towards the pool. Barbara stood up and followed with Fiona and Dan. "I hope the water isn't cold," Fiona said.

It wasn't. After testing the temperature with her toe Barbara lowered herself in at the steps, very aware that the two young men were both watching while pretending not to. She glanced briefly down and noted that her breasts were very obvious, so she quickly slid in to hide herself. Once in the water she relaxed. For the next few minutes she stood in the shallows with Fiona while Lofty and Wendy swam up and down. Fiona then set off to swim along the pool, so Barbara followed, taking care to keep her head out of the water so as not to get sore eyes from the chlorine.

On reaching the other end Barbara paused to catch her breath. The others by then were already on their way back. Suddenly a person, swimming using a powerful backstroke, bumped into her. A man's head swivelled around and she found herself looking into a pair of grey eyes in a handsome freckled face. As the young man wiped water from his face a peculiar feeling caused Barbara to look harder at him.

The man shook his head and took hold of the edge of the pool. "Oh, I say, I'm sorry," he said, an English accent quite clear.

Barbara shrugged and said, "Sorry. My fault for getting in your way."

She was deliberately gruff as she did not want to encourage a strange man to make a pass at her. However, it was such an obvious ploy to get to speak to her that she had to smile.

The man did not seem to take the hint. He smiled and said, "I do apologize. Are you one of the locals?"

"My mother told me not to speak to strange men," Barbara replied, but not as frostily as she wanted to because there was something appealing about the man's beguiling grin.

The man pretended contrition. "I do know we haven't been introduced but my father told me that faint heart never won fair lady and you look so pretty that I wanted to meet you. My name is Mark."

Barbara was about to snub the man and swim away when something in her mind clicked. She frowned and looked hard at the man. "Have we met before?" she asked.

Mark shook his head. "I don't think so."

Then recognition came to Barbara. She glanced around to confirm her suspicion and looked hard at Mark's companion. He was holding on the edge of the pool ten metres away. When he noted Barbara looking at him the man looked away and it was exactly what she wanted as his profile became clear. A spurt of surprised recognition and puzzlement made Barbara edgy. She turned back to Mark and said, "I do know you. We have met. You are the British commando lieutenant my platoon ran into during a field exercise at Dotswood last week."

Mark looked surprised. "Me? A commando! Are you sure?" he asked.

Barbara stared hard at him and in her memory saw the camouflaged face and was certain. "Yes I am. You were not amused, and you led your patrol away to the west before my OC could arrive. It was you."

Mark grinned and nodded. "Yes, that was me. I didn't recognize you. You er... look much better in a swimsuit than in a camouflage uniform. You are some sort of army cadet officer, aren't you?"

"Yes, a Cadet Under-Officer," Barbara replied.

She was both intrigued and puzzled. Having never spoken to a commando before she wanted to discuss some aspects of training but knew she should just go away. However, she felt curiously drawn to him, liking the friendly face and obvious manly physique.

"Are you a commando?" she asked.

Mark nodded. "Lt Mark Guy, B Troop, Special Boat Squadron, Royal Marines. We are in Australia on exercises."

SBS! A real Royal Marine Commando! Barbara thought, impressed in spite of herself.

Having seen Mark in the field with his men she was sure he was the genuine article and not some poser spinning her line. She was still puzzled though, so she asked, "So what are you doing in Cairns?"

"Having a few days leave before our next exercise," Mark answered. Then he smiled and said, "Are you a local?"

"Yes," Barbara replied.

"We're only here for a few days," Mark said. "What tourist attractions do you recommend we see?"

Sensing what was coming, Barbara pursed her lips in amusement. "Go and see a travel agent and get some brochures," she said.

"I was hoping you might show us around," Mark answered.

"Don't get fresh!" Barbara snapped. But she was not really angry. He was much too handsome—and she was tempted.

Mark threw up his hands in mock horror. "Oh, don't be like that!" he cried. "A man has to seize what opportunities he gets."

A comment Barbara had once heard about 'never miss an opportunity' and 'you never catch up on the ones you miss out on' flitted through her mind to firstly annoy, then to amuse her. In spite of herself she found she liked Mark and his direct style.

Maybe? she wondered, then felt guilty for being disloyal to Roger.

For just a second, she considered having a holiday affair with Mark, sensing that he would be able to teach her all about physical love—and that then he would go back to England and out of her life. Shocked at her own wicked thoughts Barbara shook her head. "I am not that sort of girl."

"Oh, I didn't mean it like that!" Mark said. He was so obviously open about it that Barbara stayed.

"So, how long are you on leave for?" she asked, the naughty ideas swirling back.

"Five days," Mark answered.

Barbara thought for a minute, then listed a dozen tourist sights worth seeing: Green Island, the Great Barrier Reef, Barron Falls, the Atherton Tablelands. "You would need a car for that," she added.

At that Mark looked diffident. "We have a hire car," he said, then asked, "So, would you mind very much if I asked you to come with us as a guide?"

Barbara had to laugh and was tempted. But she shook her head. "No. My parents wouldn't allow it," she said.

Mark grinned. "No harm in asking," he said. "What about a date?"

"I might be too young," Barbara replied teasingly. She knew she was being disloyal to Roger even thinking about it, but equally she was peeved at his non-appearance and knew that deep down she was hungry for a bit of romance.

"You look old enough to me," Mark replied, his eyes skimming down her front.

Barbara realized she had stood up so that her bosom was out of the water and she felt a flush of heat. "Don't give me the 'big enough, old enough' story," she snapped, but with amusement, not anger. Then she saw his eyes flick to her boobs again and realised what she had said.

"Big enough for sure!" Mark replied, grinning even more.

Barbara blushed and slid down into the water but, to her own surprise, did not feel offended, only aroused. She crossed her arms to hide her front and stuck out her tongue. "Don't be rude," she chided. Her conscious mind told her to swim away, but she didn't.

"I wasn't!" Mark pleaded, his eyes laughing. He looked down in mock contrition, then up and asked, "So how about it? I would love to take you out to dinner."

To her own surprise Barbara thought, *And I'd love to go.*

She hesitated, then said, "I will think about it."

Again, she sensed she should leave before she let herself get in too deep. Reluctantly she made herself turn and begin breast stroking away.

Mark called after her, "Barbara, we are staying at the Captain Cook Motel. If you change your mind, give me a call."

On an impish impulse Barbara turned her head and met his eyes. She nodded and smiled. Then she swam back along the pool to rejoin the others.

As she reached them Fiona grinned and gestured with her head towards Mark. "Who's that 'Mr Smoothie' Barbara?"

Barbara smiled and said, "He is a Royal Marine Commando from the Special Boat Squadron."

The others all knew enough about the famous SBS to look momentarily impressed. Then Dan made a face. "Oh bull! He will just be some joker telling you that trying to impress you Barbara."

Barbara shook her head. "No, he's the real thing. He is the lieutenant we met during the field exercise at Dotswood," she answered.

"What lieutenant?" Fiona asked.

Barbara turned to Dan and reminded him. "Remember when we were advancing from the Triangle back towards the Gravel Scape the afternoon of the big exercise? We ran into a patrol of British Commandos in all that burnt-out scrub."

Dan's face changed. "Oh yeah! I saw them. What are they doing here?"

"Having some leave before their next exercise," Barbara replied.

"What were you talking about?" Fiona asked.

"He was trying to win on," Barbara answered, blushing and smiling at the same time. She turned to look and saw Mark and the other young man laughing to each other.

"Roger won't be impressed by that," Fiona replied, but she gave the two commandos a speculative look.

Barbara watched as Mark and the other man heaved themselves up out of the water. Their broad shoulders and rippling muscles instantly convinced her that both were indeed commandos and very fit.

There might not be much Roger could do about that, she thought.

"Maybe he needs to pay a girl a bit more attention," she said.

She smiled while she said it and Fiona met her eyes and nodded in understanding, then again turned to admire the two commandos as they walked across the lawn to their towels. Suddenly Barbara felt a wave of goose bumps rush up her body as something that had been niggling at her became apparent.

He called me Barbara! she thought. *How did he know my name is Barbara? I didn't tell him.*

A horrible feeling of suspicion welled up and she stared at Mark in dismay.

Chapter 15

TESTING A THEORY

Fiona looked at Barbara in alarm and grabbed her upper arm. "Barbara! Are you alright?"

Barbara nodded and bit her lip, then again looked towards where Mark and the other young man were drying themselves with towels fifty paces away. "Yes, why?"

"Because you went all still and your face went as white as a sheet," Fiona replied.

Barbara suddenly began to shiver and she put her hands to her face, conscious of it feeling tight and drawn. As the horrible suspicions swirled in her head she replied, "He called me Barbara. How did he know my name?"

Then another disturbing idea came to her: had Mark and his friend been waiting for her; was the meeting deliberate?

They could have only done that if they knew I was going to the swimming pool this afternoon, she reasoned. That got her trying to remember how she had organized the pool meeting. *By phone,* she thought. Then a wave of cold fear swept through her. *Is someone listening to my phone? Are those Commonwealth Security people bugging my phone?* she worried.

It was a deeply upsetting thought, but she suspected that such people would have both the legal authority (or could get it) plus the technology to do such a thing. She now sat down and put this idea to Fiona and Dan. Willy and Marjorie sat up from cuddling and listened in surprise. They all turned to look at Mark and the other young man who were now spreading towels preparatory to sitting on them. Barbara saw that Mark had noted the heads turn to look at him but that he tried to pretend nothing had happened. That deepened her concern even more.

She now described the visit by the security men and her suspicions. At that both Wendy and Fiona gasped and said that they had also been visited by the same two men. That shook Barbara even more. "They must be watching me," she said, her lip trembling with anxiety.

"But why?" Lofty asked. "Why don't you just tell them?"

That made Barbara feel uncomfortable and confused. "I thought I had but they don't seem to believe me. They keep coming back at me and I find it really annoying," she said.

What she did not feel like doing was describing her own apparently petty reactions at various times. There was also the irritating thought that with all the modern technology they must have available the army should be able to search the small area around the Gravel Scrape to find the 'thing'.

Willy shook his head. "I think you are being paranoid," he said. "It will all be just a coincidence."

At that Barbara shook her head emphatically. "I don't think so. I think I am being spied on and they are trying to find some way to tricking me into telling them what they want to know."

"Be easy to test your theory," Fiona suggested.

Her support warmed Barbara and she smiled. She could tell that Lofty, Wendy and Dan, all of whom had been involved with her in rescuing Fiona from the religious fanatics back in June, believed her.

"How would we do that?" Lofty asked, pleasing Barbara even more by implying that he and the others were with her.

"All Barbara has to do is make a few phone calls to meet us at various places and we get there early and see who turns up," Fiona replied.

"And photograph them," Dan added. "Secret agents don't like being photographed."

"We could get into trouble," Wendy cautioned.

Dan chuckled. "You will if you let Lofty do what he wants!" he replied.

At that Wendy withdrew her hand from Lofty's leg and poked her tongue at Dan. "Oh poo to you!" she retorted, blushing very red, before meeting Barbara's eyes and giggling.

"That's enough of that sort of talk children!" Willy said with mock severity. "Now, where can we arrange to meet; who will be there and who is going to take the photos?"

They discussed this for a few minutes and Marjorie's suggestion of keeping it simple and public was settled on. "'Sizzlers' restaurant tonight at seven," Barbara said.

It was decided that Roger would be invited, along with Fiona, Lofty and Wendy. Dan would be the outside spy and photographer. Willy and Marjorie were to watch from a distance and pretend not to be part of the group.

"We will pretend to be two lovers cuddling in a dark corner," Willy said.

Marjorie giggled. "We won't be pretending," she added, then giggled again and went red.

The others laughed and Barbara experienced another spurt of jealousy. She said, "We also need a few simple codes to arrange things by phone in emergencies."

This led to more discussion and quite a few silly comments and jokes which showed that all of the others were excited and interested. Barbara found she was feeling much better and even looking forward to a bit of entertainment.

If the spies want to give me a hard time they can earn their pay! she thought.

The subject was discussed for a few more minutes and then another swim suggested by Dan. However, nobody felt like going back in so Barbara pulled on her T-shirt and shorts, making sure she had her back to Mark while she did.

"I will go home and phone Roger now," she said.

"I will come with you," Fiona added.

"Oh, I'll be alright," Barbara reassured her. She had not felt any anxiety as to her own personal safety up till then, but Fiona obviously felt concerned.

Fiona shook her head. "Doesn't matter. I will come anyway," she insisted. "You can give me afternoon tea."

So it was agreed. Barbara stood up and picked up her towel and bag, taking care not to glance towards Mark at all. She knew that Willy was doing that, while pretending to kiss Marjorie (or actually kissing her and pretending to be totally absorbed by it, she corrected).

Walking towards the front entrance and thinking she was being watched caused Barbara an absurd reaction. Tiny trembles went up and down her back and she was acutely conscious that her body was being studied. That made her feel awkward and stiff and she blushed at the thought of her buttocks trembling and of her funny walk being noticed. It was a relief to pass through the entrance and out to the bike racks. She and Fiona quickly unlocked their bikes and set off, pedalling towards Barbara's home.

Barbara found it a pleasant ride and chatted happily until they turned into her street. It was only when she noticed that the white car with two men sitting in it was still parked in front of her neighbour's that her anxiety returned.

As she and Fiona pedalled towards the car she said, "Don't look at that car but it was parked there when I left home and it had two men sitting in it."

Fiona nodded but did not turn her head. The pair pedalled by, Barbara memorizing the car's registration number. Then she saw something that added to her suspicions: the white van was still parked in front of the Jessup's. She mentioned this to Fiona as well.

Fiona nodded. "Just as well I came with you," she murmured as they rode up the short driveway at Barbara's house.

"What will we do about them?" Barbara wondered.

"Nothing yet, they might be entirely innocent. We will just watch from your house for a while," Fiona said. "They might be just two men meeting socially."

Barbara agreed but the germ of an idea wriggled impishly in her mind. She put her bike under her house—a lovely old high-set 'Queenslander'—and led the way up the backstairs. Inside the house Barbara checked that they could just see both the car and the white van through the front windows without being obviously seen themselves, then went to organize afternoon tea.

When, an hour later, the car with the two men in it was still parked along the street Barbara put her first plan into operation, after explaining it to Fiona. On hearing it Fiona blushed and then giggled in embarrassment. "Oooh Barbara! That is a wicked idea!"

After checking the phone book Barbara telephoned the police station. "We will sew some confusion and stir up the State versus Federal rivalry a bit," she said. When the police answered she gave the name and address of one of her neighbours, Mrs Carlyle, then said, "There is a strange motor car parked out in the street. It has been there several hours and there are two men sitting in it acting suspiciously."

"What do you mean by suspiciously, lady?" the policeman queried.

"Well... er... I don't like to say. I mean it embarrasses me... but I think they are two homosexuals doing... er... doing whatever those people do. I rang up because I thought they might be trying to pick up young boys in the street," Barbara said.

"Have you seen them speak to any young boys?"

"Er... no. But what these two men are doing is disgusting. I think you should investigate," Barbara replied.

Because Fiona was biting her lip and giggling so much she had trouble keeping the chuckles out of her own voice. Satisfied she had set things moving she hung up and then burst out laughing.

"Now, let's see if anything happens."

Nothing did for half an hour. Both girls began to lose interest and Barbara thought her phone call had not been convincing enough. Then sickening doubts began to seep in.

I might be causing harm to perfectly innocent people, and I gave a false name and address to the police. I think they can trace where phone calls came from if they want to, she thought.

That got her worried about being in trouble for wasting police time or for making malicious or hoax calls.

Just as she was really starting to regret her plan Fiona nudged her. "Look, a cop car!"

Barbara joined Fiona at the crack in the curtains just in time to see a Queensland police car pull up behind the parked car. Two uniformed officers got out and walked forward to the parked car and stood over the windows. A moment later the two men in the car climbed out with obvious reluctance. Both wore long trousers and white, long-sleeved shirts but the only thing Barbara could really see from that distance was that both appeared to have moustaches, dark hair and brown complexions.

The two men both appeared agitated and seemed to argue with the police before producing wallets or documents. The police studied them carefully, then handed them back. The two men were then allowed to get back into their car. This was then driven away and the police climbed back into their car and followed it.

"Well, that was interesting," Barbara commented. "It wasn't what I expected at all."

"What did you think would happen?" Fiona queried.

"I thought the men would just show their secret service ID and tell the coppers to go away," Barbara answered. Then she added, "Actually

I didn't expect the police to arrive at all. If it is a properly co-ordinated operation the Secret Service people should have warned the State police."

"You watch too much television!" Fiona replied.

Barbara laughed. "Don't we all! Now, what about that white van?"

"Might belong to the people in the house," Fiona suggested.

"The Jessups? I doubt it. I have never seen it before," Barbara said.

"If you know them why don't you call and ask?" Fiona suggested.

Barbara wasn't sure if that was a good idea but finally decided it was worth a try. *If there are Secret Service people in the house they will lie to me but I might be able to tell that,* she thought. *And if they aren't then Mrs Jessup might call the police herself.*

So Barbara looked up Mrs Jessup's telephone number and dialled it. The phone then rang for so long that Barbara thought she might be out. Mrs Jessup abruptly answered. "Who is calling please? Oh Barbara Brassington. Yes Barbara, what can I do for you?"

"Sorry to bother you Mrs Jessup but I have noticed a white van parked outside your house all day and I got worried that it might belong to burglars or something," Barbara replied.

"Burglars! Oh no... I... er. No, it is just being left there for a few days by a friend," Mrs Jessup replied.

Barbara thought she had heard someone speaking in the background but wasn't sure. But the hesitation had convinced her. "Thank you, Mrs Jessup. Sorry to bother you. Goodbye," she said. After hanging up she related the words to Fiona and added, "Now I am sure something fishy is going on. She sounded very nervous and I am sure she just made that story up."

"So what do we do about it?" Fiona asked.

"Nothing for now," Barbara answered. "We just act as though we don't know we are being watched."

Fiona looked doubtful, and said, "Do you think you are safe Barbara?"

Barbara nodded. "Yes, with all these government people watching me. So, now I will call Roger."

Roger's mother answered the phone. "Oh, Barbara dear! Yes, Roger is here. He is all upset because he wasn't able to meet you. Our car broke down and he has only just walked back from the service station. He was going to call you. I will put him on," she explained.

Roger was all apologetic. "I made it halfway to the swimming pool and the motor just conked out," he explained. "Then I had to organize the RACQ to come and tow it to a motor mechanic's. I tried ringing you, but you weren't home. I have just walked home. Sorry."

Barbara was partly mollified by the explanation but still felt slightly jilted. She asked if he wanted to come to Sizzlers.

Roger sounded doubtful. "But we were only out last night."

"So? It is holidays," Barbara answered, somewhat nettled by his lack of enthusiasm. "Don't you want to see me?" she needled.

"Oh, alright," Roger replied. "I will ride my bike."

His tone of voice really annoyed Barbara. "Don't bother if that is how you feel! Don't put yourself out on my account!"

"Oh Barbara! I didn't mean it like that. I'm sorry," Roger replied, his voice all anxious contrition. "I will be there. I will ask Lofty to pick me up."

Barbara had never spoken so sharply to Roger and she now felt guilty about it. "Wendy might not like that," she quipped. "I will get dad to drive me and we will pick you up."

"OK, what time?" Roger asked.

Having agreed on times Barbara ended the conversation. She felt she did not want to talk to Roger at that moment.

Maybe I don't love him? she wondered. *If he really loves me he should want to see me every night.* That made her think hard as she realized she should feel the same way—and she didn't. *Maybe it is over?* she wondered.

That made her sad and she bit her lip. Then the niggling doubt that maybe she had never really loved Roger pushed its way to the top of her consciousness. That was an uncomfortable thought and she quickly suppressed it. An image of Mark Guy's fit, muscled body and handsome face caused her even more concern.

Pity he is an enemy, she thought.

Fiona raised an eyebrow. "What was that sigh for?" she asked.

Barbara was reluctant to discuss her love life but suddenly found she needed to talk and poured out her worries and nagging doubts. Fiona nodded and agreed. "He looked like a real hunk that Pommy Commando. It might have been fun to go out with him."

"I still might. I am sure he would ask me if we 'accidentally' meet again," Barbara replied. And then she found she was hoping he would be at Sizzlers so the opportunity might arise. She knew where he was staying but thought that her calling him would be much too forward.

He would think I was fast and loose if I did that, she reasoned. Which got her all hot with shame and arousal as she pictured what might then develop.

Soon after that Barbara's father came home. Fiona only stayed for a short while longer, making Barbara aware that she obviously thought she was in some sort of danger and should not be alone.

As she mounted her bike Fiona reinforced this by saying, "You be careful Barbara. Keep your door locked and don't let any strange men in."

Barbara laughed but agreed. "I will be careful," she reassured her. "See you at seven."

She did. After having a bath and dressing with particular care in clothes she thought were smart casual but still very attractive she had her father drive her to Roger's. Roger was again all apologetic but made up for his earlier attitude by saying nice things about her clothes and appearance. Barbara's father then drove them both to the restaurant and dropped them off, promising to pick them up when they phoned.

As soon as he had driven off Barbara carefully studied all the people in sight, while pretending not to be looking at all. To her disappointment there was no sign of Mark Guy or his companion. Fiona, Wendy and Lofty joined them and reported they had not seen any sign of the British commandos either. This was all news to Roger, so they had to explain their suspicions to him. He was horrified and not at all amused at the story of how the police had moved the two men on.

The group stayed outside chatting for nearly half an hour before moving in. The only people they saw in that time that they knew were Dan and Pat Sheehan. They sauntered past and Pat gave them a mere nod. His presence gave Barbara a sense of reassurance. So did the presence inside of Willy and Marjorie. They were seated at a side table and had obviously been in the restaurant for some time. Barbara noted with scandalized amusement that Marjorie was wearing a halter neck dress with a very low-cut front that went almost down to her waist. It really showed off her cleavage to best effect and drew the eyes of all the males in the room when she walked past.

She does look very attractive, Barbara conceded, noting that Marjorie had very sensibly worn a dress long enough to hide most of her legs. Seeing how loving and attentive Willy was to her caused a few twinges of what Barbara could only name as jealousy. *I hope Roger cares as much for me,* she wished.

Neither Willy nor Marjorie acknowledged them. Barbara made sure their own table was well away from them. There was no sign of Mark Guy inside, so Barbara relaxed and began to enjoy herself. Food was ordered and the conversation quickly steered to cadets and then to camp. That led to a discussion about the crashed satellite and to the current situation of government agents apparently watching Barbara.

"I can't imagine why," she said. "I've told them as much as I can, and you people know just as much. Any of you could lead them to where the stupid thing crashed."

"Not exactly," Fiona replied.

"Near enough. You all walked across that bit of ground several times," Barbara answered.

Roger frowned and shook his head. "I think you should tell them again," he said.

"No. They don't deserve it," Barbara replied. "They just want to steal the secrets. It belongs to the French."

"So, would you show them?" Lofty queried in a humorous tone.

He had his arm around Wendy's shoulders and that made Barbara feel jealous as well. Wendy had worn a dark blue dress which had no back and the front of which was tight under her bosom, then covered all of her chest, to fasten around her neck. It made it obvious Wendy wore no bra and every time she moved her whole front quivered.

Wobbles alright, Barbara thought, remembering Wendy's school nickname. With more than a hint of jealousy Barbara noted that Wendy was pressing happily against Lofty.

Once again Barbara experienced a strong surge of desire and was ashamed to admit to herself she wanted a man to hug her and to give her some physical romance.

Maybe Roger will try later? she thought hopefully.

But he didn't. Instead they had an argument. It arose as the group made their way outside after the dinner. Wendy started it by asking what they were doing the next day.

"What would you like to do?" Fiona asked.

Wendy grinned and looked up at Lofty, rubbing against him as she did. Fiona snorted, then laughed. "Yes! You can do that any time. What about us?"

Wendy grinned even more and snuggled up to Lofty. "We will too," she said.

It was Lofty's turn to laugh but he went red with embarrassment, although he gave Wendy a loving squeeze. "What about a picnic?" he suggested.

Barbara listened and watched with growing frustration and jealousy. She badly wanted to be hugged and kissed and could feel a deep urge to have her body loved. She said, "What about a beach party tomorrow?"

As she said this she gave Roger a quizzical look. To her disappointment he shook his head. "Sorry. I have to work at home tomorrow. I promised Mum I would fix up the back garden; and we are going to see Aunty Vera. We could go on Wednesday."

"Oh, all right!" Barbara replied, conscious of a deep sense of frustration and disappointment.

The friends discussed places to go and it was decided that Ellis Beach or Simpson Point might be the best locations. Times and who was to travel with who were agreed and then Barbara asked, "So what about tomorrow?"

Wendy and Lofty said they had already made arrangements so Barbara looked at Fiona. Fiona shrugged and replied, "We might go shopping?"

"When?"

"After lunch?" Fiona said.

So it was agreed. Lofty and Wendy then made their farewells and climbed into Lofty's car. As they drove off they grinned and Wendy blew kisses. She was looking very excited and Barbara was sure that she and Lofty were going off to park and have sex. The thought of that made her even more jealous, even though she was anxious that Wendy did not get herself into trouble.

She will be alright. Lofty loves her and will be careful, she told herself.

Thinking about what sex might feel like got her quite aroused and that added to her frustration, particularly when Roger made no moves to take her off somewhere private. Instead he just stood and held her hand until Barbara's father arrived. They all climbed into the car, dropping Roger off first, then Fiona.

Thus, it was a very frustrated and irritated girl who slid into her bed half an hour later. Thinking about what Wendy and Lofty might be doing at that very moment made her squirm with desire and jealousy. Barbara was so aroused that she did not wear any pyjamas and for quite a while she lay there, gently stroking her own heated body, her moods alternating between unhappiness at her situation and sharp arousal. Knowing that the man who took her virginity would have to be very special made her feel depressed as she sensed that Roger was not that man.

It will have to be just right, she told herself, pushing aside the uncomfortable thought that tonight she was so horny that she might give in to almost any good-looking male who made a pass.

Feeling confused and frustrated she eventually dropped off to sleep.

Chapter 16

SURPRISES

Barbara's father woke her in the morning. He knocked gently on her door till she answered. Into her sleep fuddled consciousness came the awareness that the sheet had slipped off her and that she was nude. She quickly pulled the sheet up, even though she knew her father would not open the door. Ever since her mother had left Barbara had been very careful never to let her father see her naked, sensing instinctively that it would be unfair and stressful.

Poor dad! Mum's been gone for two years now. He should get himself a girl friend. He must need some love too, she mused.

Though still physically innocent, she understood enough to appreciate that a male's sexual and emotional needs were different. That got her thinking about her own needs. She stretched and tenderly ran her hands over her bare skin, wondering if Wendy had made love to Lofty. That got her worrying again about the whole business of sex and love and of when and how she might surrender her virginity.

I will be eighteen in three weeks time—an adult, she thought.

Knowing that the age of consent was sixteen bothered her. *Am I normal?* she worried, well aware that girls like Marjorie had been having sex almost every day since they were thirteen, even though it was against the law.

And Wendy is only just sixteen now, she mused.

It was all worrying stuff, but she appreciated she was reaching that stage in her life when relationships and romance might become very important.

"But do I like men that much?" she muttered as she sat up.

But one man she did love was her dad, so she pulled on a dressing gown before going to the toilet and then to the kitchen. She found him picking up his briefcase and noted that it was already half-past eight. "You should have woken me earlier, Dad," she said.

He smiled and gave her a kiss on the cheek. "You are on holidays, and you were sleeping like a baby, so I let you."

That comment bothered Barbara. *Did he look in to my room and see me naked?* she worried.

Hiding her concern, she smiled and returned his kiss and he said goodbye. "Have a good day," he said as he went down the back stairs.

Only then did Barbara remember the secret agents and the white van. Quickly she walked through to the front of the house and looked out. The white van was still parked in front of the Jessup's and she did not know whether to believe Mrs Jessup or not.

Maybe I am getting paranoid? Maybe they have lost interest. Perhaps it is all just in our imagination? she thought.

She watched her father back the car out and drive off, then returned to the bathroom. For the next ten minutes she enjoyed a shower. For her own secret pleasure, she allowed herself to relax while she enjoyed soaping her own body. It was a habit she had got more and more into recently and each time she fantasized that it was some 'Prince Charming' doing it to her in some romantic setting.

Afterwards she dried herself then walked nude back to her room, carrying her dressing gown. Once there she stood in front of her full-length mirror and critically examine her body. Try as she might she could not really find fault with what she saw. She had to admit she had an attractive female form. Very tenderly she slid her hands over her body, luxuriating in the tingling sensations and sheer pleasure of it.

Knowing she had the house to herself Barbara decided to enjoy the sensual pleasure and naughty thrill of being naked, so she did not dress. She padded back to the kitchen, enjoying the cool air on her bare skin and the feel of the floor on her bare feet. Knowing that there was a slight possibility of one of the back neighbours seeing her through the windows added to her sense of dare. While standing at the sink filling a glass with water she peeked out but saw no sign of anyone. After filling a bowl with cereal and milk she settled at the kitchen table to eat a leisurely breakfast.

She was just finishing this when she heard a car drive into the driveway. That got her heart skipping fast and she got up and hurried to the front to check who it was. By then time she looked out through the Venetian blind her heart was beating rapidly and she got ready to scuttle to her room to get dressed. Her first thought had been that it was her father returning to collect something he had forgotten but the engine noise had informed her it wasn't. Nor was it Roger, although the impish idea had already flitted across her mind of meeting him nude and pretending to be surprised.

To her surprise she saw two men in their twenties she had never seen in her life climb out of the car. The first impression was that they were more secret agents but their clothing and hairstyle caused her to shake her head.

Long dark trousers, long-sleeved white shirt, dark tie, polished leather shoes, short haircuts, she noted. Then she thought, *Religious people—Mormons or Jehovah Witnesses. Oh, I don't want to be bothered by them,* she thought crossly.

But how to get rid of them? Then a wicked idea crossed her mind and she blushed at the very temerity of it.

No, I couldn't, she told herself.

But it did seem a good tactic to get them to leave. For just a second, she had dark thoughts about the possible consequences of arousing men's passions and the possibility of rape but another glance at the men as they started up the front steps made her shake her head.

Not these guys!

By then her heart was hammering rapidly at the sheer wickedness of the dare. As she heard the front doorbell ring Barbara began to hop from foot to foot and her heart rate shot up even more.

I can still run to my room and get dressed, she thought.

For a moment she hesitated, but then a streak of stubborn irritation held her there. Her mouth was now quite dry and the palms of her hands were so sweaty she felt the need to wipe them on the curtains.

Taking a deep breath, she stepped over and opened the front door, using it to screen most of her body. Peeking around the door she croaked, "Yes, what do you want?"

Both men stared and looked surprised and embarrassed. One quickly got control of his eyes and face. In a curiously neutral voice but with an American accent he asked, "Miss Barbara Brassington?"

By now Barbara was regretting her actions and was flaming with shame. She stayed mostly behind the door but noted the men's gaze flicking down and she became hotly aware that they could probably see part of her right breast.

"Yes," she mumbled.

The man, clean-cut and looking in his late twenties, held out a leather

ID wallet. "Chuck Wilson, Central Intelligence Agency. This is Howard Otis."

Barbara was stunned. *Not Mormons! CIA!*

Panic and shame flooded her but an instant spurt of annoyance stopped her from asking them to wait while she got dressed.

"So?" she asked, guessing immediately that they were going to ask her about the satellite.

"Can we come in?" Chuck asked. By now he was blushing a bright red and trying hard not to look at her.

"No," Barbara heard herself answer, quite surprised at her own temerity. "I haven't got any clothes on."

"We will wait while you get dressed," Chuck replied stiffly.

"Thanks, but I am happy the way I am," Barbara said.

"I would prefer it if you made yourself decent," the man replied in a slightly censorious tone.

The suggestion that she was somehow indecent angered Barbara and stiffened her resolve. "I am in my own home. I will wear what I like," she said, moving so that more of her naked body was visible.

The men's reactions were all that she had imagined. Their eyes goggled in disbelief and ran up and down her body. One gaped but the other managed to keep his face neutral and he was first to get control of his eyes. But the refusal obviously threw the man. A slight frown crossed his brow.

"May we ask you some questions?"

Now standing partly exposed in the doorway, Barbara nodded. "Yes." Her heart was pounding with anxiety, but stubborn annoyance held her there.

"We'll wait till you get dressed," Chuck said, tactfully looking away.

That really annoyed Barbara. His attitude made her decide to use her nudity as a weapon as it obviously upset the men.

"You'll be waiting a long time!" she snapped. "What do you want?"

"I want you to put some clothes on," Chuck said, now obviously angry and very embarrassed. His companion was equally red, but his eyes kept flicking to her body and the tip of his tongue began to dart out to lick at his lips.

"If you want to talk to me you will have to accept me as I am," Barbara heard herself reply stiffly.

Chuck went even redder. He managed to meet her eyes. "You should get dressed," he insisted.

"Why?" Barbara snapped defiantly. She was now deeply regretting her dare but there was no way she was going to back down now.

"Because it isn't right. Women should dress with modesty at all times," Chuck said.

The edge in his voice gave Barbara some satisfaction. *Good! He is losing his cool,* she thought. Knowing they were from the CIA was causing her waves of deep anxiety, almost fear.

This fuelled her anger and she snapped back, "Oh yeah? Who says so?"

"It says so in the Good Book," Chuck replied stiffly.

"The Bible you mean?" Barbara snorted. "I don't believe that bit. It was written by men a long time ago to justify them keeping women under their thumb."

At that Chuck looked shocked. Then anger mottled his face and he said, "You should not speak like that."

"Why not? I thought Americans believed in freedom of speech and religion. Are you here to convert me to being a Mormon or to get me to tell you about the French satellite?"

With that she placed her fists on her hips and deliberately moved to be fully visible. She knew she was making the men angry and aroused but her fear and irritation seemed to just make her want to provoke them even more.

Her bluntness seemed to take Chuck by surprise. For a moment he obviously struggled to master his thoughts and emotions then he replied, "The satellite."

"Why should I tell you? What's it got to do with you?" she demanded to know.

"National security," Chuck replied, his eyes flicking to her body.

Barbara snorted with disbelief. "Whose national security? It's a French satellite, isn't it?"

"Australia is an American ally," Chuck answered, ignoring her dig.

"I thought France was an ally of yours too?" Barbara retorted. "Are you going to steal secrets from your friends? Doesn't your 'Good Book' say 'Thou shalt not steal'?"

At that Chuck went red and took several deep breaths but did not answer. Barbara was aware that the other CIA agent was surreptitiously running his gaze up and down her body. Now she was glad she had remained nude as she sensed it gave her a powerful weapon against such otherwise intimidating men.

Then Chuck really infuriated her, and lost his case completely, by saying, "We are willing to pay for information; willing to pay a lot."

Barbara gave him a withering look and snapped back scornfully, "How much? Thirty pieces of silver?"

Chuck blushed again and a look of fury crossed his face, but he managed to control himself. He glared and said, "So you won't help us?"

"No. Now please leave."

"We will report you," Chuck threatened.

Barbara managed a laugh although in truth she now felt sick with anxiety. To end the conversation, she shut the door firmly then locked it. She heard the men mutter something and then their footsteps as they went down the steps. For a moment she felt dizzy as she leaned her back against the door and gulped in deep breaths. She found her heart was hammering as though she had just run a race. Then she thought she was going to vomit but managed to steady herself. Waves of scorching shame alternated with surges of deep anger.

On hearing car doors closing she moved to peer through the Venetian blinds. All she saw was a glimpse of Chuck's angry face as he reversed the car down the driveway. To her intense relief the car just drove off, to vanish around the next corner. As she watched it go Barbara's gaze settled on the white van. The uneasy suspicion returned that 'they' were still watching her. She remembered TV shows where the police had set up their electronic listening gear in a van.

Is it that? she wondered.

Then she broke down in a fit of trembling and had to sit. It took her ten minutes to calm down, the shame becoming the dominant emotion, leavened by an impish memory of the men's surprise and obvious discomfiture.

I'm as bad as Chloe! she thought, then shook her head. *No, Chloe would probably have invited them in and fed them cakes!*

Feeling slightly better, Barbara considered what she had done. Now sickening anxieties of being in trouble with the authorities began to churn in her stomach.

The police might charge me with indecent exposure, she worried. Then she shook her head. *No. I doubt it. I'll bet those two won't be game to even mention that I had no clothes on.*

A sudden need for someone to talk to sent Barbara to the telephone. With shaking fingers she dialled Fiona's number. To her relief Fiona was at home.

Barbara at once asked, "Fiona? Can I come over?"

"Sure. Is everything alright?"

"I'll tell you when I get there," Barbara replied. "See you in twenty minutes."

Barbara now felt a twinge of fear at being home alone. Being naked added to this. *I could get raped,* she thought.

That thought sent her to her bedroom and she dressed in jeans and shirt, then laced on her joggers. After closing up the house she made her way down the backstairs and got her bike. She wheeled it out and then locked up the underneath of the house. Taking a surreptitious glance at the white van she mounted the bike and pedalled out onto the road.

The shortest route to Fiona's went past the white van. For a moment Barbara considered going the other way but then she set her jaw.

That is just being weak, she told herself. *Besides, I might be just imagining things. There may be nothing in it.*

So she rode close by the van, giving it a hostile glare as she did. There was no-one in the cab and she could not see into the back so all she could do was ride by, although she had to resist the temptation to whack the side as she passed. That gave her an idea and as she rode on towards Fiona's she turned it over in her mind, liked it, added to it, and then chuckled.

At Fiona's she refused to come in. "Get your bike and come for a ride," she said, again thinking about spy movies she had seen where the enemy had planted eavesdropping devices. Fiona was not keen but agreed. She asked her father for permission, collected her bag and bike and joined Barbara on the front lawn.

"Where to?"

"Just a ride to begin with," Barbara answered.

Fiona only lived a few blocks from the Esplanade, so they went in that direction, then sat on a park bench in the shade of a tree. Satisfied that nobody had followed them and that they could not be overheard even if they had been Barbara related the morning's visit. She was careful not to mention being nude and feared that she was blushing so much that Fiona might guess that something else had happened.

To her relief Fiona did not seem to notice anything. Her reaction was to get all anxious about Barbara's safety and suggest again that she tell the authorities. At that Barbara shook her head. "No way! This is supposed to be a free country. I don't like being spied on; and I won't be a party to deception and theft. The satellite is French, so they can have it."

"Tell them then," Fiona suggested.

"I might," Barbara agreed. But she had only a vague idea of how to do that. She knew that foreign governments had embassies in Canberra and that there were even people called consuls, but she wasn't at all sure how to find out. Instead she said, "Never mind the stupid satellite; will you help me?"

"Oh alright, but I think we should get Roger, and Lofty and so on to help."

"We need some water-soluble paint," Barbara said. "Let's go to the shops and see if we can buy some."

So the two girls set off in search of a shop that sold the type of paint they wanted. After pedalling fruitlessly around for half an hour Barbara finally thought of looking in the telephone book 'Yellow Pages'. That gave them an address out along Mulgrave Road, so they set off for that. Along the way they stopped for a cold drink. Luckily the shop on Mulgrave Road did sell what they wanted but it turned out to be a bit more expensive than Barbara had bargained on.

"I don't have much cash left," she said, ruefully counting the small amount left in her purse. "Let's go and find an ATM."

So the girls pedalled back into the main part of the city. After collecting more cash Barbara suggested calling their friends to organize. "We will use a public phone and meet them on the Esplanade where we can't be overheard," she said.

So she took out her mobile phone and called. That was a frustrating experience. The first person Barbara called was Roger, but the phone rang out with no answer.

"Well, he did say he was going to visit his Aunty," Fiona reminded.

"Oh, rude words to his Aunty!" Barbara cried in annoyance.

Fiona took over the telephoning and soon had Lofty, Wendy, Dan and Pat all agreeing to meet them within the hour. That done the two girls then rode to the Esplanade and parked their bikes under a shady tree where they could look at the sea. After sitting waiting for twenty minutes Fiona suggested another cold drink, indicating a shop half a block away. Barbara agreed so Fiona went to buy cold rinks and ice-creams while Barbara sat and minded the bikes.

For the next few minutes Barbara sat and stared out to sea, her mind roving over options concerning the satellite. While she sat there quite a number of people, some obviously overseas tourists, walked by. Thus, it was a surprise to Barbara to find two of them stop in front of her. Her mind took in the baggy shorts and bright Hawaiian shirts before she recognized one of the faces.

"Mark!" she cried, amazed and suspicious that he was there. "What are you doing here?"

"We were just walking along enjoying the sights and we saw you," Mark replied. "It is a very pleasant surprise."

"I don't believe you. You are spying on me and following me around," Barbara snapped accusingly.

Mark's grin faded, and he looked hurt. "No, we aren't! We are just on leave."

"You are not!" Barbara snapped. "You want me to tell you where the satellite is."

"That would be nice," Mark replied. "But believe me, it wasn't my motive for stopping to talk to you. I just think you are really pretty and I'd like to get to know you. Nobody told me to try to talk to you."

Barbara blushed at the compliment and felt herself weaken as she took in his handsome face and friendly smile, but she shook her head. "You are just saying that. You are just trying to butter me up to get me to tell," she said.

"I am not!" Mark protested.

His companion grinned and then added, in a very 'North of England' accent, "He isn't you know Miss. He reckons you be the Bee's Knees."

Mark turned a look of mock severity on his companion and said, "Thank you Corporal Tomlinson. I will do my own smooth talking thank you. Now you trot along and leave us for a while."

"Yes sir." Cpl Tomlinson grinned and started walking. As he did he called back, "Don't you trust him Miss. A girl in every port he 'um got."

171

"I have not!" Mark answered, laughing as he did.

Barbara had thawed a bit by this and decided that perhaps Mark was telling the truth.

He's a real charmer, she thought.

But just to stir things along she said, "Do you have a surveillance team watching us? Are you wired for sound? Have you got a miniature camera?"

Mark shook his had. "No. None of the above. I am not a spy."

"Well somebody has been spying on me, and if you people want the satellite you had better hurry up because two American secret agents from the CIA tried to bribe me this morning," Barbara said.

At that Mark's grin vanished. "You don't say! Now that is bad news. Tell me more."

Barbara did, relating everything she could remember, except for the fact that she was nude. As she talked she watched his face closely but failed to detect the faintest trace of a smirk which might have indicated he knew about her not having any clothes on.

Mark listened and then shook his head. "No sense of humour those American chappies. They are all right-wing, clean-cut, all-American boys who have no sense of proportion and despite their protestations of morality are usually most un-Christian in their attitudes."

On hearing that Barbara could only nod in agreement. Her own experience was too limited but what he said rang true to her. She began to think he really had nothing to do with the satellite at all and wondered if she should accept his offer to dinner.

He was obviously thinking along the same lines because he again asked her for a date. Barbara shook her head but was tempted. "I am too young," she said. "And you are too old."

"I'm only twenty-three," Mark replied. "And you must be at least eighteen."

"Only seventeen," Barbara answered. "I am still at school." She now found she was anxious lest he make some comment about her 'being old enough'—or some smart crack about schoolgirls—which would indicate he only had sex on his mind.

Instead Mark made a face and said, "Alright, so I will come and ask your mother."

He is either a very skilful liar or he is not a spy, Barbara decided.

If he was a spy his people must know that mum does not live with us anymore.

Instead she said shook her head again and noted with a mixture of regret and relief that Fiona coming back. She pointed to her. "You had better go. Here comes my friend."

Mark looked at Fiona and smiled, then said, "So what about dinner?"

"I'll think about it," Barbara answered, unable to resist returning his smile.

"Your friend can come too. We can easily find her a nice fit young commando," Mark replied.

He did not take the hint but stayed and introduced himself to Fiona. Fiona's reaction caused her some amusement as she was clearly charmed. But then Dan and Pat arrived, and they were obviously not amused. On being introduced they looked impressed and both then bombarded Mark with technical questions about the Royal Marines and what the commandos did. Next Lofty and Wendy arrived and Mark finally gave up.

"I'll see you around then," he said, looking wistful. "If you change your mind give me a call."

Barbara nodded and wondered if she would. It was with a stab of genuine regret that she watched Mark's very fit form vanish around the next corner. Then she had to explain to the others what had been happening. Their consensus was not to trust him. She then told them about the American secret agents and the white van. "The white van is our target," she explained.

When they heard her plan the others became quite excited and chuckled with mirth. After organizing themselves the whole group set off for Barbara's. This took half an hour to reach. First Barbara and Fiona pedalled along her street past the white van to her house. They pretended to ignore it and went into the house. After checking through the house for any sign there had been intruders they peeked out the front and then waited.

Ten minutes later Dan and Pat walked along the footpath to the van. They then split up and got quietly to work with the spray cans of paint. Within a couple of minutes, they had painted in big letters on both sides and the back doors and windscreen the words SECRET SPY VAN. They then wandered on along the block and vanished around the next corner.

By then Lofty had parked his car fifty paces back from the van and he and Wendy were pretending to kiss.

Well, not pretending actually, Barbara noted.

Dan and Pat reappeared on their bikes and rode fast along the street to the van. They stopped and Dan began banging on the sides while Pat started to rock the van. Both then jumped on their bikes and rode off.

For a while Barbara thought that they had made a mistake and she became quite anxious.

At least the paint will wash off easily, she told herself to calm her anxieties.

But then a car drove up and stopped behind the van. A man got out of the car and looked angrily at the writing, then went to the back of the van. From where she was Barbara only got a glimpse, but it was obvious that the man had opened the back door and was talking to someone inside.

"It was a spy van!" she cried in dismay.

Fiona looked very pale and nodded. "Oh Barbara! You had better be very careful."

The van and car then drove off. Fiona watched them go and then said, "I don't know if that was a good idea. Now they know we are aware of their surveillance and they will pick another method that will be harder to detect."

"I don't care. It is all just silly," Barbara replied. She felt genuinely insulted and outraged at being spied on. It made her even less willing to co-operate. The others all returned and joined them and Lofty confirmed that there had been two men in the back of the van with a lot of electrical equipment. He was also deeply concerned for Barbara's safety.

"I'll be careful," she said, but she did feel just a little scared.

The others were obviously worried and wanted to stay with her but at that moment the phone rang. It was her father, and Barbara was quite surprised. He rarely rang her, and she was even more intrigued when he asked her to come to his work to see him.

"There is something I would like to discuss with you," he said.

That got her even more curious, so she asked Lofty for a lift. Pat, Dan and Fiona rode off on their bikes and Lofty drove Barbara and Wendy to town. All the way Lofty kept looking in his rear vision mirror to check if they were being tailed. He dropped Barbara off outside her father's office and she thanked him and Wendy.

"See you at the picnic tomorrow," she said.

Intrigued by her father's unusual request Barbara hurried inside. Her father's secretary showed her straight in and she went to his office. As she walked in she saw there was another man sitting in one of the arm chairs talking to her father. Her father was smiling and as she stopped she noted a smile break out on the man's face. The man stood up and she had a fleeting impression of a very muscular, tanned, young man in his twenties. He wore a well-cut suit and had short dark hair and brown eyes with a real twinkle in them.

Heavens! He is good looking! she thought, aware that her heart rate had increased.

Her father stood as well and said, "Barbara, I would like you to meet Lieutenant Raoul de Berg of the French *Commandos Marines*. He is taking us out to dinner."

Chapter 17

RAOUL

For a moment Barbara could only gape in surprise. Her initial reaction was irritation at the mention of the satellite but then her eyes met Raoul's. A wave of emotion such as she had never before experienced swept through her, leaving her warm and slightly breathless. Raoul added to that be bowing slightly and taking her hand. He then bent to kiss it, sending more surges of warmth through her. She had read about Frenchmen and seen this in the movies, but it was quite another thing to actually have it done to her.

As he straightened up Raoul met her eyes again, his twinkling. *"Enchanteur Mademoiselle,"* he said, adding, "You are far more beautiful than I expected."

Barbara blushed and looked at her father. He was smiling, which reassured her, but she felt flustered. "Oh, you are just saying that to butter me up!" she cried.

"Butter me up?" Raoul queried, raising an eyebrow.

"To impress me, to flatter me, to weaken my resolve," Barbara said.

Raoul nodded and smiled. "Thank you. My English is not that good, at least not in the idiom, in the slang. But yes *certainement*, I would like to butter you up."

"You just want the satellite," Barbara replied, unsure how she felt and still feeling emotionally off balance.

As she spoke her eyes registered his muscular upper body, his tanned and cheerful face and the bright hazel eyes. He was so handsome that she was almost speechless.

"I did until I actually met you," Raoul replied. "Now I must say that it was worth the trip just to feast my eyes on your loveliness." As he said this he half-turned and smiled at her father who smiled back, obviously amused and not disapproving.

Barbara could only snort, and say, "And what if I won't tell you? I haven't told our own people, and I haven't told the British, or the Americans."

"Then I must use all my charm to butter you up some more," Raoul replied, "And if I fail then meeting you is ample reward."

He said this with such sincerity that Barbara could only blush again. She shook her head but was interrupted by her father. "Americans?" he asked.

Barbara nodded and described the morning visit. Once again, she made no mention of being naked and was glad she was already so flushed that the new wave of shame did not show. Her father looked worried and shook his head and Raoul looked serious.

"I suppose it is inevitable that the Americans have to be involved. They are the Big Boys and will not want any challenge to their power," he said.

Barbara frowned. "What do you mean?" she asked.

Raoul shrugged. "The Americans are the new Roman Empire. They want to be in a position of such unassailable military superiority that no-one can threaten or challenge them, or disobey them either. It is very worrying for true lovers of liberty."

Her father then asked, "Do you think Barbara is safe?"

Raoul looked thoughtful and then nodded. "From the Americans, yes, and the British. You did say the British did you not?"

"Yes, I did," Barbara replied. "A Royal Marine Commando lieutenant named Mark Guy."

At that Raoul's eyebrows went up fractionally and he shook his head slightly. "Marines! I would have thought that the British would send James Bond for a job like this."

"Aren't you some sort of marine?" Barbara queried, remembering the introduction.

Raoul nodded. "*Oui.* I am a marine."

"What unit do you belong to?" Barbara asked, genuinely interested.

Raoul smiled and said, "How did you meet this Englishman?"

It took a moment for Barbara to realize that Raoul was not going to tell her his unit which immediately made her suspicious.

I'll bet he's some sort of Special Forces, she thought.

But she then explained how her platoon had found the British commandos at Dostwood and then how he had spoken to her at the swimming pool and at the Esplanade.

"I wondered how he knew my name. I thought he must be a secret agent," she explained. Then she turned to Raoul. "Are you a secret agent?" she challenged.

Raoul laughed. "*Non*! I am but a simple soldier of the sea."

"So why are you here?"

Raoul shrugged. "I suppose because I was conveniently in the area. Now, I ask again, will you be my guests for dinner?"

Barbara met his sparkling eyes and nodded. *Why not?* she thought. *Daddy will be there, and it is only business.*

"Thank you," she said. "But I'm not really dressed for going out."

Again Raoul laughed, the sound seeming to shiver right to the very centre of Barbara's being. He grinned and said, "Ah, *la femme*! *Mademoiselle* has nothing to wear!"

At that Barbara could only huff. She looked to her father for help and he smiled again and said, "We can go home and change."

Raoul nodded. "That would be a good idea. You could then meet me at my hotel at perhaps seven o'clock?"

Barbara's father agreed to that and she nodded. Now she was feeling a sense of tingling excitement that made her tremble slightly. Raoul smiled his thanks and then said, "Thank you, and if I may ask, please do not mention to anyone that you are meeting me. I am not in your country legally. If that bothers you then please tell me and I will leave at once. It would not be fair to implicate you in something illegal. You may then tell the relevant authorities."

That was a surprise to Barbara and she felt a shiver of worry. She looked at Raoul and said, "You snuck ashore off a ship."

Raoul only shrugged and kept his smile. "I do not say," he explained. "Other people besides myself are involved and I do not wish to cause harm to them, or to the good relations between my country and yours."

Barbara nodded and, to her own surprise, agreed. *Marine Commando,* she thought. *He might have come ashore from a submarine or something.*

It was only later, while driving home with her father that the full import of that struck her.

This satellite must be very important if all these countries are trying to get it; and if the French can divert warships and are willing to risk harming international relations. It was certainly serious food for thought and left her quite undecided about what to do. *Do I tell the French, or not?*

Only when the car turned into her own street did Barbara remember the white van. She saw that there were no vehicles parked in the street and wondered if she should tell her father what she and her friends had done. She also worried about whether the spies, whoever they were, were now watching her from somewhere else.

As they got out of the car in the garage at home Barbara's father said to her, "You don't mind going to dinner?"

Barbara shook her head. "No. It should be interesting. Er... Daddy..." Her hesitation caused him to look at her. She bit her lip, then went on, "Er... please don't mention any of this while we are in the house."

"Why not?" her father asked in surprise.

"Because I think we are being spied on and the house may be bugged. I am sure the telephone is being tapped," she replied.

Her father stopped and looked hard at her, a frown creasing his forehead. "Tell me more," he demanded.

There was nothing for it then but for her to relate all that she knew and suspected. When she finished, he frowned. "You have been busy little bees!" he said. "I wish you had told me sooner."

"We didn't want to bother you," Barbara said, "And we didn't think it was that important."

"I hope you are safe," her father said as they resumed walking.

That got Barbara feeling anxious, but she forced a smile. "If I tell the French where the satellite is then that should be the end of it," she said.

Then her worries shifted to the much more personal and feminine level of feeling concerned about her appearance. First, she looked at her fingernails and shook her head.

These need trimming and painting, she noted, aware that they had been cut short and unpainted all of the cadet camp. *Now, what can I wear?*

After thinking for a while she dug out the green evening dress she had worn to the famous school dance. She had not worn it for nearly two years and suspected that it would no longer fit her. It took a bit of squirming to get into it but it did fit—like the proverbial glove. A long look in the mirror got her biting her lip.

Heavens! It accentuates every curve. She turned and examined herself critically from every angle and shook her head. *No, too revealing. But what else do I have? And why do I care?'* she asked herself, suddenly aware that she wanted to look her best for Raoul. *He is only a man after all, even if he is a Frenchman.*

But it was no good. To her own dismay she found her desires defied logic and then she shrugged and giggled with impish mischief.

So he can enjoy the view, she thought, noting how the front of the dress pushed her breasts up and out, causing quite a dramatic cleavage. That got her blushing but wishing she had some suitable jewellery to wear with it.

A pearl or emerald pendant, she thought.

So the green dress was what she wore, with a simple gold chain necklace and black shoes. When her father saw her, he nodded with approval.

"That looks very nice dear. It will certainly take his mind off satellites."

At that Barbara blushed and wished she hadn't worn such a provocative dress. "Oh Daddy! Is it too revealing? Do you think I should change?"

Her father laughed and shook his head. "No. You look really attractive. Anyway, you are only young once. Enjoy it while you can," he advised.

Barbara wasn't quite sure but agreed. She said, "You make sure you stay next to me all the time," she said.

Then, to her own surprise and consternation, she found she was slightly breathless and more than a little anxious as they drove back to Raoul's hotel. This changed to blushing pleasure when she saw his eyes light up as she walked into the foyer. He was wearing a plain white, long-sleeved shirt with tie and long slacks but still looked very smart and handsome. When he again bowed and kissed her hand she positively glowed with warmth. Then she blushed again when he produced flowers.

"Oh, you shouldn't have!" she cried, embarrassed, flustered and deeply pleased all at once.

"My pleasure," Raoul replied, bowing again.

As he did Barbara was acutely conscious of his eyes feasting on her bosom and she half-wished she had not worn the dress, and half-wished to flirt some more. She also noted her own breathless reaction. Usually when males ogled her breasts she felt hot and resentful but this time she was moved by a deep feeling of arousal and an urge she refused to consciously acknowledge. But she did accept that she was not offended by his gaze and blushed even more.

Raoul then offered her his arm and she took it, feeling slightly giddy. "Shall we go in?" he asked.

For a few moments Barbara could not answer. She was vaguely aware that she was staring back, drawn into his gaze as though by a magnetic force. In all her seventeen years she had never met a man like him. When she realized what she was doing she blushed fiercely and then nodded, her throat constricted and her heart thumping rapidly.

I think I am in love! she thought in wonder.

Raoul led her into the dining room. It was a five-star hotel with a *maitre d'* and all the trimmings: candles, dim lights, soft music (real music from a small orchestra!) and Barbara was half-overcome by shyness. Raoul added to her palpitating heart by murmuring, "You are what I have always dreamed of, a woman on my arm who brings a room to a standstill when she walks in."

Barbara felt her cheeks scorch with pleasure and concern. She glanced anxiously around the room and noted at least a dozen pairs of eyes on her. It made her so acutely self-conscious that she had trouble walking and all her muscles felt stiff and awkward.

A smiling waiter in white jacket and bow tie bowed them to a table and positively beamed when Raoul addressed him in French. Luckily Barbara had studied French for 5 years at school so could follow the conversation. Raoul explained, "This is Francois. He has worked in the best hotels in Paris."

When Raoul held her chair and helped her to be seated she blushed some more. Raoul sat on her left and her father on her right. Barbara bent over to put down her handbag then hastily sat up, flaming with shame when she realized just how much of her bosom bulged out when she bent forward.

Oh, I wish I hadn't worn this dress, she told herself. That got her casting about for a plan of escape. Her thoughts were interrupted to discuss drinks.

"Wine?" Raoul queried, raising an eyebrow to her father.

Barbara was about to say no when her father smiled and nodded. "Just a glass I think," he said.

"Dad! I'm not old enough," Barbara hissed anxiously.

"Piffle! Count it as part of your education," her father replied. He ordered a sweet white wine for her.

Barbara was handed the menu card and scanned it, noting first that it was written in both French and English. Then she said, "There are no prices. I hope this doesn't cost too much. It all looks very expensive."

Raoul laughed gently and said, "Please do not concern yourself about cost. You are my guests, and besides, it is the French government that is paying, and I am sure they know how to dine in style."

Her father added, "If you need to worry about the prices of food you can't afford to stay at this hotel."

Barbara nodded and felt very immature and ignorant. To ease her embarrassment, she pretended to relax and looked around the room. "So how will the government know what you spent?" she asked.

"I will present the accounts of course," Raoul replied. He was still smiling and leaned over to point to his suggestion for the main course. "Do you read French?" he asked politely.

For a moment Barbara considered keeping her knowledge of that language secret but then she nodded and said, "A little. I learnt some at school."

Their eyes met again, and she was quite astounded at how fast her heart hammered and how dry her throat felt.

This is silly! she told herself, but there was no denying the very real physical effect Raoul had on her.

The wine arrived, and Barbara sipped tentatively at it. She had some experience of drinking at parties but had long ago decided she liked neither the taste, nor the effects, of alcohol. But this was quite different, and she was pleasantly surprised. She sipped again and then leaned forward to study the label.

"You approve?" Raoul asked anxiously.

Barbara nodded, then pouted. "It is probably just a sneaky trick to get me to talk."

Raoul laughed and again Barbara felt her heart lurch. *He is just so nice!* she thought.

The conversation moved to a few polite questions about school and home and then to local tourist attractions. That reminded Barbara of Mark Guy and she could not help wondering what dinner with him might be like. To change the conversation, she began to ask about France and

Raoul's home and family. She half-expected him to be evasive and to clam up but instead he became quite animated and happily described his home near Toulon, his younger brother Vincent, the pet cat and the old donkey left by a not very reputable old uncle.

Barbara began to relax and enjoy herself. A description of how Raoul and Vincent had been caught stealing the Cure's peaches caused her to gurgle with laughter. Barbara noted her father smiling with happiness and wondered if she had been drinking too much wine (She was on to her second glass by then). Raoul laughed with her and his eyes sparkled with pleasure.

The food was also a delight and far more quickly than she imagined possible two hours slipped by. It was only as they were finishing desert that Raoul brought the conversation back to the satellite. He sighed and, with a look of genuine regret on his face, said, "*Mademoiselle*, I am sorry to say that I must now ask you if you will help me in my quest."

"Quest?"

"To recover the missing part of the satellite."

Put so directly Barbara found herself mixed in her feelings. To gain more time she said, "Why should I?"

"Because the satellite belongs to France," Raoul replied.

"You must have the plans. You can always make another," Barbara countered. She was remembering what Major Conkey had said about satellites and she did not much like them.

"We could," agreed Raoul. "I think what we really want is for the secrets to remain out of the hands of those who might use them for possibly evil purposes."

Barbara looked sceptical and asked, "Oh yes, who?"

At that Raoul looked slightly uncomfortable and baffled. After a moment's thought he said, "Certain Middle Eastern countries, and a few countries run by military dictators and tyrants. Iran or Syria for example, or Dagestan."

That made Barbara wish she had paid more attention to world events. Not wanting to appear ignorant to Raoul she nodded and looked thoughtful. It certainly sounded like a reasonable explanation. But she still wasn't convinced so she said, "What about America?"

Now Raoul did look serious. "Them too. They are now in the position of being the world's great power. They have no serious rivals and one consequence of that is that they are tending to become bullies. There is a danger that they might become tyrants and use their power to push their own culture at the expense of smaller states."

That also made sense to Barbara, so she asked, "What if the thing you want was destroyed in the crash?"

Raoul shook his head. "The information I was given indicates the part in question was specifically designed to survive such an event. It was ejected ten kilometres before impact. Even more important to know is that it is not in the hands of foreigners. So I ask you again, please help me find it."

Barbara knew she was weakening but rationalized it by telling herself that the thing really did belong to France. What bothered her was that Australia, Britain and America were all apparently trying to get it for themselves and she had a niggling concern over somehow letting down her own side. She bit her lip and then asked, "How could I help you?"

"Describe exactly where you were and what you saw," Raoul replied, "And perhaps draw a map with distances and directions on it. Could you do that?"

"Of course, I could!" Barbara replied, her pride nettled. "I am a Cadet Under-Officer."

"Cadet Under-Officer? Please explain," Raoul requested.

Barbara spent ten minutes telling him about how the Australian Army Cadets was organized, its rank structure, training and methods. Raoul listened carefully, nodding from time to time and asking a few questions. He then said, "I understand your pique. I also was a cadet when I was younger."

"Younger! How old are you now?" Barbara asked. She knew that the question might give away her interest in him as a man, but she felt she just had to know.

Raoul smiled and said, "Twenty-four."

Barbara could only nod while she did the sums in her head.

Only seven years older, she thought, then realized what the 'only' implied.

At that moment her father stood up. "I need to visit the toilet," he said. "I will be back in a minute."

As her father walked away Barbara felt a little surge of anxiety, which was almost immediately replaced by the delicious thought that she and Raoul were alone. He met her eyes and smiled, and she could not help smiling back. Then he reached forward, and she found herself taking his hand. It felt warm and nice to hold.

He looked into her eyes and said, "Pardon me for being so forward, but I want you to know that I think you are the most beautiful girl I have ever seen. Quite frankly, I could not care less whether you tell me about the satellite or not, but I do care that I get to see you again. I think I would like to fall in love with you."

Chapter 18

LOVE?

Barbara's mind raced as fast as her heart. *Love!* she thought. *Oh yes! I could fall in love with this man.* But memories of past hurts, and cynicism and suspicion of Raoul's motives rose to spoil her leaping spirits.

"Oh, you are just saying that to get me to co-operate," she said.

Raoul shook his head vigorously and looked very serious. "No. I don't care about the satellite. But you, I think I could fall very badly in love with."

A surge of warmth seemed to engulf Barbara and she tried to tell herself it was just the wine. *I've drunk too much,* she told herself as desperation grew towards panic. But she knew she had not. Her own heart was hammering and all she could see were his twinkling eyes and smiling lips. She leaned towards him and looked earnestly into his eyes.

"You aren't just saying that?"

Raoul again shook his head. "No. I think you are wonderful. You are beautiful, and intelligent, and you have spirit."

"I might not like men," Barbara replied, trying to keep up her crumbling defences.

"Now that is a challenge!" Raoul answered with a smile. "May I?" that last because he now held both her hands and was leaning across for a kiss.

In near panic Barbara gasped, "My father might come back."

"I take that as a yes?" Raoul queried.

Then he gently caressed her right cheek with the back of his hand. Barbara seemed to be drawn to him by an irresistible force and she found herself squirming with desire. Somehow their lips met and she closed her eyes and surrendered to the sheer pleasure of it all.

After a minute or so they drew apart. Barbara was amazed and found she was panting as though she had just run a race.

This is ridiculous! she thought. *I only met him this afternoon.*

Raoul sighed, then said, "That was very nice. May I see you again?"

Barbara badly wanted to say yes but there was still that niggling suspicion. In an attempt to keep control of her emotions she said, "What about your satellite?"

"Oh I... I... I swear about the stupid satellite!" Raoul replied. "You are worth a dozen satellites."

"Only a dozen?" Barbara said then laughed. She felt so happy she wanted to shout it out to the whole room.

Raoul smiled and then suggested meeting the next day. "You are on holidays are you not?"

Only then did Barbara remember Roger and she burned with guilt. "Oh, not tomorrow! I arranged to go to the beach with... with... er... with some friends."

"With your boyfriend eh? Lucky man!" Raoul answered. He sounded genuinely jealous.

"Sorry," Barbara murmured. And she was too. She badly wanted Raoul to be with her, to kiss her again, to hold her.

Raoul shrugged. "No matter. Of course, you would have a boyfriend! I would have been surprised if a girl as attractive as you did not have one. So, if we meet again then it must be just for business eh?"

"I truly am sorry," Barbara cried, and she felt her throat choke up and became anxious lest tears start. There was a minute's silence during which both sat and looked into each other's eyes.

It was Raoul who broke the silence. "Will you tell me how to find the satellite please?" he asked, reluctantly letting go of her hands.

Barbara nodded, and was unable to speak for a moment, so sharp was the pain in her chest. Then she sniffled and straightened up. "I will draw you a map. Or, better still, I will mark a map very accurately."

"When?" Raoul asked.

"Tomorrow night? Perhaps we could meet somewhere?"

At that Raoul gave a wry smile. "I would love that, but what about your boyfriend? He might not approve."

Once again guilt surged in Barbara and she felt such a sharp stab of regret she nearly broke into tears. To meet such a man and to be denied!

Maybe just a little romance? she wondered, then felt even more guilty.

In her confusion the only thing she was sure of was that she wanted to be with Raoul again. She said, "Where could we meet?"

"It will be a Wednesday. So what place is quiet, yet public enough for us not to be noticed?"

For a minute or so Barbara thought fast, mentally ticking off possible venues. Finally, she opted for a coffee shop on Sheridan Street at North Cairns.

That is close enough for me to ride my bike and should be just busy enough to make us inconspicuous.

She suggested this and gave her reasons. Raoul listened and then nodded approval. While they were settling the details Barbara's father rejoined them. That allowed her to calm down a bit, but she found it was now an effort to pretend to act normally. Her very being seemed to be tingling and she knew she would help Raoul, even if it meant breaking the law.

The trio moved to a pleasant lounge overlooking the sea to enjoy coffee and mints. The conversation again switched to Raoul's home and life. Barbara learned that he had joined the marines at age seventeen and that he had graduated as a Sous Lieutenant at twenty. Since then he had travelled all over the world and had already been to several international 'hot spots': once to the Balkans peacekeeping, once to West Africa helping suppress arms smuggling, and once to Mali to fight Islamic terrorists.

Barbara frowned. "But Mali is a long way from the sea. What were marines doing there?"

"We operated on the River Niger in small boats," Raoul answered.

"It sounds very exciting," she commented.

"It is," Raoul agreed. "It is exactly why I enlisted."

Barbara's father asked if he intended to make the marines his career. Raoul nodded. "*Oui.* But of course. I am going to retire as *l' Inspector General.*"

His obvious determination and sincerity made Barbara smile. So did her father but he then said, "It is getting late. I think it is time we said goodnight."

Raoul shrugged and nodded. Barbara was sure that the message in his eyes was that he did not want her to leave; that he really wanted to spend the whole night with her. To her own shocked surprise, she found she wasn't offended by the idea, rather aroused.

I'd better watch myself or this man will get me into bed! she thought.

The farewells sounded offhand and casual but to Barbara they were laden with vibrant tension and she again believed that Raoul was thinking the same as her.

Just as well Daddy is here, she told herself. *Anyway, I am too young.* But that wasn't very convincing, not when she knew that Marjorie was having sex with Willy almost every night. *And probably Wendy and Lofty are too,* she added.

Even having considered such an intimate state made her blush with shame and scandalized arousal. When the moment came to leave Barbara almost flung herself into Raoul's arms. Instead she kept a firm grip on her facial muscles and arms and hoped that she sounded suitably nonchalant.

As she and her father walked back to their car her father commented that Raoul seemed very nice. "A perfect gentleman anyway," he said.

"I suppose so," Barbara replied, trying to sound off-hand.

She didn't want her father to suspect how affected she'd been. Then she thought of a comment she'd heard Fiona use, that a gentleman was only a wolf with patience, and she blushed with shame again.

At home she checked that there were no cars in the street, then worried that they might have been tailed to the meeting with Raoul.

The secret agents might be on to him now, she thought.

That bothered her considerably, as did the idea of helping a foreigner to break the law. But, having said she would help Raoul, she now felt committed. She dug through her webbing and camp file and found two copies of the photocopied 1:25 000 map and one of the 1:10 000 scale enlargement. All were a bit dog-eared and had pencil lines for navigation drawn across them, plus mathematical calculations and notes scribbled on their backs. She always kept such things as mementos.

After some careful thought she pencilled a neat little X on the 1:25 000 scale map at the point where she had seen the piece of wreckage. That done she placed the map on her bedside table and prepared for bed. She carried on with her usual routine: teeth cleaning, toilet; saying goodnight to her father, then into her bedroom. But this time she varied it by not wearing her pyjamas. Even contemplating such an action made her blush but a sense of excited naughtiness seemed to grip her.

Having slipped off her clothes Barbara stood and critically examined her body in the full-length mirror. What she saw, she liked. She was also peculiarly aware that her whole body seemed to be tingling in a most unfamiliar way. Very gently she cupped her breasts and squeezed them. Then memories of the American Secret Agents caused her to blush with shame, at the same time as she squirmed with a naughty gladness. Concern about her getting into trouble for exposing herself briefly spoiled her mood before she shrugged and thought about Raoul. To her own embarrassed surprise, she knew she had an urge to let him see her nude.

Slowly she pirouetted in front of the mirror, while sliding her hands down her body. As she did she remembered that she might be under surveillance by secret agents. That made her cover her front and look anxiously out the side window. Because trees obscured the neighbours houses she had never bothered with blinds or curtains but now the glimmer of light from a window in the house at the back made her peer out. But the light was difficult to see and leaves mostly blocked the view.

"No," she decided, but it left her feeling exposed, so she turned off her light and climbed into bed.

As she lay in bed she gently slid her hands down over her body, her imagination replacing them with Raoul's.

What will it be like? she wondered, then realised what she had said.

To ease her guilt, she told herself she had been thinking of some hypothetical future husband, and not Raoul, but it was his face that kept forming in her mind's eye. It was also his tanned, fit body that she fantasized at touching and which she imagined pressing against her.

"He said he could easily fall in love with me," she murmured, savouring the memory of the kiss.

Love! Just thinking about it set her heart pounding. And all the thoughts were not just pure romance. To her own subsequent shame, she found her hands caressing her own body. *Oh! If only!*

Those thoughts and actions got her quite aroused and she alternately burned with desire and shame. Then she remembered Roger and burned with guilt. It was made worse by being aware that, in her mind, Roger was just a nice boy, but Raoul was a real man.

A real man! He will love me for sure.

Thinking such romantic thoughts, she drifted off to sleep. It was a deep, restful sleep from which she woke refreshed but also warm with arousal from a very erotic dream. Barbara did not normally have dreams like that and it left her feeling both heated, and ashamed. What Raoul had been about to do was not something she had never let any boy even try before!

Memories of that dream mingled with fantasies about the previous evening's dinner to keep her happy and excited, except when she remembered she was joining Roger and the others for a picnic. Then guilt and concern replaced the pleasure. But there was a whole morning to fill in so she busied herself with household chores: vacuuming, dusting, washing, polishing and generally tidying up. She also cleaned out her webbing and pack, washing and re-packing her mess gear, stove and other small items normally kept there. The webbing and pack were then hung up under the house.

I wonder if I will ever use them to go camping again? she thought, touching them regretfully. *I will have to hand them back to the Q Store soon anyway.*

Her boots she dusted and put in the cupboard and her camouflage uniforms were packed away. She then prepared for the picnic, packing towel, sunscreen, cold cordial and snacks. Over her one-piece swimsuit she wore only shorts and T-shirt, plus sandals and a straw hat.

After lunch her father drove her over to Roger's. On arrival there her father said goodbye. "Be home for tea please," he said.

"I will be. I have to meet Lieutenant de Berg this evening at seven thirty," Barbara replied. She almost called him Raoul but changed just in time, not wanting her father to suspect she was so taken by him.

As her father drove away Roger met her at the front gate. Seeing his cheerful smile caused Barbara a distinct twinge of guilt and she understood enough to realize that was why she hurried forward to give him a hug. As they rarely exchanged such affection Roger was surprised and that also reinforced what Barbara was thinking—that Roger was a good friend but not her true love. She could not help contrasting his chubby frame with the muscled fitness of Raoul. Even Mark Guy's image danced briefly in her mind to torment her guilty conscience.

Roger led her in under his house. This was a lovely old high-set Queenslander similar to her own home but underneath was the 'Train Room'. Over the years Roger and his friends had constructed a huge model railway and looking at it reinforced the message that Roger was still really just a boy. It also caused Barbara to feel sorry for Roger. His friends of the 'Hiking Team': Graham, Peter and Stephen, were all a year ahead and had left school. Not one was still in town. Graham had gone into the Regular Army and Peter and Stephen to universities in the south.

Poor old Roger! He's is a bit left out now, she thought. He had friends in his own class and at cadets, but it was clear to her that they were not as close.

Once again, her guilt caused her to act uncharacteristically and she moved to study the model railway. It was really quite a magnificent construction, taking up almost half the underneath of the house. It was built in five distinct sections. Closest, and built on a solid timber frame at knee height, was a coastal plain with sugar farms, a sugar mill and a small town and port. Behind that was a range of mountains up which a line wound its way through tunnels. Barbara knew that this represented the Kuranda Range. Behind the mountains, at chest height, was an area of farms and forest with three small towns and a timber mill. The back section was a range of dry hills through which a tiny N-gauge railway wound its way. This was the mining area west of the Atherton Tablelands.

A dozen electric trains were parked on various sidings. It was plain from the dust which had collected on them that Roger had not played with the railway in months. Noting that caused Barbara another wave of sadness. For something to say she asked if the trains could be run.

Roger shook his head. "Not really. All the tracks have dirt on them and need cleaning." Seeing Barbara's mystified look, he explained. "If the rails aren't clean there is poor electrical contact and the motors either won't run, or they jerk along." As Barbara nodded he went on. "Where were you last night?" he asked.

"I went out to dinner with Daddy," Barbara replied. Even as she said it she despised herself for not telling the truth and she blushed.

"Where did you go?" Roger asked.

Barbara told him, and he raised his eyebrows. "That's supposed to be very posh. It must have cost an arm and a leg."

"It probably did," Barbara answered. "I don't know. I didn't pay. But it was certainly lovely."

As she said this her mind was swamped with images of Raoul and that wonderful kiss. Stabs of guilt caused her to blush some more. Luckily, she was saved from further questioning by the arrival of Lofty, Wendy and Fiona. After cheerful greetings they all trooped out to Lofty's car and climbed in. Barbara made sure she sat between Roger and Fiona and she made a point of snuggling against Roger, hoping to feel the magic of love and arousal. Instead she just enjoyed a pleasant drive with her friends.

Twenty minutes later, they pulled up outside the kiosk at Ellis Beach. Barbara had been there dozens of times so the view of the Coral Sea framed by coconut palms barely registered. Roger bought her a soft drink and an ice cream, and the friends gathered under the trees at the front to chat and eat.

"Where shall we go?" Lofty asked.

"Along to the north end of the beach," Wendy replied.

"What's wrong with here?" Roger asked.

Wendy reddened and giggled. "I wanted to do a bit of sunbathing and there is that nice little beach among the rocks around the point," she said.

Lofty smiled back at her and nodded. Barbara did not care where they went. There were a dozen lovely picnic spots along that section of coast and one place was as good as another to her at that moment. She was mildly amused by Wendy's sunbathing suggestion and decided she would join her if she did not mind.

So they drove another couple of kilometres north along the Cook Highway and parked at the edge of the beach near a rocky point. There were a few other picnickers, but the main sweep of beach was mostly deserted, just four kilometres of white sand fronting the sparkling blue sea. Bags were carried down to the shade of a she-oak at the top of the beach and they settled there on their towels for a few minutes.

Wendy pulled off her T-shirt, revealing a white one-piece swimsuit. She asked Lofty to apply sun cream, a task which he attended to with loving relish. By then Barbara had taken off her own T-shirt but she then found herself feeling unusually reticent. When Roger suggested he apply sun cream to her back and shoulders she smiled and said yes, but actually did not feel like such attention at all. It was another set of well-muscled hands she wanted to do that task.

A swim helped to ease the social situation but not for long. Barbara did not particularly like swimming in the sea. Having grown up in Cairns she had a phobia about jelly fish stings and was also quite paranoid about sharks. Even though it was not the 'Stinger' season she still could not relax in the water. Seeing Lofty and Wendy playing together, touching and hugging, did not help. Jealousy and frustration both nettled her. After about twenty minutes she made her way back up to the tree and towelled herself dry.

Wendy joined her and said, "I want to go around behind those rocks there to do some sunbathing. I want to wear a strapless gown to the formal and don't want any strap marks showing. Would you like to join me, Barbara?"

"If you want," Barbara agreed.

"I'll come too," Fiona said.

"What about us?" Lofty asked with a cheeky grin.

Wendy poked her tongue and said, "You boys can just relax here for a while."

"Aaaw!" Lofty wailed in jest.

"You get to see more than enough as it is," Wendy said to him, then realized what she had said and coloured a deep red. She made a face at the others. "Oh, poo to you! Come on girls," she cried.

Snatching up her bag and towel, Wendy set off along the beach. Barbara saw Lofty blush and noted that he was aroused. Normally she was offended by any overt displays of male sexuality or lust, but now she just felt glad for Wendy and experienced a pang of yearning. The thought that it would be nice to have that effect on a man who loved her made her look at Roger. But he was just... well, just Roger. Feeling curiously sad, Barbara jammed on her straw hat, scooped up her towel and sun cream and followed with Fiona. The two boys sat down to talk.

The girls strolled along, chatting and happy; except that Barbara was only pretending. For some reason she felt quite tense. She had been nude with both Fiona and Wendy before so did not think it was any anxiety about that (She was sure Wendy meant nude sunbathing!).

The girls walked a hundred metres north to where a low point of rocks ran down to the sea. They clambered around this, staying just above the tide level and dodging the small waves that swilled and sloshed up near their feet (This was the Coral Sea, with no real surf because of the Great Barrier Reef). Around the point was a small beach studded with numerous large rocks. The beach was backed by a rocky hillside covered with a belt of dry bush, effectively hiding it from vehicles travelling along the highway.

The next problem was to select a spot they all liked and which was suitably secluded. In finding this they walked a bit further than they intended, going nearly another hundred metres. Having decided on a nice sandy stretch between two large outcrops of black and grey rock the girls spread their towels. With a lot of cheerful but obviously nervous chatter they sat down. Then shyness temporarily overcame them. Wendy broke this by looking at the other two and saying, "You don't mind if I strip off do you?"

Barbara had to smile and then remembered herself standing nude at the door and went red.

What a hypocrite I am, she thought.

She shook her head, and after a careful look in both directions along the beach, moved to peel off her own bathers. As she rolled them down she glanced at the others and felt a rush of thrill and pleasure.

The others did likewise, with a lot of nervous but excited glancing. Then they sat side by side and talked. Barbara knew she was being aroused by the situation and by the sight of the other girl's naked bodies and that bothered her.

Do I prefer women to men? she wondered.

Wendy began to smear sun cream on her front and Barbara found that even more arousing and she experienced deep urges she did not want to admit to. The conversation shifted to the boys when Fiona said, "What will we do if the boys try to peek?"

Wendy shrugged. "They don't have to peek. They could have joined us if you didn't mind."

That thought got Barbara all confused. The idea of Roger being nude with them did not seem to fit. *I can't see him doing that,* she thought. But she could imagine Raoul—and that got her daydreaming an exciting fantasy.

Fiona looked nervously at them both and then said, "I've never been nude with a boy, have you?"

Wendy looked at her in amazement. "Yes," she answered.

"With Lofty?" Fiona queried.

Wendy nodded. "Lots of times," she admitted.

"Oh, Wendy! You be careful," Fiona said, her face alive with embarrassed interest.

"Oh piffle!" Wendy retorted. "Lofty and I have been doing it for years. We know how to be safe."

Barbara blushed at that and wondered if she ever would, or could, do such a thing. Then she thought of Raoul and knew she would. Wendy rolled on her front and handed up her tube of sun cream.

"Would you put some cream on my back please Barb?"

Barbara took the tube and began to squirt dollops of cream on Wendy's bare skin. Wendy giggled and squirmed and Barbara found it very suggestive. Then she knelt beside her and began smearing the cream smoothly around. This was something she enjoyed doing, and which she liked having done to her, so she did it gently but firmly, combining it with a little massage. Fiona sat beside them, chatting on about men and what they liked.

Fiona must be getting a bit frustrated and randy, Barbara decided.

Then Fiona looked around and grunted with annoyance. "Oh drat! Here come some men."

Barbara looked up, following the direction of her gaze and saw two men walking down from the edge of the bush towards them. Both men were fully dressed in casual clothes, long trousers and shirts, and straw hats. Her initial reaction was annoyance and embarrassment but then her eyes took in the pistols the men carried in their hands and she felt her stomach contract in fear. Instantly irritating thoughts about perverts were swept aside.

Oh no! This looks like trouble!

Chapter 19

STUNNED

Barbara stared at the approaching men with growing horror. She now saw that they were both 'Middle-eastern' in appearance: swarthy complexions, black moustaches and dark eyes. Instinctively she knew they were not just ordinary perverts come to leer at girls.

They are the two spies who were watching my house, she thought.

Then, as they got closer, she recognized them as the two men who had spoken to Major Conkey on the Mingela Road at Dotswood near the One Mile Creek dip.

"Trouble," she muttered. "Bad trouble. Get dressed."

Wendy murmured in mild protest and lifted her head to look. Fiona, who had been sitting facing the sea while she rubbed sun cream on her front, glanced over her shoulder, then rolled onto her knees and snatched up her towel to try to cover herself. Barbara groped for her bathers, her eyes on the two men. She saw their eyes glitter and one briefly licked his lips with the tip of his tongue. But it was the guns that had Barbara scared, not the possibility of sexual assault. Both men had automatic pistols fitted with silencers.

Fear flooded Wendy's face and she blanched. "Oh my God!" she gasped. She squirmed over onto her back, her fleshy body all quivering as she did. She sat up and began trying to pull on her bathers.

Barbara was now all in a fluster, almost paralyzed by fear. Part of her mind wanted her to cover her nudity, but the other part was overwhelmed by the growing terror which told her that sex was not a part of this. That the men were coming to get her she had no doubt. She tried to hold her bathers so as to get into them but could not find the openings for her feet. So she gave this up and grabbed at the edge of her towel and attempted to cover herself. As she was kneeling on it this was less than successful and she crouched to hide herself.

The men came to a standstill a few paces away, their eyes raking the girl's bodies as they scrambled to cover themselves. The man on the right met Barbara's eyes and gave what looked like an evil grin.

He removed a cigarette from his mouth and pointed it at her then said, "You come with us."

Barbara could only nod. She sensed that resistance would lead to instant violence. *I must wait my chance,* she thought, her mental faculties almost swamped by nausea.

By now Fiona had covered herself with her towel and she knelt back, her arms tucking the cloth under her armpits.

"Who are you? Go away!" she cried indignantly.

The second man pointed his gun at her. "Be quiet little girl, or I will shoot you."

Barbara had some difficulty understanding him because of his accent but the gun, and his hard eyes, made his meaning chillingly clear. She swallowed and then said, "Don't do anything, Fiona. They mean it. They are spies after the satellite."

The first man, obviously the leader, frowned at her. He replaced his cigarette and puffed at it. The second man was distracted by Wendy's attempts to get her foot into her bathers. In the process her huge breasts swung and bobbled, and Barbara noted the men's eyes ogling them with obvious lust. But her real fear was that the spies might shoot both Wendy and Fiona to stop them talking.

Crack!

The leader of the spies suddenly spun round and fell hard against the rock beside Barbara, then slumped on his back on the sand. Barbara noted the red drops and the wide, staring eyes but it took a moment before the stunning realization came to her that the man had been shot. Not only shot, but shot in the head and very obviously dead. A thick flow of dark, red blood began welling from the back of his shattered skull, staining the sand and soaking into it.

The second spy turned and gaped at his companion. His mouth opened, and the cigarette almost fell out. Then understanding dawned and he spun round. At the same instant Barbara understood that this was real. She tensed to try to grab the man's arm or gun so that he could not harm or threaten Fiona or Wendy. Even as she did the man realized his peril and began to turn back towards her.

Crack!

This time Barbara saw the bullet strike and was stunned. Chunks of hair, bone and flesh were flung up in a fine, pink mist from the side of the man's head. The impact was so violent that the man was hurled to the ground at her feet. There he gave several spasmodic twitches before a final shudder, after which he lay still. A look of stunned amazement was fixed on his face and the cigarette remained stuck to his bottom lip.

This can't be true, Barbara told herself, so unreal and unlikely did it all seem. But deep down she knew it was and realized she had been half-expecting something to happen. Horror caused her to choke up and gasp for breath.

Both Wendy and Fiona stared at the man in shock. As a spurt of scarlet squirted from his shattered skull Wendy's eyes opened wide and she screamed. Fiona began to sob and gasp, crying.

"Oh my God! What is going on? What is happening?"

By then Barbara had recovered from her first shock and her racing mind told her that she and her friends were in great danger. Whoever had shot the men could obviously see them.

"Get down!" she yelled, dragging at Wendy's arm. Wendy lifted terror-stricken eyes to meet Barbara's but reacted to her command and flung herself flat on her towel. By then Barbara was also down beside the rock, her eyes scanning the bush on the hillside. That was the direction the shots had come from, but she found she was so scared and flustered that her eyes could not focus to search properly.

Wendy screamed again and huddled against Barbara, her eyes fixed on the face of the first dead spy, who lay on his back only a metre from them. Barbara glanced back and saw that Fiona was still kneeling and was staring in stunned disbelief at the dead men. "Fiona! Get down! Get behind the rock," Barbara shouted.

Then she turned her attention back to the bush. Part of her brain had already made the technical assessment that whoever had shot the two spies was a very good shot and that, if they wanted to, they could just as easily shoot her or her friends. That got her sweating with pure fear and thinking about cover.

The shots came from over there, she decided. *So we need to get on the seaward side of the rocks to be under cover.*

She turned and gestured urgently, "Get back! Crawl around to the back of the rocks."

Neither Wendy nor Fiona moved. Both seemed to be transfixed by the sheer horror of it all. Barbara swore and looked around, seeking frantically for a rational plan. Her eyes took in the open hand of the first dead spy. Lying near it on the sand was his pistol. Thinking to use it for self-defence she crawled forward. The discomfort of the sand sticking to her bare skin she ignored.

As Barbara reached out for the pistol movement among the rocks fifty metres away caught her eye. A running man burst into sight, scuttling from rock to rock towards her. The man wore dark long trousers, and a white, long-sleeved shirt and tie. Over the outside of his shirt he wore some sort of camouflage vest festooned with pockets, pouches and a radio. Across his front he clutched a wicked looking, black, automatic rifle with a telescopic sight. His short haircut and clean-cut appearance made connections click in Barbara's synapses and she gasped.

"The American Secret Service agent!"

As he got closer the American, Chuck Wilson Barbara remembered, snarled, "Don't touch the gun! Lie down!"

Barbara's fingers had been about to close on the butt of the pistol but faced by the threat of Chuck's rifle she froze. Chuck arrived with a dash, casting a sour, disapproving glance at the naked girls. He bent to check the pulse on the first spy, then placed his fingers against the neck of the second. "Both dead. Keep us covered," he said.

Barbara at first thought that Chuck was speaking to her but then she saw that he had a throat microphone and a wire trailing down from an earpiece.

He is talking to someone else, she thought, her eyes again scanning the bush at the top of the beach.

Chuck scooped up the first spy's pistol, clicked the safetycatch on and thrust the weapon into a pouch on his vest. Then he looked at Barbara. "Get dressed!" he snapped.

By now Barbara knew she was on the edge of hysteria. She was trembling and deeply shocked. It took all her will power not to break into sobs. Gasping in deep breaths she glared defiance back.

"Get stuffed!" she retorted. Outrage was now being added to fear to fuel her anger.

Chuck scowled back then gestured towards the sea. "Get back behind these rocks you girls. You are in terrible danger."

He grabbed at Barbara's arm, but she twisted free, the sweat and sun cream on her skin making her slippery enough to break his grip. Rather than allow him to grab her again she turned and scrambled back behind the rock. Her towel and bathers she left lying on the sand. Chuck glared but then grabbed at Wendy. She stared at him wildly, her face streaked with tears and her bosom heaving as she gasped for breath. With a strong heave Chuck got her up and pushed her. She went sprawling on the sand over behind Barbara. Then Chuck reached for Fiona. Shrieking with terror she shook him off but went into a crouch behind the other rock. In the process she stood on the hem of her towel and lost it. Terrified she paused to snatch at it but Chuck pushed her behind cover.

Chuck scuttled over beside Barbara and levelled his rifle around the side of the rock, facing back towards the hillside. After a quick glance to check they were all crouching down he reached for the radio hooked onto the front of the vest. "Hawk, this is Stingray. Get that helo round here quick, over," he said.

Barbara did not hear the reply by 'Hawk' but Chuck answered. "Four enemy. Two dead and two more up beside their car on the highway. They have A. K.s, so be ready to give covering fire, over."

By now Barbara was trembling violently as shock and fear swept through her. Her mind felt stunned, but she was able to work out that Chuck was talking to someone in a helicopter. She was also appalled to learn that there were two more spies up at the road and that had Kalashnikov automatic rifles. Having seen them a hundred times on the TV news she knew exactly what he was talking about. The thought sent chills of dread through her.

Wendy now grabbed at Barbara. "Barbara, what is going on?" she cried, her voice rising to a shriek.

"Spies," Barbara replied, her breath coming in hot gasps as though she had run a race. "This guy is an American Secret Agent." She indicated Chuck, who frowned at her, then resumed scanning the hillside.

Chuck muttered something into his radio in reply to a question and then turned his head to the right. Out of curiosity Barbara followed his gaze. A faint tremor in the gentle breeze confirmed that she was thinking and a moment later, when the tremor became a noticeable vibration she knew she was right.

I did hear correctly. He was talking to a helicopter. And here it is! she thought.

Into view swept a grey painted helicopter. It was very low, just above the waves, and came around the next headland to the north very fast. Not being particularly interested in aircraft Barbara had only a rough idea what type it was but it looked to her like a Blackhawk. She had flown in army Blackhawks several times so was familiar with the machines. What she did note as it got closer was that it wore no obvious markings, being painted a dull grey all over. Only as it turned in and came to a hover just over the edge of the beach did she make out the faint lettering saying NAVY.

She could only gape in surprise as it settled and soldiers in dark green and brown camouflage uniforms and wearing webbing and helmets began to jump out. A door gunner sat crouched behind a twin machine gun on a pintle mounting. The soldiers were armed to the teeth and obviously meant business. The whole impression was hi-tech: helmet night vision mountings, night sights on the automatic weapons, radios, and odd attachments fitted to webbing and weapons.

Americans, Barbara decided, seeing the AR15 rifles and dark green/ brown camouflage.

They were obviously talking to Chuck and taking orders from him as he pointed to their leader and the soldiers—marines, Barbara corrected— scattered and went to cover among the rocks. Chuck then turned to face back up the slope and began talking again on his radio. Barbara crouched to protect herself from the stinging grains of sand being stirred up by the rotor wash. She was still so stunned she was merely noting, rather than reacting, to events. But she did note that the downdraft had blown away her bathers and towel, and that several of the marines were continually glancing at her and the other girls in wide-eyed amazement.

Then she saw the second Secret Agent break cover and come running down the beach. He had some sort of sub-machine gun clutched in his hands but what really struck Barbara was the pair of binoculars slung around his neck. They looked large and powerful.

They have been watching us! she realized with dismay.

That stirred indignation. Under the stress of fear and sickening disgust this began to evolve to a smouldering, unreasoning anger.

Chuck now turned and pointed to the helicopter. "Get in!" he shouted.

That shocked Barbara even more. By now she was feeling really angry, as well as scared. That stung her to defiance. "No! You go away and leave us alone," she shouted back.

She saw Chuck's eyes flick to her naked body, then away and she realized that her nudity was bothering him.

He is embarrassed, she decided. *Good, the bloody prude! I will show him!* Quite deliberately she relaxed from covering herself, using her nude body as weapon.

Chuck went very red then shook his head angrily. He tried to keep his eyes focused on her face. "You can't stay," he yelled. "It is too dangerous. There are more Dags up there with guns. They want to kidnap you and will probably kill you."

Barbara believed him but got stubborn. "Dags?" she cried.

"From Dagestan, in Central Asia," Chuck shouted back. He stood up and reached across to grab her arm.

Barbara knew her geography well enough to place roughly where Dagestan was, and she knew enough of current affairs to know it was a military dictatorship in the grip of Moslem Fundamentalists. Even so she resisted Chuck's attempt to seize her. Once again, she slipped out of his grip but he was both determined and angry. He shouted and next moment Barbara found herself gripped from behind by a pair of camouflage clad arms. One of the marines had her in his grip and he was strong.

For a moment Barbara froze as her mind tried to grapple with the reality of it all. Even now anger and indignation were her main emotions, more at being man-handled than the fact that the marine's arms were tight up under her breasts. She found herself lifted off her feet and carried towards the helicopter. The indignity of it made her furious. Kicking and squirming did no good. She was powerless in the man's grip. To add to her humiliation, she could see the faces of the helicopter crew leering at her nakedness.

A crewman reached out and grabbed her arms. She started to struggle until common sense told her that she needed to get away from the place and the American helicopter was probably the safest option at that moment. With an effort of will power she forced herself to relax and be guided into a seat. The fact that her breasts got a good squeezing and bumping in the process was only dimly noted. Then she found herself staring at the dark tinted visor of a flying helmet. The crewman was saying something, but she could not hear him. All she was aware of was his groping hands down at her hips.

She looked down and saw he was trying to fasten a seat belt around her. It was obvious he was getting a good, close look at her more intimate details as he did this. His gloved hands were busy just above her groin. That both angered and amused her. Waves of warmth swept through her: shame and arousal. To end it she helped, and he soon had the belt pulled over her stomach and clipped up. He then pulled the ends to tighten it before turning back to the door.

Barbara now looked out and saw Wendy and Fiona both running towards the helicopter, and both in the grip of a marine. Wendy was in front and her breasts were bouncing so wildly Barbara could not help remembering that her school nickname was 'Wobbles'. She was making no attempt to cover herself and looked quite bewildered and frightened. The burly marine had to push at her bum to help her up and Barbara saw him grinning as he got a good close look. Wendy was helped up by the crewman. In the process he could not help bumping her bosom. Wendy did not seem to notice, just slumped thankfully down in a seat and threw Barbara a look of relief.

Fiona still clutched her towel over her breasts but the rest of it was trailing in the wind exposing her lower body and legs. Barbara could not help admiring the delightful curves of Fiona's hips and thighs.

Gee, she is shapely, she thought. Fiona looked very pale but had herself back under control.

As she was helped into the helicopter both the Secret Agents ran over. Barbara saw the younger one glance at Fiona's buttocks and then purse his lips and look away. That both amused and annoyed her.

You ignorant dick! she thought. *God made women shapely for men to admire and you turn your nose up at one as pretty as Fiona!*

While Fiona was being moved past her to another seat a roaring noise made Barbara glance outside. She saw that a second helicopter had arrived and was settling on the beach. Two marines ran to it and scrambled in and the engine note changed to a deeper roar. Even as Fiona was settled in her seat the helicopter lifted off. Barbara knew what to expect but still found it a peculiar sensation. To her it all felt very insecure and she tensed.

The helicopter did not lift far. Instead it backed away and turned sideways so that the door gunner could aim his machine guns better. Barbara saw that the remaining marines had grabbed the bodies of the two Dag spies and were carrying them down to the second helicopter.

Shouldn't they leave them for the police investigation? she wondered.

As the helicopter lifted higher Barbara tried to lean out to see if Lofty and Roger were watching. However, the machine turned the other way and she did not get a clear look. All she could then see was the sea and the mountainous coastline stretching away to the north. Then the helicopter put its nose slightly down and began racing fast out to sea.

Chuck now seated himself opposite Barbara and fumbled at the seat belt, helped by the crewman. The other Secret Agent seated himself opposite Wendy and the two marines sat on the outside, weapons pointing out. Barbara swivelled her head from side to side to confirm her first impression.

We are heading east, straight out to sea, she decided. *Where on earth are we going?*

Chapter 20

A PROMISE

Barbara leaned forward and shouted above the roar of the helicopter's engines, "Where are we going?"

Chuck leaned towards her, studiously avoiding looking at her naked body. "You'll see. Won't be long."

"I want to be taken ashore," Barbara replied. "Take us to Cairns please."

"It isn't safe," Chuck replied.

That annoyed Barbara. Already her emotions were in turmoil: shock, disgust, fear, indignation, shame; and now smouldering outrage at the way she had been manhandled onto the helicopter. She rubbed at her breasts and bent to examine them to see if they were bruised. There were certainly red marks. Partly she did this to discomfort Chuck and his sidekick as she could tell they did not approve and were deeply embarrassed. To her own subsequent shame, she felt an unreasoning desire to hurt.

She pointed back towards the rapidly receding coastline, aware that already the mountains were almost lost in the haze. "I want to go back to the shore. You have no right to take me anywhere against my will. That is abduction."

That comment had come as a result of her mind turning over the events of the last few minutes. It really bothered her that the American Secret Agents had been following them and keeping them under surveillance, but it had been the helicopters that had crystallised her ideas.

This wasn't some spur of the moment rescue, she reasoned. *These helicopters were waiting close by, flying around.*

Chuck made no answer to her accusation and pretended to have difficulty hearing as he cupped his ear. He then spoke to the crewman who rummaged around under the seats and then held out three buoyancy vests. Fiona accepted hers gratefully and quickly slipped into it, then adjusted her towel over her lower body. Wendy also took one but getting it on became a major distraction. She had to lean forward and do a lot of wriggling. This caused her boobs to bobble and sway and then the jacket was too small to do up over them. She blushed fiercely and then squashed her breasts together using the jacket. In the end she held her arms over her front and hunched up. All this provided a diversionary spectacle that had the two Secret Agents deeply embarrassed and pretending not to look, the crewman shaking his head in disbelief, and the two marines openly leering.

All that annoyed Barbara even more and made her stubborn. She took the lifejacket and held it over her front but made no attempt to put it on. The crewman made gestures, but she just shook her head and ignored him. Finally, Chuck yelled at her: "Put the lifejacket on!"

"No!"

"You gotta."

"Why?"

"Safety Regulations," Chuck replied angrily.

"Not my regulations. I didn't ask to be put on this helicopter. I am here against my will. Take me back to the shore," Barbara retorted. Driven by the urge to resist she deliberately lowered the lifejacket and allowed her breasts to sway with the motion of the machine.

I'm as bad as Chloe! she thought. Then she smiled as an impish urge to be naughty and to tease took hold.

Chuck looked very angry at being disobeyed and for a moment Barbara thought he would order the crewman to forcibly dress her. He was obviously deeply embarrassed and looked away. Barbara felt a pang of sympathy.

Poor man. He probably has a really nice mother and sister and has been brought up all religious and strict.

Still Chuck persisted. He ordered the two marines to take off their shirts. To do this they had to hand their weapons to Chuck and his offsider, then take off their webbing. Once this was achieved Chuck passed one shirt to Wendy and held one up for Barbara.

"Put the life jacket on and wrap this shirt around you," he said.

Barbara had been admiring the rippling muscles of the marine opposite her but now met Chuck's eyes and shook her head defiantly. She could see that both Wendy and Fiona looked apprehensive, even scared. She was feeling frightened herself, but also very angry.

Anger flared in Chuck's eyes, but he kept his face under control. "I don't want to have to force you," he said.

"You could ask nicely! You could say please!" Barbara retorted.

At that Chuck did blush and the sight of the marine grinning did not help his temper. "I'd like you to," he managed to say.

"Why should I?" Barbara asked, adding, "And don't give me any of that religious stuff as a reason."

For a moment Chuck breathed deeply and appeared to grind his teeth. His companion looked hurt. Chuck then said, "Because we will get into trouble when we arrive."

"You will be in trouble," Barbara replied, "For kidnapping and sexual assault."

At that Chuck looked shocked. A worried frown crossed his face. His companion spoke up. "Say! That's not fair. We saved your life. I had to kill two men to rescue you."

"Thou shalt not kill!" quoted Barbara. Then she said, "So we add two counts of murder to the charges."

As she said this the pattern of the sea changed. The helicopters had been racing low over the surface of the ocean, almost skimming the waves, but now the colours changed abruptly. Barbara looked out and saw lighter colours, the patches of brown and pale green and knew instantly where they were.

We are crossing the Great Barrier Reef, she thought. *We must be going to a ship.*

She had suspected that, but when the ship suddenly came into view off to starboard she gasped. *An aircraft carrier!* she noted.

Chuck saw her look and turned his head, then looked back at her. "Nearly there. Now will you please cover up?"

Barbara was so amazed that she nodded, another spasm of worry adding to her already apprehensive emotions. This was real, it was big, and it was way outside her experience. She saw that Wendy had pulled her shirt on, just managing to get a couple of buttons done up but leaving quite a cleavage exposed. For the moment Barbara decided to play along, the germ of an idea forming as she put the life jacket on the floor.

Chloe will be proud of me, she thought as she slid her arm into a sleeve of the shirt.

As she slipped the shirt on the young marine openly admired her breasts and even Chuck's offsider kept flicking his eyes to them. To keep her advantage Barbara deliberately made her boobs quiver and wobble as she adjusted the shirt. Then she held it closed across her front. She did not button it up, nor did she pick up the lifejacket.

By then the helicopter had come to a hover above and beside the aircraft carrier. Barbara had often seen such ships on TV, but she was now quite amazed at the massive size of the thing. It was like a mountain of grey steel sticking out of the ocean. The flight deck was crowded with aircraft and helicopters and there seemed to be dozens of men working there. Then the helicopter swung inboard and began to settle. Through the starboard door Barbara saw the huge 'island' superstructure come into view with its forest of masts and aerial. It seemed to her that every open space on it was crowded with watching men, most in mottled blue and grey uniforms, the others in marine camouflage. Seeing them firmed Barbara's idea.

The helicopter settled onto the flight deck and men wearing bright coloured suits, helmets, goggles and ear protection appeared at the door. The crewman stood up and leaned over to undo the girl's seat belts. One of the marines jumped down, followed by Chuck and his offsider. The weapons and webbing were passed out and then the girls were invited to step down. A set of steps had been unfolded for them. Fiona went first, gripping her towel tightly but putting out one hand for a deck crewman to steady her with. She was led across the deck towards a doorway where a cluster of men were standing watching.

Wendy climbed down next. As she did she had to use one hand to try to hold down the hem of the shirt, which kept blowing up in the downdraft from the still spinning rotors. Barbara clearly saw her bum a few times, as did the men helping and watching. Then it was her turn. By then she was breathing so fast she was almost hyperventilating. An emotion she had never experienced was gripping her and she seemed to be all a-tingle, her mind separate from her trembling body.

She waited till Wendy was well clear of the steps before standing up. The shirt she gripped with one hand, using the other to keep her balance. At the door she paused and looked around, noting that all the men working on the nearby aircraft were watching. The grey painted jet fighters parked in a row she recognized.

Harrier Jump Jets, she thought. *Now, let's make these guys jump!*

Chuck was standing few metres away talking to an officer in cams. A crewman held up a hand to steady her so she accepted the offer and took his hand. Stepping carefully down Barbara noted the men crowding the little platforms on the superstructure. She also noted that the wind was strong, more than a stiff breeze. It was blowing the hem of the shirt up and she could feel the wind cold around her buttocks. That suited her too.

To her own surprise the most obvious feeling she had was the tactile one of the roughness of the flight deck on her bare feet. But she was deeply angry and feeling very rebellious. She now acted on that. As soon as the crewman released her hand she stepped clear and shrugged the shirt off, letting the wind whip it away. She then stared defiantly up at the window and balconies above, before striding forward.

There was a sort of shocked pause as men stared and obviously did not believe what they were seeing. Mouths dropped open and eyes widened. Barbara stopped and turned to watch the second helicopter. It was now coming down to land further back along the flight deck. Then Chuck's furiously angry face appeared in from if hers.

"Get dressed! Cover yourself!" he screamed.

Barbara pretended not to hear and cupped her hand to her left ear. Chuck seized her elbow and spun her round, then pushed her towards the doorway. That angered Barbara even more. For a moment she stalled, resisting his efforts to propel her along. Suddenly hands seized her from behind and she felt cloth being wrapped around her. In the process the man's arms squashed her boobs.

Anger flared and Barbara spun round, her hand lashing out.

Smack! She struck the man's face hard, then instantly regretted it. He was a young sailor and he was holding the shirt for her. The hurt and stunned look on his face caused her an immediate surge of sympathy.

The poor boy! He didn't expect that. He was only trying to help, she thought, noting at the same time that he was not only fresh-faced but actually very good looking.

Full of instant contrition, she bent forward. "I'm sorry. I just reacted. Please help me."

The boy looked baffled as well as hurt but he nodded and held the shirt open. Barbara turned her back on him and slipped her left arm into a sleeve. As she got it on she moved to hold the sailor's hand across her bosom. She then held it there while she slid the other sleeve on. Driven by the thrill and arousal she gripped his hand and squeezed it to her breasts, then released him and turned to face him. By now he was looking flustered as well as stunned. She noted the clear, red outline of a hand on the side of his face so leaned forward and quickly kissed the cheek.

"Thanks," she murmured.

Then she spun on her heel and strode towards the door. Now she was regretting her exhibitionist impulse. Ahead of her she saw faces, which were more gaping mouths than anything. Among them she recognized Wendy's and Fiona's shocked faces. By this time Barbara was so emotionally disturbed that she knew she wasn't thinking straight. But she managed to walk defiantly across to the doorway ahead of her. As she did sailors and marines parted before her, making her feel that the situation was even more unreal.

Through the door hurried more men, some in bright yellow coloured suits and with red cross armbands. Each held open a blanket. Barbara realized their intention as they rushed over and tried to enfold her in one. It caused her temper to explode again and she fended off the first man's attempts.

"Leave me alone! Keep your hands off me!" she screamed.

She knew she wasn't acting rationally but was so angry she did not care. The navy medic looked surprised and baffled but tried again. This time Barbara dodged and swung a slap at him. Her hand just clipped his cheek and a look of hurt surprise appeared. Still not comprehending the man tried again. This time Barbara sprang at him and raised her hands like claws to scratch at his face. The man was lucky she did not scratch him, and he stepped back just in time.

Another man appeared in Barbara's vision: middle-aged, dressed in khaki and holding a peaked cap in his left-hand. His mouth was working furiously, and he yelled at her, "Git yourself covered up girlie!"

"No! Go away! Let me go!" Barbara shouted. She went into a defiant crouch with her hands still curled into claws. As she did the shirt she wore flapped open and she didn't care.

The man looked very angry. "You obey orders on my ship," he shouted, his eyes flicking to her body and his face mottling a deep red. "Now cover yourself up and stop prancin' around like a two-bit whore."

The insulting name took a few moments to sink in but when it did it roused Barbara to a new pitch of fury. "Don't you call me disgusting names, you arrogant foreigner! I didn't ask to come to this ship and I'm not one of your sailors, so I'm not taking orders from you."

The man looked deeply annoyed and Barbara knew instinctively that he was some sort of senior officer. With an effort he mastered his anger and shouted back, trying to make himself heard above the sound of a helicopter's engine.

"This is a rescue mission. We are trying to help you. Now please co-operate."

As he finished the man nodded to someone beside Barbara. Before she could react, strong arms enfolded her in a blanket. In the process her arms were trapped and that sent a new surge of anger through her already over-charged system.

"Let me go!" she shouted angrily, but to no avail.

The engine noises mostly drowned out her protest and the men ignored her anyway and she found herself hustled through the doorway. In the process someone trod on her right toes, the pain so intense that she cried out and found her eyes swimming with tears.

By the time she could see properly again she had been pushed through another doorway into some sort of briefing room. The aircraft engine noises diminished sharply but were partly replaced by the steady humming of air conditioning and other shipboard motors.

In the background she heard an angry voice calling, "All you men get away from this area. Get back to your work stations, now move!"

Good! Barbara thought. *I've stirred them up.*

But then she began to shake and cry as the shock began to set in. Images of the men being shot returned with savage clarity to stun her with dismay and disbelief. A woman who must have been a navy doctor from her actions and her khaki uniform began to examine her in a small cabin to one side.

"Are you alright?" the doctor asked. "Do you need anything?"

"To be let go, and to be treated right," Barbara replied. She knew she was shaking and unsteady, but being spoken to helped her start to get a grip on herself.

"I'll just check you over," the doctor said, starting to unwrap the blanket.

"Keep your hands off me!" Barbara snapped. "I'm fine."

"It's alright. I'm a doctor," the woman replied. "Now sit down. You are in shock."

Barbara tried to protest but found herself slumping into a seat. "So I should be!" she retorted, "Seeing men just gunned down and murdered, then being manhandled and kidnapped."

The female doctor gave her a hard look at that and snapped back, "You got any complaints you better show me the bruises honey."

That both annoyed and steadied Barbara. She did want to look for bruises but did not want this woman seeing her body. She held the blanket tightly around her. The doctor raised her own eyebrows quizzically and then reached out and took hold of Barbara's wrist. Barbara made no attempt to stop her when she proceeded to take her pulse.

The doctor then nodded and said, "I'll just give you a little sedative."

That really alarmed Barbara. "No way! I'm not having you people drug me," she replied fiercely.

The doctor just kept taking her pulse, then her blood pressure, before pointing to a bundle of blue camouflage navy clothing.

"Fine then. Just slip these on and let us know what size foot you've got."

The doctor stood up and left the cabin, closing the door behind her, but not before Barbara noted a female sailor standing outside. Barbara then sat and considered what to do next. For a while her emotions just swirled.

For several minutes she just sobbed and trembled. Slowly she calmed down. Thinking back she knew she was on the edge of hysteria as ghastly images of the shootings filled her mind. She found she was both deeply ashamed at her brazen displays but also glad she had. For a while she rebelled at the idea of getting dressed, thinking to remain naked and defiant, but then she suddenly drained of energy and decided to co-operate to that extent.

Still shivering from the shock and excitement, she stood up and took off the blanket and shirt, then examined her body. There were several small bruises, but she wryly noted them and decided that they would not amount to much if she complained. She then picked up the clothing. This was just a pair of dark blue long trousers and a long-sleeved shirt, both standard US Navy issue with no badges on them. With a shrug she pulled them on and did them up. Not having any knickers or bra on made her feel uncomfortable but she did feel better and more able to face whatever was coming next.

That was a half-hour wait. Barbara just sat and tried to relax, her mind going over and over the shocking events of the last hour. Alternate waves of shame at her exhibitionism and feelings of deep satisfaction at having acted that way coursed through her. What then began to gnaw worryingly at her was being separated from her friends. At first, she had not even realized it was happening but now she badly wanted to know how they were and where they were. On top of that she began to feel concerned about all the people she knew must now be worrying about her: Roger, Lofty, her father. Then she remembered she was due to meet Raoul that evening and she really began to fret.

At length the door opened, and the female doctor came back in, followed by a female sailor in the blue camouflage work dress. On seeing that Barbara was dressed the doctor nodded with approval and gave her another quick check. The female sailor laid out three pairs of trainer shoes of different sizes, and some socks. Barbara tried the footwear on and found a pair that fitted. Quickly she pulled on the socks and laced up the trainers. Then she accepted the offer of a cup of coffee, but only with some reluctance, still being suspicious of being drugged.

The coffee was good, strong and sweet. It lifted her and she felt much better. More time went by and then a male officer came and told her to follow him. A male marine in cams took up a position behind her and followed them, irritating but also amusing Barbara.

What on earth do they think I might do? she wondered.

The group made its way along a corridor, passing half a dozen doorways, before ascending a flight of steps. All along the way they passed men working or walking by and it was obvious from the looks they gave her that her exploit was common gossip. It made her feel both embarrassed and pleassed.

Good! she thought. *They are wary of me and aren't just going to treat me as though I am a silly little girl.*

The trio stopped at a polished wooden door, outside which stood another male marine, this one in camouflage and wearing a helmet and side arms. There was a brass nameplate on the door, but it was some sort of acronym and Barbara did not have time to decipher it. The marine sentry knocked and the door was immediately opened. Barbara found herself in a large and well-appointed conference room, so well furnished that she found it hard to remember she was on a ship.

If she had felt intimidated by the simple HQ building at Dotswood and the lieutenant colonel there she now felt almost awed and overwhelmed by the gathering she confronted. There were seven men in the room, all looking grim and powerful. Barbara quickly glanced around, hoping to see Fiona or Wendy but there was no sign of them. She was ushered to an armchair facing a solid looking, grey-haired man dressed in khaki. A glance revealed two silver stars on the man's lapels.

Major General, she thought, then remembered that US Navy wore khaki as uniform on ships. She had to dig through her mind to come up with the naval equivalent rank and that helped her steady her shaken nerves. *Rear Admiral?* she decided.

The man stood up and offered his hand. "Rear Admiral McKinley," he said gruffly.

For a moment Barbara shied away from accepting the man's hand, but then she took it and held it for a brief shake. She was then offered the seat. Gratefully she lowered herself into the chair, her legs starting to shake. That made her glad of the long trousers. As she settled herself she glanced around the room, noting the two CIA agents, now in clean clothes, a navy officer in white with black epaulets and gold rank bars, two others in khaki with what looked like silver eagles on their epaulets, and a junior officer who was obviously some sort of aide or secretary.

There was a moment's silence then Rear Admiral McKinley said, "Well Miss Brassington, you have had an eventful few hours."

"I've had an eventful couple of weeks," Barbara replied. She was sure she could see what was coming.

They are going to soft soap me and then ask me to help them find the satellite, she thought. That got her all worried because she felt she had promised Raoul she would help him find it.

Rear Admiral McKinley smiled and nodded. "So I gather. Would you like to tell me about it?"

Something about the man irritated Barbara. Memories of being spied on, bribed and then the ghastly events on the beach flooded into her mind. Despite her fear she shook her head.

"Not really. I'm sure your spies have told you all about it. I just want to go home. Please take us back to the beach. My boyfriend will be getting very worried by now."

A flicker of irritation crossed the Rear Admiral's face. He said, "That is all being taken care of. We do not think it safe for you to go back."

"Why not?" challenged Barbara. She thought she knew, but wanted it confirmed.

"Surely you realize that those men were going to take you prisoner?"

Barbara nodded. "Who were they? Where were they from?"

At that Chuck leaned forward, met the Rear Admiral's eye and shook his head. The admiral said, "I'm not sure we can tell you that."

That did annoy Barbara. "Why not? It was me they were threatening! Don't give me that 'National Security' bull. If you want me to talk you have to give something too."

Both Chuck and Rear Admiral McKinley looked peeved. Chuck then said, "Dagestan. They had been watching you for days."

It took a moment for the implications of that to sink in. Then a deep anger began to splutter. "You mean you knew about it all that time and waited till the last minute to act?" she cried.

Rear Admiral McKinley frowned and leaned forward. "Say, that's a bit unfair. You might at least thank these gentlemen for saving you. They had to kill two men to do it."

"Thank them!" Barbara cried. "What you mean is that they used us as some sort of bait. You could have warned us instead."

Chuck coloured but stayed calm. "We tried to, but you er... you didn't want to listen."

"So you spied on me and my friends! You and your friend lurked in the bush spying on us like a pair of peeping-tom perverts. Then you set that ambush up. You must have, because helicopters don't stay hovering in the air for hours close by for no reason. You must have listened to our telephone conversations and planned the whole thing. I'm sorry. I'm not impressed and I'm not grateful. Anyone who can kill men without a flicker of an eyelid but blush when he sees a girl with no clothes on is morally deficient."

At that both Chuck and his fellow agent blushed deep red with embarrassment. A darker red suffused the Rear Admiral's face. Barbara went on, "I don't approve of foreigners coming into my country and carrying on their private wars. You could have left all of this to the Australian police. I'm sure they are efficient enough to deal with the situation. All you seem to have done is killed a couple of people and then fled the country. I want the Australian authorities informed."

The anger on the Rear Admiral's face became more obvious, the lines around the corners of his mouth and around his eyes deepening. He gestured to the naval officer in white. "This is Commander Grundy, Royal Australian Navy. He is your liaison officer. Everything is being passed on to your government. Your state and federal police are both being kept informed. That is how I can tell you that your friends and family are safe."

Hearing that made Barbara feel quite silly. It also deepened her already deep fear of the situation. This was obviously high-level government stuff and she was caught in the web, ignorant of most of the facts. To gain time and to show she did appreciate her family and friends being looked after she said, "Thank you for that. Now, can I go please?"

Rear Admiral McKinley pressed his lips together and tried to look calm and affable. "Of course, but first we would appreciate your help in finding the missing satellite."

That put Barbara squarely on the spot. She knew her only possible objection was that she had made a promise to Raoul.

Is my integrity more important than the security of my country?' she wondered.

It was an agonizing choice and she felt peculiarly torn. In her turmoil she tried to wriggle off the hook by temporizing. "I showed those army people at Dotswood," she said.

"They say you weren't very helpful," Rear Admiral McKinley replied.

That annoyed Barbara. "What rot!" she cried. "I took them right to the spot. I pointed to where the stupid satellite had hit a tree. I showed them on the map. I even showed my friends and Major Conkey where it was, or at least the approximate area."

"They have searched the area you indicated and say they cannot find it," Rear Admiral McKinley replied. "They deny you showed them. They said you were very unhelpful, insubordinate and obstructive."

"Who is 'they'?" Barbara retorted. "If it was that lieutenant colonel then he was just rude and arrogant. He couldn't even read a map! And we stood within ten paces of the thing while I pointed to it. But all he and that ignorant warrant officer could do was snicker because... because I was having a pee when the satellite crashed, and it gave me a fright."

Rear Admiral McKinley frowned as she mentioned going to the toilet. "How would they know that?" he asked.

"They wanted to know what I was doing there, why I was alone in the bush at night and at that place at that exact time," Barbara replied. She then described in detail how the navigation exercise had been organized, where her check point was, who was at it, and how she had walked away to go to the toilet.

That seemed to mollify the Rear Admiral somewhat and he said, "I was told you refused to show them at your HQ when they asked you to locate the place on a map."

Burning memories of the SAS soldiers sniggering at the video caused Barbara to blush and grit her teeth angrily. "That's not quite true," she replied. "I went there to show them and found them snickering over a video they had secretly taken of me doing a pee in the bush. I was so humiliated and offended I ran back out. But I did then show Major Conkey where it was, when he burnt the video."

"Video?" Rear Admiral McKinley queried.

Barbara felt her cheeks scorch with embarrassment, but she now described how she went down to One Mile Creek to do a pee and later found the SAS soldiers watching it on video.

"The disgusting perverts!" she added.

At that Rear Admiral McKinley frowned at a clearly embarrassed Commander Grundy, who said, "Sorry Admiral. We weren't told any of this."

"I'll bet!" Barbara cried. "The bloody cowards!"

Rear Admiral McKinley cleared his throat then said, "I see that you have been somewhat badly treated."

Barbara flared again. "Badly treated! I have been manhandled, kidnapped, terrified, almost sexually assaulted, and insulted!"

"Insulted?" Rear Admiral McKinley asked. "By whom?"

Barbara had now recognized one of the US Navy officers with the eagles on his collar. She pointed at him. "By him. He called me a very hurtful name."

The officer seemed to blanch and shrivel. Rear Admiral McKinley turned in astonishment and barked at him. "What is this Captain Turner? What the hell happened?"

The captain looked stony faced. "It was when she stepped off the helicopter admiral. She was undressed and I... I tried to get her to cover up," he replied.

Barbara was scared stiff, but she tried to conceal it with a display of bravado. She curled her lip and retorted. "You didn't have to call me a tart! All you had to do was be nice and ask."

The captain went very red and spluttered, "I didn't call you that. I... er... I."

"Called me a two-bit whore!" Barbara snapped. "Now apologise if you want my help."

For a second Barbara thought the man might refuse but one glance at the admiral caused him to swallow and he said, "I'm sorry. I was just offended by such a brazen display. I did not mean to imply you were a..."

"A prostitute? Hooker?" Barbara cut in. "I suppose you sailors might know what they look like. Personally, I've never met one."

At that the captain went purple in the face and looked deeply offended but Barbara detected a hint of a grin on the face of the admiral and Commander Grundy hid his mouth behind his hand. Even Chuck had to control a look of malicious glee.

Captain Turner took several deep breaths and was obviously both very angry and afraid. He then said, "I was just concerned about your modesty and about not having any complaints or problems on the ship. So when I saw you out on the flight deck with nothing on I just reacted. I'm sorry."

Barbara stared hard at him. As she did the images from a music video she had once seen flitted across her mind. "If it was good enough for Cher to prance around almost naked on a battleship in front of a lot of sailors I don't see what the problem is," she retorted.

It was instantly apparent that all the men present had seen the video of a very scantily clad Cher singing and dancing on the deck of a battleship and even straddling the mighty big guns in one suggestive scene.

The Rear Admiral nodded and said, "I remember that. So will you please accept our apology?"

Barbara saw that she had scored her point. In fact, she was now starting to tremble with reaction and a niggling fear of being in trouble for her lewd behaviour was starting so she nodded.

"Yes," she agreed.

Rear Admiral McKinley coughed and leaned forward. "Er... good. I think that has cleared up that little misunderstanding. Now Miss Brassington, or do you prefer Miz?"

Barbara just shook her head and gave a wry smile. She was now feeling more in control, both of herself and the situation. *They are only men after all,* she reminded herself.

Rear Admiral McKinley appeared to relax slightly and he nodded then asked, "So, may I again ask you to help us find the satellite?"

That put Barbara squarely back in the middle of her dilemma. *Do I break my promise to Raoul, or not?*

Chapter 21

A PROMISE TO KEEP

For several seconds Barbara sat and wrestled with her conscience. *My promise or my country!* she agonized.

She was just about to say no, when a compromise occurred to her that she clutched at, even though she knew in her heart it was just that.

I can tell them, and still tell Raoul. He might be able to find it before them.

To gain time she said, "What I don't understand is why you can't find the thing. I mean, with all those soldiers and helicopters and so on, and you must have modern metal detectors and all that scientific stuff."

Rear Admiral McKinley shrugged and replied, "Well they haven't. They say they have searched and re-checked every square inch of the grid reference you gave them, but nothing. They did say that the metal detectors were not giving the best results because there is apparently a lot of old iron in the area, barbed wire, shrapnel from World War Two artillery firing, rubbish like that. What they have suggested is that you may not have given them the correct grid reference."

That really annoyed Barbara. One of the things she really prided herself on was her navigation and map reading. She snorted. "Oh what piffle! Get me a map and I will show you again."

A map was immediately passed forward by the young officer. Rear Admiral McKinley gestured and the small table between him and Barbara was immediately whisked clear of objects. The map was spread out and turned so that she could read it. At a glance Barbara saw it was a copy of the same map she had used during annual camp, the Dotswood 1:50 000 that Major Conkey had said was inaccurate. She quickly located Keelbottom Creek and slid her finger along it till she found the Mingela Road. Within seconds she had her finger tip on the area where the Gravel Scrape was, even though it was not shown on this map either. For a fleeting moment she was tempted to give a false location to save her promise and to help Raoul but being a liar did not sit easily on her conscience either so she checked the actual spot as well as she could. It took her only a few more seconds to calculate the Grid Reference. She gave this as a 'six figure' reference and the young officer, Commander Grundy and Chuck all wrote it down.

The map was then turned so that the others could study it. There were satisfied grunting and murmuring, which made Barbara burn, feeling she had broken her promise. Rear Admiral McKinley beamed and nodded.

"Thank you, Miss Brassington. That should be a real help." He turned and said to the young officer, "Get that radioed to the search HQ immediately Jerry."

The young officer nodded and moved to a telephone on a side table. Rear Admiral McKinley turned back to Barbara. "Now young lady, we had best see to your welfare."

That puzzled Barbara. "What do you mean sir?"

Rear Admiral McKinley looked serious. "Well, you are at risk, so to speak. The plan is to keep you safe until the thing is found and the incident is over."

"Keep me safe?" Barbara replied, a sickening feeling beginning in her stomach as she tried to imagine what those words meant. She had an idea and her worst fears were immediately confirmed.

"Yes, keep you in a safe place so these damned Dags can't threaten your life," Rear Admiral McKinley replied.

"Do you mean here, on this ship, as a prisoner?" Barbara asked, aghast at the implications.

Rear Admiral McKinley looked uncomfortable. "Well, not as a prisoner. I think the term is 'Witness Protection', isn't that so Commander Bragg?"

The other US Navy senior officer nodded. "That's right Admiral." He then looked at Barbara. "I'm Commander Bart Bragg; of the JAG Corps; the Judge Advocate Generals Department. We are the navy's legal department."

"I've watched *JAG*," Barbara answered, alluding to the TV series. "Sorry, but you aren't as handsome as Commander Rabb. Where's he?"

It was a feeble joke and Barbara only used it to gain herself time to think. She was now torn by two completely different sets or emotions and ideas. Part of her was terrified by the whole situation she found herself in and welcomed the offer of protection; but the other part was now distressed by having broken her promise to Raoul.

I must get in contact with Raoul, she thought. *I must honour my promise to tell him.*

There were grins at the joke and the mood in the cabin visibly relaxed. Rear Admiral McKinley called for refreshments and another door opened and several stewards came in with trays of coffee, water and biscuits. Captain Turner excused himself and quickly left the cabin, but not before giving Barbara a wooden-faced but sour glance.

Barbara returned to her previous question. "Do you mean I will be kept here on this ship?"

"That is a possibility," Rear Admiral McKinley conceded. "Or we could have you and your friends flown to a safe US base somewhere; Hawaii or Guam for instance."

That possibility both thrilled and appalled Barbara. To gain more time she asked, "What about my father?"

"Him too, if it is deemed necessary."

"Why can't we be kept at a safe place in Australia?" Barbara asked.

Rear Admiral McKinley nodded. "That is a possibility as well."

"I would prefer that," Barbara replied. "I would like to be taken home to collect some things as well."

Chuck shook his head. "That might not be a wise idea."

"I would still prefer to be in Australia," Barbara answered. Then she asked, "How long might this witness protection go on for?"

"Hopefully only for a week or two," Chuck answered.

"You don't sound too sure," Barbara answered. Secretly she was appalled and she remembered a TV program about people who had been forced to take on completely new identities and move to other towns; never letting on to their relatives or friends that they were still alive. The thought of never seeing her friends again, of having to go to a new school with a false name, of having to leave cadets, all flooded her with a feeling of despair that almost caused her to burst into tears.

Rear Admiral McKinley answered her. "We will see what we can do. Now, would you like to have some coffee and cookies?"

"Cookies?" Barbara queried. Then she giggled and said, "Oh, you mean biscuits. Yes please. And I would like to see my friends please."

"Sure. They will be right along," Rear Admiral McKinley agreed. He nodded to the junior officer who again went to the telephone. The admiral poured Barbara a cup of coffee and turned himself into an affable host. Chuck and his offsider excused themselves and left the cabin. Commander Bragg and Commander Grundy both joined the social circle and the admiral began asking polite questions about Barbara's school.

Barbara answered a few questions and then said, "Excuse me for asking, but I don't even know what ship I am on."

"The USS *Wasp*," Rear Admiral McKinley answered.

"It's an aircraft carrier isn't it?"

"Of a sort," Rear Admiral McKinley replied. "She's an L.H.D.; a Landing ship, Helicopter, Dock. She is designed to transport and land a Marine Expeditionary Unit. So she carries lots of helicopters to do that, plus a couple of Air Cushion vehicles, Hovercraft you would call them, and a few other boats. Lieutenant Roberts here can give you all the details, if you are interested."

Barbara looked at the junior officer, who smiled back, somewhat nervously. *He's actually quite handsome; in a clean-cut, 'All-American college-boy' way,* she thought.

She said, "I saw some 'Harrier' jump jets on the flight deck."

Lt Roberts answered. "Yes, A.V. 8 Bs we call them. They are for providing close air support to any landing force. We have nine AV8Bs embarked at the moment."

"And the helicopter that picked us up; it looked like a Blackhawk?"

Lt Roberts nodded. "A close relative, an SH-60B 'Seahawk'. We have a dozen of them on board."

"Could I have a bit of a look around?" Barbara asked, both for something to say and to gain more time to think.

Rear Admiral McKinley nodded and answered. "A tour of the ship? Not a problem. Lt Roberts can take you on that."

Lt Roberts nodded and looked keen, causing Barbara to smile. *They really are only men,* she thought, *Or rather big boys. He wants to show off all the war toys!*

There was more description of the ship and discussion of life at sea before the cabin door was opened and Fiona and Wendy were ushered in by a female junior officer. They both wore the same blue camouflage clothes and looked quite apprehensive till they caught sight of a smiling Barbara. Then they grinned with relief and hurried over to her. She stood up and hugged them both, a few tears now sneaking out.

Rear Admiral McKinley also stood up. When the greetings were over he said, "I'd like to thank you ladies for your assistance. Now, I extend the hospitality of the ship to you. I will leave you in the good hands of Lt Roberts and Ensign Reeves. They will show you around and settle you into your quarters."

"Quarters? Aren't we going ashore?" Barbara asked. The idea of having to stay on the ship got her all anxious.

I have arranged to meet Raoul tonight! she thought.

The admiral frowned. "You can of course, but I am not sure if arrangements have been finalised for your safety. Until they are you can stay on the ship."

He said 'stay' as though making it an offer but Barbara had an uneasy feeling she would not be given a real choice. To test it she said very firmly, "I want to go home."

"Yes. We will see to it. As soon as the Australian authorities have things organized. Get on to that please Commander Grundy," Rear Admiral McKinley replied. "Now ladies, I am afraid I must be rude and leave you. There is work I have to do. Thank you again and I hope you are well looked after."

With that Rear Admiral McKinley left the cabin. Barbara caught a quizzical look in Fiona's eye and could only give a faint shake of her head, hoping she would go along with her plan. Wendy just looked and acted relieved. The three friends were then ushered out of the cabin and taken on tour of the ship by Lt Roberts and Ensign Reeves.

Under other circumstances Barbara would have been fascinated by it all and would have loved the tour. Now she was just very self-conscious and also very anxious, noting that the sun was already low.

It will be dark in an hour or so, she thought, very conscious of the 1930 meeting time she had agreed on. *Oh! How can I get a message to Raoul?* she fretted.

As she walked along her mind turned over various possibilities including talking to her father by telephone and somehow conveying a coded message to him.

The tour was thorough and extensive. Barbara had been on shipboard tours before, but never quite like this. There were all the usual long corridors full of machinery noises and strange smelling draughts of air, the walls—bulkheads, she corrected—festooned with the usual wiring, fittings, boxes, hoses and pipes. All the while they met people.

They seemed to lurk in every compartment, giving Barbara an almost overwhelming impression of crowding.

How do they live like this? she wondered, marvelling that humans could inhabit such a place for weeks and months on end.

The tour took them from deck to deck, showing recreation rooms, a galley, storerooms, rooms with pieces of equipment in them, the aircrew briefing room, then the flight deck. It was cool and windy out there and Barbara was quite astonished at the way the horizon rose and fell. The motion of the ship had not really been noticeable before that and it almost made her queasy to watch. While they were out in the open she again noted how the sun was sinking rapidly towards the western horizon. She also saw that there were three other warships with them, smaller destroyer type vessels, but they were too far away and she knew too little to be able to identify what they were.

Next they went down to the hangar deck. That did amaze Barbara: the sheer size and complexity of it, the lights, aircraft, machines and busy men. From there they went down another couple of decks and peeked into the engine rooms but did not go down into them. They were steered around the marines and crews living quarters and passed dozens of locked doors with signs saying 'Authorized personnel only'. Then Lt Roberts checked his watch and began leading them back up flight after flight of stairs.

What made Barbara particularly self-conscious were the looks. Almost every person they met or passed seemed to leer knowingly at her, making her blush and feel very ashamed and uncomfortable.

Serves me right! she told herself. There was no doubt she was a shipboard celebrity. *Chloe should have been here. This would have really suited her,* Barbara thought ruefully.

And then they were shown into the Control Room; the Action Information Centre. Barbara had been in one once before on a visiting warship whose name she could not even remember, so she had some understanding of what all the TV screens and radar displays were all about. But this was different. All of the equipment was functioning and manned. Amid the dim blue lighting were dozens of people busily watching the screens or tapping at keyboards. Even these people all gave her interested, knowing looks.

Lt Roberts pointed and explained: "That system keeps track of all aircraft within several hundred miles of the ship. Those controls over there are the ship's air defence system and they are data linked to our escorting destroyers so that the right ship responds to a threat with the most appropriate weapon." He moved on and pointed again. "These are the underwater warfare systems—anti-submarine."

Barbara had to smile at the American pronunciation of 'ant-i'. She nodded and tried to appear calm and relaxed but now hung back and stood behind Wendy and Fiona most of the time.

Lt Roberts next stopped in front of a huge video monitor that took up half a bulkhead. On it was shown the outline of the east coast of Australia and the islands on the other side of the Coral Sea. A number of coloured and numbered symbols stood out clearly. "This is the situation map," Lt Roberts explained. "From our electronic intelligence sources, radar, satellites and so on we keep track of every ship within a thousand nautical miles of the ship. By flicking a switch we can show the deployment of every ship in the US and allied navies, plus most other fleets."

The operator did this and huge world map appeared. The screen was then switched back. Fiona peered at it and then asked, "Where are we?"

Lt Roberts leaned across and pointed to a small cluster of blue symbols off the Queensland coast halfway between Cairns and Townsville.

We are going south! Barbara noted.

Lt Roberts pointed to a white symbol nearby. "That is a merchant ship, a bulk carrier going north; and the red one way out there, that is a Russian fishing boat. There is usually one of them trailing us. They aren't really fishing trawlers at all. They collect intelligence."

Then Wendy pointed and asked, "What are the three blue ones near us?"

Lt Roberts laughed, then said, "They are three French warships; a Landing Ship Dock a bit like us named the *Mistral*. She carries marines too. With her are a frigate and a supply ship. They sailed from New Caledonia two days ago. I guess they are hoping to get lucky and want to get their satellite back." At that he laughed again and added, "Fat chance!"

Barbara had a vivid image of Raoul as he said the word 'marines' and then she burned. She was now ashamed of herself for being so weak as to give in and show the location on the map. She was also irritated by the American's apparent contempt for the French.

I must show Raoul. At the very least I can warn him the Americans might have the satellite and his government can ask for it back, she told herself.

She pretended not to be interested but did note that the American Task Force appeared to be in a position to block the French from getting closer to the Australian coast.

On leaving the control room the girls were led to a cabin and told they could use it. It was a double bunk cabin which also had its own en-suite shower and toilet and there was a settee and chairs. After a visit to the bathroom they were then led along to the wardroom to be fed. This was also an embarrassing affair as all of the officers there turned to look at them and then pretended not to be interested, while continually scrutinising them. Lt Roberts and Ensign Reeves sat with the girls while they were served with a delicious hot meal: Turkey and grits, then desert.

The food was good and Barbara knew she would have been really enjoying the experience except that the wall clock showed it was now 1645 hours and she knew there was a French naval Task Group only a hundred nautical miles away.

How can I contact Raoul? she fretted, all the while pretending to be tired and relaxed. That was her new plan; to lull the Americans into thinking she was now worn out and no longer interested or annoyed.

Not that she had to pretend too hard. She really was exhausted. The horror of the afternoon kept recurring and she broke into bouts of shivering and occasional cold sweats. Her eyes began to droop and she found it a relief to be led back to the cabin. Here she flopped onto one of the bunks, deliberately avoiding conversation with her friends.

The cabin is sure to be bugged so that the Yanks will hear everything we say, she thought.

The two officers left them, but not before Ensign Reeves requested they not leave the cabin. The sight of a female sailor in the corridor outside reinforced Barbara's impression that they were not free to leave.

Only then did the girls talk freely. "Oh Barbara! You were so naughty!" Fiona cried.

Barbara blushed but managed a wry grin. "If Cher could do it on a battleship I can do it on an aircraft carrier," she replied.

Wendy laughed with embarrassment and described her own feelings. As she chattered away Barbara wanted to warn her not to say too much in case the cabin was bugged. But she got no chance, so the girls had a good girl talk about the horror of the shootings and their own emotions. A good cry and group hug followed. Then Barbara lay back and closed her eyes, her mind and emotions in turmoil.

She fell asleep, but on being shaken awake Barbara experienced a real panic attack. It was the first she had ever suffered, and it shook her badly. For a few minutes she could only sit and shake, alternately sobbing and biting her knuckles. Ensign Reeves, who had been responsible for waking her, sat and tried to comfort her. Fiona and Wendy then joined in. When Fiona put her arms around her Barbara gripped her fiercely and then sighed with relief as understanding of where she was and that she was safe came back to her.

Fiona stroked her hair. "You will be alright Barb," she said.

Barbara could only nod and cling to her. "Sorry about earlier," she whispered. "I think I must have been in shock."

"It was certainly horrible," Fiona agreed, shuddering at the memories.

Ensign Reeves, who was all concern, now said, "I didn't mean to give you a fright. I was sent to tell you that you are being taken ashore."

That news immediately made Barbara feel better but she made an effort to hide this. She looked around, hoping to see a clock, but none was visible. As the cabin had no portholes she was further irritated, unable to tell what time of day it was.

How do people live in such claustrophobic conditions, she marvelled.

Unwilling to betray her impatience she sat forward and 'casually' glanced at Fiona's wrist watch. That took some reading too as she seemed to have trouble focusing. Then her vision came clear.

Only 1730! she thought in amazement. She felt as though she had slept for hours but realized it must have only been about twenty minutes.

Still feeling groggy, she asked, "When?"

Ensign Reeves gestured towards the flight deck. "The helo is winding up now. I was sent to bring you up."

Barbara could only nod and pretend to be worn out, not that it took much acting. Both Fiona and Wendy accept the news quietly and Barbara wondered if they had been spoken to about Witness Protection. From the way they were acting she suspected not.

They probably aren't in the danger I am, she reasoned.

The girls were led up a flight of steps and along a corridor to a room where they were handed bright red lifejackets. This time Barbara made no fuss but pulled it on and allowed Ensign Reeves to do it up. Ear protection was added and then Ensign Reeves shook hands and thanked them.

"Good luck," he said. A seaman in a bright yellow vest and safety helmet and visor then led out through another door onto the flight deck.

There Barbara had her anxieties increased. The sun had set and dusk was fast setting in. The only aircraft with its engine going was the large twin rotor helicopter parked in front of her. Standing nearby, wearing life jackets and ear protection were Commander Grundy, Commander Bragg and Lt Roberts. Barbara had vaguely expected some sort of farewell by the admiral but he was nowhere to be seen and the girls were led straight across the windy deck to the door of the helicopter. Barbara went last and climbed the steps with a mingled feeling of relief and regret.

Inside the cabin of the helicopter there was a crewman who pointed to a row of seats along the side. To her annoyance Barbara saw that Chuck and the other CIA agent were already seated there, dressed in clean civilian clothes. Chuck looked up and gave wry grin but the engine noise precluded conversation, for which Barbara was thankful. She sat down between Lt Roberts and Fiona. Wendy went next, then Commander Grundy. Commander Bragg sat opposite and the crewman, after checking all seatbelts were done up, joined him.

Within a minute the engine noise had increased and the helicopter trembled, tilted and then lifted off. Barbara had a fleeting glimpse of the dark grey superstructure, dimly lit by the last of the daylight and by numerous lights, then the dark sea swept into view underneath. The helicopter settled on an even keel and the flight began. Barbara had no idea where they were going but did not ask. She stuck to her policy of pretending to be exhausted and no longer interested.

Might be going to Townsville, she thought. That got her thinking hard. *Who do I know in Townsville who might help me? How can I get away from Chuck and his sidekick?*

She determined not to include Fiona or Wendy in her plans. As the helicopter flew on, the cabin lit only by a row of dimmed lights, Barbara sat back with her eyes closed and began to plan.

How do I get word to Raoul? she wondered. *How can I keep at least part of my promise?*

Chapter 22

FRIENDS

The helicopter flight lasted nearly half an hour. It was noisy and relatively boring as there was nothing to see outside except dark sea. For most of the time Barbara sat with her eyes closed and pretended to be asleep. She did doze a bit but most of the time her mind and emotions were in turmoil. For a while she talked to Fiona, but, between the ear protection and the engine noises, it was difficult to make herself understood without shouting. What she did gather was that Fiona was deeply shocked by the killings and was still feeling a deep sense of unreality. That was partly how Barbara felt so she had no trouble understanding.

Through the porthole Barbara glimpsed lights in the distance. These grew steadily closer and she craned to try to see out.

Where are we? she wondered.

Knowing that vitally affected her possible actions. With some relief she detected the shape of the coastline and the dark silhouettes of mountains. They looked familiar and there were too many lights for it to be any other place. Sure she was not mistaken, she sighed with relief.

Cairns! Thank heavens!

A few minutes later the helicopter tilted and circled on a landing approach. It slowed and lifted its nose to the peculiar landing hover which Barbara had experienced before. Then it lowered to the tarmac. Through the porthole Barbara saw rows of light planes parked outside buildings. She then knew exactly where she was: the General Aviation side of the airport. That suited her and she relaxed a bit, preparatory to the next step in her plan. Fiona's watch now showed 1830 hours.

I still have sixty minutes to get to the RV in time, Barbara thought. Now her whole body seemed to tingle with anticipation and she tensed, ready to take advantage of any opportunity.

The engines were switched off and then the door opened and steps lowered. Seat belts were undone and the girls took off their hearing protection and stood up. Wendy stumbled and looked stiff and groggy. She had dozed off and looked very waxy in the yellowish light from the lights outside. Barbara grabbed her and steadied her, holding her tight until she had her balance.

Chuck indicated they should wait and his companion stayed with the girls while he and the naval commanders climbed out. Through the window Barbara saw the headlights of three cars. These stopped just outside and she silently cursed. She did not want to be transferred under guard straight to a car. Lt Roberts and the crewman collected the lifejackets and he wished them well. Wendy asked about the uniforms and Lt Roberts laughed.

"Keep them, compliments of the US Navy. I hope you appreciated our help and our hospitality," he said.

Barbara now did, having recovered from the initial shock and having had time to think about what had happened, so she said so, but she was still torn and even more determined to keep her promise to Raoul. She was bothered she might be acting against her country's best interests, but she still had the niggling suspicion that the possession of the satellite's secrets was more of a power play than a threat to Australia. She half-believed Raoul's assessment that the US simply did not want any competitors so that they could be top dog. She was also mildly ashamed that her own country just seemed to always do what the Americans wanted. But she was honest enough to admit to herself that she really did not know.

Chuck now reappeared at the door and beckoned to them. Reluctantly Barbara made her way to the door and climbed out. What she saw confirmed her suspicions. Standing beside the three cars were the two Australian Security men she had met: Mr Cavendish and Mr Blaketon. Three other men in civilian clothes sat in the driver's seats.

When the three girls were standing near the cars Chuck gestured and said, "I think you have all met Mr Cavendish from ASIO? Good. Now, we are going to take you to a safe place for the night. He assures me that all your friends are safe and so are your families. The two Dagestani spies who were waiting at the car have both been taken into custody and we think they did not know what happened and did not have time to report to their own people. For that reason we think you may be fairly safe; except you Miss Brassington. You were the one they were targeting and watching as your name kept coming up in the reports. So we may have to keep you safe for only a few days. Once we have the satellite then I am sure all the spies will lose interest."

Barbara swallowed and felt a surge of emotions. *If I make sure the Americans get the satellite then I will be alright,* she thought. It was a powerful temptation.

She said, "So you think we may not have to change our identities and stay hidden for ever and all that stuff."

"We never said you would have to do that," Chuck replied.

"No, but you hinted at it," Barbara said, noting the open-mouthed dismay on Wendy's face. Fiona, having the constant fear of the religious cult seeking her out for vengeance, clearly understood.

Chuck nodded and then said, "That might be so. Now, my strong advice to all of you is that you never mention any of this to anyone— not to your family, not to your friends, certainly not to the media. You could not prove any of it anyway, and we will obviously just deny any accusations. So will the Australian authorities."

He glanced at Mr Cavendish, who nodded grimly and said, "Just keep your mouth shut. Just tell people that you were washed off the rocks by a wave and that an American navy helicopter was lucky enough to see what happened and picked you up. Tell your friends that the helicopter took you to the ship for a medical check up because the ship was closer than the hospital. Just don't make a big deal of it, and try to forget."

Chuck agreed with this. "Remember, not a word. This is national security stuff and you may never be able to tell anyone. So, unless we give you permission, say nothing. That will help keep you safer as the Dags won't know what happened. You open your mouth they might find out. Then they might come gunning for you out of spite. The Dags are Moslem fanatics remember, and they won't take kindly to being beaten by girls."

It was a chilling prospect and Barbara broke into goose bumps. She was now feeling both physically and emotionally exhausted but was also very keyed up. Minutes were ticking by and she was still determined to try to see Raoul.

I will tell him, she decided.

Both the naval commanders then said thank you and shook hands before the girls were ushered to the cars. What Barbara had feared now happened; one girl was taken to each car, separating the group. Barbara did not want that and protested, saying she wanted to stay with her friends, but Mr Cavendish just said they were being taken to their own families, and that each family was in a different place. For a moment Barbara stood at the car door and glanced around. She had vaguely hope to be able to make a run for it and get away among the planes and buildings but now saw that was hopeless. Now she saw that she had no choice but to get into the car. To her annoyance Chuck slid in beside her in the back seat while Mr Cavendish climbed into the front beside the driver.

Oh! How can I escape? Barbara wondered as the car began moving.

To lull Chuck into a false sense of alertness Barbara now slumped down and tried to maintain the impression that she was worn out and submissive. Her self-control was then tested by the route the cars took. On reaching the entrance to the airport they turned left and proceeded into the city along Sheridan Street. Barbara had half-expected that and could only grit her teeth with frustration as they drove straight past the coffee shop where she was hoping to meet Raoul—now within only thirty-five minutes!

As they drove past the coffee shop Barbara stared hard, hoping to catch sight of him, but saw no sign of him. Then she slumped back and brooded over how long he might wait, and how she might contact him if he did not.

At his hotel I suppose? she decided.

At James Street they turned right and soon after that Barbara noted that the other two cars were no longer following them. That depressed her even more as she really did want to stay with her friends if possible, if only for the emotional support.

Five minutes later the car pulled into the concrete yard of a block of non-descript flats in Earlville. These were two stories high and had enclosed garages underneath. The car drove in and the garage door shut electronically behind them, even before the car's engine had been turned off, and long before Barbara could have jumped from the car and run out. Feeling baffled, battered and defeated she climbed slowly out and followed Chuck and Mr Cavendish to a doorway. The driver locked the car and came behind her. The door led to a stairway that went up to the next level. The stairs opened into a flat; a very ordinary 2-bedroom flat with a small kitchen-lounge room and a bathroom and toilet.

Barbara's father was waiting there and she sobbed with relief and threw herself into his arms. Knowing that both Chuck and Mr Cavendish could hear she acted the part of an upset little girl who has been through a traumatic experience—not hard in the circumstances. There were tears and hugs and her father stroked her hair while she clung sobbing to him.

"Oh Daddy! It was horrible!" she wailed, more tears flowing.

Then, over his shoulders, she caught sight of the wall clock. 7:15 pm.

Damn! Too late! Raoul will probably be there now. How can I contact him? she wondered.

With a massive effort of will she regained control of her emotions, while still pretending to be very upset. "Daddy," she whispered. "You must help me, but don't let these men know."

She felt her father nod and he gripped her tighter. "My poor little baby Bubs!" he comforted loudly, then whispered, "What do you want?"

"Have you got your mobile phone?" she whispered back.

Again he nodded. For a moment he fumbled in his pocket, extracting a handkerchief to dab at her face. He released her from the hug and looked anxiously, deep into her eyes, while nodding some more. Then he half-turned and said to Mr Cavendish, "Thanks for bringing her back safe. I really appreciate it." At the same time his other hand, now hidden from the men, slipped a small mobile phone into her trouser pocket.

Barbara felt a surge of warm affection. *Good old Dad! He trusts me enough not to ask questions.* She then sniffled loudly and pointed. "Is that the bathroom? I need to go."

Mr Cavendish nodded. Barbara walked past, rubbing her eyes and head bent forward. Her father at once began asking loudly for an explanation and moved to sit on the far side of the lounge room. Barbara went into the toilet and closed the door. She knew exactly what to do from watching police dramas on TV, but her hands shook while she did it. First she flushed the toilet. Then, while the sound of running water was at its loudest, she punched in the numbers on the phone and waited. As she had planned, the noise of the cistern refilling itself covered the sound of her voice.

She had thought long and hard about who to phone. It could not be Fiona or Wendy, for obvious reasons. Nor did she think it reasonable to call either Roger or Lofty as she felt sure the security people had been listening in to their telephones. Other people she had briefly considered were school friends in her own class and even her own cadet platoon sergeant, Dan Russell. But Dan, while she was sure he could be relied on, didn't have a car. Pat Sheehan, the CSM, did, but she did not know him well enough. But there was one friend she felt sure would help, without questions: Willy Williams. Willy had been in love with her all through Year 8 and Year 9 and obviously still had a special affection for her—as witnessed by him risking his life to rescue her at Mt Mulligan in March.

But when the phone kept ringing Barbara felt her hopes plummet.

Oh no! Willy might not be home, she thought, picturing him in the arms of Marjorie—and experiencing both a flash of jealousy and a surge of arousal as she did.

Then the phone clicked and Willy's voice answered. "Yes, hello, Willy speaking."

Barbara's relief was so great that for a moment she found it hard to speak. She had to swallow to moisten her throat. "Willy! It's me, Barbara. Please listen and don't interrupt or ask questions," she hissed, urgently aware that time was critical.

"Barbara? Questions? Sure," Willy replied, obviously intrigued.

Barbara bit her lip and then took the plunge. "Listen Willy, I can't talk freely. I will explain it all later but I need you to do something really important, and it might get you into trouble and, might break the law," she said.

"Stuff the law!" was Willy's reassuring response. "If you want something done then I am your man."

"Good man!" Barbara answered, only later realizing she could have said 'boy' but had instinctively used the other term. "Can you get your Dad's car and use it to pick me, without too much fuss or too many questions being asked?"

"No problem," Willy assured her.

"Good. Now, please don't mention it is for me, not to anyone, do you understand, not to anyone, not even Marjorie," Barbara said.

"Sure. My lips are sealed," Willy replied.

"Good. Then please pick me up at the corner of Mulgrave Road and Balaclava Road at Earlville in fifteen minutes. That's at seven fifty. If I'm not there wait half an hour, no more, then go home. And Willy, please bring me some old clothes, a pair of shorts and a shirt, and some money."

Willy's voice showed he was plainly intrigued. "Money?" he answered with a chuckle. "And I thought you wanted me just for my good looks!"

"Willy! Don't joke. I need some money. Please!" Barbara replied, both cheered and annoyed by his flippant response.

"All girls want money," Willy replied with mock resignation, adding, "You sound destitute."

"I am. You will understand why when you get here, now get moving!" Barbara snapped.

She was painfully conscious that the toilet had stopped its noises, so she ended the call, quickly used the toilet then flushed it again. After slipping the phone back into her pocket she walked back out to the kitchen, ignoring the men, while she looked for a glass. To her relief they did not seem to take any notice of her. She filled a glass with water and had a big drink, refilled it and then carried it to a lounge chair.

Barbara lowered herself into the chair, aware that she was trembling from emotion and anticipation and hoped the men would all think it was just exhaustion and shock—which it partly was. While sipping the water she carefully studied the room. Her next problem was to slip away and she wasn't sure if the doors and windows were somehow locked or not. She hoped not, and thought that the logic of the situation was that she would be glad to be safe inside and would not try to leave.

Her chance came almost immediately. The men all stood up and Chuck and Mr Cavendish both moved to the front door. They stood there for a minute giving last minute instructions to the driver, who was obviously another Commonwealth Security agent and their bodyguard. While they talked Barbara leaned over and whispered to her father.

"Dad, I'm about to run away. Don't worry, and try to stall these guys. You know who I am going got meet. Tell these people I have run away to be with my lover and that you think we have eloped. They can stop worrying about me."

Her father raised his eyebrows but remained calm and nodded. "Your lover eh? You sure you know what you are doing?" he asked quietly.

Barbara nodded. Then she stood up and said loudly. "I feel sick. I'm going to lie down. Which bedroom is mine?"

The agent, who had just closed and locked the front door behind the departing backs of Chuck and Mr Cavendish, pointed along the short corridor. "The second one; and remember, for your own safety leave the curtains drawn and don't open the windows."

Barbara nodded and walked along the corridor. Behind her she heard her father ask to have the TV turned on and then about getting some coffee.

Dad is going to help by making some noise, she thought gratefully. *Now, can I get out?*

She feared that the windows might be locked or barred in some way, or even alarmed. As soon as she was in the bedroom she closed the door, judging that people would think that a reasonable thing for a girl to do, if only for privacy while changing. Then she went straight to the window, pulled the curtain aside and looked out. The window appeared to be an ordinary sliding one and had a simple interior snap catch. Below it was a long, narrow back yard with clothes lines in it. A high paling fence lined the backyard, separating it from the back yard of an 'Old Queenslander' house. A few trees overhung the back fence.

"I think I can climb over that fence," she muttered, "But can I get down without hurting myself?"

Very aware of the minutes slipping by Barbara did not hesitate. She unlocked the widow and quietly slid it open then leaned out. It looked easier than she expected. There was a narrow concrete ledge at the height of the first floor, some sort of overhang or awning, and each back yard was separated from its neighbour by a dividing fence. Barbara saw that she could easily reach across to the top of that fence.

Without any delay she swung her leg over the window sill and climbed out. A minute later she was clinging to the top of the dividing fence at the point where it joined the back fence, having walked across the timber beams to which the palings were nailed. By then her heart was hammering fast with excitement and she was perspiring. The timber was rough on her hands but she ignored that. A quick heave and she had her leg over the back fence. Then she turned, twisted around and lowered herself down the other side. For a moment she hung by her hands before dropping to the grass.

Out! she told herself exultantly. But had she been seen?

She crouched and listened but there was no sound from the flat. Then she was gripped by fear—wondering if she wasn't making a terrible, possibly fatal, mistake. She even considered trying to climb back, but shook her head. After a minute she took a grip on herself.

I have to do this, she told herself.

It was relatively dark in the back yard of the house so she walked forward confident she would not be seen. Dogs were her main concern but no yapping or barking broke the usual suburban evening noises. Lights indicated that there were people home in the house but she could not see any through the windows. A glance behind her showed a light in the kitchen window of the flat and she briefly glimpsed her father's head but then it was gone and so was she. She hurried around the side of the house and jumped the front fence into the next street.

Barbara could not believe how easy it had been. Sure that her escape must be quickly discovered she set off along the street at a run. It was a street that she had never been in before but she knew the general layout of the suburb and quickly made her way around several side streets to Balaclava Road. Here she paused at the intersection to get her breath and to check for pursuit before hurrying along it towards the main road. The lights of Mulgrave Road showed clearly a couple of blocks ahead but she was thankful for that as they guided her and she was able to avoid any stumbles on the grassy footpaths.

However, on reaching the main intersection, she was faced by a dilemma: stand out in the open and risk being seen by any pursuers; or to hide in the shadows and risk Willy not finding her quickly? Being dressed in the US Navy blue camouflage made her feel extremely conspicuous. She opted for the shadows and stood in the narrow lane between two shops, standing where the headlights of cars did not shine on her but where she could see out to check for Willy.

And there he was!

Barbara gasped with delight as she recognized the car which had swung in to park in front of the next shop. After a quick look both ways she walked quickly over to the car, even before Willy had switched off and opened his door. He looked around in surprise as she knocked on the passenger window, then he reached across and opened the door. As she slid in he restarted his motor and turned the headlights back on.

"Barbara, are you alright? Are you in trouble?" he asked.

"Yes, and yes, now no questions please," Barbara replied.

She was almost overcome by a wave of affection and relief and could only slump into the seat. As she fumbled with the seatbelt she gestured to get moving.

"Drive! North Cairns, Favio's Coffee Shop, quickly!"

Willy set the car in motion and pulled out into the traffic. Barbara started to pull the seatbelt across, then stopped. "Did you bring me some clothes?" she asked.

Willy glanced at her and grinned. "I did. They are on the back seat. Mind you, I did wonder what you might be wearing. Where did you get those togs?"

"Off the US Navy," Barbara replied, twisting around to reach for the clothes. They were a pair of baggy shorts and a short-sleeved shirt with a bright floral pattern on it.

Willy raised an eyebrow in surprise. "I wasn't sure if the clothes were for you or someone else," he commented as he slowed to turn left into Anderson Street. "So I brought some of my Mums. So how come you got clothes from the American navy, what happened to yours?"

For a moment Barbara considered not answering, remembering the agent's advice, but then she giggled and blushed at the memory of walking across the flight deck of the aircraft carrier.

"I lost mine and got rescued by an American helicopter. It's a long story. I will tell you later, and don't tell anyone about it please."

Then she blushed again and hesitated. She wanted to change but knew that Willy would be able to see her in the lights from the streetlights, traffic lights and headlights. The knowledge that she had no bra or panties made her flame with embarrassment. But after thinking about it for a minute she smiled and shrugged.

So what? He's always wanted to see me without my clothes on, I'm sure, and I'll bet he sees Marjorie without hers all the time. With those thoughts she unbuttoned the shirt.

As she struggled to shrug it off she saw Willy glance and then goggle. "Barbara!" he cried in a strangled gasp.

"You just keep your eyes on the road," she chided, but she smiled. A delicious sense of thrill ran through her and she felt she was starting to understand Chloe.

She would be proud of me, Barbara thought as she dropped the navy shirt and reached for the floral shirt, hotly conscious that her bare breasts were visible and that the movement of the car was making them even more noticeable by making them bounce and quiver.

Despite her asking, Willy glanced across at her. "What happened to your bra?" he asked.

"I thought I told you to keep your eyes on the road," Barbara replied with a laugh, even more hotly aware that she was enjoying herself. She began to struggle into the floral shirt. This was awkward to do in the car and resulted in some fairly revealing squirming about.

"Sorry," Willy said, but she noted his eyes flicking sideways to glance at her.

As Barbara slid her arm into a sleeve, she said, "It's alright. I don't mind if you look. You've earned it. Anyway, Marjorie's are bigger aren't they?"

Willy grunted and nodded but apart from a brief flicker did not look again. He concentrated on driving the car—till she peeled off the trousers.

"Bloody hell!" he muttered. "That's not fair!"

"Poor Willy!" Barbara said, blushing hotly as she struggled into the shorts, very conscious of not having any knickers on. As she did the shorts up, she said, "After you have dropped me off would you mind going 'round to my place to get some things for me?"

"Sure. What do you need?"

"A bra and some panties would be nice," Barbara replied. "And also a set of cams, my army boots, socks and basic webbing—and make sure the waterbottles are full. And on my bedside table is a map photocopy that we used on annual camp. Bring that too please."

"What will I tell your Dad?"

"He won't be there. He is back there, but he knows what I am doing. You will have to use the spare key to get in, and try not to be seen," Barbara replied. She then described how to find the spare key and where the various things were. By then they had reached Sheridan Street. As they turned left into it Barbara looked at the clock on the dashboard. It read 19:55.

Oh dear! Will Raoul still be there? she wondered.

Chapter 23

ON THE RUN

A s the car approached the small shopping centre where the coffee shop was Barbara had another mild panic attack.

Am I being stupid? Am I doing the right thing? she wondered.

She wasn't sure, but what she did know was that she wanted to see Raoul again, and she wanted to try to keep her promise.

Barbara pointed to the shops. "Just pull over here please Willy. When you come back with my stuff park along the side street there. If you see a cop car near these shops then get out of here. Just go home and forget you ever knew me," she said.

"Why? What have you done?" Willy asked anxiously as he brought the car to a standstill at the kerb.

"I'm not some sort of horrible criminal, if that is what you are worrying about," she replied. Not wanting to explain more she opened the door and stepped out. Willy reached across. "Here is a hundred dollars," he said, passing her some notes.

"Oh Willy! Thank you," Barbara said, almost overwhelmed by a surge of affection. "Now get going and don't be seen with me." Suiting her own actions to this she started walking along the footpath.

Willy stared hard at her, then waved and set his car in motion again. Within seconds it was swallowed up in the rush of traffic along Sheridan Street. Barbara stopped and tried to calm her nerves. She knew she had not committed herself and could back out. But her stubborn streak took over and she clenched her jaw and walked on towards the coffee shop.

Now her heart was hammering as hard as it had when escaping. *Will he be there? Does he really like me? Will he go for my new plan?* she wondered anxiously.

And there he was!

While still twenty paces away Barbara saw Raoul walk out of the well-lit doorway of the coffee shop and turn away from her along the darker footpath. Barbara let out a little sob and broke into a run.

"Raoul!" she cried.

He stopped and turned, squinting against the light. Then she reached him and flung her arms around his neck. That caught him by surprise, but he was strong and steadied them both, then hugged her.

"Hmmm! *Mademoiselle, ma cheri!* This I like. But what is ze matter? Where 'ave you been?" he murmured into her ear.

For a minute Barbara could not answer. All she could do was cling to Raoul. Never in her life had any man other than her father had this sort of effect on her but now she just felt safe. She began to shiver and sob. Raoul held her with strong but tender arms and she gripped him tightly as all the awful images of the day flooded through her overstrained mind.

"It was… sob…. hor…. hor…. horrible!" she wailed at last. "They…. they just shot them in cold b…. b… blood."

"Shot them? Shot who? Who shot who?" Raoul asked, still hugging her to him and gently nuzzling her hair.

"The Americans… C.I.A. agents. They…. they shot two spies, two Dags they called them," Barbara sobbed between sniffles. Shudders still wracked her body and she gripped him even tighter.

"C.I.A.! Dags! *Sacre bluer! le Dags*" Raoul cried.

"You've heard of them?" Barbara asked, lifting her tear-stained face away from his shoulder to look at his face.

Raoul nodded grimly. "*Oui.* I mean yes. Zey are the very bad news. Zey are *l'fanatique, l'extremist.* Were zey watching you?"

Barbara nodded, then paused while more sobs wracked her breathing. "Y..y..yes. They tried to kidnap us. The Americans shot them and rescued us. Then they took us away in a helicopter—to an aircraft carrier."

"Aircraft…. *Mon Dieu !* You ze interesting day 'ave had. I sink you had better tell me all about it," Raoul replied. He looked carefully in both directions, then asked, "Did zey bring you 'ere? Are you alone?"

Barbara nodded and snuggled against Raoul's chest. "Yes, I'm alone. I ran away from the safe house they took us to."

"Ran away ! Safe house! Zey have you in a safe place under guard to protect you and you run away? But why?"

At that Barbara looked up into his eyes. "Because I promised you that I would tell you where the satellite was, and now…"

Her lip trembled and she burst into tears again. With an effort she controlled herself and between more sobs she told him how she had given in and told the Americans.

"I feel so awful. I have let you down and I just feel weak and stupid," she sobbed.

At that Raoul hugged her tightly to him and gripped her head. "Ah! Little petal! *Ma Cheri!* You have done wonderfully. For someone your age you are a marvel. Now, perhaps you had better tell me all about it, if you want to?"

Barbara looked up, tears of joy now welling out. "I want to," she said.

Raoul gestured to the coffee shop. "In there? Is it safe do you think, or have you been followed? Are you perhaps being watched even now?"

Barbara shook her head. "I don't think so," she said.

Raoul had another careful look around and nodded, then eased her arms from around his neck. "Zat is very nice, quite wonderful, but also very distracting to a man," he murmured. He took her arm and steered her back towards the door of the coffee shop.

Barbara would have been happy for him to keep his arms around her all night but she understood and fell into step. "I almost missed you didn't I?" she said.

Raoul nodded. "Yes. I had waited and was just about to give up, would have waited outside for a few more minutes in hope perhaps. You are very lucky. Then I would 'ave had to take risks to contact you again."

"I kept looking at the time and getting more and more upset," Barbara confessed. "I really did want to see you. Anyway, I would have called your hotel."

By then they were inside and Raoul steered her to a quiet table in a corner where they could watch the door. He shook his head. "My hotel! Non. You would me not 'ave got. I 'ave moved to a new place. Zat one was too conspicuous and I feared zey might be onto us. I 'ave moved to a less obvious residence."

Barbara noted that 'us' but merely filed it away. She sat down with a sigh of relief and broke into a fit of trembling again. Raoul signalled to the waiter and asked her, "'ave you eaten?"

When Barbara shook her head he ordered more coffee and toasted cheese sandwiches. As soon as the waiter was out of earshot he reached over and gently folded his hand over hers. That felt wonderfully comforting and Barbara began to calm down, with spasmodic fits of shivering. When the coffee and food had arrived and been paid for Raoul quietly led her into telling him the story. To her own surprise she even included the bits about being naked on the beach and about walking nude across the flight deck of the aircraft carrier.

Raoul burst into loud chuckles and slapped his thigh. *"Eh! Tiens!* How I wish zat I had there been! I mean to watch ze faces of *l'matelots Americains, ze* sailormens. And to see you too. You must 'ave looked *tre magnifique.* You are so very beautiful. They must 'ave been stunned."

Barbara had to smile and the thought crossed her mind that she would not mind this man seeing her nude. That made her blush and feel shocked at herself. Raoul then looked serious, "Zis aircraft carrier, it has a name?"

"*Wasp,*" Barbara replied. "It is some sort of marine landing ship."

Raoul nodded and looked thoughtful. "*Oui.* I know her, a Landing ship 'elicopter, Dock. I 'ave seen several of her sister ships."

"They took us on a tour," Barbara explained, "and in their control room I saw a big radar screen that showed three French navy ships. They said one of them was a landing ship for marines. Is that your ship?"

Raoul smiled. "Zat I cannot say. So zey are watching the ships of France eh? Can you remember the position, the deployment?"

Barbara nodded. "Yes. The Americans are between them and the coast of Australia and are just outside the Great Barrier Reef. The Americans were about halfway between Cairns and Townsville and were heading south."

Raoul was impressed and said so. "That is very good. You the famous lady spy you now are eh?"

Barbara blushed with pleasure. "It wasn't that hard. It was all up on a big coloured map."

Again Raoul nodded and then said, "So, after the aircraft carrier, what happened then?"

Barbara now described the flight ashore and the trip to the safe house. She also repeated what Mr Cavendish had said about not telling anyone and how her life could be in danger if she did.

At that Raoul looked very grave. "He is quite correct. You have taken a great and foolish risk. Perhaps you should just go back as quickly as you can. I will drive you to near there."

"But I promised to help you," Barbara replied.

"Thank you for that, but I fear now we will be too late. l'*Yankees* will now use all their technology to find our piece," Raoul said. He then looked diffident and continued, "However, I did bring the map in the hope you could show me the spot." He took out a folded Dotswood 1:50 000 and opened it on the table.

Barbara had a sip of coffee to gain time to steady her nerves and then pointed to the place. When Raoul took out a pencil to mark the place she reached across to take it. Their fingers touched and for a moment he paused and looked into her eyes. To Barbara it was as though electricity was flowing from him to her and she felt uplifted.

"I can show you," she said.

"Thank you," Raoul said, handing her the pencil, still looking at her.

"No, I meant show you, actually take you to the spot," she added.

Astonishment showed on Raoul's face. "*Alors! Zat* is a wonderful gesture, but it is far too dangerous, and quite unnecessary. I am sure we can navigate to zis spot. You must go back to your father and l'custody of *l'surete*."

Barbara shook her head vigorously. "I don't trust them, and I don't believe them. Besides, I think the satellite should go back to France. It is yours. I feel bad about what I have done and want to make it up."

"But it is not necessary," Raoul insisted. "I do not place you at such risk."

"Will you know if the Americans or Australians locate the satellite?" Barbara challenged.

Raoul nodded. "Almost immediately. They keep up the pretence of being our friends and we have officers at the search HQ at Dotswood."

Barbara nodded. "Well, as I see it, I am not safe until the satellite is found. So I will take you there and show you."

Still Raoul refused to listen. "You can do that by taking your own Australian Army people there and showing them," he argued.

Barbara curled her lip. "Oh them! I tried to. No, I want you to have it, if the Americans don't beat you to it."

"But it is dangerous. Besides, you are just a young girl, a very pretty one too, which makes it even harder. I cannot just travel around with you. It is not right."

"I'm not going back to that flat, so you may as well accept my offer," Barbara said firmly.

Raoul sighed, then shrugged. "You eat your food before it gets cold.".

At that moment, the wail of an approaching police siren caused them both to stiffen in their seats. Barbara swallowed the mouthful she was chewing and tensed ready to run. But the police car gave no hint of slowing and then raced past along Sheridan Street, heading northwards.

"I don't like the sound of that," she said.

Raoul shrugged. "It may be nothing, a road accident perhaps? Now eat up and I take you back before zey find you are gone."

"I'm not going back," Barbara repeated stubbornly. "I am staying with you. I have sent for my bush gear and I will go with you to Dotswood. We can be there tonight and be back by this time tomorrow if we get moving."

"Your bush gear?" Raoul asked.

"I asked Will... er... my friend, to get my camouflage uniform and webbing, and a map," Barbara replied.

"Your uniform!" Raoul asked in astonishment.

"Yes. If I am in uniform then no one will notice from a distance. I will just be another soldier searching," Barbara replied. She had thought about that and was confident she could just stroll around as long as she stayed a hundred or so metres away from any troops.

A look of admiration showed on Raoul's face and he smiled. "I still think I must take you back to your father."

"You will have to tie me up and force me," Barbara warned. "I've made my mind up."

Raoul looked very thoughtful, then glanced at his watch. He then looked at her and asked, "Do you sink zey will know you are with me? Do zey know I am in the city?"

"I don't know, but I doubt it. My father knows, but he won't tell, and I haven't told anyone else about you," she replied.

Raoul twisted his lips thoughtfully, then said, "I sink zey are on to me. Zat is why I shift my address. So maybe I must move anyway." Then he shrugged and looked at her, obviously baffled. "Maybe I just leave you here and you go home?" he suggested.

Barbara shook her head. "No. I am going with you."

"But you can't!"

"Why not?"

"It is not safe. It is not proper. I fear for your safety; and I fear for your reputation," Raoul replied.

"I think I am in more danger here in my home town," Barbara replied soberly. "These Dags know I live here, and where, and who my friends are. I need to end this, and quickly, or life will become unbearable."

Raoul thought about that and then nodded. "Maybe you are right. Come, let us go outside and talk about this some more." He stood up and went to pay the bill. Barbara waited, and watched him, admiring his lithe stride and handsome profile. She knew she was being stubborn, stupid and romantic but did not care.

Outside Raoul pointed along the relatively dark side street. "Zat is my car, or rather ze car zat I hire. But first I must discuss zis with my *superiors.* Zey may not agree to your plan, in which case I take you back at once. I might anyway, for I care for your wellbeing, Little Rose." With that he walked a few paces away and took out a mobile phone. A ten minute conversation followed, all in rapid French. Barbara was too far away to hear most of it and the French was too fast for her school level to understand. So she stood and kept looking anxiously around. Now that she had put her plan to Raoul she badly wanted to carry it out, if only to be with him longer.

At the end of the conversation Raoul shrugged and snapped the phone shut. Then he walked back to her. "Zey say what I fear zey might say. Zey are all 'artless bureaucrats in l'*Commandement des Operations Speciales*. But you would expect zat. Zey accept your offer. So how do we do it? What is your plan?"

Barbara was so pleased she almost embraced him again. Instead she took a deep breath and outlined her idea: drive to Dotswood via the 'back road' (Across the Atherton Tablelands to Ravenshoe, then through Mt Garnet and down the Kennedy Development Road, then east across the Burdekin River at Battery); find the satellite (she was sure she could walk direct to the spot in minutes), then drive home again. How Raoul then got the satellite out of Australia was his problem but she felt sure he could arrange it, with three French warships off the coast, one carrying helicopters. He smiled at that but made no comment.

After hearing her plan he nodded and said, "Alright. So we wait for your bush gear to arrive. Then we drive to my resort and collect my equipment and my other team member. Then we set off. How is zat eh?"

'Wonderful!' Barbara wanted to say, but she just nodded and said. "Good". Then she said, "You had better wait out of sight till my friend drops off the gear."

"I wait in the car," Raoul agreed. He left her standing there and walked the twenty paces to where a dark coloured car was parked in the relative darkness halfway between two streetlights.

Now that her plan had been accepted Barbara tingled with excitement. She knew it was a race against time and pictured arriving at the Gravel Scrape area next morning to find hundreds of Australian soldiers, or US Marines, all with metal detectors and shovels.

We will look silly then, she thought. But still, it was worth a try. The thing had not yet been found.

Then she became increasingly nervous. As the minutes ticked by with no Willy the tension grew. Once she thought she heard another police siren in the distance and that got her biting her lip with anxiety.

They must have discovered my escape by now, she decided.

Willy arrived from the opposite direction this time. She saw him turn left from McLeod Street and pull up almost behind Raoul's car. A soon as she saw him Barbara began walking towards him, trying to act calm and relaxed. Willy saw her at once and switched off his car's headlights. As she went past Raoul's car he looked at her and raised and eyebrow. She nodded and continued on. Willy climbed out and lifted a garbage bag full of gear from the back seat.

"Here you are," he said.

"Any problems?" Barbara asked, taking the bag.

Willy shook his head. "Not at the house, but after I drove off a car pulled out and followed me. I think it was that car which just went past along McLeod Street. I think they are onto us."

That bit of news made Barbara feel awful. *Oh no!* she thought. *Now I have gotten Willy into trouble.*

She said this to him and he just grinned and shrugged. "Don't worry," he said. "I will just tell them I am a burglar."

That annoyed Barbara. "Willy, don't be silly! This isn't a game or a joke. They will sus out in two secs that you know me; that you are in the same class at school."

"So? I'll tell them the truth, that I'm your friend and I helped you."

Barbara bit her lip and felt tears start again. Having such a good friend made her feel very special. She shook her head then said, "No. Yes. That is your story. Say I asked you to get me some clothes and things and that I am running away with my boyfriend. Tell them that my boyfriend could not do it because he has never been to the house, and you have. Say you do not know who he is, and that my father does not approve, which is why we are running away together. You do not know where we have gone."

"Are you really running away with your boyfriend?" he asked.

His tone was light and bantering but Barbara could tell he was hurt and feeling stressed. She bit her lip and shook her head but said, "You will just have to trust me."

Willy nodded towards the car in front. "Is that him there?"

Barbara made no answer to that but said, "Get going please, before that other car comes back and sees us together."

"You are going to find that satellite aren't you?" Willy said, standing his ground.

Again Barbara did not answer his question. "Get going!" she said, her lip trembling.

Willy stepped forward and hugged her, then gently kissed her forehead. "You take care," he said.

Tears sprang out. Barbara sobbed and then tried to make a joke of it. "Don't you let Marjorie catch you doing that. Now get going."

Willy nodded and released her. "Phone me if you need anything. Here's my mobile number. You won't risk getting my parents or Lloyd."

Barbara took the slip of paper. She then said, "I have my Dad's mobile. You can call me on that. Here is the number. Got your phone?"

Willy shook his head. "I will memorize it," he said. "If they catch me they will find the number in my phone."

So she told him and he repeated it four times. Then he leaned forward and gave her a quick kiss on the cheek before climbing back into his car. Barbara stood and watched as he switched on the motor and lights. As she did a car swung into the side street from McLeod Street. For a second its headlights shone full on her. On an impulse Barbara reached forward and opened the door. The car suddenly slowed and Barbara saw the driver look at her. Then it accelerated on around the corner. As it did Barbara was sure she saw the driver look back and thought he had a radio or mobile phone in his hand.

Oh what a dill I am! she thought, *Standing here on the footpath with a garbage bag full of gear!* She saw Willy looking at her quizzically.

"Are you coming with me?" he asked.

"No. It was just a trick to make him think I was going with you," she replied.

"Good plan!" Willy said. "I will lead them on a chase. Get into your car, quick!"

Barbara sobbed and wanted to hug Willy but instead she slammed the door and ran to Raoul's car, reefed the back door open and tossed the gear inside, then clambered into the front. "Drive!" she said, noting that Raoul already had the motor running. "Go back the other way."

Raoul switched on the lights and did as he was told, doing a U-turn and heading towards McLeod Street. As he did he said, "So?"

"That car. I think it was the one that was following Wi... my friend. I think the driver saw me and was using a radio," Barbara explained. As she said this she noted Willy's car drive off in the other direction.

Raoul chuckled. "Ah! So the chase begins eh?"

"Go left," Barbara ordered as they reached the intersection with McLeod Street.

Raoul did as he was told. "My accommodation, it is in the other direction, at Clifton Beach."

"That's alright. We can just go round the block," Barbara said.

As they did this the same car came driving back around the corner. It passed them. Barbara swivelled her head to look and saw Willy's car just rounding the corner into Sheridan Street. The car followed it. Barbara pulled out the mobile phone, then studied Willy's mobile number in the light from the dash and punched in the numbers. A few seconds later Willy answered. Barbara said, "Willy? It's me. I think they are onto us. A car followed you."

"I know," Willy replied. "I'll give him a bit of a run around. Which way do you want me to lead him?"

Barbara thought for a second. *They will expect us to go south along the Bruce Highway.* she thought so she replied, "Go out along Mulgrave Road to Gordonvale, if you don't mind?"

"It will be a pleasure. Stay in touch, and take care," Willy replied. The phone went dead. Barbara sighed and then said to Raoul, "Go left at the next, then left again along Sheridan Street. My friend is going to lead them the other way."

Raoul nodded, then swung the car around the corner. "Good. Now, you put on the seatbelt. If we 'ave the chase you per'aps need it eh?"

As they swung into the cross street the heart-pounding sound of another police siren came to them. It was coming along Sheridan Street from their right so Raoul slowed. The police car came into view, lights flashing and going well above the speed limit. It raced across the intersection and kept going. Raoul drove along to the intersection with Sheridan Street and swung left. As he did Barbara saw the brake lights on the police car come on and it swung left into the street where they had been parked.

Barbara looked at the police car. "They are onto us alright," she said.

A sickening feeling gripped her stomach and she swallowed nervously. *Oh my God! We are on the run!*

Chapter 24

WHICH WAY?

By now Barbara's heart was racing. She bit her lip and gripped the handle on the door. Raoul accelerated along Sheridan Street, taking care not to exceed the speed limit. As they reached the next intersection Barbara saw two uniformed Queensland Police officers leave their parked car and walk over to the door of the coffee shop. To her relief they did not look in their direction and the car was soon past the corner.

"They will soon know we have been there," Barbara said. "My ginger hair is just too obvious."

Raoul nodded and gave a grim smile. "*Oui,* and zey will start to wonder who is the man you meet."

"I told Willy to tell them you were my boyfriend and that we were running away together," Barbara replied. She related the details of her cover story.

Raoul smiled and nodded. In a bantering tone he said, "So your father does not approve of me eh? Ah well! What a pity. But..." He stopped speaking and Barbara wondered what he had been going to say. Instead he said, "This Willy, he is in love with you."

Mentally Barbara kicked herself for having let slip Willy's name. Then she blushed and hotly denied any such thing. "He is not! He had a crush on me a few years earlier. He's got a girl friend named Marjorie."

"He still the great affection for you has, otherwise he would not do such things on trust," Raoul replied. "I can imagine that," he added. "A man could very easily fall in love with you."

That really got Barbara's heart going and she blushed with pleasure. *Maybe he does like me a bit?* she thought hopefully.

By then they had passed the traffic lights at the swimming pool. The next two sets of lights, at Collins Avenue and the turn-off to the International Airport, both held them up, causing Barbara to fret with anxiety. Then they were hurrying on out past Aeroglen and onto the Cook Highway. Every few seconds she looked back to see if they were being pursued.

By now Barbara was thinking hard. If the police were looking for her would they set up road blocks, and if so, where?

The Barron River Bridge? she thought.

That got her all anxious again, so she warned Raoul and peered through the windscreen for the first sign of any road block. But the traffic was flowing fast and freely and they sped across the long concrete bridge without any trouble. Then it was on across the canefields and flat land north of the city.

There was no sign of police at the roundabouts at the turn-offs to Machans Beach, Holloways Beach or Yorkeys Knob. Barbara did not expect them, but her local knowledge told her that the stretch of highway between the Caravonica roundabout and the one a kilometre further north at Smithfield was the best choke point. Again she warned Raoul, giving her reasoning. He nodded and thanked her and they both stared carefully in that direction as they came to the Caravonica roundabout.

Raoul took it slow, ready to either turn left towards Kamerunga, or to go back towards the city, but there were no police in sight on the straight in question. Barbara sighed with relief as they turned north. At the next roundabout, at the Smithfield Shopping Complex, Raoul also drove slowly, exiting to go north along the Cook Highway. As they came out of the roundabout Barbara looked left along the main road which led up over the mountains to Kuranda, the way she planned to go later, and sucked in her breath in dismay. The flicker of blue lights showed right at the bottom of the mountain.

"There is a police road block there," she said.

As she spoke the glow of more brake lights told her she was right. Cars were coming to a stop in a long line. The sight of that caused her to shudder.

If we had gone that way we would be stuck in that line of cars and would have had to turn off into the shopping centre car park.

Raoul drove on north, his eyes flicking constantly to the rear vision mirror and to scan the route ahead for the first hint of trouble. Barbara sat 'on the edge of her seat' with tension, wondering what to do if they did meet a road block.

What story can I tell? she wondered.

Having changed clothes would help but she knew that her red hair was very distinctive. That got her wondering how to hide or disguise it.

She was also starting to have niggling doubts about the situation she had placed herself in. *I am in a car with a man I hardly know and on the run from the police. He could do anything to me and there would be no one to help me,* she thought.

But that fear was counterbalanced by her instinct that Raoul was trustworthy. Several times she glanced at him, noting the firm jaw and handsome profile.

Suddenly the phone rang. It was so unexpected that she jumped and almost dropped it on the floor. "Hello, hello? Yes. Yes Willy, what?"

Willy answered her at once. "Can't talk. They've got me. There is a police road block at Gordonvale. It covers both the Bruce Highway south and the Gillies Highway to the Tablelands. Got to go. Good luck."

The news made Barbara sick. She felt very upset at having been the cause of Willy getting into trouble. Raoul asked what he had said and she passed him the information. "They must be closing off all the roads," she said. It was an awful feeling, of a net closing, of being trapped by powerful forces outside her control. She became very agitated and tensed ready to flee into the bush on the mountainsides if they were pulled over.

In the event they reached the turn-off at Clifton Beach without any problems. Raoul turned right off the highway and drove in along several side streets to a very pleasant little motel type resort tucked away among palms and bushes near the beach. The car was parked in front of a unit and he switched off and climbed out.

"You wait here. I will only be a few minutes," he instructed.

He went to the unit, opened the door and went in. Barbara sat and tried to relax. She realized she had been perspiring and felt hot and tired. She wound the window down and felt refreshed by the cool breeze. The sound of waves breaking gently on the beach came to her and she sighed. Then she froze.

A man had come around the trellis from the next unit and gone to the door of Raoul's unit! A big, stocky man in civilian clothes.

Barbara's heart leapt into her mouth and she flustered. How to warn Raoul? What to do? Was he a secret agent? Were they caught?

The man knocked on the door and said something. To Barbara's immense relief the door opened slightly and the man went in. She faintly heard Raoul's voice before the door closed again and he was speaking French and seemed quite relaxed.

His fellow agent? Barbara wondered.

He was. A few minutes later both men came out. They were carrying several suitcases and bags and came straight over to the car. Barbara sat tense and anxious while she looked at the newcomer. He was a stocky man in his late thirties or early forties with a cheerful face and short grey hair. Something about him radiated toughness and reliability.

Raoul opened the back door and said, "This is *Sergeant Chef* Henri Boucher. He is my second... er second, er.... two. I. c."

Barbara heaved a sigh of relief and smiled in return. When Sgt Chef Boucher held out his hand she automatically put hers up to be shaken, only to have him bow and kiss it.

"*Enchantement, Mademoiselle,*" he said, grinning.

Barbara blushed with pleasure and decided she liked him at once. Raoul then gave Sgt Chef Boucher rapid instructions in French, the gist of which were to go ahead of them along the highway.

He turned to Barbara. "Which way should we go, Miss Barbara?"

"North," Barbara replied instantly. To try to go back through the city was to get caught. She explained, "There are four roads: one south, the Bruce Highway, one north, the Cook Highway. There are also the two roads leading up to the Atherton Tablelands: the Gillies Highway from Gordonvale and the Kuranda Range Road. We know they have closed the Gillies and Kuranda Range, and the Bruce Highway. That only leaves the Cook Highway."

Sgt Chef Boucher took out a road map and held it in the light so Barbara could see it. She pointed to the roads she had mentioned. "We might still be able to get away by going up the Rex Highway from near Mosman," she explained. "Then back through Mareeba."

Sgt Chef Boucher looked doubting. He grunted and said in heavily accented English, "If the police have closed three of the roads they are very likely to have closed the fourth. Where might they do that best?"

Barbara thought for a moment. "Almost anywhere from Buchans Point on would do, the road is squashed between a steep mountainside and the sea," she said.

"That is what I thought," Sgt Chef Boucher agreed. "That is the road we came in along is it not *Mon Lieutenant*?"

"*Oui sergeant,*" Raoul replied. "So we must proceed with care. You will drive ahead, slowly. We will stay about half a kilometre behind."

Sgt Chef Boucher grinned. "Better than leading into a minefield like that one in Iraq, eh *Mon Lieutenant?*"

Raoul grinned back and lightly punched the sergeant's arm. "Don't scare *Mademoiselle* with your old soldier tales," he chided.

With that he took out a small pocket radio and called up. The other set was in Sgt Chef Boucher's pocket, which he pulled out and replied. Both men nodded and Sgt Chef Boucher walked off to a car parked in the next car port. He climbed in and Raoul took his seat and started the car.

The two cars pulled out onto the street and turned left towards the highway. Raoul drove slowly and allowed Sgt Chef Boucher's car to accelerate out of sight. A minute later they followed him out onto the highway, turning north.

They had only been driving for a few minutes when Sgt Chef Boucher came on the radio. Barbara had to strain to understand the French but she got the message: there was a police road block at Buchans Point!

That dashed her hopes and she felt even sicker. Raoul told Sgt Chef Boucher to keep going through it and then to come back to where they had started from. Raoul then pulled the car into the next right turn lane and did a U-turn. "Back to the resort," he said. "Then we will think up the Plan 'B'."

"Will Sgt Chef Boucher be alright?" Barbara asked.

"I think so yes. He has a Dutch passport and has nothing particularly suspicious in his luggage," Raoul replied.

Which means we have? wondered Barbara, but she did not ask. Instead she asked, "Dutch?"

Raoul nodded. "The Dutch have a very good marine corps in their navy, and we have often done exercises with them. It helps to speak their language."

"Which is why you speak English so well?"

"Thank you, not so well I think sometimes, but yes. We often train with the British Royal Marines, or with the Americans, who also speak a form of English."

Barbara laughed at that, having heard plenty of their 'form of English' only that afternoon. *Was it only this afternoon?* she marvelled. It had been a long day and it obviously wasn't over yet.

At the resort Raoul parked the car in front of the unit and switched off. "You had better get out," he said.

He climbed out and extracted a suitcase from the back, then led the way to the door. Barbara noted that the key had been left in the lock and as soon as she stepped inside she saw a sheaf of bank notes lying on the bed. Raoul followed her gaze and said, "To pay for the rooms. We had not checked out and we are not the thiefs."

"Thieves," Barbara corrected. "I did not think you were."

"I must now to the beach go," Raoul said. "Please come with me."

The beach! At night with Raoul! she thought.

Startling images of the beach that afternoon sprang into her mind, mingled with moonlight, romantic ones, leaving her feeling dizzy and tight in the chest.

"The beach?" she echoed.

Raoul saw her concern and shook his head. "You will be quite safe. The Dags will not get you. I will keep you safe."

"It might not have been the Dags I was worried about," Barbara said.

It took Raoul a moment to grasp her meaning. Then he blushed and shook his head. "Please, I did not mean anything like that. It is to use the satellite radio equipment. I need a place where I can see the sky but no-one can see me, and I wanted you to keep watch."

"Oh, pity," Barbara replied, managing a smile.

Raoul stopped trying to extract a bag from his suitcase and looked very serious. "Please *Mademoiselle*, do not be the tease. You are too attractive and it would be too easy for a mere man to misread the signs and make a mistake. You are quite safe. Cross my heart as the English say."

Barbara blushed at the compliment, then stood and watched while Raoul checked the canvas satchel. He then took another small carry bag from the suitcase and slung it over his shoulder.

"We are ready. Can we go?" he said.

They went out the front, Raoul locking the room behind him and this time keeping the key. Barbara walked happily along beside him as they made their way along the front of the motel. Raoul led her along a dimly lit garden path into a garden which fronted on to a road. Beyond that was the esplanade and beach. Moonlight glittered on the water and a gentle, cool breeze was wafting in. A streetlight fifty metres away gave some light, as did the moon.

"Please warn me if anyone comes," Raoul said. He did a quick check that nobody was lurking in the shadows. "I was checking for lovers, not secret agents," he commented. Then he took a small torch from the carry bag and opened the satchel on a picnic table. Barbara was fascinated, and also concerned lest someone come. Out of the satchel came a small metal satellite dish on a folding stand. This was all opened out, then plugged into a small laptop computer.

Raoul then seated himself and opened the lid of the laptop. After switching it on he began typing. Barbara alternated between watching the garden path and road and watching his face. It was lit up by a faint green glow and that seemed to accentuate his rugged good looks even more. The satellite dish oscillated slowly, then stayed aimed up at the sky to the east. Satisfied the equipment was ready Raoul typed in a long message. He then pressed a button and sat back.

"Is that a type of radio?" Barbara asked.

Raoul nodded. Barbara then said, "But can't the Signals Intelligence people pick it up?"

"A burst transmission," he explained. "The message goes out in a millisecond, and in code, and split across several frequencies. There is no chance anyone but my receiver could intercept or decode it. The best anyone else could do is detect that there had been a transmission somewhere in this region."

Barbara remembered dimly hearing some such information during a lesson on radio antennae so nodded, trying to appear as though she understood. Raoul then watched as the screen lit up with a message. He bent and read this, then bit his lip and began typing again.

A car came into the resort car park and both of them stopped and went tense. A minute later the hand held radio crackled softly and Raoul spoke quietly in reply. Footsteps sounded and Sgt Chef Boucher appeared among the palms.

"Ello! Down on the beach eh? Do not trust him *Mademoiselle. Mon Lieutenant,* he is the very devil with *la femmes.*"

Barbara blushed, mirroring her own fantasy. "Oh piffle!" she snorted. "He's just using the radio."

She then looked at Raoul and got a shock. He was holding an automatic pistol! For a second her heart thudded in alarm, then she saw him smile and lay it on the table.

Phew! she thought. *He is just being cautious.* But it was still an unpleasant shock to learn that he was armed. Then she shrugged and told herself not to be silly. *Of course he would be. All spies carry guns. The sergeant will have one too.* But it made her feel scared and was not reassuring at all.

Sgt Chef Boucher joined Raoul and the signalling went on. From time to time the two men muttered quietly in French and they both read the messages and discussed them and their replies.

After about twenty minutes Raoul packed up the radio equipment and said, "That is enough. Back to the room." He slipped the gun back into the carry bag, along with the torch, and led the way back through the garden.

Once they were back in the room Raoul locked the door from the inside and invited them to be seated. "Coffee?" he asked. Barbara sat down on one of the two beds and nodded. She suddenly felt very tired and thirsty. Sgt Chef Boucher moved to make the coffee. While the water was boiling they discussed the situation.

Raoul said, "Not only are the authorities looking for you *Mademoiselle* but they have closed off the area where the satellite is believed to be."

"Closed it off?" Barbara asked, a sense of sickening failure sweeping through her.

"Road blocks by the Military Police have closed off both ends of the Mingela Road. So now we cannot drive there. Sorry, but your plan is no longer workable."

That really hurt. Barbara realized she had been staking a lot on helping Raoul and tears prickled. She shook her head, unwilling to give up. "Couldn't you fly there? What about a helicopter. There are some on your landing ship, surely?"

Raoul gave a short laugh. "Ah! *Mademoiselle* Firebrand would have us break international law! She thinks we should fly the military aircraft of one country into the airspace of another without permission. I believe in most circumstances that it considered a hostile act."

Barbara felt both very ignorant and young. She retorted, "I was only trying to help."

Raoul nodded "I know. Sorry, I am teasing, but that is just what we asked. Yes we do have helicopters on the ship: 'Super Frelons' and 'Super Pumas'. Both types have the range for the job but at the moment they cannot fly off without being tracked by that mer... merd... er... I swear... that American aircraft carrier. It is now only about ten kilometres from our ship."

"So there must be another way?" Barbara said. "Can't we drive to near the area and walk in? I can walk twenty or thirty kilometres in a day cross-country."

"Perhaps. I have been asked to come up with options because the 'Big Wigs', they think you are our best chance. They want us to try and will get back to us. So, we can relax for an hour. In the meantime we need to plan extricating ourselves from this area."

"Just walk," Barbara answered. She had been thinking about that was well and this gave her a chance to recover somewhat in Raoul's eyes.

"Just walk?" he said, his voice just on the edge of sarcasm and his eyebrows raised.

Barbara turned to Sgt Chef Boucher. "Did the police at the roadblock ask you for any identification or anything?"

Sgt Chef Boucher shook his head. "*Non*. They just check in the back and in the boot. They are looking for a red-haired teenage girl, not a middle-aged man."

"Good!" Barbara cried. "So you can drive up to the other side of the mountains and we will walk up and meet you."

"Are you serious?" Raoul asked, somewhat less sceptically.

"Yes," Barbara replied confidently. "These mountains are nothing. You can walk up almost any of the ridges in about two hours. I know a walking track just near here that we went over on a cadet exercise one weekend. It will get us past the roadblocks for sure."

As she said that, Barbara vividly remembered climbing straight up over the coastal mountains back in June when she and her friends had been searching for Fiona in the 'Smiley People's' territory.

There wasn't even a track that time. She and her friends had just climbed a ridge. She described this to Raoul.

"There are forestry roads up on top," she explained. "We can do it easily. All Sgt Chef Boucher has to do is go up the Kuranda Range Road and turn right along the Black Mountain Road. When he gets to McKenzies Pocket he turns right and follows the forestry road to Forgan Smith Lookout. If I had a map I could show you."

Sgt Chef Boucher produced his road map and Barbara saw that the Black Mountain Road was marked on it as a dotted red line. She carefully described how to find the right turnoff. "If you come out in open sort of forest after driving through jungle for a few kilometres you are there. If you cross a little concrete bridge among she-oaks, you have gone too far by a hundred metres."

"She oaks?"

"Needle leaf trees. Not broadleaf rain forest trees, but not pine trees," Barbara explained. She had walked along the road to Kuranda and did not remember any other turn-offs that went anywhere, except back at the houses near the town.

Raoul looked impressed. "Alright. We might try that. But if HQ says no then I am driving you to the nearest police station."

Barbara nodded. "Thank you. Thanks," the second because Sgt Chef Boucher handed her a cup of coffee. She sipped at it and immediately felt better. The plan was discussed in more detail, such as what to do with the second hire car. Raoul decided they would just park it somewhere.

"Outside the Smithfield Police Station," Barbara suggested. "The coppers won't notice it then, not for quite a while."

That elicited a belly laugh from Sgt Chef Boucher. "*Magnifieque!* Not just beauty, but brains as well, eh *Mon Lieutenant*?"

Raoul appeared to blush. "That will do thank you *sergeant chef*. Now, time to get set up again. Let us go."

The trio again made their way out to the front garden. It was still deserted and the street and beach beyond appeared empty as well. Raoul set up the satellite radio and set to work. After a few minutes a message appeared on the screen. Raoul read it and his face changed. He looked very serious and shook his head doubtfully a few times. Then he called them both over.

"This is heavy stuff. Paris has made the decision, not the Pacific Commandant. They really must want this bit of kit back!" He whistled softly and shook his head again. "Miss Barbara, are you willing to do a night parachute jump?"

That really stumped Barbara. She could only gape for a moment while her heart thudded and all her fears swirled. "I... I... er.... Won't you be able to go if I don't?" she asked.

"We will go anyway, with or without you," Raoul replied. "It will just be easier with you to guide us. Now please *Mademoiselle* Barbara, think carefully. This is dangerous stuff. You could be killed or seriously injured. The French Government offers full compensation for any accident but you know governments, particularly when they are making an electronic offer."

Barbara was scared stiff. She looked at Raoul and asked, "Do you want me to do this?"

He bit his lip, then said, "I want you to be safe. But yes, it would make it easier. It is just that I will not find it easy living with myself if you get hurt."

Oh my God! A parachute jump, and at night! Barbara thought. *Will I or won't I?*

Chapter 25

MOMENT OF TRUTH

Barbara felt so dizzy she was glad she was seated. This was, she knew, one of those moments in life when a person is confronted by a challenge they must face, or forever despise themselves.

Can I do it? she thought. *Am I brave enough?*

Then she looked at Raoul and knew she must. *No matter what, I will do it for him,* she told herself.

"Yes, alright," she answered.

"You are sure?" Raoul asked.

"Positive," Barbara replied somewhat more firmly. "But where are the aeroplane and the parachutes coming from?"

Raoul smiled. "They will be provided. We are to advise on the best location. The time will be sometime tomorrow night," he answered.

That bothered Barbara. "But we might be too late by then! The Americans will have had a whole day to find the satellite!"

"That cannot be helped," Raoul answered. "These things cannot be organized that swiftly. Now, let us finish our planning on getting safely out of this area. I accept the plan to walk up over the mountains. The next question is when is the best time?"

Sgt Chef Boucher grunted. "Why not now? The sooner the better."

Barbara thought about it then shook her head. "No. Most of the track we have to follow is jungle and it will be very difficult to walk that in the dark. We should start in daylight."

"Dawn then?" Sgt Chef Boucher suggested.

Again Barbara shook her head. "No. At that time of day your car will be almost the only one on the road. You will be conspicuous and more likely to be stopped at a police road block, or remembered. So will we be. People will notice the unusual. I think we should start at about eight o'clock, when everyone is going to work. Then you will be lost in the crowd and be will be less noticeable."

"I agree," Raoul said. "That will also give you a good night's sleep. You look like you need it."

"I've had a hard day," Barbara agreed, very aware that she was starting to yawn and feel drained of energy.

Sgt Chef Boucher looked worried and said, "But that gives the authorities all night to track us down. We could get caught in our beds."

"Possibly," Raoul agreed. "But I think the risk worth taking. After all, we are just two Dutch tourists. No, we stay here. Now, we will book another room for me and you *Mon sergeant*. That way *Mademoiselle* can have the privacy of this apartment."

At that Barbara sat up, appalled. "Oh no! Please don't leave me on my own. I will be too terrified to sleep if you do."

"But, but it is not right for men to sleep in the same room as a young girl," Raoul protested. "Think of your reputation."

"Then if you won't, Sergeant Chef Boucher can stay here," Barbara replied. The very thought of being alone, knowing there were prowling foreign agents who might kill her, terrified her.

Sgt Chef Boucher looked horrified. "*Non! Non!* Not me. Think what will happen when *Madame Boucher* gets to hear of it! *Mon Dieu!* I would be out on my ear, with the dog house, as the *Anglais* say. Rather fight the Afghans than endure that sort of scolding. It would go on for years. She would never let me forget it," he wailed.

The thought of the tough commando sergeant being tossed out by his wife so amused Barbara that she gurgled with laughter. Sgt Chef Boucher looked offended, then laughed.

"You do not believe me? You do not have to live with *Madame!* So, the lieutenant must stay, not me."

"Please!" Barbara begged, looking earnestly at Raoul.

Raoul looked around the room. "Both of us then."

Sgt Chef Boucher shook his head and did not agree but Raoul over ruled him. "That will be the safest. And that way one of can be awake on guard at all times." He then turned to Barbara. "And *Mademoiselle* I promise that you will be quite safe from any improper advances. There will be no attack upon your virtue. Sgt Chef Boucher and I shall sleep in this large bed and you in that small one."

Barbara nodded but was secretly appalled at her own disappointment. The thought of sharing a motel room with Raoul had caused her a surge of romantic desire that quite amazed her. To hide her emotions she said, "And I will share the guard duty."

"But no! We are guarding you," Raoul protested.

"Piffle! I'm a cadet under-officer. I've had years of piquet duty. So I will do my share," she insisted.

Raoul looked at Sgt Chef Boucher and shrugged then said, "So be it. Two hours on, and you will start, then Sgt Chef Boucher, then me, agreed?"

Barbara nodded and gave him a grateful smile. Raoul smiled back and then said, "Good. Now, let us get to sleep and try to get a good night's rest."

At that Barbara gave an enormous sigh of relief. "Thank you!" she cried. Then tears started. Sgt Boucher stood up and made his way to the door. "I will collect the luggage and leave you to deal with this situation *Mon brave officier,* " he said. Then, as he closed the door, he met Barbara's eye and winked mischievously.

Barbara puffed up with indignation, but he was gone. She then turned to Raoul. "You don't mind do you? There isn't a *Madame de Berg* is there?"

"No. Not even an intended. Just a girl in every port, such as all good sailor men have," Raoul replied wryly. "I will also get my belongings from the car. Is there anything you need?"

"I will see what my friend brought me," Barbara replied.

She was now tingling with excitement again. Never in her life had she spent the night in a room with two men, let alone one as nice and as male as Raoul! She moved to follow him outside but as she stepped through the door he called to her to stay inside. As he did Barbara saw a woman at the next unit give her a sharp and disapproving look. The implication sent a wave of shame through Barbara. Burning with embarrassment she hurried back inside.

That woman thinks I am a prostitute, she told herself. Disgust and shame coursed through her and she sat and felt ill and exhausted.

Raoul brought in the garbage bag of belongings and his own luggage. Sgt Chef Boucher locked the car and carried his bags in then locked the door to the room. Raoul looked at Barbara and said, "Are you alright?"

"A bit embarrassed, and very tired," she admitted.

Raoul suddenly seemed very shy and diffident. "This will be alright; I mean two men in your room? We do not wish to offend you," he explained.

Barbara had to smile at that. "It will be alright," she reassured him. "I am used to males from being in the army cadets. They smell, they snore, and they fart."

"*Mademoiselle!*" Raoul cried, apparently shocked. Sgt Chef Boucher chuckled and nodded.

Barbara giggled then turned to examine what Willy had provided. To do this she tipped everything out on the bed and spread it out. To her relief her webbing was there and a quick check showed that all of her bush toilet gear was in it: the toothbrush and toothpaste, soap and such like. Willy had found two pairs of knickers and a bra, a pair of socks and her army boots. As well there were a DPCU 'Austcam' shirt and trousers, the US Navy cams, and a cloth bush hat. Best of all the 1:25 000 scale map was in a basic pouch, along with a $50 note.

Oh Willy! What a wonderful friend you are! she thought.

Further digging showed that her hexamine stove, matches, toilet paper, mess gear, torch and First Aid kit were all still in her webbing, along with her 'Silva' compass and a protractor.

I am as ready as I will ever be, she thought, trying to thrust the challenge of parachuting out of her mind.

Raoul unpacked some clean clothes and then some toiletries and took himself to the shower. Sgt Chef Boucher stood where he could watch the outside through a tiny gap at the side of the windows curtains. Barbara turned down her bed and lay back, planning to have a shower after Raoul.

Within seconds exhaustion claimed her and she dropped off to sleep.

Only to stir back to muzzy consciousness when she was touched. She woke to find Raoul leaning over her and pulling the bedclothes up to cover her. He had showered and changed into clean clothes and turned off all the lights. Barbara twitched with alarm till she realized who it was and what he was doing.

Raoul smiled. "Stay asleep my lovely," he said.

Barbara tried hard to reach up, to keep him in her consciousness, but she was just too tired and her arms, which were trapped under the sheet, seemed to be too heavy to lift. *I'm supposed to do guard duty,* she thought. But she drifted back into a deep sleep, filled with dreams, both good and bad.

* * *

It was a bad dream that jerked her awake in the middle of the night—a nightmare filled with spurting blood and chunks of white bone and reddish hair flying as bullets whacked into skulls!

Barbara cried out, and knew she had. And then arms enfolded her and a warm, gentle hand began to stroke her hair.

"Sssh! Ssssh! Calm down. It is only the dream."

A dream? Barbara thought, struggling to ungum her sleep filled-eyes. The room was in darkness, but enough light came in through the curtains for her to be able to see quite well.

"Raoul?" she asked.

"Yes. Now relax. You are safe," Raoul replied.

As realization came to her Barbara reached up and gripped him, hugging him tight, aware that her own body was trembling and covered in perspiration. Her heart was pitter-pattering very rapidly and she had to gasp for breath.

"It's alright," Raoul soothed. "Calm down and go back to sleep. It was just a nightmare. You are safe."

"Oh, hold me please!" Barbara whispered.

To her great relief he did. His arms hugged her to his strong warmth and she felt suddenly safe again and began to relax. She would not have minded if his touch had been more intimate but his hands stayed firmly on her back or head and his arms around her shoulders. After a few minutes she got control of herself and calmed down.

Then she realized that Sgt Chef Boucher was also there, sitting in a chair near the window and pointedly not looking in their direction. Embarrassment surged through Barbara and she bit her lip. She moved to get up. Raoul released her and helped her to sit up. He then brought her a drink of water.

"I was going to have a shower," she muttered.

"You fell asleep. That was what you really needed. Now go back to sleep again."

"But I am supposed to be on guard," Barbara answered.

Raoul shook his head. "Later. It will do the wicked and lazy *Sergeant Chef* good to take your place for a couple of hours.

Barbara looked at Sgt Chef Boucher, who turned to face her. He grinned and in reply to her query said, "You need the sleep *Mademoiselle.*"

"Please wake me when it is my turn please," Barbara asked. She wanted to say hold me to Raoul but could not bring herself to be so forward with Sgt Chef Boucher just there.

But Raoul took her hand and gently stroked it. "You rest," he said.

She lay back and, at his insistence, closed her eyes. Very slowly she drifted off to sleep again, pleasantly aware that he was watching over her.

* * *

Barbara opened her eyes and wondered where she was. All her muscles felt stiff and she groaned slightly as she stretched. She realized she was lying on the bed in the motel. Sprawled on the next bed was Raoul. On the bedside table near his hand was the automatic pistol. There was no sign of Sgt Chef Boucher.

The sight of Raoul sent a warm glow of affection through Barbara. She sat up and moved across to look down at him.

Suddenly she became aware that his eyes were open and he was looking at her. "What's wrong?" he asked.

"Nothing, except that Sgt Chef Boucher is not here and you have fallen asleep," Barbara answered. She saw his eyes widen with interest as they flicked down. Before she thought about it she glanced down herself, and instantly went hot with embarrassment. She was still leaning over him and while she had slept several of the buttons on her floral shirt had come undone! Her breasts were half-exposed!

Oh heavens! Do I make a big deal of this or not? her mind asked.

She wondered, but only for a fraction of a second, if he had noticed, then knew he had. There was just enough light coming in from outside to make the view quite visible. Then she realized she didn't care. But she did understand that she was in the grip of strong desires she had barely experienced but which were very powerful. She felt an intense urge to bend down and kiss this man.

For several seconds they stared into each other's eyes. Barbara sensed that she was in a situation that could very quickly get out of control.

Alone, in a room with a strange man, she thought. *And what a man!* she added.

She knew she was breathing fast and was dimly aware that her lips were parted and just aching to be kissed. "Oh, hold me!" she whispered, reaching down to hug him.

To her intense disappointment Raoul shook his head and stopped her. Very gently he held her shoulders, his eyes looking into hers questioningly. By then Barbara was almost panting and she could feel the heat building in her body. Fire seemed to surge through her. Dimly she sensed that she would let this man do anything he liked to her. To her own detached amazement she found she did not care what the consequences might be.

Raoul reached up and kissed her forehead, then very gently eased her away. "Oh! Oh!" he groaned. "I was right when I said a man could easily fall in love with you. And I think I have. For that reason I say, not yet. We must first get to know each other properly. Then we let the nature take its course, eh?"

Barbara felt a sharp pang of regret, but also another surge of warmth. She understood that he was not rejecting her; rather that he cared for her and did not want to hurt her. Then little waves of shame began to lap at her consciousness.

Oh dear! What have I done? she asked herself.

She stepped back, her face burning. "I'm sorry. You must think I am a really cheap throwing myself at you like that."

Raoul sat up, still gripping her shoulders. "*Non.* I think you are wonderful. I also appreciate that you are very young, that you are very nervous and anxious. Perhaps too you are over-tired and suffering from the shock after the terrible events of yesterday. I am not sure if physical love is the right cure for that at this moment. Anyway, I do not want to lose your affection by taking advantage of you when you are emotionally vulnerable."

"Oh! You are wonderful!" Barbara cried.

She gripped him to her, pressing her bosom against his chest. *He is just the nicest, most thoughtful, caring man,* she thought. And definitely a man! She realized that he had become very aroused.

"I could love you," she whispered.

That made him smile and kiss her cheek. "I think that is very good. And when this is over, I would like to get to know you. Now, perhaps we had better both cool down before we do something we might regret?"

At that moment Barbara was willing to do anything he suggested, and was shocked by the self-revelation that came to her.

I really am normal, she told herself.

She had always suspected that when the right man came along it would all be alright—and it was! It was such a relief she wanted to shout for joy.

Once again Raoul took control of the situation. He moved away, half-rolling over to look at his watch. "What time is it?" he asked.

Suddenly Barbara was ashamed of herself. She stepped back, pulling her shirt closed as she did. Raoul tactfully kept looking at the bedside clock while she fumbled with the buttons. He muttered that it was only 2 o'clock. Next he stood up and looked through the curtains, then grunted and opened the door. "Come in and sleep Henri," he called.

Barbara blushed fiercely as she had forgotten about Sgt Chef Boucher. *Thank heavens he didn't come in while I was throwing myself at Raoul,* she thought, more heated flushes of shame sweeping up her neck.

To help ease the situation, she said, "I will do the next two hours on guard."

Sgt Chef Boucher raised an eyebrow. "Is *Mademoiselle* rested enough?"

"Yes," Barbara insisted.

Raoul nodded and said, "Bed *Mon brave.* Let *Mademoiselle* have a turn. But only for one hour please. Now, time for a few more hours sleep."

With that he flopped back on the bed and closed his eyes. Sgt Chef Boucher went through into the toilet. Barbara moved to sit in the chair near the windows. She felt suddenly drained of desire and hot with shame. But she could not get Raoul out of her thoughts and she kept glancing to look at him. She saw that he was looking at her. After a minute or so he nodded and smiled, his eyes still holding hers.

Quietly, so that Sgt Chef Boucher might not hear, Barbara whispered, "Good night. Sweet dreams."

In reply Raoul grinned and said softly, "Stop that, or I think perhaps you are a witch. You beguile me so, I go weak. I so desire you. Now let a poor man sleep and don't keep stirring up the animal passions."

Barbara smiled at him and nodded. At that moment Sgt Chef Boucher came back into the room and moved to lie on the bed beside Raoul.

I wish that was me lying there, she thought, then blushed at her own wickedness.

To change her thoughts, she sat forward and peeked through the gap in the curtains. Outside was still and quite but the very silence reminded her of their peril and she felt the tension increase.

As she sat on guard, Barbara heard Raoul roll on his side and fidget until he was comfortable and then steady breathing. For a while she sat there, warmed by the dying glow of her arousal, her mind reliving those delightful minutes of revelation.

And she ignored the one hour and stayed on guard until 0400. She then woke Raoul. To do this she shook his shoulder, feeling quite hesitant about it because now she was ashamed of her earlier forwardness and worried that it might have given him a bad impression.

He might just think I am a cheap slut, she thought.

Raoul opened his eyes and looked at her, his face alert and questioning. Barbara stepped back, and said, "Your turn on guard."

He nodded and rolled out of bed, apparently wide awake. To hide her confusion Barbara moved to the other bed and lay down. She was tired but sure she would not sleep. To avoid any embarrassment she lay with her back to Raoul, her mind replaying the last two days and wondering about the future.

During which she fell asleep.

* * *

It was a dream such as Barbara rarely had: warm hands gently caressing her body; she was aflame with desire and ready for the thrust of her man—and she woke up!

There he is, she told herself with a loving sigh.

She was lying on her side facing him. Raoul was sound asleep, lying on his side facing her. For a several minutes she studied him, noting the charming, boyish good looks on his relaxed face, the bulge of muscle in his upper arm where the sleeve of his shirt had pulled up, the foot poking from the sheet.

Is he the one? she wondered, aware that she was feeling distinctly aroused.

She found herself gritting her teeth with a most unfamiliar emotion: frustration! For the first time in her life she had woken up ready for love, and knowing it.

Then noises outside brought her back to reality. She saw that it was daylight and realized that it had been the sound of a car starting up that had woken her. A glance at the bedside clock told her it was almost 7 o'clock. There was no sign of Sgt Chef Boucher and no sounds to indicate he was in the bathroom.

I had better get up, she thought.

Very quietly she slid out of bed, her eyes still lovingly fixed on Raoul's face. With an effort she resisted the temptation to lean over and kiss him.

Come on girl, get a grip on yourself, she chided. *Remember the Dags are outside, and the police. Now have that shower.*

Barbara found a bra and undies in the jumble on the floor, then dug out her toilet bag before moving to the bathroom, all the while glancing to make sure she was not waking Raoul—and half-hoping she would. It was a typical motel bathroom and included the toilet. Feeling very daring she left the door unlocked. First she went to the toilet, blushing when she realized that flushing it must wake him. Then she stripped and moved to the shower.

That was bliss. The warm water quickly refreshed her and she began to hum quietly, the sheer joy of thinking she was in love driving out other thoughts. Slowly she soaped herself, enjoying the stimulation of touch and imagining it was him doing it. Her eyes examined her body, noting the small bruises from the previous days manhandling.

Manhandling alright! she thought, remembering the various incidents.

That also got her aroused. First, she thought of being nude with Wendy and Fiona, then of the helicopter flight and finally the scene on the flight deck.

However, did I find the nerve to do that? she marvelled, both thrilled and ashamed at the memory.

Suddenly there was a knocking on the door. "Hurry up girl," Raoul called. "I have a need to go to the toilet."

An impish thought crossed Barbara's mind and she called back, "You can come in. I won't look."

"I do not wish to offend you," Raoul replied.

"I won't be, and don't you look," Barbara answered.

A glance showed her that the frosted glass walls and door of the shower cubicle would still allow a fairly good view, but that only added to her feelings of excitement. By then she had begun to breathe faster and knew she was being very naughty and daring. She turned her back and held her arms over her bosom, her whole body tingling.

The door opened and Raoul came in. Barbara glanced over her shoulder, hotly aware that he could see all of her bare back and buttocks. She saw him glance at her, then away. He was only wearing a towel around his waist and looked very fit and manly. He moved to the toilet bowel and she could only see part of his back. But she heard the splashing, even above the sound of the shower, and that caused her to blush.

As the toilet flushed Raoul called, "Hurry up woman. You have been in there ten minutes at least. I have to shave." He made his way back to the room, sliding the door closed as he did.

Normally a male calling her 'woman' would have annoyed Barbara, but this time it sent her an entirely different message. She laughed, and it was on the tip of her tongue to suggest he join her in the shower.

Oh! What's come over me? she asked herself, shocked at her own naughty thoughts.

But she knew what it was—love.

She turned off the shower and pulled the glass screen aside. While drying herself she kept hugging warm thoughts to herself and marvelling at the change. In a searing revelation it came to her that she wanted this man to see her naked, that she wanted him to make love to her. She knew she was now breathing fast, that her desire was aroused, and that she was potentially making the most important decision of her life, all under stress. But equally she knew she did not care. Thoughts of regret, of disgrace, of disease, of pregnancy, were all swept aside. In fact the words 'have his babies' crossed her mind several times.

Then he called again, asking her to hurry up.

Before she realized what she was doing, she called back, "You can come in, if you want to." She held the towel across her front and stood waiting.

Raoul, wearing only a towel, appeared in the doorway. He stopped, surprised delight on his face. Then he blushed and began to turn away.

"Oh! *Pardon.* I am sorry," he said.

"Raoul," was all Barbara could croak. Her throat had constricted and gone dry and blood was pounding in her ears.

Raoul stopped and looked back, his eyes searching hers, and also sweeping over her half-covered form. "You are so beautiful!" he cried, wonder and admiration on his face. Then he shook his head in disbelief and turned away muttering, "Beautiful, but too young."

"Oh, don't say that! I'm not a little girl!" Barbara croaked. She stepped towards him, dropping the towel.

"Oh! I can see that!" he gasped, his eyes lingering on her bosom.

Men! Barbara thought, but she loved it.

She put her arms around his neck and he put his on her hips. It felt so nice, so natural. They came together slowly. Their lips met. His bare chest brushed her nipples. Then they were pressed together in a passionate embrace. For long minutes they kissed and their hands stroked and rubbed each other. She could tell that Raoul was very aroused and she pressed against him. But Raoul only caressed her back and squeezed her buttocks, making her cry out as passionate desire surged in her. Her whole body seemed to tingle and she yearned for him to move his hands to her front.

Then they eased apart, a look of delight and desire on his face. That really set Barbara on fire. Waves of heat seemed to scorch through her. She found she was gripping him tightly. Then they were pressed hard together, and she knew she wanted it.

"Oh please!" she croaked in a stifled sob.

"Are you sure?" he asked as they stopped kissing, both panting with arousal.

Barbara nodded. She knew it was a moment of truth. *I am a normal woman and I want this man to make love to me, and I want him to do it now,* she thought. She was so aroused she felt sure she was willing to do anything he suggested—except what he did say!

Raoul shuddered with aroused desire, but gently and firmly held her away from him. "Are you a virgin?" he asked, stepping back and taking her hand.

Barbara nodded.

At that he shook his head. "Then we will not go further, however wonderful it may be for me. It would be wrong and I like you so much I do not wish to spoil it and have regrets."

"Please! I'm sure. I love you!" she cried.

"Then when the right time comes I will be gentle," he said, making her love him even more.

Chapter 26

TENSION

So inflamed with desire was Barbara that she ached with urgent need. She trembled and a deep anxiety gripped her. Strong emotions boiled within her and she clung tightly to Raoul, still hoping he would act. But Raoul just held her and then shook his head and eased himself away. A look of great sadness crossed his face and he shook his head again.

"No," he said. "This is not the right time. I think, maybe, that I am the right man for you, but if I am, then we must not spoil things."

"Raoul!" Barbara gasped, writhing in frustrated urgency, but half-agreeing with him. She knew she was overwrought and not thinking clearly. But Oh! How she ached to have him do it!

Raoul leaned forward and kissed her forehead. "You are too special," he muttered. "I have never met a girl like you in my life. If you are the one, then I want to woo you correctly. I think that this is the wrong time for both of us. You are tired and under great stress, and I am a soldier on a mission. Let us save ourselves for a more romantic time."

"Oh Raoul!" Barbara cried, half in frustration, and half in relief.

New waves of love seemed to engulf her, and she thought he was the most wonderful man she had ever met. She knew she wanted him to make love to her—and she knew that what he said was right. With a sigh of frustration and love she hugged him to her again.

When he finally freed himself he looked at her in a most serious way, and said, "After this is over, I will come back and we will have a holiday together, and I promise I will make everything perfect for you."

Wonderful images of being with Raoul in a palm fringed tropical resort, free to make love all day and all night began to flood through Barbara's mind, helping to ease the tormenting waves of frustration that were still surging through her heated body.

At that moment the small sliding door above the side bench slid open. The effect on both was startling. Raoul sprang aside, snatching up the pistol and aiming it. Barbara crossed her arms over her bosom, her heart in her mouth as fear replaced sexual desire in a gasping surge.

A tray was slid in onto the bench. On the tray was a plate of food, drink containers and the utensils to eat with. All that was visible of the person doing this, because of a small timber partition, was a hand. This withdrew and the sliding door snapped shut.

The effect on both bordered on the ludicrous. "Breakfast," Raoul said, looking foolish. "I forgot that I ordered it." He gestured to the gun as though to apologise.

When the first shock wore off Barbara gurgled with laughter. "It's alright," she said. "I think you look great."

"I feel very foolish," Raoul admitted while putting down the gun and adjusting the towel. "I did not mean to offend you. Now please don't look."

To her own surprise Barbara found she was not annoyed at the sight of the male body. Previous bad experiences had caused her some very negative reactions in the past. But now an intense urge to bond with this man surged in her and she stepped forward and embraced him.

"You didn't offend me," she said, snuggling against him and putting her arms around his neck. Their bodies came together and she kissed him and then sighed. It felt so right, and so natural, that she just felt a warm glow.

Raoul held her tightly, his face alive with wonder and love. By instinct they came together again to kiss. As their lips touched and Barbara was thinking how nice he smelt, and how good it was to be naked and with the right man, there was a knock on the door.

From outside came Sgt Chef Boucher's voice. "'ello in there! Are you awake yet? Can I come in?"

Once again the effect was comical. Both jerked apart. Raoul jumped up and began picking up items of clothing, searching for his trousers. Barbara scuttled back into the bathroom and slid the door across. As she did she saw Raoul drop the towel and snatch up his pants and begin hopping around as he tried to pull them on. As he did she was granted a side view of his very erect male member and the sight caused her a surge of interest, arousal and relief.

He's normal, she thought, amazed at her own reactions.

Seeing him struggling to pull up his trousers caused Barbara to burst into breathless giggles. Raoul gave up, tossed the pants aside and grabbed the towel off the floor. As he did he grinned at her and shook his head.

"Don't be naughty! Close the door," he whispered. Loudly he called, "Come in!"

"Ok!" came the answer. "Unlock the door please"

Barbara thought she detected chuckles in Sgt Chef Boucher's voice as she closed the bathroom door. She blushed and felt her heart hammering with excitement and desire. She began squirming quickly into her clothes. Out in the main room she heard the door open and Raoul say, "We will 'ave our breakfast first."

Sgt Chef Boucher said something in a guttural foreign language. Raoul snorted and answered in the same language, then laughed. Barbara raised her eyebrows.

What did he say? she wondered. But she could guess. *I'll bet he made an improper male suggestion.*

Barbara really blushed then, but also giggled. She felt very naughty, and very happy. For a few minutes she stood and stared at herself in the mirror, feeling the burning in her cheeks, as though she had a high fever.

Oh, he is wonderful! she told herself. Then she hugged herself and smiled. *I'm normal! Oh, thank God!*

With those thoughts to boost her she dressed. She pulled on the floral shirt and shorts, then tidied her hair and washed her still heated face. Then a wave of shyness and shame almost overcame her. It took an effort to step out of the bathroom.

Sgt Chef Boucher gave her a big grin and said, "Good morning *Mademoiselle*. You slept well?"

"Yes thank you. Did you?"

"Enough. Thank you for doing the piquet duty," Sgt Chef Boucher replied.

Raoul was waiting, the towel around his waist and his clothes and toilet bag in his hands. He gave her a smile, easing her fears and causing another gush of adoration. He gestured to the food tray. "You eat the breakfast," he said. "Sgt Chef Boucher has had his and I can go to the shops but red-headed girls cannot."

Barbara accepted the logic of this and sat down at the bench. Raoul went into the bathroom to shower and shave. The breakfast was bacon and eggs with toast, plus coffee and fruit juice. The fruit juice was pineapple, which she thought too sour and which she would not have normally drunk, but she quaffed it down. The first sight of the greasy bacon had caused Barbara's stomach to churn but then hunger took over and she almost wolfed it down. While she ate her breakfast Sgt Chef Boucher kept guard and chatted, explaining that he had gone back to his room only after doing guard duty.

"I wanted things to look normal to the motel management," he said.

By the time Barbara had finished eating breakfast Raoul had returned, wiping his jaw on a towel. He was now dressed in jeans and an open-necked casual shirt.

"Good girl!" he said with approval. "Did you leave me any coffee?"

She had and he drank it while she packed her belongings back into the garbage bag. Raoul then finished dressing and packing, slipping the pistol back into the small carry bag. Knowing what was planned Barbara had a huge drink and made sure her four watebottles were full. Raoul also had a drink then moved to the door.

"Are you ready?" he asked her.

Barbara stood up and nodded. Now she was embarrassed and not a little ashamed of herself. She avoided meeting Sgt Boucher's eye as he opened the door and went out. As soon as Sgt Chef Boucher was out of hearing Barbara met Raoul's eye.

"Thank you," she whispered, meaning for treating her with such consideration.

He obviously understood as he moved over and gently kissed her forehead. "I meant what I said," he replied. "I intend to find out if you are the girl of my dreams. I want to love you. Now, enough of this, to war."

At those words Barbara was almost overcome with emotion. Her chest went tight and her throat choked up. She was sure she was in love. Her whole being cried out with joy and she wanted to hug and kiss him but could only nod. Raoul eased them out of the situation by picking up his cases and going out. Barbara followed.

Sgt Chef Boucher was waiting beside his car. Barbara hurried to the other side of Raoul's car. But Raoul pointed to Sgt Chef Boucher's car. "We go in that one," he reminded her. Barbara felt herself brought down to earth with a bump as she remembered the plan. With a nod she moved her gear to the back door of the other car and busied herself placing it in. Then she climbed quickly in and huddled down in the seat.

Raoul went off to pay the bill and Sgt Chef Boucher climbed into the front of the car. He turned to look at her, his face concerned.

"You are alright then, Little One?" he asked gently.

"Yes thanks. I have had a good night's sleep and eaten breakfast."

He met her eyes and then nodded with understanding. "Be brave," he said. "We will try to keep you safe."

Barbara nodded and then felt fear grip her as chilling memories of the Dags being shot on the beach flooded into her consciousness. Then the thought of doing a night parachute jump added to her fears. It took her an effort to stop from hyperventilating.

Sgt Chef Boucher said, "I listened to the morning news on the radio. There was no mention of any police hunt for you. Not that we would expect that. This is all security stuff, not criminal eh?"

"Perhaps the roadblocks are gone?" Barbara suggested.

"Maybe, but we not risk it eh? We go with your plan," Sgt Chef Boucher replied.

He sounded so cheerful and confident that most of Barbara's fears abated and she sat back and breathed more easily. Raoul returned, exchanged a few quick sentences with Sgt Chef Boucher about the plan to dump the other car, then smiled at her and went to his own car. Both cars were started and they moved off. Barbara found she was gripping the seatbelt and biting her lip.

Here we go! she thought, her anxiety level shooting right up.

The first part went with what seemed to be almost laughable ease. Both cars drove out to the Cook Highway, turned left and drove south towards Cairns. They just slipped into the flow of morning traffic. A few kilometres later they went around a roundabout and Raoul drove his car to the front of the Smithfield Police Station. There was a police car parked out the front but no sign of any officers. Raoul parked the car and casually strolled off along the footpath. By then Sgt Chef Boucher had turned into a service road and then pulled over in front of a shop a hundred metres to the north. Raoul just walked to the shop, went in and made a couple of purchases, then walked calmly out and climbed into the front of their car.

"*Voila! Un mysterie for l'Gendarmerie,*" Raoul said with a chuckle. He turned and smiled at Barbara. "You are fine Little Cabbage?"

Barbara could only smile back. Then she asked a question that had been bothering her. "Do you think I should use my mobile phone to get friends to check if there are still road blocks?"

By now she had remembered Willy and was feeling extraordinarily guilty.

Raoul shook his head. "*Non*. They could intercept that. Turn your phone off and save the battery for an emergency. We will run with your plan. It seems to me a good one. Now, you direct us."

Barbara took out her phone and did as she was told. Sgt Chef Boucher set the car moving and pulled back out onto the highway, this time heading north again. Once again it all seemed unreal and too easy. They saw no police cars and everything was peaceful and normal. At Evergreen Street Barbara directed them to turn left. Then she had to really concentrate and she bit her lip and stared through the front.

"First left, then right at the T-junction" she directed. Sgt Chef Boucher did as she said and she had the satisfaction of recognizing the street and of seeing the mountains directly ahead. She pointed and said, "That ridge there, the one straight in front of us. We go up that. Now turn left at the next T junction and then right up a steep little side street."

Two minutes later the car swung around at the end of Tobias Close. Sgt Chef Boucher pulled the car over and stopped beside a chain which blocked off a concrete driveway which led uphill through the jungle.

"That's our track," Barbara said, relief flooding through her.

She and Raoul climbed out. Barbara anxiously eyed a house across the court, wondering if anyone was watching, but there was no-one in sight. Not even a barking dog. With her heart beating rapidly and with sweaty hands she hoisted out her garbage bag and hurried up the concrete driveway. Raoul slung the canvas satchel over his shoulder, hoisted on his small carry bag and, after a few more quick words to Sgt Chef Boucher, strolled after her. By the time Barbara had gone fifty paces the car had driven off.

By then she was already puffing, as the slope was steeper than she remembered. Raoul quickly caught her up. "Slow down," he said. "Remember ze tortoise and l' hare. Slow and steady wins ze race on hills."

Barbara knew that but in her anxiety had been hurrying. Now she slowed down, hoisting the garbage bag to a more comfortable position. Raoul held out his hand. "You may give me that. It is better if I carry it."

That ruffled Barbara's gender feathers. "I can carry it," she panted back.

"I 'ave no doubt you can," Raoul replied. "But I the commando am, not you. I am very much fitter and I would prefer you keep your strength for when you need it."

Barbara compressed her lips in a stubborn gesture, even though she knew he was right. "I'll be right," she replied.

"Please," Raoul answered. "To me this is just a stroll. In *l'Fusiliers Marins* we run fifteen kilometres before breakfast some days, and that with the rifle, webbing and helmet. This mountain range, how high is it?"

"The Macalistair Range? About four hundred metres," Barbara replied.

Raoul grunted. "With full pack and webbing, water and five days rations we climb it in one hour. Like this I expect my men to be up it in about twenty minutes. Now please be sensible. You are already puffing like ze old steam train and the sweat is starting."

It was too and Barbara had to admit she wasn't as fit as she should be. Even so it irritated her to admit that males were stronger or more capable. Then common sense told her to agree and she nodded and handed him the garbage bag. By then they had passed a sharp turn back to the right which led up an even steeper section of roadway. There was now bush on both sides and already Barbara felt safer.

The cops won't catch me in this, she thought, remembering all those cadet exercises and the desperate adventures of a few months earlier.

She said, "Do you think I should change into my camouflage uniform?"

"Is there such thick jungle that you need the protection?" Raoul asked.

"No. It is just a walking track. Some of it goes through long grass but mostly it is quite clear," she answered.

"Then I think you should stay dressed as you are," Raoul replied. "In a uniform you attract comment. Dressed as we are we are just two hikers seeing the sights."

Barbara accepted that. By then they had reached a section of the road which was behind the back fence of a house. She found she was so puffed she had to stop to get her breath back. Raoul made no comment on this but merely looked around, commenting on what a grand view the people who lived in the house must have. A minute's rest was enough and Barbara plodded on. Two minutes later they reached a flat area on which stood a large steel reservoir. At the right-hand end of the cutting at the back of the flat was a faint foot trail. This led up into typical coastal savannah woodland: long grass, grasstrees and numerous eucalyptus trees.

Once on that track Barbara really felt safe. *I can just bolt into the bush,* she told herself, quite confident she could hide or escape from most pursuers. *After all, I've had a bit of practice!* she thought wryly.

After that it was just two hours of plod, rest, plod. The track was narrow, forcing them to walk in single file, but as it followed the ridge top it was easy to follow. Fitness, rather than navigation was the delaying factor. There were a few grassy stretches where Barbara kept a wary eye for snakes but mostly it was through rainforest and easy to see where she was putting her feet and quite unobstructed.

As they went up the ridge the scenery got better and better, with long views out over the Coral Sea and back towards Cairns. Barbara looked at it during her frequent short rest stops and found her emotions curiously mixed. It was her home territory and she loved it. Now the thought crossed her mind that France might have nice scenery too.

That made her glance at Raoul. He caught her glance and returned a smile and said, "You are looking very thoughtful and sad Ginger-haired One. Is something the matter?"

"I was thinking that I may never see my home again," Barbara answered. "I might have to live somewhere else with a new identity; that is if these Dags come after me, or my own country might not want me if I help you."

Raoul nodded. "You may be right, but I hope for you it is not so. But take heart, there are many beautiful places in the world. France owns many of them and I am sure you will now always be welcome there."

That was a really scary thought to Barbara. She tensed, feeling that Raoul was going to say more, but he just met her eyes, then shrugged. "Come. Sgt Chef Boucher must now be waiting for us on top. We must be about halfway up this mountain."

They turned and resumed their trek up the mountain.

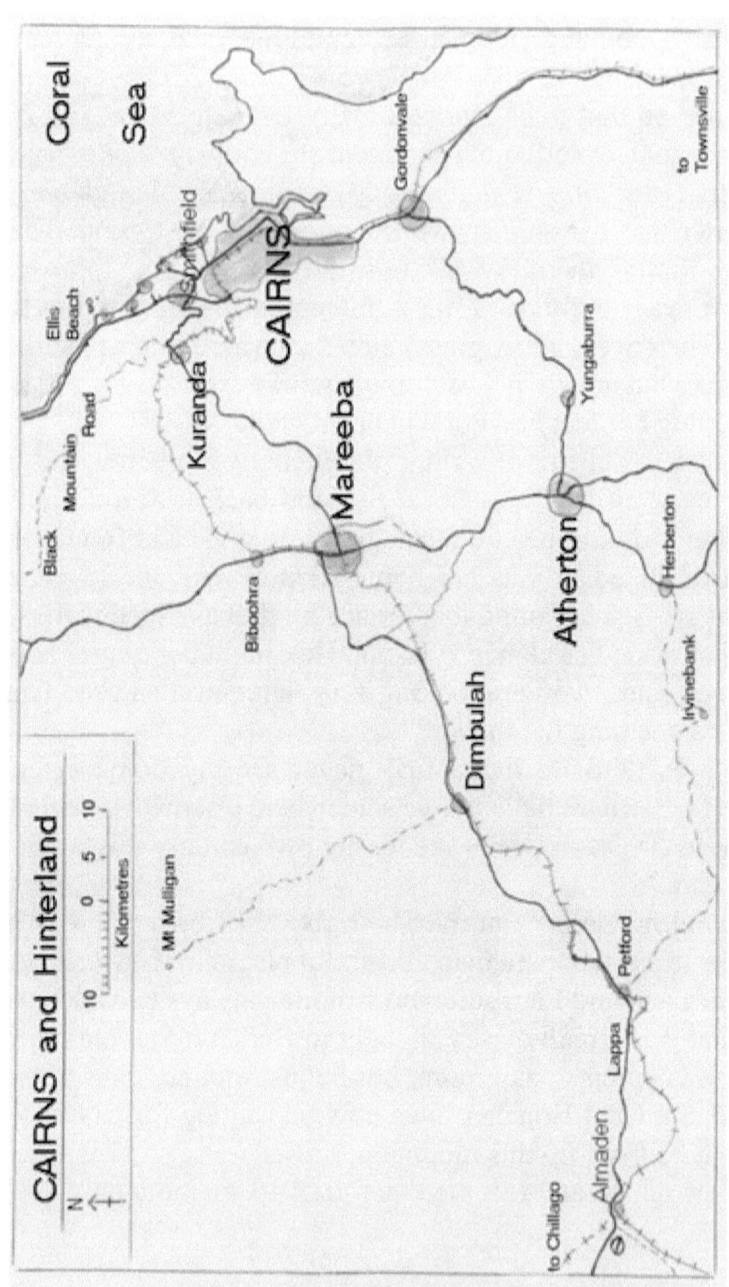

CAIRNS and Hinterland

N

Kilometres
10   0   5   10

Coral

Sea

to
Townsville

Gordonvale

Smithfield

Ellis
Beach

CAIRNS

Kuranda

Black

Mountain

Road

Mareeba

Yungaburra

Biboohra

Atherton

Herberton

Dimbulah

Irvinebank

Mt Mulligan

Petford

Lappa

Almaden

to Chillago

Chapter 27

DECISIONS

After another half-hour's walk, the pair entered proper rainforest and the slope steepened appreciably. Barbara had to stop more and more frequently and felt worried lest Raoul think she was weak. He took out one of her waterbottles and they quickly emptied that. Then they plodded on up. The jungle canopy now restricted the view to occasional glimpses. Wait-a-while appeared. Barbara wasn't sure if Raoul had ever seen it and pointed to one of the tendrils.

"Watch out for those," she cautioned. "They really rip you and they are too strong to break."

Raoul examined the tendril, with its curved barbs, with interest. "Most unpleasant. What is it called?"

"Wait-a-while or wait-a-bit," Barbara replied. She had met it too many times for it to be any favourite of hers. She shuddered at some of the memories. "I think I prefer open country," she commented.

They plodded on up. Barbara kept up the pretence that it was not an effort lest Raoul despise her for being weak. From time to time she admired his well-muscled male form, the broad shoulders and slim hips.

He is very handsome, she told herself. Then the mischievous thought crept in that they were alone in the jungle. *We could make love,* she thought.

Several times she imagined contriving some 'incident' to set up a situation for that purpose but then she was ashamed of herself for having such immoral thoughts. It came as a shock to her to find just how easily she could imagine doing things she had previously sternly opposed allowing.

The old saying is right—rape is the wrong man—and I think Raoul might be Mr Right!

They walked on. The track levelled out and Barbara knew they were now nearing the top of the mountain. "This is a place called Forgan Smith Lookout," she explained. "This track was blazed by the early pioneers back in the Nineteenth Century to get to the goldfields further inland."

"Lookout?" Raoul queried, looking around at the dense jungle which now hemmed them in.

Barbara laughed then explained that the clearing had overgrown in the last hundred years. "So Major Conkey said," she added.

"Major Conkey?" Raoul queried.

"The OC of my army cadet unit. He is also my history and geography teacher," she explained. She then related some of the early history of the region as they walked. Raoul knew none of this and was more than politely interested, although Barbara had to often explain English terms, or Australian slang.

The track wound through flat jungle for half a kilometre but was easy to follow, except for two fallen trees they had to clamber over. Abruptly the vegetation changed and they came out on an overgrown vehicle track with a dense pine forest beyond. This had a real jungle of undergrowth, mostly wild raspberries, and Barbara knew from hard experience that it was a horrible environment to try to push through on foot. Vivid images of pushing through a similar forest further north in June when they were escaping from the Smiley religious cult caused her to shake her head and shiver. That had been a really horrible experience.

"Pine trees?" Raoul queried.

"Planted in plantations by the Forestry Department," Barbara replied. "The natural vegetation was much nicer. This is McKenzies Pocket. We go this way."

She led the way to the right. The track was badly overgrown with prickly wild raspberries and several times she scratched her legs. Raoul then took over the lead, trampling the worst of it out of the way. Now they had the rainforest on their right and the overgrown pine forest on the left.

"Do you think Sgt Boucher will be alright?" Barbara asked.

Raoul nodded. "We are very familiar with places like this. We both spent months in *l'Cote d'Ivoire,* and in *Afrique Central,* Central Africa that is, and also in Rwanda and Mali."

"What were you doing there?" Barbara asked as she clambered over another fallen tree and made a short detour into the edge of the jungle.

"Peacekeeping in Rwanda, fighting rebels in Central Africa and Mali, and trying to catch diamond smugglers and gun runners on the Ivory Coast," Raoul replied matter-of-factly.

Barbara knew enough to be impressed to the point of awe. This man really was a warrior, and a man of the world. It made her blush to think of her romantic fantasies of a few hours earlier.

He must think I am nothing but a silly little schoolgirl, she thought. Which made her thankful they had not had sex; and then to speculate on how many women he had made love to. *He must be experienced,* she told herself, the memories causing her to blush with arousal and shame.

Her thoughts were interrupted by their arrival at a road junction. A dirt road led in from the left through the pine forest and the track joined it. Parked beside the road was the car. Sgt Chef Boucher was nowhere in sight but as Barbara and Raoul walked out into the open area at the junction he called softly from the cover of the forest and stepped out, a pistol in his hand.

"You made it alright then?" he commented.

Raoul appeared quite unsurprised by his sudden appearance. Instead he looked at his watch. "Ten thirty. Two and a half hours. *Mademoiselle* has done well. Any problems Henri?"

Sgt Chef Boucher shook his head. "*Non, Mon lieutenant.* There was a police road block at the bottom of the mountain but they only looked in the back of the car and in the boot. They did not say what they were looking for. Mme Barbara was right, there was so much traffic they looked quickly only. Then I just drove here. Your excellent description led me straight to the place *Mademoiselle.*"

"Thank you," Barbara replied. "What do we do now?"

"We communicate with our *superiors,*" Raoul answered. He unslung the satchel and Barbara now understood that the radio equipment must be top secret and not the sort of thing to let fall into the hands of another government.

That is why Raoul carried it, rather than risk it in the car, she decided.

That he was a shrewd and clever man was even more apparent to her. That thought made her feel even more immature and young.

How stupid of me! she thought, *to throw myself at him like that. He must think I am just a little tart, and a silly one at that! It would have served me right if he had just screwed me and enjoyed it.*

Feeling ashamed of herself and quite depressed, not to mention more worn out than she liked to admit, Barbara sat in the car and watched while the two Frenchmen set up their satellite communications equipment and went to work. For nearly half an hour they worked, with much head nodding and shaking, and a deal of tooth-sucking evident before they packed the equipment away.

As Raoul placed the satchel in the back seat beside her Barbara asked, "What happens now?"

"We must locate a suitable airfield and inform our HQ," Raoul replied.

"What do you mean by suitable?" Barbara asked, although she had a fair idea.

"Somewhere where a fairly large aircraft can land without many people noticing. The landing strip must be a minimum of seven hundred and fifty metres long. You wouldn't happen to know any such places would you?" he replied.

That got Barbara's mind going. "Somewhere out in the dry country to the west," she said. "Most of the cattle properties have airstrips, but I don't have any idea how long they are."

"We need some accurate topographic maps," Raoul said. "Do you know where to obtain such things?"

Barbara did. "There are shops in Cairns, and I am sure there is one in Atherton," she answered, remembering Graham Kirk buying one there two years earlier.

Sgt Chef Boucher answered, "I think perhaps this Atherton, rather than another trip to Cairns and back. If we keep going through the police roadblock they perhaps get suspicious."

"This Atherton, where is it?" Raoul asked.

"About an hour's drive," Barbara answered. "Get me your map and I will show you."

A glance at the map convinced the two Frenchman. Raoul said, "Atherton it is. Let us get moving. We need this information by mid-afternoon. Can you direct us to Atherton Barbara? You don't mind me calling you Barbara do you?"

At that Barbara almost sighed with relief. "It is better than the endless *Mademoiselles,*" she replied.

They climbed into the car, Sgt Chef Boucher driving, with Raoul beside him and Barbara in the back behind Raoul. By then it was 11:20. At Barbara's direction they first drove back through the pine forest to the Black Mountain Road. As they arrived at the road junction she tensed in an agony of indecision. She knew that the shortest way was left, back to the Kennedy Highway near Kuranda, but she was anxious lest there be a police check point at the big bridge across the Barron River just near there. She knew of another road, having used it on an exercise two years before. That led via a roundabout route through the State Forest, across the Barron River at Oak Forest, then back to Kuranda. But that road, the Myola Road, came in at a set of traffic lights only a kilometre west of the same bridge.

Is the extra hour or so of driving worth the effort? she pondered.

Finally, she decided they should take the risk so they turned left onto the Black Mountain Road and drove the six kilometres to Kuranda. As they reached the junction of the Kennedy Highway and turned right she was gripped by anxiety. Her eyes blinked as she tried to focus into the distance to see if there was a police check point at the far end of the half-kilometre long highway bridge.

There wasn't. Nor was there one at the traffic lights at the main intersection. As the car sped on westward along the highway Barbara sat back and trembled with relief. She explained her fears to Raoul and he nodded. "Are there any other places we should avoid; bottlenecks where the police find it easy to check traffic?"

"Mareeba probably," Barbara said. She did not know Mareeba well but knew it was the hub of a dozen roads, with only two bridges across the Barron River. Then her mind went back to the same exercise and she remembered walking the back roads and a dawn march. At that she relaxed. "We can take secondary roads to by-pass it," she said.

So they did. At the Emerald Creek Road they turned left and went south till they came to the road which followed the irrigation pipeline. There they turned right and went along this, soon afterwards crossing Tinaroo Creek, which Barbara vividly remembered as one of their campsites. The road then climbed a long, gentle slope to a wide, flat hill topped on their left by a farm surrounded by trees. There was a road junction there.

We turned right here during that exercise, Barbara remembered. She directed Sgt Chef Boucher to drive straight ahead.

As they did Barbara had a series of vivid flashbacks. Off down to the right Barbara could see across the open fields to where a powerline went across the other road and on through savannah bushland.

That is where CSM Kirk led our patrol that day, she remembered.

That had been the time she had seen Willy and Marjorie frolic naked in the river. The army cadet recon patrol of three had just reached the bank of the Barron River, quite a small stream at that point, when they had heard voices and hid in the long grass on the river bank. Into view had come three of the exercise 'opposing force'—air cadets: Willy, Marjorie, and a girl named Vicki. Vicki had gone away and both Willy and Marjorie had stripped and gone for a swim, which included a lot of pashing and sexual play.

Thinking about it now got Barbara hot and aroused. At the time, she had been both fascinated and extremely embarrassed. Pressed against Graham Kirk, with Parnell on her other side, she had been very concerned that they could see all of Marjorie's ample charms. She had wanted to warn Willy, but things had developed too quickly and it would then have been too embarrassing, so the trio had just lain in hiding and watched.

Barbara had not thought that Willy and Marjorie would do anything serious, and she had been both appalled and fearfully embarrassed when the lovers had walked up onto the small beach ten metres away and begun to have sex. Barbara remembered being at first disgusted and angry. This was because the way they were doing it, with Marjorie on top, had been the way Barbara had caught her mother in adultery one afternoon.

Then, to her own shame and amazement, she had become fearfully aroused. The revelation of the dark corners of her own personality had shaken her badly and had helped her keep a very tight rein on her emotions and desires ever since.

Thinking about the incident led to her conjuring up a fantasy of her and Raoul being beside the river and she became quite aroused. Despite feeling frustrated she found it a relief.

At least I know I'm normal, she told herself.

But now the monster of sexual passion had been roused again! Vivid images from her recent experience with Raoul in the motel caused her to become very heated, and also very ashamed.

Thinking about Willy also made her wonder what had happened to him after the police pulled him over. Remorse helped her to regain some control of her overheated emotions. She was now so worked up she was fidgeting with desire. Part of her mind told her it was just that she was thinking that way because she was so stressed and tired.

It is just the shock of the horrible things I saw and being so afraid that is making me think so irrationally. I must get control or I will get hurt, she told herself.

The need to navigate helped shift her thoughts back to more mundane things. The car went down a long slope and then wound down a steep gravel road into the gorge of the Barron River. After crossing a short concrete bridge it climbed up the other side and then came out in open farm country. After a couple of kilometres they crossed a railway line, then came to the Kennedy Highway again. Barbara said to turn left.

By this time they were halfway between Mareeba and Atherton and the road was very good. They sped through the little farming settlement of Walkamin and on southwards. Ten minutes later they were at Tolga and a few minutes after that they emerged from the strip of jungle called 'The Tolga Scrub' and Atherton came into view.

"Where to now?" Raoul had asked as they drove into the main street.

"The place we want is in behind the Court House and Police Station," Barbara had replied. Then she realized what she had said and added, "Oh no! We had better not go there."

Raoul laughed and shook his head. "On the contrary. It is like your plan for the car. The last place the police will be looking is in their own back yard. Where is this place?"

It took a couple of wrong turns before Barbara directed them to the Department of Natural Resources building behind the police station. Driving into the small car park sent her heart rate shooting up and she hunched down in the back.

Raoul told Sgt Chef Boucher to stay in the car, ready for the quick getaway. He then asked Barbara what maps she thought he might need. Her mind had been turning that over and she now suggested the two rows of 1:100 000 scale maps including Mareeba and Atherton and the country to the west.

"That might cost a bit," she added diffidently.

"How much?" Raoul had asked, frowning.

"Maybe a hundred dollars?"

At that Raoul laughed. "Do not worry. If it cost ten thousand I am sure we would still buy them," he said. He checked his wallet and then went into the building. Once again Barbara sat and was gripped by anxiety. She also felt even more naive and immature.

Of course the French government isn't going to quibble over a few hundred dollars with so much at stake, she told herself.

That 'reasonably large aeroplane' had been on her mind and she had decided that the only place it could be flying from was French New Caledonia, and, as that was at least a thousand nautical miles away (she knew that from geography) then it had to be a big, multi-engine plane.

Something like a 'Hercules', she thought. *And they cost millions of dollars. So the maps are nothing.*

At that moment a police car drove into the yard. Barbara did not see it a first but she noticed Sgt Chef Boucher turn to look. When she followed his gaze her blood seemed to freeze and she tensed, ready for flight. Sgt Chef Boucher put his hand to the ignition key but shook his head. "Stay calm *Mme* Barbara. They have not seen you. They are just parking their car. *Non!* Do not turn your head to look at them. Just sit low. Ah! Now they are leaving the car, two *Gendarmes,* and now they go into a back door of *l'Prefecture.*"

Barbara sat there with her heart hammering and her mouth feeling dry. Worse still she felt the urgent need to do a pee. That embarrassing need came to dominate her thoughts, so that when Raoul re-appeared with a roll of maps under is arm she felt more stressed than relieved.

As he climbed into the car he said, "Ok, where to now?"

Barbara burned with embarrassment but managed to say, "A place with a toilet please."

Sgt Chef Boucher nodded and started the car. Barbara stayed low as they drove out along a narrow lane past the parked police car. This brought them out on a wide street. Sgt Chef Boucher grunted and pointed to the left. On the opposite corner was a public toilet. He drove over and parked as close as he could, on the other side street. Barbara had a careful look around but no police were in sight.

Raoul climbed out and looked casually around, then turned to her. "I also will go. Now, stay calm Barbara. Act naturally, or you make yourself stand out. Walk slowly, as though without a care in the world."

That took some doing but Barbara managed it. She climbed out of the car and strolled to the toilet block, pleasantly surprised at how cold the air was. After relieving herself and washing her face she walked back outside and looked in both directions. Only then did she notice that the toilets were attached to some sort of tourist information office. As she glanced towards it the door opened and two men in casual civilian clothes walked out, both laughing and holding handfuls of coloured brochures.

Then Barbara saw one of the men turn and stare at her. He looked vaguely familiar but Barbara could not place him and felt rising alarm. The last thing she wanted at that moment was to be recognized. Then the man called her name.

"Why hello Barbara. Fancy meeting you here."

It was Mark Guy. Barbara was flabbergasted. All she could do was gape. Her mind seemed to go blank as fear flooded it.

What do I do? she wondered.

Luckily, she retained enough awareness to see that he was smiling and did not seem at all threatening. The grinning man beside him she now recognized as the Yorkshire corporal.

"Hello," she replied feebly. As the first shock receded she began to wonder why he did not immediately arrest her or something.

Instead Mark stopped walking, his face still all smiles. "What brings you to this part of the world?" he asked in a friendly tone.

Barbara opened her mouth, could think of nothing to say, closed it, then opened it again. She gestured to the tourist pamphlets. "Same as you, just touring around," she said. All she wanted to do was flee back to the car but her now racing mind told her that would attract suspicion.

Unless he already knows why I am here and is just making small talk to cover them bumping into me, she thought. The idea that somehow she had been tracked to Atherton snuck in, to frighten her even more. *But how could they?* she wondered.

Mark shook his head, but kept smiling. "You could have been our guide. That would have been nicer than depending on tourist information shops. I'm sure you know all the best places to go," he said.

"I do," Barbara replied, trying to return the smile but feeling as though the result was a sickly grin.

At that moment, Raoul came out of the other toilet. Barbara glanced towards him and her heart leapt into her mouth as Raoul's hand went to his carry bag. For an instant she feared that Raoul was going to pull out the pistol and start shooting. Instead he merely raised one eyebrow and strolled over to her.

"Friends?" he murmured, taking her hand.

"No, just a couple of people I met in Cairns," Barbara replied.

She saw Mark's smile slip a little and quizzical little frown furrowed his brow as he looked at Raoul. Barbara felt her heart hammering and in an attempt to appear natural but to end the scene she said, "My boyfriend."

"Lucky man!" Mark answered, giving Raoul a wry grin.

"Excuse us," Raoul said. "We must go." So saying he led Barbara firmly past Mark and his corporal and across the side street.

Mark made no attempt to stop them. Instead he merely shrugged and said good naturedly, "Another time maybe?"

As they crossed the side street Barbara glanced at the car. She noted that Sgt Chef Boucher was still sitting in it, apparently quite relaxed and not watching them but she was sure he was very alert.

What is Raoul planning? she wondered, but she trusted him enough to keep walking.

On the other footpath Raoul turned her to face across the main street. Barbara understood why—if it was a trap and they kept walking along that side of the street it would be straight past the police station. Raoul kept a tight grip on her hand.

"Who are those men?" he asked.

Barbara had trouble answering. The meeting had been so unexpected and had raised such a flock of questions that her heart was palpitating and her throat constricted. She swallowed and croaked, "That was the Royal Marine Commando lieutenant, Mark Guy. The other man is his corporal."

There was a break in the traffic and Raoul hurried her across to the median strip. As they did Barbara glanced to her right and saw that both Mark and his corporal were still standing outside the tourist office, apparently looking at the brochures.

Raoul shook his head and muttered, then said, "I think he recognized me. I have seen him before, during a NATO exercise on Sicily last year. We were not introduced but he was at the same briefing. Ours is a fairly small professional world, so I think he at least knows he has met me before."

"Do you think they were following us and accidentally bumped into me?" Barbara suggested as they hurried across the second part of the road to the far footpath.

"I do not know," Raoul replied. "But now we must make sure they do not follow us further. We must lose them."

"How will we do that?" Barbara asked as they set off up the footpath of the major road leading uphill away from the main street.

"To begin with, just keep walking," Raoul answered, squeezing her hand and smiling.

Chapter 28

COMMITTED

Barbara glanced quickly back towards the tourist information office, taking particular care to note the car parked out the front. "That blue car must be theirs," she said.

"Yes. Do not look. Do not show any interest," Raoul answered.

"What about Sgt Chef Boucher? He did not see those two British commandos and will wonder where we have gone," Barbara said.

"He will do what is needed, do not fear. Ah! Here is a shop. Let us see if we can buy some food," Raoul said.

By then they had reached the end of the next block and he steered her into a small shop. It sold a variety of fast foods as well as drinks and confectionary. "You do the ordering," Raoul said. He then took out his small radio and went to peer back through the shop window towards where Mark and his corporal still stood on the footpath.

A teenage girl came through from the back of the shop to ask what they wanted. Barbara looked at her and was horrified.

I know you, she thought.

The girl's expression said exactly the same thing. The girl said, "Oh, hi CUO Brassington! How are you? What are you doing here?"

Oh blast! thought Barbara. The last thing she wanted at that moment was to meet someone she knew, let alone an army cadet from the Atherton unit!

"Hello Robyn," she said. "I'm fine. We are just driving around the Tablelands."

Robyn, a sergeant who lived in the nearby town of Tolga and who had been in the same accommodation building during the December Promotion Course, nodded and asked what she wanted. Barbara named her purchases and Robyn began preparing them, all the while sneaking appraising looks at Raoul.

Barbara purchased pies, sausage rolls and hot chips. Three soft drinks were added. By then Raoul had finished speaking to Sgt Chef Boucher and he walked over and placed a baseball cap on her head.

"For you, to cover your pretty red hair," he said with a laugh. He then saw the look on Robyn's face and raised his eyebrows.

Barbara flamed with pride and embarrassment. "This is Robyn," she explained. "Robyn is in the army cadets."

Raoul nodded and smiled but said nothing, just handed over the money. By then Barbara's mind had been racing and she came up with a story.

She said, "Er... Robyn. This is my boyfriend, but my dad does not approve of him and doesn't know we are spending the day driving around the Tablelands. Please don't tell anyone you have seen me."

"I won't," Robyn replied, her eyes lighting up with interest.

Barbara picked up the plastic bags full of food and turned away, her face red with embarrassment. Raoul smiled at Robyn and winked, then followed Barbara, taking a bag off her and then taking hold of her hand in its place. "We are the lovers," he whispered. "We must act the part."

Barbara giggled and blushed, feeling both naughty and ashamed. "Was it alright to say that?" she asked anxiously.

Raoul laughed. "To tell a girl to keep secret your secret boyfriend of whom your poor father does not approve? *Merci!* As good to take out a full page advertisement in the local newspaper. She is all agog to rush off and tell her friends this delicious secret."

"I'm sorry," Barbara answered, blushing and feeling very silly. "It seemed like a good idea."

"It is. It fits with the story your other friend was to tell. It will serve. Do not worry my love. I like it," he answered.

Those words were balm to her hurt feelings. *'My love' he called me,* she told herself. She snuggled closer, pressing against his arm.

"Where are we going?" she asked.

"Sgt Chef Boucher is going to meet us further along this street," Raoul answered.

The pair walked on up the footpath hand in hand. Barbara enjoyed that, feeling as though she did not care who was trailing her. Just being with Raoul made her feel special and safe. By then they were out of sight of the two British commandos and she saw no further sign of them. Two blocks later they found Sgt Chef Boucher sitting in their car in the car park of the local swimming pool. The car was hidden from the street behind bushes and among a dozen other cars

"This is as good a spot as any," Raoul said, sliding into the front seat. "Which way did they go *Mon Sergeant Chef?*"

"North along the main street, sir," Sgt Chef Boucher replied. "I don't think they saw me and they did not appear to follow you. Nor did any other car."

"I wonder if that meeting was coincidence?" Barbara asked.

"How could they possibly have known where we were going?" Raoul asked. "We did not know ourselves until we came here."

"Maybe they can read your radio transmissions?" Barbara suggested.

Raoul and Sgt Chef Boucher both shook their heads emphatically and said *Non*. "Besides, we did not mention where we were heading for," Raoul added.

Barbara then said, "What if they put one of those radio tracking devices in our car?"

Both men looked doubtful and shook their heads. Raoul said, "I think per'aps just a coincidence, but even so, we will keep the eyes skinned."

"Peeled," Barbara corrected, then, "Where are we going to next?"

"First we eat, then we study the maps," Raoul answered.

For ten minutes they had lunch and then Raoul took out the roll of maps. "I 'ave eight maps," he said. "Now, we need the airfield at least one kilometre in the length and well away from any farms or towns."

It was an interesting new experience for Barbara. She was used to reading such maps but had never scanned one for such a specific object before. She took the map Raoul handed to her, saw it was the CHILLAGOE 1:100 000 and nodded with familiarity. Slowly she then began running her finger up and down the grid lines in a systematic search.

Within seconds she had found a landing ground. She held the map for Raoul to see and asked, "What about here? This one beside Emu Creek?"

Raoul peered closely, then shook his head. "Too close to those buildings, and I don't like the look of all those hills around it. This is to be a night landing and take-off."

Barbara blushed and felt foolish but was then gratified when Sgt Chef Boucher also had one vetoed. Raoul muttered and held up his map. "I like this one," he said, showing her the Mt Garnet airfield.

"What about the town?" Sgt Chef Boucher asked.

"About five kilometres," Raoul measured. "I think far enough for the noise not to be heard much," Raoul answered. "Anyway, keep looking and if we do not find a better one it will have to do. If nothing else it is on the road to where we want to go."

Barbara continued her search, amazed at how much empty bush there was, and how rough much of the country appeared to be. She found another airstrip at Sunnymount but it had buildings on both sides. Two more beside Koorboora Creek she found had 'not usable' printed beside them, so rejected them. Then her eyes lighted on one next to the name MOUNT LUCY. This time she double checked before speaking. The airstrip was at least one thousand, five hundred metres long and four kilometers from the nearest buildings.

'Almaden,' she read.

I know that place. We stopped there for lunch on that school field trip to Chillagoe last year.

Into her mind came the image of a dry and dusty little settlement at a rail junction: a quaint old wooden railway station, hotel, and half a dozen houses scattered around among open bush.

The hotel was really nice and served delicious home-made pies, she remembered.

She held the map for Raoul to look at. "What about this one? It is only three or four kilometres from the town of Almaden but there is a range of hills in between."

Raoul took the map and studied it carefully, scanning the whole area. "I am also looking for the approach to be over relatively deserted country," he explained, "and this place looks perfect for our needs. Do you know this place?"

Barbara nodded. "Not the actual airstrip," she answered, "But I have driven along the road from Almaden to Chillagoe a couple of times." She explained the family weekend trips and school excursions.

Raoul nodded and looked more carefully. "The road, what is it like?"

Into Barbara's mind came images of a very good bitumen road with almost no traffic. "It is about an hours drive from Mareeba," she added, after explaining what the road was like.

Raoul looked even more thoughtful. "I would have preferred more traffic. If we are one of the few cars on the road we are more conspicuous and people might remember. Now, do we need to go to this Mareeba place or is there another way?"

Again Barbara's local knowledge came to her aid. She shook her head and answered, "No, we don't have to go through Mareeba. There are several secondary roads that cut across from near here."

She clearly remembered the exercise against the Air Cadets and Navy Cadets at Walsh Bluff and Ariga the previous year. She asked for the ATHERTON map and pointed to the roads she meant.

"This one, following the irrigation channel," she said, tracing along it with her finger.

"It will do. Let us get going," Raoul said.

"It means going north along the same road the two Pommie commandos went along, at least for part of the way," Barbara answered.

"Pommie?" Raoul asked.

Sgt Chef Boucher laughed and replied, "*Australie* slang for *l'Anglais.*"

Raoul smiled thinly and repeated, "Pommies. I must remember that one. OK, let us make the tracks."

"Are we going to this Almaden airfield?" Barbara asked, a bit surprised at the speed of the decision.

Raoul nodded and handed her the ATHERTON map. "You guide us please. Yes, we must do *un reconnaissance*. If it is not suitable we must another place find and the sooner we know the better." He looked at his watch. "1315. The aircraft will be taking off in a couple of hours. There is a need for speed."

Barbara could only nod and take a deep breath. Thinking about that aircraft and what it implied got her heart speeding up and her body tensing with anxiety.

I hope I have the guts, she thought. For perhaps a second she considered backing out and asking to be let out but then she shook her head and despised herself for being a coward. *I don't want Raoul to think I am scared, or a weakling,* she told herself, resolving to make the parachute jump *even if it kills me!*

For the next hour and a half they drove non-stop. First they returned to the main street and went north along it, all the while keeping an eye out for the British commandos. Once out of town they headed north through the Tolga Scrub and the town of Tolga, then on towards Mareeba. Barbara concentrated on careful map reading. Once across Rocky Creek she warned Sgt Chef Boucher.

"About a kilometre ahead, we cross an irrigation channel and immediately turn left."

They almost overshot the turnoff, the turn made dangerous by several following vehicles which were impatiently trying to overtake. Once on the bitumen side road beside the West Barron Main Channel there was no traffic at all and she relaxed a bit. Raoul turned from time to time and carefully scanned the distance.

"I look for the distant shadower," he explained.

But no car followed them. They drove along the road, taking several sharp bends too fast for safety till Sgt Chef Boucher understood the nature of the road. At Ariga they turned right and went north past the Lotus Glenn Correctional Centre.

I hope I don't end up in there, Barbara thought unhappily.

The knowledge that she was probably breaking the law by helping foreign agents weighed her spirits down for a while.

Five minutes later, they reached the Mareeba-Dimbulah Road and turned left. From then on it was mostly just a hundred kilometres per hour drive with few bends. They slowed to pass through the small and sleepy town of Dimbulah and Barbara was assailed by memories: the holiday work on the nearby tobacco and fruit farms, with all its attendant drama and comedy; and the frightening experience further north at Mt Mulligan the previous March.

For a few more kilometres they drove fast across rolling, mostly open, farm country and then slowed again to cross Eureka Creek at the Muldiva Crossing. Soon after that the farms ended and they had nothing but savannah grassland or woodland on either side.

After twenty minutes of this Raoul shook his head and said, "Certainly much emptiness."

"Dotswood is this sort of country," Barbara said. "Only flatter."

"Like the southern part of Chad," was Sgt Chef Boucher's comment.

The tiny settlement of Petford was next, then the range of rugged, dry hills leading up to the even smaller settlement of Lappa. After that the vegetation changed somewhat and they got long vistas of seemingly endless bush and rugged hills.

Australia is certainly a big place, Barbara thought. Once again memories assailed her as she stared northwards to the rugged jumble of the Featherbed Range. *I wonder how Frank and Nerida are getting on?* she thought, stark images of the two Aboriginal teenagers who had run away in a desperate attempt find themselves and to preserve a part of their culture flooding her mind. It made her feel very sad and not a little anxious for their safety. *That was two months ago. I hope they are alright.*

The deserted gold mining area of Koorboora was passed, and then more ranges of steep, rugged hills. Ten minutes later they arrived at Almaden. As Sgt Chef Boucher slowed near the first houses of the tiny town Barbara pointed to the right. "There is a hotel just there if you want a drink or something to eat. They are lovely people and the food is very nice."

Raoul shook his head. "No. We need to be unremarked and to pass through un-noticed. Which way?"

Barbara indicated the signs reading CHILLAGOE and Sgt Chef Boucher turned the car that way, crossing the Cairns Railway and then heading out of town along a bumpy gravel road. A couple of minutes later they crossed the Forsayth Railway and then passed the turn-off to Ootan. The road was very dusty and badly corrugated.

Barbara licked grit from her teeth and said, "This gravel only goes for a couple of kilometres. Then it is bitumen again," she said.

It was as she said. They followed a good bitumen highway through a small range of rocky scrub-covered hills. Now Raoul was map reading and he warned Sgt Chef Boucher to get ready to turn left. A minute later they came to a road junction. A gravel road led off to the left into ordinary looking savannah woodland. The car was turned off the highway and it followed this road. There had been no other traffic on the main road and Barbara felt sure they were safe for the moment.

A kilometre along the side road they came to the airfield. It was a dirt strip in a long, grassy clearing surrounded by ironbarks. There were no buildings and no sign anyone else had been there for some time. Raoul climbed out and examined the ground, then remarked that there were no wheel tracks visible on the dirt road.

"This will do us," he said. "We hide the car and ourselves, then we wait."

The car was driven to the east end of the strip and parked in the bush on the far side, facing back the way they had come. Then Raoul and Sgt Chef Boucher got out the satellite radio equipment and spent half an hour communicating. With nothing to do but sit alone with her thoughts Barbara became more and more nervous and afraid.

I can still back out, she told herself.

Her anxiety was so great she even considered walking away through the bush and back to Almaden. Once again she rejected that idea. What she found curious was that she felt perfectly safe with the two Frenchmen. It was the thought of the impending challenge that was stressing her.

"Will I be able to do it?" she asked herself. The anxiety got her breathing fast and sweating with what she had to acknowledge was fear.

Raoul walked back smiling. "That is done. Now we wait," he said. He seated himself in the back of the car beside Barbara. After a couple of minutes he reached across and took her hand. That got Barbara's heart hammering rapidly again. To her surprise, he said, "You do not have to do this you know. You can back out if you wish. After we take off you can take this car and drive home."

"I haven't got a driver's licence," Barbara answered, knowing as she said it that it sounded foolish.

"No matter. We can drive you closer to the town and leave you with some money," Raoul replied.

"No. I said I would do it and I will," Barbara replied, gritting her teeth with determination.

Raoul patted her hand and squeezed it. "You are a very brave girl," he said, adding, "I 'ope you do not come to regret your decision."

After that they tried to rest. It was 1600 hours by then and they had five hours to wait. A rug was spread on the ground in the shade but the roughness of the ground, and the red ants, made that less than successful. So they sat in the car, trying to sleep. Time dragged slowly, and Barbara became sick with nervous exhaustion.

I can't back out, she told herself, *I have made a commitment.*

Another of her waterbottles was drained as the afternoon temperature was still high. *Must be over thirty degrees,* Barbara estimated. She was drowsy from the heat and the droning sound of insects but the fear, discomfort and flies all kept her awake. For her it was a horrible afternoon, both her body and her mind being strained and tested. Even going off into the bush to do a pee did not bring relief. She was embarrassed, knowing the men knew what she was doing, and she kept getting memories of being watched by the SAS. That gave her what she knew were irrational fears but she could not help looking anxiously around her, wondering if, even now, she was being spied on.

At last the sun went down, resulting in a brilliant red sunset. Silence settled with the evening. As darkness set in Barbara became more and more tense till she felt sure she must vomit or collapse. She tried gamely to hide this and kept chattering about some of her other adventures. These quite amazed Raoul and he kept asking for more details of her life.

When Sgt Chef Boucher went off for a few minutes into the night Raoul said, "I hope you do not mind me asking all these questions, but I do want to get to know you. If you do not mind I would like to come back to meet with you after this is over."

That sent Barbara into an emotional whirlpool and she felt almost dizzy. "I'd like that," she said. After a few minutes of quietly hugging that prospect to her she asked, "Should I get changed into my camouflage uniform now?"

Raoul nodded. "*Oui.* It would be for the best."

Feeling quite self-conscious Barbara went to the other side of the car and stripped off her shorts. The breeze around her legs made her very conscious of her gender and she quickly pulled on the long camouflage trousers and did them up. Then, after a check that Sgt Chef Boucher could not see her in the starlight, she took off the floral shirt. For a moment she stood and looked down at her bosom, relishing the memories of Raoul looking at them. Then she blushed with shame and slipped on the camouflage shirt. When that was done up she sat and tugged on socks and her army boots and then laced them up.

Being dressed in uniform caused a noticeable change in her emotions. Suddenly she felt calmer, more in control, more confident. Feeling much better she bundled the civilian clothes into the garbage bag and went back to join Raoul and Sgt Chef Boucher.

Raoul ran a very appraising eye over her. Nodding with approval, he said, "You look very good, very much the soldier. What do you think *Mon Sergeant Chef?*"

Sgt Chef Boucher smiled and nodded. "Very much. The badges, what do they indicate?" he asked.

Blushing with pleasure and pride Barbara explained the 'Blue patch' cadet badges on her upper sleeves and then her Cadet Under-Officer rank slides.

And then it was time. Raoul stood up and collected his suitcase, carry bag and satchel, then said, "We must get into position. As soon as the aircraft stops we get aboard. Stay close to me."

Barbara said yes, then hoisted on her webbing and picked up her garbage bag and walked with him to the edge of the grassy clearing. There she stood beside Raoul. He smiled in the starlight and gave her hand a squeeze. Sgt Chef Boucher collected his own gear and then checked through the car using a torch, making sure there was nothing left in it. He then joined them. The three stood side by side and stared into the starry western sky.

A radio crackled and Sgt Chef Boucher answered. Barbara stiffened with mounting apprehension. Then she heard the drone of aero engines off to the west and saw Sgt Chef Boucher turn on a torch. The radio came to life and Sgt Chef Boucher said something quickly in French. Barbara heard the engine notes change and she strained her eyes to try to detect the approaching aircraft against the stars. Before she even realized it was down, a large transport aircraft thundered into view on the ground, having touched down near the other end of the strip.

Oh my God! Barbara thought in near desperation. *What have I got myself into?*

In the starlight the aircraft looked huge, but as it got closer she saw that it was only twin-engined. "Is it a Hercules?" she asked, almost having to shout above the growl of the engines.

"Transall," Raoul replied.

That meant nothing much to Barbara, but she saw it was a high wing monoplane and was painted a dapple camouflage pattern. The aircraft rolled across to the far side of the strip, then abruptly swung across in front of them. As it did Barbara had a fleeting glimpse of heads in the cockpit before the angle changed and all she could see were flat panes of Perspex with starlight reflecting on them.

The aircraft turned right around till it was facing back along the runway. By then Barbara could see it had a large opening at the rear, a sloping ramp and dim red interior lighting. The details were then obscured as the slipstream filled the air with dust. She squinted and covered her eyes and tried to spit out grass and grit that was blown into her mouth. Some dirt got into her eyes, which began to water. In mounting panic she rubbed at them.

The engine noises suddenly reduced dramatically. The buffeting wind and dust dropped. Then Raoul grabbed her hand and started walking. Barbara began walking with him but almost every instinct in her was to break free and run away. Instead she made herself stride across to the back ramp. Sgt Chef Boucher was there first and hurried aboard. Raoul then stepped up and passed his suitcase to a man standing there. The man took it and hurried forward, shoving it into a webbing container. Barbara then found herself stepping up, her heart in her gritty, dry mouth and her nose assailed by all those aircraft smells of oil, fuel, rubber and plastics.

The man, obviously a crewman by his flying suit, helmet and intercom on a long lead, hurried back and took her garbage bag and then seized her other arm and helped her forward into the cargo bay. By then Barbara was so scared she was moving like a zombie. In the dim red light her watering eyes were filled with dozens of rapid impressions: grim-faced, heavily armed soldiers with camouflaged faces sitting along the other side, web cargo straps, and seats, dangling straps and cords, the curved frames of the fuselage.

Raoul helped to stow her garbage bag and webbing under the seats and then the crewman almost pushed her down. He pointed and gesticulated and she knew he was trying to tell her to put on her seatbelt. She groped for this, vaguely aware of Raoul doing the same beside her. The crewman bent to help and as he did Barbara heard the engines bellow and the aircraft began bumping forward.

We are starting the take-off run! she thought, almost overwhelmed by fear and by the speed of events.

Then she glanced back and saw that the rear ramp door was closing. With a sickening shock she realized she could no longer just get out or walk away.

Oh my God! I'm committed now! she thought.

Chapter 29

TEST OF COURAGE

Even before Barbara had her seat belt done up she could tell that the aircraft was airborne. The whole take-off run had lasted less than a minute and left her feeling so anxious her stomach heaved and she found herself gasping for breath. But it helped her to be annoyed at the fumbling hands of the crewman. She knocked his hands away from her front and took the straps and buckles herself and tried to figure out how to secure them. Raoul helped by leaning over and pointing but she did not resent that.

Then the aircraft banked sharply to the left and the G forces pressed her into her seat. As the aircraft straightened out on a new course the opposite effect sent her stomach up into her throat. She had never been airsick, but nor had she ever experienced a take-off like that! Next to her was a round window and she tried to turn her head to look out but the dim red interior lighting was just strong enough to cause reflection and to make it all but impossible.

Then the aircraft turned to the right and climbed steeply, its engines thrumming with vibrant power. Abruptly it levelled out, again sending her stomach to her mouth. Barbara found she was in a cold sweat and breathing very rapidly. There had been times in the last few years when she had been truly terrified but she found her present situation really scary and she half-regretted her decision to help. The other half of her emotions began to respond to the sheer thrill of it all.

This is unbelievable, she told herself. *Here I am in a foreign aeroplane helping another country, possibly against my own, and enjoying myself!*

With something of a jolt she realized that it was only a day and a night since she had been helicoptered back from the American aircraft carrier. The kaleidoscope of experiences swirled in her mind and made her shake her head.

A door in the forward bulkhead opened and a man in a flying suit, to which were fastened officer's epaulets and pilots wings, came through. He spoke briefly to the crewman, who then pointed to Raoul and to one of the tough looking soldiers seated opposite. At his beckoning they both undid their seatbelts and stood up, gripping overhead straps for support. Then the crewman walked over to Barbara and indicated she should also undo her seat belt. Having only just got the thing done up she was mildly irritated but she sensed something important was happening. She unclipped the belt and stood up. The crewman steadied her as the plane rocked in turbulence.

A pointing hand sent her staggering after Raoul and the other two men through the doorway. She found herself in a well lit corridor with doors on both sides and a short flight of steps at the end. She guessed these led up to the flight deck. The pilot opened a door on the right and led the way in. Raoul and the soldier followed. Barbara made her way to the door and looked in, all the while clinging to whatever handholds she could find as the aircraft turned steeply again and then bounced about in more turbulence.

The cabin was very small and contained a table with bench seats on either side. A fourth man, also in an olive drab flying suit, was already seated there with maps spread out on the table in front of him. Raoul slid in beside the pilot and gestured her to join him. The tough looking soldier, who Barbara now saw in the white light was dressed in a camouflage uniform and with dark green webbing, sat opposite her against the corridor bulkhead, then took off the American style Kevlar helmet he was wearing.

The cabin door was closed and that muffled the sound of the motors so that ordinary conversation was possible. Raoul introduced himself and shook hands with all the men. He then turned and indicated Barbara. Speaking in very rapid French he introduced her and explained her army cadet uniform. The man with the maps—the aircraft's navigator she now learned—pointed to her rank slides and raised his eyebrows.

"Cadet Under-Officer," she replied.

He nodded and she heard the word 'cadet' a few times, accompanied by nods and smiles. Her French was just good enough for an outline understanding of what was being said. She was next introduced to the pilot, a captain. Raoul then indicated the soldier sitting opposite her.

"This is *Sous Lieutenant* Henri de Blainville of *la due 'eme Regiment Etranger de Parachutistes,* for short Two R. E. P. In English the Second Parachute Regiment of the Foreign Legion."

It took a second for the full implications of what Raoul had said to sink in, then Barbara felt a wave of insecurity and awe almost amounting to fear. *The French Foreign Legion!* she thought. She had heard and read enough to know that they were one of the world's most famous elite fighting units—and here she was leaning forward to shake hands with one of them!

In her flustered state she became flippant. "Why not marines?" she asked Raoul in a joking tone.

Raoul laughed. "The required equipment had to be flown from.... er... from somewhere else and this aircraft could not land on my ship."

Barbara nodded and sat back, trying to appear cool and detached, while inside she boiled with feelings of immaturity and inferiority. S-Lt de Blainville returned her look with what appeared to be arrogant contempt, mingled with male sexist appraisal of her shirt front. To Barbara he was like a creature from another planet. His rugged good looks were topped by a very close-cropped crew cut and he appeared to be so muscly he was almost bursting out of his shirt. She noted that his camouflage uniform had a different pattern to her own; darker brown and some patches of darker green, but not nearly as dark as American or British 'woodland green' camouflage uniforms. Clipped to his webbing were several small black cases which she thought were a radio and a GPS.

The pilot now took charge and they all turned to the maps. The top map was a 1:1 000 000 aviation map. Barbara saw that a pencil line had been drawn on it with a planned course. The line came in from the Coral Sea well north of Cairns, over the rough country between Mossman and Cooktown. It then came south to Almaden across the Mitchell River and Featherbed Range. Now it went west and then south before crossing the Kennedy Highway south of the Mt Surprise turn-off. The line had frequent short detours to avoid the cattle station homesteads and crossed the Burdekin River just south of a place called 'Battery'.

The pilot pointed to Dotswood and asked Raoul in French, "Where do you recommend we drop you?"

Raoul replied, "How close is it reasonable for you to approach?"

"We are flying at only one thousand metres above the terrain and with our engines throttled back and silenced. I would estimate that ten kilometres is as close as we should go."

Raoul pointed to the map, and said, "Somewhere about here?"

The pilot and navigator studied the area and the navigator then spread an Australian DOTSWOOD 1:100 000 scale map on the table. They all leaned forward to study it and Barbara saw the fingers all pointing to the same general area. The navigator said, "Here, to the south of this place called Mount Bluey?"

Raoul frowned and twisted his lips in concentration, then nodded. "It looks reasonable. No farms are shown anywhere in the area. Here, then, in the headwaters of this Thorntons Creek."

S-Lt de Blainville grunted and pointed to the map. In French he asked, "What does the green actually represent? Is it forest or what?"

Barbara understood and replied, "Savannah woodland. Trees and grassland."

S—Lt de Blainville looked mildly surprised and turned to her. "The trees, how close together are they?"

Barbara thought hard, picturing the vegetation around Dotswood. "Sometimes the canopies touch, but mostly they are a few metres apart; savannah woodland rather than savannah grassland," she replied.

"That is not so good. This will be dangerous then," S—Lt de Blainville replied. "Is there not some open farm land or a clearing we can use for a DZ?"

The thought of parachuting at night had already been gripping Barbara with fear but now she had vivid images of crashing down through ironbarks, the branches splintering into jagged ends that tore at her flesh, her stomach and...

The horrifying images she conjured up sent her into a new level of almost paralysing anxiety. The men scanned the map but she shook her head, and said, "There won't be any farms. That is all cattle country. The only fields with crops would be a lucerne paddock near a homestead."

That had to be translated and explained and the men studied the map some more. Finally they decided on the only 'open' area shown which was nowhere near a marked building. This was the lower end of Thorntons Creek and barely ten kilometres from Dotswood.

While they were deliberating the aircraft changed course several times and Barbara guessed they were weaving a zig-zag course between cattle station homesteads. She made a rough estimate of the distance and said, "It is about four hundred kilometres. How long will it take us to get there?"

She noted Raoul give her a look of respect but it was the navigator who answered. "About forty minutes from now."

Barbara knew she must have looked surprised, or even dismayed, because the pilot added, "This aircraft, it can fly at four hundred kilometres per hour."

"Do you have to land to refuel somewhere?" she asked, genuinely curious as to how this operation was being mounted.

Again it was the pilot who answered. "*Non.* This aircraft can fly eight thousand kilometres without landing. On this trip we plan on only about five thousand."

Barbara tried to calculate the distance to and from New Caledonia. She knew there were many other French owned islands out in the Pacific but did not know of any closer.

The pilot watched her face and said, "You are curious to know where we come from and to where we go back."

"Caledonie Nouveau," she replied.

There were smiles but no answers so she guessed she had been correct. The pilot then asked, "You would now like some refreshment, yes?"

Barbara said she would, and a visit to the toilet. There was a general shuffling of seats. The navigator left and Barbara was shown to a tiny toilet. This had all the chemical smells, hissing noises and cramped confines she associated with aircraft toilets. On returning to the cabin she was handed a cup of coffee and served with a plate of hot rolls. The pilot chatted cheerfully, while sipping his coffee. Raoul was in a jovial mood and even the grim-faced S-Lt de Blainville smiled a couple of times.

The coffee almost came straight back up again as the aircraft bumped and surged through more turbulence and then changed course again. With an effort of willpower Barbara kept it down and tried to keep smiling, hoping that what the men could see was not a sickly grin. She was scared to the point of being terrified but was determined not to show it and to go ahead with the jump.

The emotions were further tested and got much worse when Sgt Chef Boucher came to the cabin with an armful of camouflage uniform clothing and boots. Raoul and he sorted out shirts and trousers to fit and went off to change, leaving Barbara alone with S-Lt de Blainville. That was difficult as she felt intimidated and inferior and had difficulty in making small talk. He did not help by being uncommunicative. It was a considerable relief to Barbara when Raoul and Sgt Chef Boucher came back, now dressed in French army uniforms. They sat down and Raoul bent down to lace on a pair of army boots.

Barbara asked, "Are you going to parachute in wearing French Army uniform?"

Raoul nodded. "Yes. That is correct."

That puzzled Barbara as she had heard that when governments sent clandestine Special Forces into other countries they usually sent them in a third country's uniform, or in civilian clothes. She said this, adding, "And I've read that if their troops get killed or captured the governments usually deny any knowledge of them and just say they must be bandits or mercenaries."

That brought a smile to Raoul's lips. He agreed but replied, "In this case I think our government are doing it deliberately, to make a point."

"But isn't that invading, an Act of War?" Barbara queried, dredging up a term Major Conkey had used in a History lesson.

Again Raoul nodded. "Yes, you are right. But I do not think Australia will declare war on France because we are caught looking for our own satellite. As I said we have liaison officers in uniform at your Search HQ and it will all just be fudged away as a mistake or misunderstanding. A few false apologies and the matter will be smoothed over. Besides, we are not planning to be seen or captured."

That caused Barbara another anxiety. "Are you taking guns?"

"*Certainement.* There is the possibility of you needing protection."

A chill of fear caused Barbara's heart to speed up. "Do you mean from the Americans?"

This time Raoul shook his head. "*Non. le Dags.*"

"But.... but the Americans shot them, or took them prisoner."

Raoul made a wry smile. "Perhaps. But where there is one, there may be more. It pays to be sure eh? Better safe than sorry?"

"What if the thing I saw is not the satellite and this is all a waste of time?" Barbara asked, voicing one of her strongest causes of anxiety.

"That has been considered," Raoul replied. "We search anyway. So, if it is not,..?" He gave a shrug and went back to lacing on his boots.

Next he and Sgt Chef Boucher were handed sets of webbing which they checked and adjusted. Then both Raoul and Sgt Chef Boucher were handed very futuristic looking automatic military rifles with all sorts of gadgets and sights attached. Both checked these for safe and Barbara was thrilled to see that the magazines were full of live ammunition.

Oh! This is getting really serious, she thought, apprehension clutching at her dry throat. No weapon was offered to her but she did not expect one anyway.

Next two small radios with earpieces and throat microphones were issued. S-Lt de Blainville handed Raoul a small tablet shaped item wrapped in camouflage. Raoul nodded and flipped it open and Barbara saw that it was a small computer like an iPad.

"What's that?" she asked as he turned it on and began to tap on its screen.

"Secret," Raoul answered. "It is a *Felin SIT COMDE.* In English you would call it a Battlefield Management System. It is a small computer linked to these radios and to some of the weapon sights by radio data link and also by satellite to our HQ. It is also a GPS navigator and shows the map with military symbols to show the tactical situation."

Barbara was amazed. She was familiar with basic GPS equipment and with car navigators but a glance at the screen on this one made her shake her head in wonder.

Raoul then went out for a few minutes. When he came back she saw that he had a small square rank badge pinned to his shirt over his lower chest. It was black with two horizontal gold bars on it. Seeing her looking at it he pointed to it and said, "Lieutenant."

Barbara nodded, having already worked that out and having noted the single gold bar on S-Lt de Blainville's chest. Out of curiosity she glanced at Sgt Chef Boucher's shirt. He now wore a black rectangle with a single diagonal gold bar.

Raoul added, "Sergeant. There are two higher grades of sergeant."

At that moment the crewman from the cargo hold came to the door and called on them to follow him. That got Barbara's heart rate shooting up again, but she followed Raoul, S-Lt de Blainville and Sgt Chef Boucher out to the cargo hold. She was dismayed to see that the Foreign Legionnaires were all strapping on parachutes and adjusting equipment.

When the crewman held up a bundle of straps and bags that she guessed must be a parachute Barbara almost froze with fear. She had to swallow to keep the bile from rising and to ease her breathing.

For the next five minutes she was helped on with the gear. Having the harness straps hanging over her shoulders and bumping against her boobs in the unsteady motion of the aircraft, made her very aware of being female. She blushed deeply when the lower straps were passed between her legs. She helped hold these as the crewman clipped the harness on and adjusted it. She could tell he was aware of her gender and that he was trying to be careful not to touch her in the wrong places but that seemed to make it even more embarrassing. Glances at the legionnaires also made her very conscious that they knew she was a girl.

Putting the parachute on brought home the reality of what she was doing in a way she had not previously felt. Her emotions now raced in a churning turmoil of fear and rising excitement. Raoul gave her instructions on how to land and what to do if she came down in a tree. That brought back the terrifying images of being impaled on splintering branches. Next, her webbing was attached by rope and placed on the seat beside her. That reminded her that her waterbottles were not all full.

It will be very dry at Dotswood, she thought.

She indicated this to the crewmen and he nodded and took the webbing away, saying he would fill them. Barbara then turned to Raoul. "Do I get a reserve parachute for emergencies, in case this one does not open," she asked.

Raoul shook his head. "*Non.* We do the low-level, combat jump, from only two hundred metres. There is not time to open a reserve chute."

Another terrifying image flooded Barbara's already crowded brain. She saw herself falling, screaming, knowing she was about to go thud.

I will be killed, she told herself. Then she briefly wondered what death would be like before shaking her head and firmly driving the images out. *Too bad. If I die, I die,* she thought.

Her attention was then taken up by being handed one of the camouflaged Kevlar helmets. It felt quite heavy to her and she briefly examined the camouflage cloth cover before putting it on. By then Raoul and all of the others had theirs on and he helped clip hers up and adjust the strap. It felt heavy and unbalanced on her head. While this was happening the aircraft began to turn and descend at the same time, making it hard for her to keep her feet. She clung to webbing straps beside her and to Raoul's arm. The crewman returned with her webbing and attached it to her with the length of rope.

A whirring noise then made her look around in alarm. To her further dismay she saw that the rear ramp of the plane was opening up, letting in a rush of cool air and allowing a shifting view of dark countryside and starlit sky.

It must be soon, she thought, again feeling herself to be on the edge of a hysterical breakdown. She swallowed and glanced around, hoping that nobody was noticing her fear.

What she now saw thrilled her even more. The legionnaires, ten she counted, had now stood up and were making final adjustments, helping each other to check and fit. In the dim red lighting they looked very grim and military. Their faces were all streaked with camouflage cream but even so she noted that one was black and another was Asian. And they were armed. The sight of those weapons sent another thrill of fear through her.

Raoul took her hand, causing her to jump in fright. Puzzled, she looked at him. He shouted in her ear. "You stand in front of me. I give you the push if you need it. We do the static line jump you see and you do not need to worry about pulling the rip cord. You understand?"

Barbara nodded, clinging gratefully to his hand while he led her over to stand behind a very tough looking black legionnaire, who gave her a toothy grin. With a shock she saw that his face was all ridged with lines of scars and that the points of his teeth were filed to sharp points. That so surprised Barbara that she got over the next moment of anxiety as Raoul snapped her rip cord to the static line, the steel wire running along just above her head.

He bent over and explained, "When the green light comes on we walk quickly forward and jump off the ramp."

Barbara nodded and he smiled and gave her elbow a squeeze. "Will you be alright?" he asked.

Again all Barbara could do was nod. Then she had to clutch at him as the plane again turned sharply. The aircraft went into a steep descent and she felt her stomach rise and with it the nausea. She swallowed several times and broke into a cold sweat. With an effort of will she slowed her breathing as she realized she was hyperventilating and feeling giddy.

I mustn't faint, she told herself firmly.

Then she swallowed again as a stab of genuine terror coursed through her. A cherry red light had come on up to the right of the now gaping back opening and all of the men in front of her stopped fidgeting and shuffling. There was a sharp word of command and they all reached up and clipped on to the static line. They then bent down and picked up their bulky bundles of webbing and weapons and stood holding these in front of themselves.

Seeing that, Barbara bent to pick up her own webbing. In doing so her helmeted head bumped the helmet of the crewman, who had bent to pick it up for her. He grinned and rubbed his helmet. She felt foolish and could only clutch the webbing close against her.

The crewman then stepped aside, pulling his intercom cord and safety harness out of the way. Then he turned and faced them and yelled out. It took Barbara a moment to translate and understand.

He said ten seconds! she thought in momentary panic.

Then it was five and she knew the test was upon her. *I can still back out,* she thought in rising panic. *I can say no!*

But in her heart she knew she was committed. Into her numbed consciousness slammed the awareness that the light had turned green and that the men in front of her had started moving.

Chapter 30

DOWN

For perhaps half a second Barbara stared in near panic at the backs of the legionnaires as they moved away from her. She saw men jumping and vanishing into the darkness and gulped. Then she made herself step forward. Part of her mind made her determined not to let Raoul think she was frightened. Feeling so scared that most of her emotions were wooden she walked awkwardly forward, almost stumbling twice as the aircraft rocked in the air.

In front of her there was suddenly nothing but the sloping ramp and blurry, moving darkness. For an instant she glimpsed the dim shape of the last legionnaire before he vanished astern. With a gulp of fear she forced herself to walk forward onto the ramp. Then the totally irrational fear of stumbling or falling gripped her. To avoid that she took two rapid strides and sprang out.

Oh God! she gasped.

As she dropped she felt like screaming and sobbing at the same time. Even as she did she flinched as the huge tail of the aircraft flashed overhead. Then she felt several sharp tugs on the harness and she began to fear that the parachute was not going to open, sending her plummeting to her death.

All the while her eyes and brain were working, in spite of her terror. Images of stars, dark hills and even the shapes of trees in the moonlight all registered on her retina. Even the sound of the rapidly receding aero engines registered. Then her brain took in that she was still falling very fast. The fear returned in a paralysing wave. She saw the trees below getting rapidly closer and thought,

I'm going to die! Oh, what a pity! (That last because she had found Raoul).

Suddenly she was jerked sharply and instantly knew that the parachute had opened. Even as she cried out with relief she remembered Raoul's briefing.

"Throw the gear!" she ordered herself.

With a determined and deliberate thrust she cast her webbing away from herself. Then she glanced up and reached up to grasp the shoulder harness. Above her she saw the dark, circular shape of the parachute as it blotted out the stars.

A surge of relief made her gasp and she then swivelled her head to look around, hoping to see some of the others, or the aircraft. None were visible and her search was rudely and shockingly terminated by something whacking hard against her left thigh. Even as she realised it was the branch of a tree she began to berate herself for not looking down, and for not adopting the arms over face position for coping with that situation, she realized she needed to brace for landing.

She was too late. Something whipped her left arm and then she hit the ground hard. Luckily she had her knees bent and was able to crumple and roll. Barbara found herself sprawled on the ground with the wind knocked out of her. It was such a numbing shock that for a few seconds she was unable to move. The helmet strap was pulled hard up under her chin and she had to lift her head to ease that.

Then relief flooded in. "I'm down! I'm alive!" she gasped. Other anxious thoughts then crowded in: being dragged by the parachute; the need to spill any air from the parachute to crumple it; the need to get out of the harness. She began to fumble with frantic fingers at the release catch.

"Undo you stupid thing!" she cried, gripping and twisting with urgent efforts.

Then she became aware that she was lying flat on the dry grass and that her parachute was not pulling her along. With an effort she sat up and twisted her head to look. The helmet blocked much of her view so she pushed it further back and tilted her head. The black mass of the parachute was draped half over the side of a gum tree or hung down onto the grass. After another few seconds of conscious thought she realized there was no breeze at all.

At that she calmed herself and was able to concentrate on undoing the catch. This time it came undone at the first twist and the harness unclipped with audible clicks and fell off her. With a gasp of relief she rolled over and rose to her knees to check. She was still gasping to recover her breath and felt a bit stunned by the fall but a quick check indicated that she was bruised but with no bones broken.

"Get up!" she told herself. "Get your webbing on in case you have to run."

By quietly ordering herself to act she was able to get her emotions and body back under some sort of control. It took a minute for her numb and fumbling fingers to unclip the rope holding her webbing but the act of untangling it and swinging it on brought back familiarity and with it reassurance and confidence. Feeling considerably better she set to work to roll up the rope. This she secured to her webbing. Then she turned her attention to the parachute. By walking away from the tree and pulling she was able to drag it free. The parachute, lines and harness were then rolled into a bundle.

That done Barbara paused and stood listening. She had expected to hear the sound of the aircraft but there wasn't even a murmur. Then she cocked her head to listen for the sounds of the others.

Stay where you land and wait to be found, Raoul said, she reminded herself.

So she sat on the parachute and allowed her trembling nerves to slowly calm down. While rubbing an increasingly sore left buttock she noted just how close she had come to the large tree while landing. With the pain came the realization of how close she had come to crashing into it. Her imagination conjured up ghastly images of having her limbs or back broken or of jagged splinters shredding her entrails. That caused her to shudder. Then she thought of the others and hoped that none had been hurt in the landing.

Two minutes later she heard the sound of footsteps and the swish of someone walking through the long grass. She crouched low and squinted in the starlight. A dark figure came into view—an armed soldier in helmet and with a weapon.

The man saw her and turned in her direction, calling softly, "Barbara?"

It was Raoul. Barbara stood up and flung herself into his arms. The embrace was difficult because both wore webbing and because Raoul was already holding his rifle, but he freed an arm and hugged her to him.

"You are safe *mon cheri*?"

Barbara knew enough French to be almost overwhelmed by that comment. *My love! Does he really mean that, or is he just saying it?* she wondered. But she clung tightly to him anyway and tried to hold back more tears.

"I'm fine," she answered, "just a few bumps and bruises."

"Nothing broken?"

"No," she croaked, looking up into his eyes. Then he kissed her.

For several seconds they clung together in a hot embrace, the warmth and reassurance flowing into her. That gave her the strength to ignore the throbbing ache that had developed down her left leg. A distant sound caused Raoul to ease himself free and look in that direction. Then he nodded and looked back at her.

"You are very brave," he said softly, kissing her again, but this time on the nose—her helmet getting in the way as he did.

More noises, then a soft call and Sgt Boucher appeared. By then Barbara and Raoul were a metre apart. Sgt Boucher saw her and nodded. "*Mademoiselle* is unhurt?" he queried.

"Only a sore bum," Barbara answered, rubbing at her thigh.

"Good. Then you have done very well," Sgt Boucher said.

Raoul said that he would get his parachute and check on the others. With that he hurried off into the darkness. Barbara saw that Sgt Boucher was wearing a small pack and webbing and had his parachute in a neat bundle under his left arm. Across his front was slung one of the French automatic rifles Barbara had noted earlier. To her it looked strange, mainly because of the long combined sight and carrying handle on the top.

"What do we do now?" she asked.

"Wait for the others to join us. Then we hide the parachutes," Sgt Boucher replied.

At Sgt Boucher's suggestion Barbara took off her webbing and lay down on her parachute. Until she relaxed she did not realize just how tense and sore she was. Her whole body seemed to tingle and shiver and the bruises now throbbed so much she began to fear she had really done some damage.

Ten minutes went by. Suddenly Sgt Boucher crouched and adopted the 'kneeling supported' fire position. Barbara saw that he had a night vision device of some sort attached to his helmet and that reassured her. Next he nodded and said, "It is only the lieutenant and a couple of the others."

Raoul arrived back, in company with S-Lt de Blainville and two legionnaires. All, she noted, were wearing night vision devices over their left eye. Without explanation to Barbara Raoul swung off a small pack and then unpacked the satellite radio from it. The two legionnaires were deployed twenty metres out as sentries by Sgt Boucher.

For the next twenty minutes the two officers made notes using shielded torches, crouching low in the grass. Both opened out one of the small computers and Barbara saw that the devices had a folding pouch that helped shield the light as they lay side by side and tapped at the screens and quietly conversed. Both then took out maps and did some navigation calculations. Then a radio was set up and Raoul typed on its keypad and transmitted and then the replies were studied as they were scrolled across the small display screen.

While this was being done three more legionnaires came in, including the big black soldier. To Barbara's concern she saw that he and the big sergeant were helping the third man, the big sergeant carrying two of the small packs. From the conversation that followed Barbara gathered that the man, a Senior Private named Pilsudski, had hit a tree branch and had a broken collar bone and dislocated shoulder.

The first aid was interrupted by the arrival of the last four legionnaires. They were carrying a large container on a stretcher. This surprised Barbara as she had not seen these items being thrown out of the aircraft. Once again she was not included in the conversations and could only pick up the general gist of them. What she did get though was a powerful impression of Raoul as a very confident and forceful leader who made rapid decisions.

The container was taken off the stretcher and the injured man placed on it. Then the big black soldier added the drum sized container to his load and four others grouped around the stretcher and picked it up. That bothered Barbara as she knew from hard experience how exhausting it was to carry a casualty for any distance.

"Can I help?" she asked

"It will be alright," Raoul replied. "These men are very fit and strong."

"They should use straps or ropes to help take the strain off their hands," she said.

"What do you mean?" Raoul asked.

"Ropes or straps at each end that go from the stretcher around the shoulders of the men doing the carrying," she explained. "Then, if one slips or loses his grip, the rope stops the casualty being dropped."

Raoul nodded. "I 'ave seen that. You are not just a pretty face are you?"

Barbara blushed and felt extraordinarily pleased at being able to help. She appreciated the huge problem the injured man must be, many kilometres from anywhere and in what was essentially 'enemy' territory. The irony that the 'enemy' was the Australian Army was not lost on her, making her feel deeply troubled.

Am I a traitor? she wondered unhappily.

The conversation had been overheard by both S-Lt de Blainville and Sgt Boucher and they both nodded and set to work to secure ropes from their webbing around the stretcher. S-Lt de Blainville gave Barbara a look of surprised appraisal.

The injured man's webbing and weapon were place with him on the stretcher and the big sergeant hefted the man's backpack onto his front. The parachute bundles were then picked up and secured and the stretcher hoisted up. The group then began to move on a compass course across the open savannah. Out of curiosity Barbara took out her own magnetic compass and noted the bearing they were moving on.

Two hundred metres on, and after three short rests with the stretcher, they came to a small dry creek. Here there was a long rest. During this they always had two sentries and the injured man was better attended to, torches being used down in the shelter of the gully. Four shovels were extracted from the container and then brought into use to bury the parachutes. This took the men nearly half an hour to accomplish, all of them, except the casualty, taking turns. Even Raoul did his share of shovel work. When Barbara offered to bury her own parachute he shook his head and did it for her, annoying her slightly.

While sitting quietly waiting Barbara massaged her wrist and left thigh. Then she sat and gazed at the stars or studied the shapes of the men around her. That they were well—trained professionals was very obvious by their silence and their continual alertness, weapons ready, eyes questing, ears cocked, even when resting. A check of her watch told her it was 2335 and that surprised her.

I thought it would be later, she mused. So much had happened in the previous two days that all her perceptions were blurred and distorted.

Before the patrol started moving towards their objective, Raoul showed her on the computer map where they were. Knowing that the device had a GPS in it she accepted the Grid Reference as accurate. Raoul pointed, and said, "We are here. We move southeast to this creek, Keelbottom Creek. I want us to be there in two hours. We need to be at the place you indicate before sunrise."

"What about the injured man? Will we be able to carry him that far in that time?"

"He has been strapped up and given a pain killer. He is going to walk for a while. Time is important," Raoul replied.

"What would you have done if he had been seriously injured?" Barbara asked.

Raoul shrugged. "We would leave him with the medic and try to extract him later. In this case the mission comes first. These men understand that. Come, let us go."

Barbara stood up and swung on her webbing, feeling slightly chilled by the risks these men were prepared to take. The group resumed moving. This time they had two scouts fifty metres out ahead: the big African and a thin man with a black moustache. Both wore individual radios with a single earpiece and Barbara noted that S-Lt de Blainville wore one as well. The two officers and Barbara came next, then the two sergeants and the injured man being helped by the medic, and last the remaining four legionnaires, who carried the container on the stretcher.

To Barbara's relief the injured man was able to walk without much help. His arm had been well strapped to prevent it moving and he tried to grin from time to time, his teeth flashing in the starlight. His pack and webbing were the problem and Barbara helped solve that by picking up the webbing. She was amazed at the weight of it, never having carried webbing that contained magazines of ammunition or the real combat load of a soldier.

The patrol then advanced at a steady walking pace. The ground was gently undulating open savannah woodland and most of the time the grass was short. There were no rocks and only a few logs and anthills so it was easy going of the sort Barbara was used to. Only the distances were longer. Twenty minutes of walking brought them to a gentle crestline. They had a short rest, then continued on. The next leg was down a slight slope for about a kilometre, then across a shallow gully and up another long, gentle slope. The only thing of interest was encountering some cattle which lumbered off into the night.

A fence was the next landmark. It was marked on the map and told Barbara they had travelled about three kilometres. Already she was feeling the strain, being both tired and thirsty. Now she was glad she had refilled her waterbottles in the aircraft as she drank deeply from one of them.

As she put it back in her webbing Barbara saw the scouts both taking off their packs. They seemed to be having trouble so she and S-Lt de Blainville hurried forward to find they were having difficulty negotiating the three stand barbed wire fence.

Realizing that they were probably not that familiar with such fences Barbara shook her head and muttered, "Watch!" She swung off her webbing. "Pass your packs and webbing across and go under on your back holding the bottom strand so it doesn't snag you," she explained.

When they looked at her she pushed her webbing under the bottom strand then knelt down and wriggled under. "Feet first," she added as she demonstrated.

"Ver good!" S-Lt de Blainville muttered and quickly told his men to copy and get on with it. Barbara stood up and dusted herself then swung her webbing on.

Taking S-Lt de Blainville's pack, she said, "They are fences to stop cattle. There are lots of them in this country and the easiest and safest way to get through is under on your back."

"You are familiar with them then," S-Lt de Blainville commented.

"Very. My cadets go under them all the time. It's like everything, easy when you know how."

"So true!" S-Lt de Blainville replied, bending to crawl under.

By now Raoul had arrived and he heard this and copied her example. By then the first scout was well on his way and the second scout followed. The others arrived one at a time and passed their pack and webbing across and went down in the dust and ash to crawl under the barbed wire fence.

The march continued, down a very gentle spur line through a stand of large ironbarks and then out onto a wide flat dotted with a few large ghost gums. Ten minutes of trudging in waist high dry grass brought them to a larger dry creek: Dunns Gully. There was another halt and the injured man had his bandages adjusted. Barbara was thankful for the break as her bruises were really throbbing by this and she feared she might be going to get cramps.

The next part of the march was up a slightly steeper slope studded with grass and small stones amid a denser stand of black-trunked ironbarks. Another crest line was reached and they halted again, the injured man showing signs of dizziness.

By then it was 0115 hours and the first glimmer of moonlight was showing away to the east. There was a short pause, during which the injured man was allowed to lie down and his dressings again adjusted. While they waited Barbara looked towards where the loom of the rising moon was showing. Hills were just visible in dark relief and that got her thinking. Trees blocked much of the view but by moving a few paces to one side her eyes found what they sought. Clear against the lighter sky was the distant silhouette of Mount St Michael.

The sight caused her to feel much more confident. *I'm not in a strange place anymore,* she thought. *I know where I am.*

It wasn't much but it cheered her to think she had at least some control over her life, and even a few options. One of them was to just walk away, but she pushed that into the back of her mind. Instead she pointed out Mount St Michael to Raoul and he was very pleased. He called over S-Lt de Blainville and pointed to it. The S-Lt gave Barbara another appraising look and nodded with grudging approval.

At 0130 the march was resumed. Barbara noted that they were right on course, aiming slightly to the right of Mount St Michael. As they went down the long gentle slope the hill was lost behind trees, so navigation was again by GPS and compass. When S-Lt de Blainville saw her looking at her own compass he frowned and pointed this out to Raoul. Raoul and the Foreign Legion officer both came back to her.

"You have a compass?" Raoul asked.

"Of course," Barbara replied. "I am a platoon commander. And I am a good navigator."

"What bearing do you think we should walk?" Raoul asked.

Barbara said, "Take out your map."

When the map was laid on the ground she noted the pencil line drawn across it and nodded her approval, then placed her compass against it and turned the milled vane of the compass housing till the red lines underneath were aligned with the Grid Lines on the map. Then she squinted in the shielded torchlight to read the number on the lubber line.

"One thousand eight hundred and twenty mils, minus one forty for

Magnetic Variation eastwards, that means one thousand six hundred and eighty mils Magnetic," she replied, aware that she was showing off.

This time a smile split S-Lt de Blainville's face. He nodded, and said, "Very good. *Mademoiselle* has the understanding. Per'aps we do find this thing."

"I will certainly take you to the place where I saw something," Barbara replied, "But I can't promise you it is what you want. It might just be a bit of wreckage."

"We will see," Raoul replied with a shrug. "Now, let us get on."

The group resumed its march. Fifteen minutes later they came to a large, dry creek lined with paperbarks. The sides were steep and difficult to climb across but the bed was sandy. They halted for another rest with sentries up on both banks. According to the map, which Raoul let her study, it was Brinagee Creek. Barbara estimated the distance still to go and saw it was about six kilometres.

It seemed a dismayingly long distance for her, but she was also aware that the paratroopers could probably cover it in one hour if they pushed themselves. By now she was feeling very tired and thirsty and had emptied one of her waterbottles.

0200 hours found the group walking across a seemingly endless flat plain dotted with large ironbarks. By then the moon was up and they were walking almost straight towards it. From her experience on night fieldcraft exercises Barbara knew that was reasonably favourable.

Anyone ahead of us will show up as black silhouettes, she thought, remembering how hard it was to see the people 'down moon'. It was only a three-quarter moon but still cast plenty of light.

Suddenly there was a disturbance ahead. Men threw themselves flat or crouched in fire positions, rifles ready. A distinct thudding sound could be heard, rapidly receding into the distance. Barbara heard S-Lt de Blainville mutter.

"*Sacre bluer!* What was that?"

At that Barbara had to smile. "Only a wallaby," she replied. Raoul looked quizzical. "A small kangaroo," Barbara explained.

At that there were chuckles and Barbara heard mutterings of the word, *Kangouroo.* S-Lt de Blainville stood up and peered in the direction the wallaby had gone. He said in a completely different tone of voice, "*Kangouroo!* I have one never seen. I would very much like to see one."

Raoul also chuckled and said, "Could have been worse. If this was *Afrique* it could have been *un lionne.*"

With murmurings about wild animals the group resumed its journey. A few minutes later, at 0215, they came to the Mirambeena Road. The scouts halted them short of it and one came back to report. Barbara crouched in the long grass and peered anxiously in all directions, wondering why they had suddenly 'propped' again, until it was explained to her. After some whispered consultation and a check of the map Raoul waved the scouts on.

As Barbara crossed the gravel road she looked along it in both directions, aware that her imagination was conjuring up all sorts of enemies. In her mind were images of the control room in the American aircraft carrier.

What if they were able to track that French plane by radar and know we have landed? she thought. *There could be troops moving to intercept us even now.*

She knew there was such a thing as 'over-the-horizon' radar but had no idea how effective or capable it was.

Then she got a shock. The country on the far side of the road was all burnt off. Dust and ash stirred up by their boots rose to tickle her nostrils and to settle as a gritty taste at the back of her mouth.

We are getting close now, she thought, picturing that frightening and exciting night and the fires that raged for the next few days.

Then another worrying thought came to her. She hurried forward and tugged at Raoul's sleeve. "What about our tracks?" she asked.

"Our what?"

"Our tracks, our bootrpints in the dust and ash," Barbara explained.

Raoul shrugged. "It is a risk we must take. We do not have time to brush them out."

S-Lt de Blainville overheard this and wanted to know what she had said. Raoul explained and he looked thoughtful and nodded, then called quite instructions to his own sergeant: Sgt Blomburg Barbara now learned. Sgt Blomburg dropped to the rear and broke a branch off a small tree and began using it to obliterate at least some of the tracks, particularly where they crossed the dirt road. As the group continued on he remained last person, brushing as he went.

A barbed wire three-strand cattle fence was encountered. They rolled under that, another unpleasant experience as the ground was covered in soot and prickles. On the other side Barbara stood up and muttered with annoyance as she tried to brush off the prickles. These were the small double-pronged types and several stuck into her. Removing them took up her attention for the next hundred metres.

Another small creek was encountered. This one was different in that it had steep rocky sides, some sort of crumbly shale or slate, and had almost no trees growing along it. The bottom was only an arm's width wide and mainly bare rock. Getting the casualty and the stretcher across took some effort as they had to scout along it to find washouts they could negotiate. While climbing up out of it Pte Pilsudski slipped and fell. A deep groan escaped his lips and he lay there shivering in pain while the medic, Lamertine, checked him.

Raoul called another halt, his manner composed. The only hint of impatience was his checking of the time every few minutes. Barbara did the same and was surprised to find it was already 0240. It was apparent to Barbara that the injured man was more seriously hurt than they had at first suspected. Raoul, S-Lt de Blainville, the two sergeants and the medic went into a huddle to discuss the situation.

It was decided to carry Pte Pilsudski again. This time Barbara insisted in taking her turn on the stretcher, a noble decision she very rapidly regretted. After only a couple of minutes her hands began to ache and she knew her muscles were giving up. To her mortification she had to admit this and they lowered the stretcher. Raoul praised her for helping and gently patted her shoulder but she was still peeved at her own physical inability. She then took the webbing again and helped carry Pilsudski's pack between her and Sgt Boucher.

A dark line of trees came into view ahead and that sent Barbara's heart rate up. *That must be Keelbottom Creek,* she thought. *We are now in the area.*

But would they find the satellite, or had she brought the Frenchmen here on a wild goose chase?

Chapter 31

IN THE DARK

It was 0250 when they reached the trees lining the bank of Keelbottom Creek. The stretcher was lowered and sentries posted while they had another rest. Raoul and S-Lt de Blainville crouched in a shallow washout and used their torches and computers to check their location. Barbara crouched to join them. Raoul pointed to the map and said, "We are about here."

Barbara nodded agreement. "I think so. We should be on my map enlargement by now."

"Map enlargement?" S-Lt de Blainville queried.

Barbara opened her basic pouch and dug out her still folded 1:25 000 map. "We used these on our annual camp," she explained.

S-Lt de Blainville bent to study the map and let out his breath in a slow hiss. "This is much better. More detail," he said. Then he looked at Barbara. "You have been here before?"

"Not this exact spot," Barbara said, "But if we keep going on this bearing in about another kilometre we will cross country I know very well. I will not need the map to guide you."

"What is the country like?" Raoul asked.

"Worse than what we have been crossing. There are thickets of small trees and several steep-sided gullies to cross." Barbara pointed to the map and said, "Particularly this one: One Mile Creek. It is awkward."

But it was crossing Keelbottom Creek that was the worst. Barbara had forgotten about the thickets of lantana and thorn trees which grew along the banks and on the sand islands in the bed of the braided stream. As the patrol pushed into the long grass her thoughts had been on the big brown snake that she had seen swallowing the other but the dense, thorny undergrowth quickly took her mind off that. The group had to push and trample their way through it. In among the trees it was much darker and the grass reduced visibility to a few metres much of the time.

Raoul was not happy and said so. "Too slow, and too much noise," he said. "It is already zero three ten."

They came out onto a dry river channel, the bed of which was sand and pebbles. Beyond it was another steep bank overgrown with cane, long grass and thorn trees. As Barbara had never crossed the creek in this area she did not know if there were any more flood channels to cross, but suspected there was. She told Raoul this but he just shrugged and signalled the scout to push up into it.

This one turned out to be even worse. There was a dense growth of lantana as well and their attempts to push through it were noisy and frustrating. Almost as annoying to Barbara was the helmet. Its unaccustomed weight was causing her a headache and sore neck muscles and it kept sliding forward to restrict her vision. Muttering with irritation she continually pushed it back. To add to her discomfiture she was scratched by thorns several times and got dry grass down the back of her shirt and even in her mouth.

Then they encountered rubber vine. For several minutes the line halted while they waited for the leaders to push a track through. Barbara did not know why they stopped but was glad to take the chance for another drink. Then the big African legionnaire came back to Raoul and explained in rapid French.

Curious about the delay Barbara asked, "What did he say? What is the problem?"

"Some sort of springy vine in a thick barrier," Raoul replied.

"Oh, rubber vine," Barbara answered. "It is a pest, a weed, introduced from Madagascar I think."

"You know it?"

"Very well!" Barbara replied, chuckling at the memories of clumps of rubber vine she had met. "Just use your secateurs," she added.

"*Secateurs!*" cried S-Lt de Blainville in exasperation. "*Mon dieu!* We are not le gardening doing!"

"We don't have any," Raoul answered. "We had better back up and find an easier route."

"I have some. Let me lead," Barbara replied.

"You should not go first," Raoul expostulated.

"Oh piffle! Why not? I lead my cadet platoon through the bush at night all the time. Here, carry this webbing," she retorted. Shoving the wounded paratrooper's webbing into an astonished Raoul's arms she pushed past him and the big African, then trampled her way forward along the rough trail. Several times she stumbled and almost tripped as vines and stalks snagged her legs but it was an environment she was familiar with and she just ignored this and pushed on till she came to where the second scout stood waiting.

By the time Barbara reached him she had her secateurs out. The second scout looked at her in surprise and opened his mouth but she just gestured him to step aside. Then she very deliberately paused.

I will look a goose if I cut the track along the island instead of across it, she thought.

So she took out her compass and checked the bearing. From thinking about the map she realized that the bearing ran diagonally across the creek bed so she did a quarter turn to the right, noted the large trees and stars ahead, then put her compass away and began to cut.

Now her experience told. Having cut rubber vine on a dozen previous occasions she knew which springy vines to snip and which to leave as too thick to be worth the effort. Mostly she just snipped the thinner ones once and then pushed through, ignoring the milky white sap that then trickled out and stained her uniform. Forward movement was resumed, one slow step at a time. But it was still faster than before, and much more silent.

After about five minutes she was through the rubber vines and into long grass again. That was much less pleasant and her fears of snakes came back with full force. All she could do was hope that the sounds of so many boots trampling along would scare the reptiles away. Having taken the lead it did not occur to her to let the scouts take over again. She detoured around several thorn trees, scratching herself on a small one she did not see. More rubber vine was encountered and she snipped a path through this as fast as she could.

Raoul pushed his way forward while she was doing this. "You are off course," he whispered.

"No I'm not," Barbara replied. She explained what she was doing and he accepted this with a nod of approval.

He then remained behind her as she cut the last of the vine and pushed through some lantana to the top of another flood channel. Here Barbara paused to listen. She looked both ways along it, straining her eyes in the moonlight. This channel was much smaller and had grass growing in its bed. Beyond it was a steeper bank topped by long grass, lantana and a line of large paperbarks.

That looks like the far bank, she thought, noting the ironbarks growing beyond the paperbarks.

She was right. A couple of minutes pushing and climbing had her on top of that bank and she found herself looking out across a wide, flat grassy area, dotted with scattered ironbarks. After putting away her secateurs she took out her compass to check the course. As she went to step off Raoul held her arm and shook his head. He indicated the African scout.

Barbara saw the sense in that so pointed out the direction to the African. He raised an eyebrow and glanced at Raoul. Raoul nodded and the African smiled and nodded, then set off across the grassy flat. As he went Barbara saw him moving his head from side to side to scan the area ahead with his night vision device. The second scout moved up beside Barbara and scanned the front with the sight on his rifle, then followed. Barbara waited till he was ten paces out, then stepped off, still navigating. Raoul and the others followed her.

It was 0340 by then and Barbara was becoming anxious. *First Light is at about 0530*, she thought, thinking back to the camp timings.

She thought she knew where she was but wasn't quite sure. As they crossed the open flat country the two scouts spread out fifty paces apart so Barbara slowed to allow them to get fifty paces ahead of her. A glance behind showed that Raoul and the others had also opened out to at least ten paces apart. He again nodded with approval. From time to time one of the scouts looked back and Barbara held her arm straight out in the desired direction. They nodded and concentrated on their scouting. She stayed focused on her navigation, glancing repeatedly at the compass held in her left-hand.

A creek line appeared ahead and the scouts vanished into it. When Barbara reached the trees and saw how large and deep the creek line was she heaved a huge sigh of relief.

One Mile Creek. Thank God!

Barbara walked and slid down the ten metres to the creek bed, following a cattle pad. At the bottom she found a gap in the long grass and easily scrambled down into the last deep section, then clambered up through another gap along a dusty animal pad. As she came out of the grass she saw that the two scouts had stopped and gone to ground at the top of the slope. For a moment her heart leapt in alarm but then she saw them looking back at her and knew they were just waiting for directions.

As Barbara walked up the almost bare slope towards the scouts Raoul called softly to her from the other bank, telling her to wait. She waved to show she had heard him but continued on up to the top of the bank. Here she knelt and looked over the crest. Beyond was a burnt-out stretch of flat country and in the moonlight she recognized the ghost gums and dry claypan. Beyond it were numerous small ironbarks and the sight of them made her happy.

I know exactly where we are, she thought. *This is the Triangle area where the company bivouacked for the night exercise.*

She gave the African scout a smile and thumbs up, then turned and made her way back down to where Raoul and the others were gathering in the creek bed. As she walked down the slope Barbara looked around, then gave a wry smile.

This is where I did my pee when the SAS filmed me, she thought.

The memory caused her to blush with shame and irritation. Worse still, it made her realize she needed to do a pee now. Having the idea in her mind made the physical need acute.

Crouching next to Raoul and S-Lt de Blainville, she said, "I know exactly where I am. We can get to the place in about half an hour."

"Good. Let us get moving. It is zero four hundred already," Raoul replied, looking at his watch.

"Just a minute. I need to go to the toilet," Barbara replied, blushing fiercely as she did. She stood up and walked away from the men along the edge of the grass. The problem then was to find a place where she was out of sight of the two scouts as well, without walking too far. She was loath to push into the long grass. Finally she selected a spot behind a clump of tall grass and took off her webbing. As she did she felt very anxious and exposed.

They've all got night vision equipment. What if they can still see me? she wondered.

Deciding it was too dark she undid her trousers and slid them down. As she squatted there, still wondering if the legionnaires with their night vision equipment could see her, the more alarming thought that there might be another SAS patrol in the area came to her. That got her anxiously looking over her shoulder. As quickly as she could she finished and pulled up her trousers.

Two minutes later she rejoined Raoul and the others. Raoul looked grave. He said, "If the map is correct it is only about one kilometre to this place. Is that so?"

"Yes, about that," Barbara answered. She took out her own map and torch and checked. Still drawn on her map, she noted, was the pencil line showing the route for the night exercise, and written along it was the magnetic bearing: 1660 mils Magnetic. She set this on her compass.

Raoul then said, "We are going to leave our injured man here, with someone to guard him. We will pick him up on the way back."

Barbara nodded, not knowing what their withdrawal plan was. S-Lt de Blainville pointed to her map. "This village called Dotswood, how many *inhabitants*?"

"It's not a village," Barbara answered. "It used to be a cattle station homestead. It is not used any more. If there is anyone there it will only be a couple of stockmen."

"Stockmen?"

"Cowboys," she replied. Barbara had to explain what a cattle station was, and the houses, sheds, men's quarters, stables, etc, that are found in such a place, then what stockmen were.

Roaul nodded and looked thoughtful as he studied the map. "And there is an airfield there?"

Barbara nodded, remembering it from the camp. "Yes a big one and in good condition—but only grass."

S-Lt de Blainville nodded and said, "Good. It will do. We go now please."

Barbara at once stood up and walked up the slope, folding her map and putting it and the torch away as she went. On top she signalled for the two scouts to get up and then used her compass to point them in the right direction. The scouts headed off and Barbara waited till they were thirty or forty paces ahead, then stepped off. Behind her came the others in a long line, widely spaced, the four carrying the stretcher with the big cylinder near the back. Sgt Blomburg came last.

They were back on flat, burnt-off ground now and the going was easy. The moon was overhead but Barbara was anxiously aware that dawn was only about an hour away. Two minutes later she stepped across the dusty wheel tracks near where 4 Platoon had been camped. Then it was on across the flat ground inside the Triangle. Knowing with absolute certainty her location allowed her to walk fast, so fast that the scouts were forced to speed up to keep ahead of her.

After another three minutes they came to the gravel road on the other side of the Triangle. "Marlow Road," she muttered, but she crossed it without stopping.

A minute later she saw the scouts both taking off their packs and saw that they had reached the barbed wire fence. The scouts quickly negotiated the obstacle and were moving ahead by the time Barbara reached it. Swinging off her webbing she went down in the dust and ash and wriggled under.

Barbara stood up and dusted herself then swung her webbing on. Taking S-Lt de Blainville's pack she was amazed at its weight. Trying not to show this she lowered it to the ground and took his webbing. S-Lt de Blainville quickly bent to crawl under.

By then Raoul had arrived and Barbara took his pack and webbing and then realized they were starting to make a cluster.

That's not good tactics, she thought, remembering Major Wickham's oft-repeated injunctions not to bunch up. So she put the pack down and turned and started walking, checking her compass as she did.

By then the first scout was fifty paces ahead with the second scout following. The other soldiers arrived one at a time and passed their pack and webbing across and also went down to crawl under the barbed wire fence.

A hundred paces further on One Mile Creek blocked their path but Barbara was able to lead the group to where the old vehicle track crossed it and get across easily.

So quickly did she cross that she was up on the other side at the same time as the two scouts, who had to climb across deeper, steeper sections of the creek bed. They looked to her and she pointed into the burnt-out thicket ahead of her. This was so dense that the scouts closed in to stay in sight. Barbara waited till Raoul and the others had caught up. As she waited she relived those glorious moments of leading her own platoon as it had advanced.

That was great fun, she reminisced. But then she remembered encountering the British commandos and a stab of worry got her biting her lip. *I wonder if that meeting in Atherton was accidental? What if they have some way of tracking me and they knew we are here?* she worried.

When the patrol reached the small gully in the middle of the thicket she explained the accidental meeting to Raoul and voiced her concerns.

He looked grave but shook his head. "I do not know how they could keep a trace on you," he said.

"What about some sort of radio bugging device," she suggested.

"In what?" he asked, "And how would it transmit? The distances would be too great and its power too small."

"To a satellite? I don't know," Barbara replied. She knew that that was how animals and fish that had been tagged with transmitters were tracked.

"I do not think so. How would our enemies have planted such a device," Raoul replied with a shrug.

That had been bothering Barbara as well. *Raoul and Sgt Chef Boucher certainly wouldn't have one on them. How could it have been hidden in our gear?* Then a chilling thought came to her: was it in her webbing that Willy had brought to her? That got her really sweating with anxiety.

But how would they have known I was going to use my webbing? she thought. *I didn't mention it on the phone. I just asked Willy to collect it.* Then an even more upsetting idea came to her. *Did Willy plant it?* That was too distressing to want to think about but she made herself. *Surely he wouldn't be such a false friend?* she wondered.

The thought of such a betrayal made her feel ill. But she did concede that the secret agents might have got to him and persuaded him by threats or by appealing to his patriotism.

No, not by threats, she thought.

Reluctantly she voiced this concern to Raoul. He frowned but shook his head. "I doubt it. They would not have had time to arrange that. Do you trust this friend?"

"Yes," Barbara replied, upset by her own horrible doubts.

"Then when we stop we can check. Come, let us get moving. Is it far?"

"Another ten minutes at most," Barbara replied.

They continued on. Still plagued by gnawing doubts and the sickening fear she might be leading these men into an ambush, Barbara led the way. She navigated using her compass but the trees were so close together they had to weave their way among them. By then the moon was just past overhead and Barbara had the uncomfortable thought that they might now be showing up as black silhouettes to anyone out on the Mingela Road near the Front Gate. She also began casting anxious glances to her left, to where she knew the sun would come up. Through the trees she began to get glimpses of the dark bulk of Mount St Michael and that cheered her.

Not long now, she thought.

The barbed wire fence which led south from the Mingela Road grid near the Front Gate was the next obstacle. The fence ran along a clearing with a vehicle track beside it and visibility was good, perhaps a hundred metres, so the legionnaires treated it as a tactical obstacle, crossing one at a time with the others under cover ready to give covering fire.

The scouts went first. Then it was Barbara's turn. Doing it tactically got her all anxious and excited and she looked nervously up and down the cleared lane as she walked quickly across it. Going under the fence was again unpleasant, all grit and soot. On the other side she stood up, dusting sand and ash from her hands. A clump of dry bushes beside a log gave her cover so she walked to it and crouched down.

While she waited she looked around. *We are only about fifty metres from the Gravel Scrape,* she decided, noting some rocks and the continuation of the burnt-out thicket.

As she looked around in the darkness a sudden tiny flare of light caught her eye. It was away to her left and was gone so quickly she wondered if she had imagined it, but then she shook her head. Her heart began to hammer with anxiety. As Raoul joined her, she took hold of his sleeve and whispered in his ear, pointing as she did.

"I just saw someone light a match over there," she said.

Raoul at once went low and signalled the others to do likewise. S-Lt de Blainville was crawling under the fence so kept moving till he was under cover near them. "What is it?" he asked softly in French.

"*Bar... er... Mademoiselle,* saw a light, a match being struck she thinks," Raoul explained.

"What is there?" S-Lt de Blainville asked.

Barbara pointed. "A road junction. There is a gate on the road leading in to the army camp."

"This army camp, it is not just there is it?" Raoul asked.

"No. It is a kilometre up the road. It is not visible from the Front Gate," Barbara replied.

"There must be a guard," Raoul suggested.

S-Lt de Blainville adjusted the focus on his night vision device. He scanned the dark bush and then muttered in French, "A cigarette. I cannot see any people, the bushes are too thick, but there is a tiny spot of heat which increases in the way cigarettes do when someone draws on them."

Raoul answered him, suggesting that there was indeed a guard at the gate. Barbara had just enough French to follow the gist of this and was able to tell them that there had been no guard when the cadets had been camped there.

Raoul nodded, then said, "Maybe not, but we were told they were closing off all the roads. So this might be a guard post. We will proceed as though it is—with great caution."

"That will make it difficult," Barbara said. "The place where the satellite is is possibly within sight of the Front Gate."

"All the more reason to be careful," Raoul answered. "Now, can you lead us by another route?"

"Easily, except for the last fifty metres or so," Barbara replied.

S-Lt de Blainville pointed along the fence and asked, "Can this fence be seen from this gate you mention?"

Into Barbara's mind came clear images of the Front Gate area. "No," she replied. "This fence crosses the Mingela Road at a cattle grid, and joins the fence surrounding the army camp at right angles. The Front Gate is about fifty metres to the right of that."

It then had to be explained what a cattle grid was but S-Lt de Blainville was satisfied. After a whispered consultation with his two scouts he signalled to the remainder of his troops to cross the fence. Raoul told Barbara to continue. She stood up and signalled to the two scouts to detour off to the right of the course they had been following. Her plan was to circle around the back of the thicket behind the Gravel Scrape. As she began moving she experienced an intense surge of excitement.

This is going to be a real fieldcraft challenge, she told herself.

Chapter 32

SEARCHING

It took only five minutes for Barbara to lead the patrol around behind the Gravel Scrape. As she did she trembled with excitement and apprehensive anticipation. Once she halted them while she did a quick check to the left. The sight of the bare earth in the bottom of the scrape was a great relief to her.

I have brought them to the right place, she told herself.

Feeling exhausted but happier she rejoined the others and moved them another hundred paces, then halted them under cover.

Crouched among charred bushes on the edge of more open country at the southern end of the Gravel Scrape she explained the layout to Raoul and S-Lt de Blainville. "The Mingela Road is about two hundred paces in front of us, just beyond a small dry creek called One Mile Creek. That is the same dry creek we have crossed twice. In this area it wriggles along parallel to the road. You can just see it over there. About two hundred metres down to our left the creek passes under a small bridge. If you put a sentry in the scrub on the other side of the bridge they can watch the road and the Front Gate at the same time. The Front Gate is about three hundred metres away."

Raoul and S-Lt de Blainville quickly discussed this. S-Lt de Blainville called in his scouts and explained what he wanted them to do. The African legionnaire headed off to the left towards the bridge, vanishing into the creek bed at the closest point. The other man, Corporal Martini, was sent to the right to near where One Mile Creek bent east to cross the Mingela Road at the Dip.

Meanwhile Raoul had grouped the others behind a clump of rocks in the burnt-out thicket. Here they lay down in a wide circle, facing out, weapons ready. Barbara was surprised to see that the odd looking French rifles had a small fold-out bipod.

What a good idea! she thought.

Having briefed these men Raoul gestured to Barbara. "Okay Barbara, please show me where you think this thing is."

After a careful look in all directions Barbara led him and Sgt Boucher forward, out onto the bare, gentle slope leading down to One Mile Creek. As she walked slowly forward, her eyes questing anxiously for the burnt tree, she noted that there was already a paleness in the sky behind Mount St Michael, which now stood out in sharp silhouette.

We had better be quick, she thought.

To her considerable satisfaction and relief she was able to walk straight to the hole where the tree trunk had once stood. "Here," she said, pointing to the black, ash-filled hole.

Raoul stared at it in the moonlight and looked puzzled. "How did this happen?" he queried.

"The satellite struck the tree and lodged in the trunk," Barbara explained. "It was glowing white hot from the re-entry friction and the heat set fire to the tree. The fire has consumed the tree and I suppose the satellite just slid down into the hole."

As she said this the awful idea that the satellite might have already been found crossed her mind, but in the darkness she could not see if the ground had any boot prints on it.

"But how would the tree burn underground?" Sgt Boucher asked.

"Lots of eucalypts are hollow," Barbara explained. "Look at that branch lying over here. I think they rot, or ants and termites eat them out, or something. Once they catch fire properly they burn right down and then underground, sometimes for days."

Raoul studied the hole, then said, "Well, there are plenty of boot prints but nobody has been digging here, so hopefully what we want is down there somewhere. Let us do a check."

So saying he beckoned to Sgt Boucher who walked over and bent down, holding a small rod in his hand. The rod was attached by an electrical cable to a small black box. Almost at once the black box began to emit a faint clicking sound.

Seeing Barbara's interested look, Raoul explained, "A Geiger counter, to check for radioactivity."

"Is the satellite nuclear powered?" Barbara asked.

"I cannot tell you, but things in space certainly pick up radiation. Ah! Yes! Listen to that. It must be down there!" he cried, the satisfaction clear in his voice.

The machine had begun to click loudly and rapidly. S-Lt de Blainville joined them carrying another gadget, a metal detector. That confirmed that there was something large and metallic down the hole.

That had Barbara puzzled. "I told the Americans exactly where to look," she said. "I even marked it on the map. You'd think they would have brought in bulldozers or mechanical diggers and dug it all up."

"That would be their style," Raoul agreed. "But they haven't, so let us get to work."

"Do we have time?" Barbara asked, indicating the faint flush of pink in the sky to the east.

"We 'ave no choice. We must try," Raoul replied. "Now, is that guard post at what you call the Front Gate visible from here?"

They looked but all Barbara could see was a clump of trees and rubber vine which hid the area from view. S-Lt de Blainville said that his scouts reported a Land Rover and two Australian soldiers at the gate. "Military Police," he added. "They look very bored, so Tribunga tells me."

"Tribunga?" Raoul asked.

"*L'Africaine,*" S-Lt de Blainville replied, "My *legionnaire* from *Gabon.*"

Barbara nodded, saying, "The man with the pointy teeth? He looks pretty scary."

S-Lt de Blainville nodded and smiled. "*Oui* The very good soldier he is."

Raoul now said to Barbara, "You wait back under cover while we get on with this."

Barbara did as she was told, walking back to join the others. She sat herself down with her back to a rock and had a big drink while Sgt Blomburg got the others organized. To her amazement two body suits of some sort of metallic silver material were removed from the container and laid out, along with two picks and the four shovels.

A sentry was posted at the rear and the other legionnaires moved forward, laying their webbing and weapons in a neat row ten metres from the hole. They remained there, seated in a line, while Raoul briefed them. Then two went forward and set to work, directed by Sgt Boucher. By then it was light enough for Barbara to see quite clearly and she became increasingly anxious as the minutes ticked by. Dawn was fast approaching!

Almost at once the work area was shrouded in a choking cloud of fine, white ash. No matter how carefully the men digging tried to pile it to one side it was stirred up. Within a couple of minutes another two men took over and the digging went on without a pause. Then Raoul and Sgt Boucher took a turn, followed by S-Lt de Blainville and Sgt Blomburg. As soon as they slowed the first two legionnaires took over again. It was an eye-opening revelation to Barbara to see how efficiently big, fit men who knew what they were doing could dig.

It was quickly apparent that the satellite, or whatever it was, was further down than they thought so the sides of the hole were attacked and broken down. Then by alternating work with picks and shovels the loosened soil was lifted out and stacked in a neat pile on one side. In twenty minutes the hole was three metres in diameter and two metres deep.

The men kept digging, even as daylight crept in. 0530 passed and then 0540. By then it was fully light and the first pink tinge was touching the summit of Mount St Michael.

Anyone on the road who looks will see us, Barbara thought anxiously. She bit her lip and even chewed her nails, until she realized that her hands were filthy with soot and grime. *I must look a sight!* she thought, ruefully studying her grimy hands and broken fingernails. Her uniform was already grimed with ash and sweat.

While they worked Barbara slid off her webbing. *I must check to see if some sort of tracking device has been slipped into my gear,* she thought. The notion that she might be the cause of these men being caught in a trap made her feel nauseous. *The enemy could be just waiting until we have found this thing and then they will swoop,* she thought.

Pouch by pouch she emptied her webbing, checking everything before replacing it. She even looked in her toilet roll and looked suspiciously at the cans of food and tube of condensed milk. But there was nothing. Feeling relieved but still anxious she swung the webbing back on.

I'm getting paranoid, she thought.

Another ten minutes of urgent toil went by. By then the men were all sweating, panting and streaked with grime and ash which stuck to their sweaty skin and uniforms. Raoul kept looking around, a frown indicating his concern. Barbara was sure he would call it off and have them all hide till the following night, but he didn't.

He is worried that the Americans will arrive and find it first I suppose, she concluded.

A metallic 'thunk' from the pick caused all their faces to break into grimy grins. The rate of work was increased and the dirt fairly flew. Sgt Boucher bent down and tested with his Geiger counter, then nodded.

"This is it," he said in French.

"Get the container and suits," Raoul ordered.

Sgt Boucher and three legionnaires ran back and set to work. Two of the legionnaires struggled into the silver suits. These included cylindrical shaped helmets with tiny visors of thick glass and huge, thick gloves which reached up to their elbows.

Radio active alright, Barbara told herself, remembering with a spurt of anger Lt Col Nevison's denial at that very spot.

Having 'suited up' the two legionnaires began walking forward, followed by Sgt Boucher and the third legionnaire carrying the stretcher and container between them. As they walked down the open slope Barbara heard a sound that sent her heart rate shooting up. She scrambled to her feet and called as loudly as she dared.

"Vehicle! Take cover!"

The men had heard it too. They at once went flat or stood behind trees. With some difficulty the two silver suited legionnaires bent and lay flat behind trees. To Barbara they were horribly conspicuous. Having warned them she moved back behind the rocks and lay down. The approaching vehicle could not have come at a worse time, she thought. It was coming from her right along the Mingela Road.

By peering through the remains of a burnt bush she was able to see. The vehicle was an army Land Rover. It vanished into the dip where the road crossed One Mile Creek, then reappeared, accelerating and leaving a tail of dust.

To Barbara's eyes the whole situation had caught them exposed. *They must see the silver suits,* she thought, biting her lip with anxiety. *And, if they didn't, there are the shapes of the men and the pile of newly dug earth!*

But the men in the Land Rover did not even glance sideways. The vehicle went racing past, lost from view half the time behind trees and clumps of rubber vines before it vanished to the left. Then Barbara clearly heard its brakes squeal and then the sound of a door slamming and voices. The distance was too great for her to make out what was said but the tone indicated the usual army banter in such situations.

They are talking to the men at the Front Gate, she decided. *Telling jokes and grumbling about how bored they are.* Then another worrying thought came to her: *If we can hear them, they might hear us!*

After what seemed an age but was actually only about three minutes she heard the Land Rover's door slam again and then its engine revved and it could be heard driving up the slope towards the army camp.

There must still be troops at the camp, Barbara decided. It was something she had expected so it came as no surprise.

As soon as the vehicle had obviously left the area Raoul gestured and got the men moving again. The legionnaires in silver suits struggled to their feet and lumbered awkwardly forward to the pit. Some sort of long-handled tongs with clamps were extracted from the container and the men then climbed down into the pit and began scraping and struggling to lift the satellite out. The stretcher and container were laid close beside the hole in readiness.

It was obviously harder than they had expected as the men had to climb out and set to work with pick and shovel again. By then the sunlight was reaching the tree tops and Barbara was very aware that time was slipping quickly by.

If another vehicle comes along we may not be so lucky, she thought.

In her anxiety she looked carefully in all directions. Suddenly her heart skipped a beat and she stared hard.

That looks like a face, she thought, noting a small circular bump showing above the lip of one of the small gullies two hundred paces to the right. It was in the gully where she had done the pee when Major Conkey had burnt the video memory chip. As Barbara watched she was sure the object moved.

I must warn Raoul, she thought.

Her heart hammering with anxiety, she stood up and hurried forward, glancing around as she did to check there were no other enemies in sight. That was a mistake because when she looked back, she could no longer see the object. By then she was close to the work and Raoul was looking at her with a quizzical look on his face.

As Barbara reached the work site she saw that one of the silver suited legionnaires was struggling to lift a shiny silver cylinder about half a metre long and thirty centimetres in diameter. The thing was damaged at one end and was obviously heavy and awkward. Even with the clamps that fitted into lugs and grooves on the casing it was still difficult.

"Yes?" Raoul asked. To Barbara he looked tired and extremely grimy but also very tough.

The sight sent a surge of love and sympathy through her. "I thought I saw someone in that gully," she said, pointing to the right.

They all turned to look. To Barbara's concern she could no longer make out the shape she thought had been a head. "I thought I saw a face," she explained. "But it is no longer visible."

"Where exactly?" S-Lt de Blainville asked.

Barbara gave an accurate, military description: "Bend in the creek; large, black-trunked tree on right bank; go half-right. See the gullies? The closest gully near those small bushes at this edge of the thicket. There is a rock or anthill."

"I see that," S-Lt de Blainville replied, raising his binoculars.

"One finger to the right of that," Barbara said. She was now feeling foolish and worrying that she had started a false alarm as she could now see no sign of any head.

"You are sure?" S-Lt de Blainville replied.

"No, I'm not," Barbara replied. "But I thought I saw a face and then movement, and whatever I was looking at is no longer visible."

"Better to be sure than sorry," S-Lt de Blainville replied. To Barbara's relief his tone did not convey contempt or disbelief. He began speaking into his headset radio while continuing to scan the area with his binoculars.

It might be an SAS patrol, Barbara thought.

Then she remembered that it was only two hundred metres the other side of the Gravel Scrape that she had stumbled on the British SBS patrol.

Maybe it is Mark Guy and his commandos? she pondered, anxious lest the British had somehow tracked them to this point. *Or maybe I am just imagining things?*

S-Lt de Blainville lowered his binoculars and turned to Raoul. "I am sending Cpl Martini to check it out," he said.

Raoul nodded and turned back to the problem of extracting the satellite from the hole. Barbara hesitated over whether to stay and watch, or to go back to cover. She decided not to distract the men and turned and walked back up to the thicket. By the time she had reached cover and sat down she saw that the satellite had been lifted clear and was, with some difficulty, being pushed into the container.

Seeing that caused her to become even more anxious, although elated. *Oh hurry up! We must get away before anyone comes along.*

As soon as the satellite was in the container, the lid was closed. The legionnaires quickly stripped off the silver suits. These were tossed into the hole. Raoul, Sgt Boucher, Sgt Blomburg and a legionnaire lifted the container onto the stretcher, then picked it up and quickly carried it up to where Barbara lay.

Seeing Barbara's questioning look, Raoul nodded and said, "Yes, this is what we were sent to get. Thank you."

"The container?" Barbara asked.

"A shield to protect the carriers from radioactivity," Raoul replied. "It is now quite safe—or so the specialists tell us," he added wryly.

Barbara saw that the silver suits had all been stuffed down into the hole by this time and two legionnaires set to work with shovels to fill the hole in. S-Lt de Blainville remained crouching behind a tree, rifle ready, while he looked away to the right through his binoculars. Raoul led the team back out to help with the shovelling. The picks were tossed into the hole and buried as well and then the remaining earth scooped in. As a final stage soot and the white ash were spread to disguise the digging area.

They were just finishing this when Barbara heard another vehicle. It was coming down the slope from the army camp. Once again she hurried out to warn them, but it was not necessary as they had also heard it.

"More than one," Raoul commented. "Let us hope it is not the pursuit coming to chase us."

S-Lt de Blainville shrugged, and said, "Cpl Martini is in those gullies now. He says there are boot prints but he cannot tell if they are recent or not."

"They might be mine," Barbara replied, feeling both guilty and foolish.

"*Non.* More than one person, he reports," S-Lt de Blainville answered.

Raoul looked around then shrugged. "Call him back in; your other sentry too. We will get out of here. Come, let us get under cover till these vehicles are gone."

By then the vehicles could be heard slowing at the Front Gate so the group ran quickly back up the slope and took cover in the small dips and behind burnt trees and rocks around the stretcher and its valuable cargo. Barbara lay down on the soot and peered through a burnt bush, her heart pounding and sweat beginning to trickle down her face.

Down near One Mile Creek she saw the African legionnaire appear. He was moving at a loping run.

He's not going to make it in time, Barbara decided, hearing the truck motors roar.

She had been hoping that the vehicles would turn right and go towards Townsville but realized they were turning towards her and coming south along the Mingela Road.

Maybe they have nothing to do with us and are just going somewhere else, she thought.

To her relief she saw Tribunga go flat in a tiny hollow halfway up the slope and still a hundred paces away. To her right Cpl Martini also took cover. The first truck came into sight. From her cover Barbara watched anxiously, noting that it was an army truck and that the back was full of Australian soldiers. A second came into sight, and then a third and fourth. To her dismay the trucks began to slow when they were directly opposite where she lay. The front truck stopped only fifty metres past the hole where the satellite had been. Tailgates were lowered and soldiers began to jump off the back.

Oh no! Surely they didn't see us? Barbara thought, her heart rate increasing again.

She tensed ready for action and broke into a prickle of perspiration. Beside her the legionnaires brought their weapons to their shoulders. Seeing that made her feel even worse.

Oh my God! There might be a battle between French soldiers and my own people, she told herself.

The idea was so appalling it made her feel sick and she looked at Raoul with pleading eyes. He looked grim-faced and merely shrugged and settled the butt of his own rifle more comfortably in his shoulder.

Barbara saw his thumb go to what she assumed was the safetycatch and her heart skipped a beat and her whole chest tightened up with sick apprehension.

Chapter 33

HOT!

Appalled at the thought that her actions might lead to the death of fellow Australians Barbara desperately tried to think of a plan to avert such a disastrous outcome. To her growing dismay she saw the other three trucks stop and the troops on them begin to dismount as well. Then she noticed something that made her feel even sicker.

They don't even have guns. What are they thinking of!

A minute later that became clear and she heaved an enormous sigh of relief. The Australian troops turned the other way and began to line out along the far side of the road.

They look like they are going to search the bit of bush where we were camped and did our night exercise, she decided.

They were. After ten anxious minutes of watching she saw the troops get organized, then move slowly forward. Some, she now noted, had metal detectors. Others had radios and some had sticks or shovels. For ten minutes the Australian soldiers searched every square metre of the ground between the road and the fence beyond. Then they moved through the fence and lined up again before advancing very slowly away from her, searching the long grass as they went.

As the line of men moved further away Barbara met Raoul's eyes and shivered. Only then did it occur to her that she must have presented the French with a real dilemma.

I won't ask him what he would have done if they had come this way and I had stood up and called out, she decided. *I might not like the answer.*

Raoul gave a grin and wiped sweat from his soot-streaked face. "We wait for a while," he said. "So just lie still please."

That gave her a clue. *For him: patriotism first,* Barbara decided. Suddenly she felt exhausted. She rested her head on her arms and lay flat. A fit of trembling shook her and then she used her will power to calm herself. *I wonder what happens next?* she thought.

A glance at her watch showed it was only 0720. *Early for those soldiers to be up and about,* she mused.

Then further reflection made her decide they had started early to avoid the heat later in the day. That it was going to be hot later was already obvious as she was perspiring and her tongue felt enlarged and sticky. Already the sun was striking at her small areas of bare skin with an unpleasant warmth.

Very cautiously Barbara rolled on her side and took out a waterbottle. A big drink helped but she also noted that the waterbottle was almost empty. After replacing the waterbotle in her webbing she lay flat and stared at the parked trucks.

Now, if they will go away we can move, she thought.

But the trucks showed no sign of moving. The niggling worry that, having searched the far side of the road, the Australian troops might search this side came to bother her conscience. Shaking her head at the situation she closed her eyes and tried to rest. In spite of feeling utterly worn out sleep would not come. Her webbing dug into her, as did stones and sticks. Continual fidgeting failed to find a more comfortable position. Then ants and flies came to crawl on her and annoy. To cap it all off the heat grew quickly more and more intense.

Barbara opened her eyes with a start. *I must have dozed off,* she thought, rubbing at dry, sleep-gummed eyelids.

Her mouth tasted foul and she saw that her skin was grimed and blackened. Her neck muscles ached from the weight of the helmet and she had a stabbing headache. Once again she felt very thirsty. She saw she was lying in the sun and very slowly wormed her way backwards into a patch of shade. This took some doing as she discovered with some dismay that the sand and stones were now so hot they hurt to touch with bare flesh. She also discovered that her bruises from the night before had stiffened up and could only be eased with some pain.

Raoul lifted his head and gave her a tired smile, then moved a metre to make room for her in a small patch of shade.

"You slept for a while," he said. "That is good."

"What do we do now?" Barbara whispered, noting that the container had been covered by a camouflage blanket of some sort.

"We wait until those trucks drive away," Raoul answered.

"What if the Australian troops start coming this way?" she asked.

Raoul looked behind them into the bush. "Then we quietly walk away in the other direction and hope they do not try to stop us."

"What if they do?" Barbara persisted.

"They did not appear to be armed," Raoul answered. "I think they can be persuaded to leave us go."

For a few minutes they lay in silence. Barbara stared at the parked trucks, willing them to leave. By now they were only visible through a shimmering heat haze. That made her aware of how thirsty she was. Once again, she took out a waterbottle and drank. In the process she found two were now empty and that caused her some concern. She also noted that Tribunga was still lying out on the bare, open flat and that he was not in any shade.

"That man will be roasted in this heat," she said, pointing to him.

Raoul nodded. "It is certainly very hot. I think as hot as Africa. Like Somalia it is. I did not know that Australia got so hot."

Raoul then offered her some food, but she felt too sick in the stomach to eat and shook her head. Once again, she tried to sleep, despite the heat, flies, ants and discomfort. 1000 hours came and went. The sun climbed higher and they all sweated and wilted. From time to time one or the other would move a bit to try to stay in what meagre shade there was. Each time Raoul insisted they move backwards, away from the road. The stretcher was dragged back a few metres, but very slowly so that the movement did not attract attention.

At 1030 a Land Rover came along the road from the south and stopped at the trucks. For a minute Barbara was hopeful the trucks would move but the Land Rover went on and the trucks stayed put. She moved to another piece of shade. Several vehicles came from the other direction, but all stopped at the Front Gate and then went into the army camp and she did not see any of them, only a dust plume to mark where the road ran up over the next rise.

At 1145 a line of Australian soldiers appeared in the bush on the other side of the road. The troops were moving towards them and Raoul hissed and got everyone shaken awake and ready to move. The Australian troops came to the fence and crawled under it, then stopped at the road. Barbara tensed, ready to act and wondering what she should now do.

She shook her head and whispered, "I wonder why they are wasting time searching over the other side of the road. I showed them very carefully where it was on the map and even gave them the Grid Reference."

He shrugged and hefted his rifle into a fire position. "Who knows?"

Barbara then summoned the courage to ask the question that had been bothering her all morning. "What do you want me to do when you go?"

"What would you like to do?" Raoul asked.

"Go with you," Barbara answered at once.

Raoul shook his head in wonder. "Ah! You are such a brave girl. You are like none of the other girls I have ever known."

In an attempt to defuse her emotions Barbara asked flippantly, "Have you know many other girls?"

Raoul grinned. "Of course I 'ave! I am a Frenchman. It is obligatory. I 'ave known many also because I am the marine, the sailor, the man with a girl in every port. Yes, I 'ave been with many girls—if you understand my meaning. But you are special. You I actually care about and want to get to know as a person."

A sharp stab of envy pierced Barbara's heart, particularly at that 'known—if you understand' comment. She understood alright, but could only feel glad. *Of course he would have sex with girls. He is a very good looking, charming man,* she thought.

Then she looked into his eyes and thought she would melt with love. Memories of her own close intimacy with him caused her heart to hammer fast.

For a moment Barbara thought they were going to kiss, heat, grime and helmets notwithstanding. A quiet call from Sgt Boucher stopped that. Barbara and Raoul both looked. The soldiers were moving to the trucks and climbing aboard.

Oh, thank God! Barbara sighed.

Ten minutes later the trucks and troops were all gone. As soon as they were out of sight Tribunga and Cpl Martini both rose from the baking ground and hobbled stiffly in. Barbara could see that both looked exhausted. They were helped into the shade further back and given water. Raoul had the container moved back fifty paces to the back of the burnt-out thicket and the group redeployed there in among the bushes, rocks and whatever shade they could find. From there the road and creek line were just visible.

"We will stay here till dark," Raoul explained. "It is too risky to be moving in daylight in this open country. Now try to eat and then have a rest."

Barbara was thankful to be able to sit up and she undid her webbing, drank the remainder of her third waterbottle and then accepted the chocolate and dry biscuit Raoul offered her. S-Lt de Blainville and the two sergeants sat with them and Barbara noted that the S-Lt kept looking at her with what she hoped was some sort of respect.

Both Tribunga and Cpl Martini had been on the edge of heat exhaustion but by soaking their unbuttoned shirts, drinking and washing their faces they slowly recovered. The other men all looked very dirty and tired and Barbara knew she must look the same. Ruefully she noted several rips in her uniform.

How am I going to explain them to Major Conkey? she wondered.

After eating and drinking some more water Barbara tried to make herself comfortable and lay down. The ground, even in the shade, was so hot that this was unpleasant but she was so worn out that she managed to doze fitfully. As before the ants, flies and discomfort kept waking her. Once a helicopter went past low over on the other side of the road. It was a Blackhawk and vanished to the south. From this new position Barbara could still just see the road and she watched several vehicles go in either direction.

Then, at 1405, the tension went up again. The trucks came back, growling down the road from the army camp to the Front Gate and then turning south along the Mingela Road.

This time they will search this side of the road, she thought anxiously.

Raoul obviously thought so too as he got everyone awake and ready to move, packs and webbing on but lying in what little cover there was.

Barbara lay on the hot sand and ash, sweat trickling from seemingly every pore and her breath coming in rapid pants as she watched the trucks driving along. Each truck left a billow of brown dust and the whole bush seemed to be coated with it, almost masking the blackness on the burnt areas near the road. But the trucks did not stop. They drove on south to the other side of the Dip. Then they stopped and the troops dismounted. From where Barbara was she could not see much but it was obvious that the search was again on the far side of the road. The only difference was that this time the trucks did not stay. They drove off southwards and were soon gone.

The group relaxed again. Barbara checked the time—1425—and tried once again to get some sleep, suspecting that she might be awake all the next night. She lay back and fanned herself, wishing she could open the front of her shirt as the men had all done.

Heavens, it is hot! she thought.

It felt much hotter than it had been the previous week during annual camp, but she had no way of checking this. The sky offered no sign of relief. There were no clouds and the sun blazed down unchecked.

She must have dozed for nearly an hour as it was 1530 when she next looked at her watch through sore, gritty eyes. Her tongue felt as though it was stuck on the top of her mouth and even a small drink was pure pleasure. She swilled the water around before swallowing it, uncomfortably aware that she had nearly finished her third waterbottle.

When she went to lie down again Barbara became aware of the need to do a pee. *This will be the first today,* she thought, adding, *That means I haven't drunk enough.*

It also raised the problem of where. As she sat up the wry thought crossed her mind that every time she went to the toilet in this place she seemed to get into trouble. After looking carefully around she stood up. The only people in sight were the Frenchmen and only two of them were awake. These were Sgt Blomburg and a legionnaire. Both were lying down facing out on sentry duty. Barbara had noted this each time she had woken and her respect for their discipline and professionalism rose even higher.

After another check that nobody else was in sight she rose stiffly to her feet. That got all the sore muscles and bruises into play and she groaned softly as she swung on her webbing. Then she hobbled slowly across to where Sgt Blomburg lay. He met her eyes with a query so she pointed into the burnt-out bush to the southwest.

"I need to go to the toilet. I will be careful."

He just nodded and went back to scanning his arc of responsibility. Barbara hoisted on her webbing but left the belt undone. Licking dry lips she walked slowly west, her eyes seeking a place not too distant that was out of sight of the men. There did not seem to be anywhere and her natural modesty made her keep walking. The whole area, as far as she could see, seemed to be just black ash, with not a blade of grass or even a single scorched bush she could hide behind. After fifty metres she still had not found sufficient cover so she walked on to where a large half-burnt log lay across beside a big tree.

This will have to do, she told herself.

She went to the other side of the log and looked back. The two sentries were still just visible but she decided the log would hide her so she put down her webbing and peeled down trousers and panties. That was instant relief as the faint breeze evaporated the perspiration. She relaxed and began, staring out across the burnt wasteland as she did. It all looked very hot and very unpleasant. Everything in the distance shimmered in the heat haze.

I hope the SAS aren't watching me now, she thought, looking around for any possible hiding place they could be in.

To her shock, out of the heat haze to the southwest appeared several moving figures. For a moment Barbara did not believe her tired eyes. Then she rubbed them and stared again. There was no doubt. About half a kilometre away to the southwest, the tiny figures of men could be seen walking through the bush. They were hard to see because of the number of tree trunks intervening and because of the shimmering atmosphere, but they were definitely men—men in uniform and carrying black objects that looked awfully like guns.

"A line of soldiers!" she gasped, "And walking straight towards us!"

For several more seconds Barbara crouched there, her mind racing and her heart in her mouth. Then she stood up, pulling up her panties and trousers. Hastily buttoning them up she kept watching the men, appalled at how many there were.

Five, six, seven, no ten or more. Heavens, there are more to the right!

Her fumbling fingers had difficulty with the buttons but she managed to zip up the fly. Shaking with anxiety she snatched up her webbing and swung it on as she started walking back towards the others. By now she was very scared, but she still had the good sense not to run.

The rapid movement will attract attention, she reasoned.

As she walked quickly across the open ground she kept looking back over her right shoulder, trying to keep as many trees between her and the advancing troops as possible, all the while biting her lip and lamenting the lack of bushes and undergrowth.

Within a few seconds she could see the Foreign Legion sentries. To her dismay she saw that they had still not seen the advancing soldiers.

Probably because they are lying down and the rise of the ground still hides them, she decided, noting the slight swell in the ground she was crossing. She saw Sgt Blomburg's face swivel to watch her. At that she pointed in the direction of the advancing soldiers and gave a 'thumbs-down' hand signal. That got his attention and he lifted his head to stare.

Barbara called out as loudly as she dared, "Soldiers, about twenty of them, coming this way. Quick! Wake the others!"

Sgt Blomburg heard her and raised himself higher to look in the direction she was pointing. The look of grim alarm that crossed his face told Barbara that he had seen the advancing troops. As she hurried in to join the group he and the other legionnaire were busy waking and warning the others. Barbara did up the belt of her webbing. As she did she saw Raoul roll over and rub his eyes. S-Lt de Blainville sat up and squinted into the glare. On seeing the troops he cried out an oath in French, then snatched up his rifle. A moment later he was crouched behind a rock and raising his binoculars.

Raoul joined him, buckling on his webbing. "What can you see?" he asked.

By then Barbara had dropped flat behind a small rock near them. S-Lt de Blainville shook his head and looked grim. "Soldiers," he replied. "And not Australians."

"Americans?" queried Raoul.

"*Non. Le Dags,*" S-Lt de Blainville replied.

At that Barbara felt her heart skip a beat, then speed up. She shielded her eyes against the glare and looked at the advancing men, now only about four hundred metres away. Now she saw that they were dressed in some sort of brown and khaki uniform and had strange looking flat caps. They also had webbing and rifles. Even at that range she could see the brown woodwork and black metal parts of AK47s.

I don't believe this! she thought. *Armed Dag soldiers walking through the Australian bush!*

But there they were, a long, extended line, angling through the bush straight towards them.

"They know we are here," she muttered. "They are coming straight towards us."

Raoul nodded. "I think you are right. You did see someone in that washout earlier, and they have called in reinforcements."

"They won't do anything surely?" Barbara said. "This is Australia."

At that both Raoul and S-Lt de Blainville gave short, sarcastic laughs. Raoul replied grimly, "They will kill us if they have to, to get this satellite."

Barbara swallowed as the sour taste of fear rose in her belly. With mounting alarm she looked at the advancing enemy—at least a platoon she now estimated.

Raoul gave rapid orders and men began scuttling to obey. S-Lt de Blainville and four legionnaires spread out facing the advancing enemy while Sgt Boucher and three legionnaires rushed to grab the handles of the stretcher. Raoul crouched and gave them the orders to lift. As they did he gestured to Barbara to get moving off towards the north.

The next moment Barbara was stunned by vicious snapping and cracking sounds all around her and by seeing dust and ash flung into the air among the men. Her bemused mind noted men falling and the stretcher being dropped. For a second longer her mind stayed frozen by the unreality of it all.

Then memories from her cadet experiences kicked in and she cried, "We are being shot at!"

Chapter 34

VERY HOT!

As the initial shock struck Barbara so did a bullet. It slashed across her hip, smacking into her basic pouch and spinning her round. She was hurled roughly to the ground, her helmet smacking her forehead. For a second she lay there stunned but then her shocked vision took in Raoul also tumbled beside her. He had also been spun around and was arched across his pack. His eyes were wide open and Barbara noted his mouth working.

"Raoul!" she cried.

He's been hit, she thought, dread rising to choke her throat. But then saw that he was alive and squirming violently to get over onto his front. Without thinking about herself Barbara sprang up and grabbed him, helping him to roll over.

"Raoul, where are you hit?" she shouted.

"Pack! Get down!" he shouted back. Then he struggled into a fire position and aimed his rifle in the direction the bullets were coming from.

For another couple of seconds Barbara stood, relief flooding through her before her eyes sorted out what they were seeing. Tiny red dots of light were flashing past with savage snapping sounds. She noted that they were emanating from the gully where she had seen the head and that there were tiny bumps there and puffs of smoke.

I'm being shot at! she thought with disbelief.

"A machine gun," she muttered. "And those are tracer bullets."

Raoul began firing back, shouting as he did. Barbara glanced around and saw that S-Lt de Blainville and Sgt Blomburg were also firing towards the gully while the other three legionnaires with them were shooting at the advancing line off to their right. She saw tiny figures go down, but whether hit or just going to ground she could not tell.

Then she realized her own danger and dropped flat, waves of terror sweeping through her with almost paralysing force.

Until she saw the blood. Right before her eyes lay one of the legionnaires, a fair skinned man, with blood coming out of his mouth. He was twitching and had clearly been seriously wounded. A glance showed Barbara that the man had been shot in the right side of his chest. Even as she watched he gave ghastly coughing groan and a shudder, then lay still, his eyes open.

"He's dead!" Barbara cried in dismay. "They've killed him!"

Then another, much more sickening thought came to her. *I killed him! I am responsible for all of this. It is my fault.*

With that appalling thought came guilt, and also anger. Right next to her hand was the dead legionnaire's rifle. She reached across and took hold of it. From her cadet training she could identify all the main parts and across her mind flashed something Major Conkey had once said about all modern weapons being designed for peasants to use.

I can operate this, she thought, squirming around to lie beside Raoul.

A glance revealed to her the safetycatch and another showed her the weapon was cocked. She lifted the rifle and cradled the butt into her shoulder. The sights came into focus: a short telescopic sight clamped to the groove in top of the long carrying handle. A surge of deep emotion—part anger, part excitement—coursed through her and she shifted her point of aim to line the sights up on one of the tiny, smoky bumps two hundred metres away.

Then she had to consciously calm herself to stop the shaking. Her breathing was coming in frantic gulps and that didn't help.

Do what you were taught, she told herself.

Very deliberately she steadied both her hands and her breathing. Then she made her eyes focus through the heat haze. Her finger moved to the trigger and she gently squeezed. Unsure how the trigger pressures worked she pulled too lightly and nothing happened so she pulled harder.

Bang!

The rifle bucked and her mind at once told her it was easy. *It is only a 5.56mm like the Steyr,* she thought. *It won't hurt me by recoiling too hard.*

She had no idea where that shot had gone but it felt good, so she aimed again and sent another shot snapping across the flat. Again she did not see her fall of shot. Smoke, heat haze and the bullet strikes fired by the others all confused the situation. Then Barbara became aware of Raoul shouting at her and gesturing behind them.

"Stop shooting and get out of here," he yelled. "Go back fifty paces and lie down."

"I'm alright," Barbara cried back. Her blood was up now and she was both terrified and wildly excited. She aimed and fired again.

Raoul's angry face appeared close to hers. "Stop! Please Barbara! Go back. We will cover you. Those men, they are trying to pin us down so that the platoon on our right flank can cut us off. We must get moving fast. So please go," he shouted.

"I can help fight," Barbara answered.

"No. Please! It is not for you to battle. And I do not wish you to be hurt. Please run."

At that moment a bullet struck the ground close in front of Barbara and a shower of hot sand struck her face. Some grains hit so hard it stung furiously and some grit went into her left eye. Another shot cracked past so close she felt the shock wave. Raoul again gestured, then turned to shout commands in French and to shoot again.

Realizing she was complicating things for him Barbara turned and began crawling back. As she did she became aware that others were moving too. Through blurry, watering eyes she saw that Sgt Boucher and three legionnaires, including Tribunga and the Asian—Tran or someone—had grabbed the stretcher. On command they picked it up and started running. To cover them the others opened a fusillade of covering fire at the gullies.

Sgt Blomburg ran to the dead Legionnaire, unclipped and hauled off his pack, then hoisted him onto his shoulders. Staggering under the weight he set off at a lumbering trot. The sight of that filled Barbara with admiration that bordered on awe. The sheer strength and determination of the Foreign Legion sergeant astounded her.

Barbara realized that no shots were snapping past close and took her chance. With a sob of fear she sprang up and ran. It was an experience she would never forget for the rest of her life. She had been shot at before but had not been in a fire fight with dozens of weapons going off. Running in mortal terror, her flesh cringing and her heart in her mouth in desperate expectation of being shot was an experience that seared itself into her mind. Dust flew, shots struck up clouds of ash and a few smacked into trees or rocks with sickening force. One bullet struck a rock near her and whined off, making a spine-chilling screech as it did. There was smoke, cordite and gun oil smell, sweat and fear—lots of fear—bowel loosening fear!

As she ran Barbara looked to her left, fearing what Raoul had said—that the enemy out that way might cut them off. To her surprise she could not see any of them and her mind registered only that one or two shots came from that direction and none of them close to her. There was distant shouting but nothing much else.

Sgt Blomburg dropped the dead legionnaire with a sickening thud, then fell flat facing back the way he had come.

He is going to give Raoul and the others covering fire, Barbara decided. On an impulse she ran out to her right to the edge of the thicket near the back of the Gravel Scrape. *I must save Raoul,* she thought.

She dropped flat and faced back, her eyes searching frantically to work out who was where and what was going on.

Barbara saw she was only twenty-five metres back from Raoul and the men with him but because of the slight curve in the ground, she could only just make out the gullies. There was a tiny blob visible there and, as she watched, a puff of smoke obscured it.

There's one, she thought. As quickly as she could she sighted on it and squeezed the trigger. *That felt good!* she thought.

This time she saw the dust fly, close in front of the blob, which vanished. She did not think she hit the man but hoped so—until the idea of shooting another human being swamped her and, making her feel so guilty she wanted to vomit. Even so she fired again, cursing the grit in her eyes that was making them water.

Dimly she was aware of Sgt Blomburg shouting. She squeezed another shot and out of the corner of her eyes saw Raoul and the legionnaire beside him spring up and bolt backwards. To cover him she fired again at where she thought the enemy were. Several shots cacked through the thicket but they came from the right. One showered her with dry, brown leaves but it had not been close.

Raoul ran back, shouting and gesticulating. He then turned when he was twenty paces behind Barbara and yelled for them to pull back. As he did he stood in a crouching fire position and opened fire towards the gullies. Barbara squirmed around and rose to a crouch and ran, weaving through the dead trees of the thicket as she did.

One bullet came close, thudding into a tree trunk and sending out a shower of splinters, but she was now so hot and excited that she was barely aware of the noise. As she ran back past Raoul she gave him a savage grin and he shook his head and smiled back, then squeezed his next shot. She ran on another twenty paces, then stopped and turned to crouch behind a rock.

There was still very little fire coming from the right and Barbara only glimpsed one tiny figure run to cover about three hundred metres away. Looking to her front she saw that the gullies were now hidden from view by the slight rise so she kitten-crawled five metres to the edge of the Gravel Scrape. As she did she looked towards the road and noted a vehicle stopping and two figures in Australian Army uniform jumping out. The two Australian MPs (she could tell that by their black armbands with red letters on them) ran across towards One Mile Creek, obviously wondering what was going on.

They will get killed! Barbara thought. *They don't understand what's going on.* A feeling of sickening dread swamped her. *I don't want to be responsible for them being killed,* she thought.

Sucking in a deep breath she shouted in her best 'sergeant major' voice. "Hey! Take cover! These are real bullets. Stop! Get down!"

The MPs stopped and stared in her direction. Barbara yelled again. "They are Dags, trying to get the satellite. Go back! Call your HQ."

To her relief the men ran to the nearest trees and went into a crouch. As they did the first bullet cracked their way. That convinced them. Both threw themselves flat and Barbara saw one pull out a pistol. When another shot smacked up dust near them they both visibly twitched, then rolled over and bolted. One leaped into the Land Rover while the other ran on across the road into the long grass. Several shots hit the Land Rover but to Barbara's relief it started moving and swung away, its wheels churning up dust and soot. In a few moments it was out of sight back along the Mingela Road, heading in the direction of the Front Gate.

Raoul was yelling again to pull back. "Come on! We are out of sight of the fellows in the gully," he shouted. "We must the clean break make."

Barbara understood that and immediately rolled over and got up. She began running but discovered she was gasping for breath; hot, rasping gasps. Her vision was hazy. Off to her left she noted S-Lt de Blainville firing in the direction of the line of troops in the distance. He was kneeling behind a tree and sending a series of aimed shots, shifting his point of aim each time.

That is really good! Barbara mused, noting how calm he looked.

Barbara ran on and found herself back at the fence. Just ahead of her were the stretcher team, dragging the stretcher and the dead legionnaire under the fence, while another legionnaire knelt and gave covering fire along the fence clearing up to her left. Another legionnaire, the signals corporal Barbara thought because of the big radio in his pack, came racing across between her and the kneeling legionnaire. As he approached the fence he swung off his pack, ready to pass it across.

Suddenly the signals corporal went sprawling backwards, his pack rolling out of his hands. To Barbara's horror he began to twitch and gasp, his mouth opening and closing rapidly. His right-hand clutched at his chest while the other still gripped his weapon. Only then did Barbara take in the detail that the rifle was actually connected to his vest by a cord.

The kneeling legionnaire at once sprang to his aid and began dragging him towards the fence. Barbara skidded to a stop near them.

Oh my God! The sig has been hit, she thought.

As she did one of the legionnaires on the other side of the fence shouted at her and then pointed. "Radio! Radio!"

Barbara bent to grab at the pack and as she did she saw that bullets were kicking up dust around the wounded corporal and the man dragging him. Her gaze flicked along the cleared lane beside the fence line and she noted a standing figure half-obscured by the heat haze and dust a couple of hundred metres away. Into her mind flitted images she had seen at the rifle range of the black Figure 11 targets the soldiers shot at. Being a cadet she had only ever been allowed to fire at circular targets but now she recognized what she was looking at.

He is shooting at us, she thought, followed by, *I must save them!*

Without further thought she whipped the rifle into her shoulder, steadied her aim on the distant figure and pulled the trigger.

As she did several shots cracked past, the sharp snapping sounds telling her they were very close. Her reaction was to fire two more shots and she saw tiny puffs of dust where her shots struck and then the tiny figure vanished into the trees to the left of the clearing. Then fear and guilt got her moving again.

He will be able to aim again in about ten seconds, she thought. Gulping and almost beside herself with fright and excitement she turned to run.

As she did she almost tripped on the pack. Gasping for breath and cringing in anticipation of a bullet striking her at any moment she bent and grabbed the pack and heaved it up, dismayed at how heavy it was. In three strides she reached the fence and the waiting legionnaire reached out and grabbed it. He swung it over his shoulder and tossed it onto the ground then reached under the bottom strand to grab the wounded corporal to drag him under the fence.

By then the legionnaire who had dragged the corporal to the fence was shoving the wounded man under the bottom strand. Barbara tried to help by grabbing the bottom strand of the fence and hauling it upwards to get it clear of the man's webbing and clothing. As she did more shots snapped past and several struck the ground nearby, throwing up showers of dust and ash. Waves of hot and cold terror swept through her.

Realizing that the clearing would be deadly to dawdle in Barbara hurled herself down on her back and began squirming under the fence, using the rifle to hold the bottom strand clear of her webbing and clothing. In her fear and hurry she rolled over too soon and got snagged. But she was so terrified that she kept rolling away without heed to the ripping trousers or the pain in her right thigh as a barb tore at it. Then she rolled again and sprang to her feet, stumbled, recovered, then threw herself behind the nearest tree.

A glance to her right showed the legionnaire she had saved now sitting with his back to a tree, his chest heaving as he took great gulps. No blood was visible but he was obviously hurt and his friend was busy rubbing hard at his left chest. Other legionnaires were standing or kneeling nearby behind trees and giving covering fire.

As she lay there, rifle ready, Barbara became aware of the choking dust, heat and smoke. The ground was so hot it burned through her clothes and sweat trickled down her face, the salt stinging her eyes. Her whole body seemed to be on huge mass of pain—stinging, aching, throbbing, gasping. Through her mind flashed the thought she had had at that exact place back in annual camp: what a terrible environment to have to fight a real battle in.

And here I am fighting in a real battle! she thought, half-unable to believe what was happening.

But Raoul was real, and she was desperately apprehensive lest he be killed or wounded and her heart was in her mouth till he had tossed his pack over the fence and scrambled under after it. As he got up he saw her and nodded, then looked around at his men, calling in French, "Up! We must run. Let us go!"

Barbara understood that the firing had died down. A quick look towards the enemy showed that a slight rise in the ground was now shielding her from most of them. But she was very anxious to get away so she got up and hurried along with the legionnaires, painfully aware that she was not fit and that her heart and lungs felt like they were going to burst with overexertion. For the first time she truly understood why soldiers needed to be so fit.

She also realized with a ghastly sense of dread how it did not matter how she felt: if she wanted to live she had to make the effort.

I can't just say I've had enough and laugh it off as a game, she realized.

There was no doubt that those Dags were real and if they caught her then her fate would almost certainly be horrible. Absolute, stunning reality gripped her by her hot, gasping throat.

The ghastly reality was reinforced when Sgt Blomburg put down the body of the dead legionnaire and hastily pulled off the dead man's webbing, rolling the body in the dust as he did. Seeing the lifeless form flopping in the ash made Barbara angry and sick but she also realized she could help. As Sgt Blomburg started to go through the man's pockets she stopped.

"I will take his webbing," she offered, reaching down for it.

Sgt Blomburg nodded, quickly shoving notebooks, pens and a wallet into his own already bulging map pockets. One of the items he pulled hastily out was a dark green beret with a silver badge on it. It fell in the dust and he scooped it up, then dropped it again in his haste. Barbara snatched it up and he gestured urgently to her to keep running.

She stuffed the beret into her map pocket then swung the webbing over her shoulders, once again being shocked by the weight of full combat gear. Gripping the rifle tightly in her right-hand she hurried after the others at a fast walk, buttoning up her map pocket as she did. Sgt Blomburg and another legionnaire, one with a green diagonal stripe on his rank badge, came after her, carrying the dead legionnaire between them. Next came the man who had been hit in the chest, Cpl Fouchet she now learned, being helped by a comrade. His pack and radio were carried between them.

Raoul re-organized them, with a scout leading, then himself and then the stretcher team. Barbara followed them, with Cpl Martini and S-Lt de Blainville bringing up the rear.

Their route led them into the thicket almost along the track they had followed that morning. Several times Barbara saw a trampled foot trail in the dust and ash but she wasn't sure if it was their own tracks or the one made by the cadets during annual camp. As they hurried along she kept glancing to left and right and back behind her. So great was her dread and physical distress she felt dizzy and wondered how much longer she could keep going without collapsing. The instinct for self-preservation helped. She was terrified and knew it.

Will we be able to get away? she wondered.

Suddenly firing began again behind her. She flinched in fear but then realized it was not directed in her direction and was off to her right rear.

That is out near the Front Gate, she decided. The firing intensified, then died away to occasional shots. Distant shouts could be heard. Barbara felt sick. *They have attacked those MPs,* she thought, getting very upset at the thought of having been responsible for their possible death.

Then she heard a Land Rover driving away in the direction of the army camp, followed by another fusillade of shots from near the Mingela Road opposite the Gravel Scrape.

Raoul had been looking back as well and said, "I think l'Dags have lost us, at least for the moment. Your warning was just in time. Another minute and they would have been too close to get out of sight over that small rise. Now, we must hurry and get right out of this area."

"Where are we going?" Barbara croaked, her throat dry and choked with dust.

"First we go to *rendezvous* with our two men left at the creek," Raoul replied. Then he really flattered her by asking, "Which way do you recommend we go?"

By then they had reached the tangle of thorn trees, rubber vines and burnt trees beside One Mile Creek. From where they were Barbara could just see the Mingela Road off to her right a hundred metres away.

This is the way Major Conkey led us in annual camp, she thought. Into her mind came the country ahead, a few gullies, a few burnt bushes, but then flat, open, burnt-off ground to the Triangle and across it. She gestured with her left-hand.

"That way, more to the left. Follow the creek line."

Raoul looked into the deep, steep-sided gully with its numerous bends. "That will be very difficult to carry the stretcher along," he said.

"Stay beside it and keep in the dips as much as possible," she replied.

"You navigate please," Raoul said.

That vote of confidence boosted her self esteem enormously. She nodded and pulled out her map photocopy. As she lifted it up to look at it the white paper reflected the harsh glare of the sun, causing her to squint, and then to remember that maps had to be kept hidden on battlefields.

In case of snipers, she thought with a shudder.

She quickly hunched the map close and looked at it, then walked across to the left. Tribunga raised his eyebrows in query and she pointed the direction. He at once set off that way at a fast walk, his head and rifle swivelling continually to search their front. The other legionnaires looked at Barbara as she passed and she saw no resentment in their gaze. They followed her, walking steadily while labouring under the weight of their burdens.

Raoul came up behind her and gave her a reassuring smile. "You are doing the *magnifique* effort under the great stress. I am very impressed."

Barbara glowed with pleasure. In her exhausted condition the praise seemed to lift her up. "Thank you," she said.

Raoul pointed to her right thigh. "I see blood. Are you hit?"

Barbara had been aware of the throbbing pain but now she glanced down at the torn trousers and saw there was a large patch of blood soaked into them. "No. I got caught on the barbed wire. It is only a scratch," she answered. Not wanting to be a burden she gestured towards the group trudging along carrying the dead legionnaire. "Are they... do they... will they bring... er... him all the way?"

Raoul nodded grimly. "If they can. It is one of the traditions of *l' Legion Etrangere* never to leave their casualties to the mercy of the enemy if possible."

"It slows us down," Barbara commented, then at once felt guilty at her own selfish desire to run away.

Raoul shrugged. "Undoubtedly, but they will fight all the better for it," he replied.

"What about the wounded man?" Barbara asked, glancing back to where Cpl Fouchet was still being helped by his mate.

Raoul glanced back and then smiled. "He will be alright. The bullet hit his ... his... I translate... er. his er," he tapped at the left pocket of his combat vest. "His radio and personal data interface. He is only badly bruised." He then called softly and beckoned. "*Caporal* Fouchet!"

Cpl Fouchet limped over still holding his chest and grimacing. "*Oui Mon Lieutenant?*"

"Show *mademoiselle*," Raoul said.

At that Cpl Fouchet nodded and then smiled. He held open the front of his jacket and shirt and Barbara was astonished to see the shiny copper head of a bullet protruding through the back of his pocket. She understood that the bullet had punched through the small computer and then hit his chest but not penetrated.

"Oh my God! How lucky," Barbara gasped.

Cpl Fouchet nodded and smiled. "Sanks," he muttered.

Barbara blushed with embarrassment and simultaneously tried to nod and shake her head. All she could do was smile and mumble. "Does it hurt?" she asked.

"I the much bruised am. The bullet it took away my wind," Cpl Fouchet explained, gesturing to the jagged hole in his shirt. Then he nodded and moved away to resume his place in the line.

The patrol continued on through the thicket, walking as fast as they could. Barbara glanced back and saw the dead legionnaire's arms and head lolling as he was carried. She shuddered and then had to grit her teeth and concentrate to keep walking when all she felt like doing was collapsing as the reaction set her limbs trembling.

After fifteen minutes of sweaty, panting slog they came out of the western edge of the thicket near the point where One Mile Creek swung round to the northeast. As no enemy had been sighted Raoul pointed into a shallow depression beside the creek. Several half-scorched thorn bushes gave some shade and cover. The group moved into it and lowered their loads to the ground, then lay down and faced out in all-round defence.

As Barbara sat down Sgt Blomburg looked significantly at her right-hand, then said, "The straight trigger finger, that is very good, but perhaps you now apply the safetycatch *Mademoiselle?*"

Barbara knew exactly what he meant. She had been carrying the rifle with her right-hand holding the pistol grip and with her right finger held straight on the outside of the trigger guard, as she had been taught to do in cadets, but she now blushed with shame a forgetting such an elementary safety precaution.

I would look an idiot if I shot myself in the foot, she thought.

To hide her shame she held the rifle up and clicked the safetycatch up. "Is that correct?" she asked.

Sgt Blomburg nodded. "Very good."

"What type of rifle is it?" Barbara asked, "I mean, what is it called?"

"*l'FAMAS,*" Sgt Blomburg replied. "An acronym yes? F. A. M. A. S. For *Fusil Automatique Manufacture d'Armes de St. Etienne.*"

Barbara nodded, looked down at the rifle. As she did she wondered how many bullets she had left in the magazine. She looked up. "How many rounds in these magazines?" she asked.

Sgt Blomberg glanced at the rifle and answered, "Twenty five in that one. But there are also thirty round standard NATO magazines on some of our rifles. You understand standard NATO?"

At that Barbara gave a tired smile, having often heard the term. She now repeated one of the most common ones her Officers of Cadets used. "Coffee, white with two sugars."

Sgt Blomberg grinned and nodded. Then he pointed to her rifle. "How many bullets did you fire?"

That caused Barbara a flush of embarrassment. She knew that good soldiers counted their rounds but very little of her cadet training had been of that nature so she had to think. "At least ten, maybe fifteen," she stammered. From his gruff and harsh tone she thought he was putting her down both as a female and as a cadet.

Sgt Blomberg pointed down. "You can check. But do it later. There should be several full magazines in that webbing. Change magazines and when we get time you can count how many in the first one."

Barbara nodded and under his tutelage took off the half-empty magazine and placed it in her own left basic pouch. As she did she realized that in his gruff way the sergeant was actually coaching her and was concerned for her. That caused her eyes to prickle with tears and she had to hold her jangled emotions in check. With hands that were trembling so much she could hardly open the clips, she extracted a full magazine from the dead legionnaires webbing and clipped it into the rifle.

"Thanks, er *Merci,*" she croaked. Then she carefully laid the rifle across her lap while she pulled out a waterbottle. To her deep concern she found three were now empty and had to start on her fourth and last. Even so she badly needed the drink and gulped down almost half the bottle. She felt much better after that.

As they rested gunfire again erupted back near the Front Gate. They all looked in that direction, then Raoul smiled. "Not our battle," he said. "I'Dags must have run into your people. That is very good. It will keep them away from us. Come, let us put even more distance between us and them."

There was a re-organization. The container was picked up and carried by straps between two legionnaires. One of these was Cpl Fouchet. To Barbara's surprise she saw that he was again carrying his pack and radio. He was grimacing but gave her a nod and then took up the load. The other soldier was his comrade who had dragged him to safety. The dead legionnaire was placed on the stretcher with his webbing and Raoul, Sgt Boucher, S-Lt de Blainville and the Senior Private hoisted it to their shoulders and set off. Tribunga and Cpl Martini led, one always able to see up over the top of the creek bank as the remainder of the party wound their away along the sheltered bed.

The creek bed grew wider as they went and the twists and turns grew less. Even so it was tough going as the bed was uneven, frequently rocky or blocked with logs or large tufts of dry grass. Down in the creek bed the air was stifling, so hot that it seemed to Barbara that she was going to collapse at any moment from heat exhaustion. *My face must be the colour of my hair,* Barbara thought, her mind now being called on to make her push herself to go on. She knew she was rapidly reaching the end of her endurance.

After another ten minutes of hard going they reached the wide depression where the Marlow Road crossed the creek.

This is where the Leadership Evaluation course began, Barbara remembered. Then she swallowed to try to clear her dry and choked throat is it came to her that now the story was real. *We are the lost patrol being hunted by the enemy,* she thought. *And they will kill us if they catch us.*

A halt was signalled and Barbara took the opportunity for another drink while slumped gasping on the sand. Despite her fear and exhaustion, or perhaps because of it, she remained mentally aware. She watched Raoul directing the scouts to search the likely sniper positions before the main group moved out across the depression. Then she smiled and felt surge of confidence.

But this patrol isn't leaderless, she decided, her admiration for him growing.

Then her heart went into her throat again as she saw Tribunga look over the top of the bank to the left, then immediately crouch down and send the 'enemy' signal. *Oh no!*

They have found us! she thought in dismay, terror rising to almost swamp her. *And worse still, they are west of us and the other Dags are off to our east. We are caught between two forces!*

Chapter 35

EVEN WORSE

Barbara stood up, shoved her map into her pocket, dusted her palms, then stood twisting the rifle in her sweaty, grimy hands. While her anxiety soared she watched Raoul scramble up the side of the bank to peek over the top through a clump of grass. As he scurried back down again her fear was ratcheted up another notch. The urgency of his body language transmitted itself to her before he spoke.

"A dozen Dags, advancing this way in extended line astride this road," he said. "We must hurry across and try to get out of their way. Quick! Barbara, go fast, hurry!"

Barbara swallowed and stated moving. Her legs wanted to run but she was too hot and worn out to do that so she trotted up out of the creek bed and across the open flat. Behind her the men hoisted the stretcher up and set off at a lumbering trot. Sgt Blomburg and Sgt Boucher followed, the container held between them.

Ten metres beyond where the dirt road crossed the sandy creek bed the creek curved to the right, then ran for fifty paces with a line of steep soil cliffs ten metres high on the left. The creek then curved to the right again. Inside the curve was a lower, flatter area in which stood several mounds of soil left from quarrying. The creek then curved sharply left again and swung around the end of a low, bare spur to go north. Several large trees grew in the depression and along the creek but, apart from a few clumps of grass right on the bank of the narrow, steep creek bed, the ground was bare dust and ash.

We need to get around that next bend and on northwards before they arrive, Barbara thought.

But God it was hot! Her breath seemed to burn and rasp down her throat and she knew she was gasping from the effort and exhaustion. It was fear that provided the spur to keep her pushing herself but it still took a real effort of willpower to keep her legs moving. She trotted across fifty metres of open ground to reach the creek bed at the point where it started to swing back northwards again. As she ran she saw Cpl Martini crawl into the grass at the base of a huge gum tree, to get into a fire position to cover them. Knowing that the enemy might appear behind her at any moment caused Barbara's flesh to crawl and her back muscles to tense. By the time she reached the creek bed again she was sobbing and ready to drop.

Tribunga popped up and gestured to her to get down. With emotions close to panic Barbara slid down into the creek bed and moved to a crouch among the clumps of remaining dry grass. In doing so she sucked in some dust and grass and began to cough and wheeze. Desperately she tried to stifle it, finally half-choking herself and bringing tears to her eyes by pushing up on the bottom of her nose.

The others arrived with a rush and Raoul gestured to keep going. Barbara rose and hurried along the narrow, deep creek bed. This section of it she knew well, having walked along it during the cadet camp. The creek bed was only one or two metres wide and was in a narrow, steep-sided ditch one to two metres deep. The grass grew along the top of both sides of this and often overhung it. Beyond the wall of grass the creek banks sloped upwards at about 45 degrees for twenty-five metres to the flat ground above. The sand was hot and very wearing to walk on so she was soon gasping with the effort again. Tribunga led the way, the others pushing along behind her as fast as they could manage in the winding creek bed. Their rapid movement was obstructed by logs or piles of flood debris.

Movement up to the left disclosed Cpl Martini and S-Lt de Blainville scurrying along out in the open just below the lip of the bank. Every ten or twenty paces one or the other stopped to cautiously peer over the top.

Suddenly the sound of distant shooting again erupted. *That sounds like it is up near the army camp,* Barbara thought.

The firing certainly sounded heavy and sustained and this time the stutter of machine guns was part of the sound. Then the sound of running feet made her look up to the left. It was S-Lt de Blainville and he was urgently signalling to get down.

"Take cover!" he called in French, adding, "They come at the run."

Barbara cast frantically around for the best cover and then crouched behind a big clump of dry grass at a bend in the creek bed. Raoul took cover a few paces from her. Through the stalks of dry grass Barbara anxiously scanned the top of the bank up to her left and even more cautiously slipped the rifle's safetycatch off. Crouched there, her heart hammering furiously and her eyes blurring and stinging with sweat, she began to pray. The rifle she gripped tightly, ready to swing it up. She retained enough self-control to remember another of Major Conkey's lessons: don't shove the rifle barrel through the bushes or you can't swing it without making a noise.

"No firing!" Raoul hissed. "No firing, unless we are detected."

He had no sooner said this than a Dag soldier appeared on top of the bank directly above Barbara. His appearance was so fast that Barbara was quite stunned by it. She was even more dismayed by the speed at which the man slithered and ran down the sloping bank towards her. All she could do was stare, open-mouthed, sure she was about to be discovered. Through the grass she could plainly see the man. He wore khaki trousers and a dark brown coat, canvas webbing of a yellowish hue, and a peculiar double layered, flat cap.

Like two pikelets or pancakes one on top of the other, she thought.

The man looked lean and fit and had a hard, bearded face and a hooked nose. His skin was brown and lined and he had a look of ferocious determination on his face.

But it was the shiny AK47 that the man carried that chilled her most. It was so obviously well cared for and carried by hands that knew how to use it that her reaction was to be almost paralyzed by dread.

It was clear that the Dag soldier had not seen them and he kept glancing along to his right. *He must run right into us!* Barbara thought.

At the last moment the man slowed, hesitated, then deviated to one side. At a flat run he ran down to creek between Barbara and Raoul, then jumped across the deep trench through a gap in the long grass. A moment later he was scrambling up the other bank. Barbara did not dare move for a few seconds but then sheer anxiety made her turn her head to watch.

As the Dag soldier hurried up the far bank she saw two more appear. These were twenty-five and fifty metres behind her and they came running down to cross out of sight around the bend in the creek. They also scurried up the far bank. All three kept looking to their right every few paces—presumably, Barbara thought, to maintain alignment on their section commander. At the crest they paused for a second to look, then hurried on out of sight over the skyline.

Oh my God! Barbara thought, sighing with relief.

"That was close," she muttered to Raoul, who nodded and wiped his brow theatrically.

The distant battle was still going on, if anything growing in intensity. Several explosions sounded and Barbara was stunned.

Surely the Dags wouldn't attack the army camp! she thought. But it certainly sounded like it. *They must think we withdrew in that direction,* she decided.

That appalled her. If the Dags were willing to fight a battle in daylight in Australia, with all the diplomatic and political consequences that must follow, then they must be desperate to acquire the satellite!

Cpl Martini had hidden behind a clump of lantana up on the left. He now crawled up and looked both ways over the top of the bank, then pointed east and gave a 'thumbs up' to S-Lt de Blainville. Raoul at once got everyone moving again.

Three sweaty, dusty minutes later they reached the two legionnaires they had left in hiding that morning. Raoul wasted no time beyond checking that the injured legionnaire, Pilsudski, could walk. He ordered the medic to help carry the stretcher and told Legionnaire Pilsudski to follow. It was plain to Barbara that Pilsudski was in pain but he just nodded and set off, his webbing slung over his left shoulder and his rifle held in that hand.

As they continued on down the creek bed Barbara realized that her emotions were all in turmoil again. Somehow she had thought that rejoining the two men left behind would be the end of it but she now realized that nothing had fundamentally changed: they were still a small group being hunted.

Once again the physical effort of walking and of keeping up began to tell. She found herself coughing and gasping, her legs feeling like lead. Her feet began to feel as though they were being roasted as the heat transferred from the sand through the soles of her army boots. By consciously monitoring her own physical state she noted that she had stopped sweating and recognized that as potentially very serious. A few gulps of water helped. While she was doing that she remembered the safetycatch and slipped it on again surreptitiously, hoping that Sgt Blomburg had not noticed.

They passed the vehicle crossing where Lofty and Wendy had run the 'minefield' stand and then entered the deep section of creek beyond.

Here they were at least in shade and the air was slightly cooler. Barbara found it an enormous relief to be out of the blistering rays of the afternoon sun, even for a few seconds. A minute later they arrived at the point where she had conducted her stand. As she did she remembered the huge brown snake—but too late to stop Tribunga from pushing through the long grass, right where she had last seen the reptile.

In a gasping croak she called, "Watch out for le snake... er... le *serpent*."

Tribunga looked alarmed and asked where so Barbara quickly explained. Raoul listened and also looked anxiously at the long grass. There was a minute's pause while he studied his map, for which Barbara was grateful as she felt ready to drop. He then pointed to the right along the bed of Keelbottom Creek. Cpl Martini and S-Lt de Blainville changed sides and clambered up to the top of the river bank. They carefully looked over the crest near the point where the dirt vehicle track came over the lip. As soon as they gave the 'all clear' Tribunga started moving along the overgrown flood channel, while Cpl Martini moved along just below the crest of the river bank.

The remainder of the group crossed the vehicle track in the wake of the scouts and began moving in single file along the bed of the overgrown dry flood channel. This was unpleasant. The whole area: banks, bed and sandy island, were covered in a thick matt of waist-high grass. Among the paperbark trees grew a thicket of bushes, thorn trees, and lantana, as well as masses of spiky flowers on two metre high stalks. As the group pushed through these they got scratched and frequently breathed in dry particles that caused them to sneeze and cough. Dry grass, leaves and prickles found their way down the backs of their shirt collars to irritate inside the shirt. By now Barbara's whole being seemed to be inflamed—flushed face, hot breath, hot feet, overheated body, everything itching, trembling and sore. To add to her woes was the constant fear of treading on a snake in the long grass.

We must be going to 'Dotswood' homestead, she decided.

Still panting from the extreme exertion, she forced herself to keep moving. That made sense to her, reasoning that the French probably intended to use the old airstrip there.

As they moved Tribunga scouted along the bed of the flood channel and Cpl Martini moved just below the crest of the river bank up to the right front. During all this time the sound of fighting came from away off to their right front. This confirmed in Barbara's mind that the Dags really were attacking the army camp.

Suddenly Cpl Martini went low and then peeked through a bush before signalling urgently. *Enemy!* Barbara noted, her heart rate shooting up to a horrible pounding pace which throbbed in her ears.

Cpl Martini signalled again and Raoul hurried up to join him. After a quick look he turned to face the waiting group, who had all crouched in the weeds, and pointed up the slope. Barbara understood the tactics of that—the high ground, such as it was, was up there, and the cover there was as good as anywhere. So she plodded up the slope, her heart feeling as though it was going to burst and her breathing so dry and hot she felt like she was choking. Blood trickled from a scratch on her left-hand.

Near the top Barbara lay down and crawled up behind a clump of grass. For a minute or so she was so distressed that she could do nothing but lie panting. Then she found her vision blurred. Her heartbeats pounded painfully in her skull and she had to wipe her eyes and then have a drink before she could get her tormented body under some sort of control. *Out of water!* she noted ruefully, screwing the cap back on her last water bottle. She slid it back into its carrier and turned to peer through the grass.

She knew exactly where she was: halfway between the northeast corner of the Triangle and the Cattle Yards near the Keelbottom Creek Bridge. The Mingela Road was only a hundred paces away across a grassy flat and beyond it, among a stand of trees, was a swampy area she had often seen but never been into. The enemy were there. She saw them at once. A long line of figures in brown and khaki were hurrying along in the same direction through the trees on the other side of the road. Her concern increased when she saw that the leading Dags were already ahead of them.

Barbara stared at the Dag soldiers in fascinated horror. She counted and reached twenty, then noted several carrying light machine guns and a couple with RPG7s. Only as she looked more carefully did some of her awe dissipate. That was when she noted that their uniforms were a mixture of assorted brown and khaki clothing.

In fact, she decided, *the Dags are a distinctly motley lot.*

Even as she watched several of the leading Dags began crossing to the same side of the road a hundred paces further along, just near the cattle grid on a small rise. As they did there was a shouted challenge in English from further along the road, from the vicinity of the turn-off to the homestead. The Dag's response to this was to dive for cover and open fire.

Barbara could only shake her head in disbelief. As she watched the puffs of blue-grey gun smoke as the AK47s stuttered and jerked she found it hard to grasp that this was real. But then bullets began to snap back overhead. These had a much sharper crack to them and sounded quite different from the ones fired at her earlier.

Steyrs, she thought. *They are Australian troops firing this way.*

Before her horrified gaze Barbara saw a Dag hit. He had stood up to run and was hit by a bullet. It struck with an audible smack and sent him sprawling in the dust. The battle then intensified as more Dags spread out and began to return the fire. Light Machine Guns began to hammer away. Then an RPG was fired, the loudness and unexpectedness of the bang causing Barbara to jump in fright.

Raoul and S-Lt de Blainville were nearby and Barbara saw Raoul biting his lip and swearing. She knew then that they had been cut off from their objective. Next another distinctive sound reached Barbara's ears and she tensed. Raoul swore again and then pointed east. Barbara risked a peek, just in time to glimpse tiny black shapes in the air beyond the homestead

"Helicopters!" she cried, her voice barely audible above the snap and crack of gunfire.

At least a dozen grey helicopters were coming in low near the old 'Dotswood' homestead, the roofs of which she could just see through a gap in the trees. The helicopters were, she estimated, about a kilometre away. But the shocks weren't over. From among the trees where the Australian troops were she saw bright green smoke starting to billow.

Puzzled she pointed to it and asked, "Raoul, what is that smoke?"

Raoul had been talking to S-Lt de Blainville and he did not hear her at first. She called louder and he turned to look. From the look that crossed his face she at once knew it was bad news. The blood seemed to drain from his face and a haggard look tensed the muscles.

"Smoke!" he echoed, then cried, "Get down!"

Still not grasping the seriousness of the situation Barbara stared in fascination at the helicopters. She saw one of the leading machines rise when the ones following were clearly settling to land. From that lead helicopter a sparkle of red flashes showed and then a stream of tracer bullets sprang towards her with terrifying speed. Barbara was so astonished at this new phenomenon that she did not even duck. Raoul moved though. He sprang across, pushing her flat and lying on top of her.

The bullets arrived with a thunderous growl. Suddenly the air was alive with flying dust, splinters, smoke, screams and vicious cracks.

Helicopter gunship!

She had seen them on TV, but the pictures were never from the receiving end. Even though Raoul pressed her flat she kept her eyes open and stared in horrified amazement. The sound was so continuous that she knew the helicopter must be firing a Gatling gun. That thought gripped her with dread as she had heard what deadly weapons they were.

Six thousand bullets a minute! her mind told her.

Several shots cracked and whined past very close but she was sufficiently in control of herself to note that most of the shots were churning up a storm of dust near the cattle grid where the front line of Dags was. One bullet cracked in very close, striking at arms length and then spinning in the grass like an enraged bee. The projectile glowed red and she noted tiny flames spring up in the grass. Smoke started to rise in thick wisps.

"Stay down," Raoul yelled in her ear.

Barbara could feel his body twitching and was aware of his hot breath and sweaty nearness. The fact that his webbing and rifle were pushing into her flesh and that his weight was pressing her into the hot sand barely registered beside the terrifying fact of being shot at.

Suddenly the firing stopped. Barbara coughed and lifted her head to gape at the helicopter. As she watched the machine suddenly moved sideways, to hover above the trees along the river bed near the bridge. Without any warning it began firing again. Barbara screamed and cringed, then realized it had shifted its fire to the other side of the road. In the most awesome, shocking display of brute force she had ever seen she watched the stream of bullets spring forward, like red water from a hose, to churn the trees and Dags across the road. Branches fell from trees, men screamed, ash and dust filled the air, cherry pink tracers ricocheted in all directions, a man was tumbled over, things flew into the air.

As the deadly hammering ended Raoul looked up. So did Barbara. She glimpsed the helicopter crossing fast towards the army camp. As soon as it was hidden by the trees across the road Raoul sprang up, hauling her down the slope by her webbing. He then gestured back the way they had come and said, "Run! But keep low and be ready to take cover."

The whole group went scuttling and stumbling back down the bank and in among the trees at the bottom. They were just in time as a second helicopter that they could not see began firing. Rockets began to smash into the area up along the road. The first explosion so frightened Barbara that she threw herself down in the long grass and prickly weeds. Raoul grabbed at her and yelled to keep running, so she scrambled up and fled, heedless of the prickles and scratches she acquired. More shocking blasts of sound rolled over them and the whole area behind seemed to churn and boil with billowing smoke and dust mixed with flying debris.

Then Raoul signalled to take cover and the group crashed into a thicket of bushes and lantana on the sandy island beyond the dry flood channel. The stretcher team came to a gasping halt, entangled in the lantana. There they threw themselves down and faced out. By then Barbara was gasping for breath and shaking like a leaf. The rocketing stopped and a spasmodic stutter of small arms fire began again. The vibration of helicopter rotors caused Barbara to cringe and through the haze and smoke she glimpsed another helicopter turn across the road and swing away towards the army camp. As it did she was surprised to see white smoke trails seem to explode out behind it.

It's been hit! she thought, but then corrected when she realized the helicopter was firing flares to decoy heat-seeking missiles. Some of the phosphorous flares fell, still smoking, into the scrub along the creek bed.

The sound of helicopters died away and only sporadic small arms fire indicated that the infantry were still in contact up along the road and near the army camp. Barbara noted that several fires had begun to burn all along the river bed, both in front and behind them. Dirty brown smoke rose in the already overheated air, causing her to cough and her eyes to ache. They were too dry to water and felt scratchy and sore.

Raoul pushed through the weeds and crouched next to her. "Barbara, are you alright?"

"Yes," Barbara croaked, her overstrained nerves and body now one tingling, throbbing ache. "Are we going to be able to escape?"

Raoul nodded but swore in French. Then he apologized before swearing again. "We are cut-off," he explained. "We must now go another way." He lay down next to Barbara, his chest heaving and face grim.

"Are they Australian troops arriving at the old airfield in those helicopters," Barbara asked, her voice a rasping croak.

"*Non*! They are your good friends the US Marines. I would say they have come from your aircraft carrier," Raoul replied.

"Is that good news or bad news?" Barbara asked.

"Both. They may not shoot us—except by accident as we just experienced, but we will almost certainly lose the satellite. I would like to avoid them if I can."

"Were you going to the old airfield?" Barbara asked, thinking that the French withdrawal plan must be to land another Transall to lift them out.

"We were, but now we go to the Plan B," Raoul replied.

"The new airfield?" Barbara wondered aloud.

"*Oui.* The new airfield," Raoul agreed.

S-Lt de Blainville had been listening to this while gulping a quick drink. He said, "We need to move from this place fast. Here the danger is and also these fires are spreading very rapidly." Then he took another gulp before grimacing and holding the canteen upside down. "That was the last of my water. Does *Mademoiselle* know where we might obtain more?"

Barbara nodded and pointed through the thicket beside them. "There is a lagoon just the other side of this sand hill. It isn't very good water though, all slime and muck," she replied, her memory dredging an image of the waterhole from annual camp.

S-Lt de Blainville shook his head. "It does not matter if the water is not very good. It can make us very sick tomorrow but I fear that some of my men may become heat casualties, you understand?"

Barbara understood only too well. She nodded and licked dry lips, then said, "Heat exhaustion. I know. I am very dry myself."

Raoul looked anxiously at her and asked, "Are you alright? You do look very *rouge*... er... red."

"I need more water too," Barbara answered, touched by his evident concern.

"Then let us get some and quickly," Raoul answered. He at once caught Cpl Martini's eye and signalled to move. The corporal and Tribunga both stood up and began pushing through the tangle of weeds and lantana. Barbara crawled to her knees and Raoul helped her to her feet. To her dismay she found she was shaking so much she could hardly stand. Then she saw she could again help. The lantana was snagging the stretcher party.

I will use my secateurs, she thought.

It was then she found the torn basic pouch all soaked with congealed blood and half-torn off her belt. Raoul looked at it as she struggled to extract the secateurs and shook his head.

"Oh Barbara! Please, you must stay at the back and be more careful."

Barbara managed a smile. "We are retreating aren't we? So the back is the front." With that she stepped across and began to snip at the lantana and rubber vines.

In the daylight it was easier. Her efforts were helped by the urgent need and by fear, fear driven by the sound of gunshots a few hundred metres away and by the spreading fires. There was no breeze so the fires were only spreading slowly but they were fierce and she knew that being caught in the thicket by such flames could be deadly. The smoke was now spreading right across the sky and she saw that it had almost blotted out the sun.

That sun had almost become her personal enemy. It was now halfway down the western sky, but was shining through the trees and smoke like a huge orange ball. The effect was to bathe everything in a rusty, reddish glow.

To Barbara it seemed like an evil portent and she shuddered and redoubled her efforts.

Chapter 36

INTO THE FIRE

Five minutes of snipping, pushing and ducking under branches had the group at the top of the bank overlooking the lagoon. One glance confirmed Barbara memories: it looked disgusting. The water level was so low it was almost a layer of mud. The water was discoloured to a black-grey tinge and was thick with dead leaves. A layer of green slime coated much of it. Whitish deposits showed as a crust around the edges of the pool and there was a dead toad floating in it.

S-Lt de Blainville just gave a wry smile. "Huh! This is fine. You should have seen some of the water we drank in Chad," he said. He at once posted sentries and sent the first couple down to refill their water bottles. "You too please *Mademoiselle*," he insisted.

Barbara slid down the steep sandy slope and then stopped to sling her rifle, copying the two legionnaires ahead of her. She then waded gingerly out till the water was just deep enough for the waterbottle to fill. As she pulled the first one out and unscrewed the cap she looked anxiously both ways along the hundred metre long waterhole. A shiver of apprehension ran through her as she saw how exposed she was to any enemy. Then she shrugged and bent to fill the bottle.

By then her boots had stirred up swirls of mud and other muck and she grimaced with disgust, remembering all the cattle and pigs that must use the waterhole. As quickly as she could she filled the bottle, then replaced it in its carrier and tugged out another. All the while the sounds of distant battle kept reminding her of their extreme danger, as did the increasingly thick clouds of choking brown smoke. Luckily most of this was drifting overhead but she became increasingly anxious, wondering if the patrol might not have to take refuge in the waterhole to escape the approaching flames. The first of these had now become visible off to her right, the crackling sound of the fire's progress also becoming audible.

There were more fires downstream too but she could not see them, just the huge columns of smoke rising up. As quickly as she could she finished filling her waterbottles. Then she bent to splash water on her face. That felt very good and brought her instant relief, making her very aware of just how hot and dry she was. Very conscious of the others waiting their turn she quickly waded ashore.

As she clambered up the bank, Barbara pointed in the direction she knew was downstream. "I will go and take over as sentry," she said to Raoul. "That way all the men can refill their waterbottles and relieve themselves without any embarrassment."

Raoul nodded and said, "Yes, but be very careful."

"I will," Barbara answered. With that she began to carefully make her way along the top of the bank. In doing so she had to step over the stretcher and she noted that the dead legionnaire now had his face covered. But the sight of a grimy, blood-stained hand sticking out caused Barbara to shiver from a chill of apprehensive dread.

I wish I had never seen this cursed satellite! she thought.

She found Tribunga kneeling behind a tree. "Go back and fill your waterbottles," she said in French, indicating her own. "I will guard."

Tribunga frowned and looked as though he would not do so but Barbara unslung her rifle and moved to a fire position behind the tree. At that the black legionnaire nodded and silently made his way back. Barbara suddenly felt very alone, even though the others were only twenty-five metres behind her and she could actually see S-Lt de Blainville and Sgt Boucher out in the water filling their waterbottles.

They are very exposed out there, she thought anxiously.

That made her very conscious of her responsibility and she peered anxiously through the undergrowth, gripping the rifle ready to use, the safetycatch off.

S-Lt de Blainville and Sgt Boucher were replaced by Sgt Blomburg and Tribunga. Then the Asian—Tran—and another corporal (*Two diagonal green stripes on the black badge?*) took their turn. Finally Raoul, Pilsudski and the medic waded out to fill theirs. Barbara watched Raoul as he frequently lifted his head to look carefully in all directions while filling his bottles. To her he looked every inch a tough, capable soldier and feelings of admiration and affection rose in her.

Oh, I wonder if he is 'Mr Right'? she thought.

A small crackling noise caused her to turn to look towards her front. Then her heart seemed to stand still and choke her throat with dread.

Only ten metres in front of her was a Dag soldier!

The Dag had walked down the sandy vehicle track to the edge of the water, his rifle held in one hand and a collection of waterbottles slung over his left shoulder on a rope. Close behind him was a second Dag, similarly laden. Even as Barbara stared aghast, her mind trying to grasp what it saw, the first Dag looked along the creek bed. He saw Raoul at once and a look of shocked surprise crossed his face. The next moment he was clutching for his rifle, trying to get it up into his shoulder.

One terrified glance told Barbara that Raoul had not seen him. She did not hesitate. *He will kill Raoul!* she thought. In an instant she swung her rifle up and sighted along the top of the barrel. Even as she squeezed the trigger, she yelled, "Raoul!"

Blat-tat-tat!

The rifle went off three times in quick succession; a short burst that threw her aim off because it was so unexpected. Barbara saw instantly that she had missed, three splashes in the muddy water behind the Dag. But the burst still served its purpose. The Dag swung to look at her, his face aghast with horror. Barbara saw his automatic rifle come into his shoulder and swing up to aim at her.

I must shoot! she thought, knowing that her own life was now in deadly peril. Through her racing mind flashed sayings she had heard but had never really believed or agreed with: *Kill or be killed. Him or me!*

But this was real and she felt frozen as she stared at that tiny black rifle muzzle. In a spasm of pure terror she pulled her trigger again. The rifle again hammered three times, just as the Dag's AK47 began to jerk and smoke. Barbara was aware of bullets striking the tree beside her, and cracking past her. In the hazy tunnel of her totally focused vision she saw the Dag twitch and convulse as bullets hammered him backwards. The water and mud behind him erupted in showers of mud and spray. To her relief (later to be relived with increasing guilt), she saw him fall flat on his back, his rifle being flung away as he went down. The man's mouth was open and Barbara noted bad teeth and a dark brown tunic now pocked by little holes.

It wasn't her rifle that had fired those bullets she realized as more shots came from close behind her. Sgt Blomburg crashed through the weeds and went into a kneeling position beside her, his rifle swinging towards the second Dag. Down beside her on the right appeared S-Lt de Blainville, his rifle also smoking. It had been his shots that had gunned the Dag down—she hoped—then felt guilty again. A quick, frantic glance over her shoulder revealed Raoul dashing out of the water, waterbottle in one hand and rifle in the other.

Then the savage clatter of automatic fire close beside her again jerked Barbara's attention to her front. She saw that the second Dag had been frozen with shock for a moment. Now he was frantically trying to unsling his rifle. He had dropped the bundle of waterbottles and Barbara experienced flashes of detail that were to remain imprinted on her mind for the rest of her life: a hard, mean looking face with a pointed black beard; mouth working as though shouting or cursing, glittering dark eyes; a lighter brown jacket with a bandolier of brown leather slung across it.

Then the man was knocked down. It was so fast and so brutal that Barbara gasped in horror. The Dag went rolling down the steep, sandy slope, his limbs flopping in such a way that Barbara was sure he was dead. The body came to a stop on the edge of the water.

More movement was visible through the screen of weeds: a third Dag!

This man was older, fatter, his chubby bearded face with mouth open, his expression a mask of alarm, rather than hate. He had been carrying his rifle slung diagonally and he was struggling to pull it off. A large bundle of waterbottles was hooked on his webbing, impeding his efforts. Sgt Blomburg fired again then swore. One hot cartridge case lodged in the back of Barbara's collar, burning her skin, but she hardly noticed. Through a haze of fear and smoke she saw the third Dag jump aside and then fall over. A moment later he was up and limping away out of sight.

Sgt Blomburg fired again; a short burst, blind through the bushes. Then S-Lt de Blainville was beside him, shouting orders. Barbara crouched against the tree, shocked and frightened. She saw Tribunga and Cpl Martini go crashing off through the weeds to her left, hurrying despite the risk. Sgt Blomburg scuttled forward to the track the Dags had come down and threw himself down facing along it.

Raoul arrived. He crouched and hugged Barbara. "Are you alright?" he cried.

Barbara looked into his eyes and nodded, all her emotions swirling in chaos. Raoul squeezed her tightly. "You saved my life then. Now, we must leave here quickly. Please get up."

As she lifted herself on shaky legs, Barbara's mind was assailed by more noises and fears. Heavy firing broke out up on the river bank behind her. She jerked her head to look in that direction but Raoul shook his head.

"Not us," he said. "That is the battle up on the road."

"Where are we going?" Barbara croaked, her eyes noting that Sgt Boucher and Pilsudski had the container hung between them and that four others had hoisted the stretcher up and were pushing their way towards her along the creek bank, cursing and sweating as weeds and lantana snagged at them.

"Away from here, in case those fellows up on the road heard us," Raoul answered, gesturing downstream to the west.

Barbara thought for a second, then said, "Go back the way we came."

"Risky. They might be tracking us," Raoul answered.

Barbara shook her head. "No. They won't be expecting that and it is the best cover. We can't walk across this flat, open country in daylight."

Raoul looked thoughtful for a moment, then slowly nodded. "You might be right. So we will do that. Please point the way, but stay back behind me. So, safetycatch on please."

Raoul pushed past her to where S-Lt de Blainville now crouched beside the track. Barbara saw at once that it was the dirt vehicle track that led down from the pump station. She had not realized they were so far along the waterhole. S-Lt de Blainville was talking on his radio to his two scouts and even as Barbara reached the track and hurried across she heard shots over to her left. These were barely audible above the firing now going on three hundred metres away along the road. She glanced that way but all she could see was a thick cloud of brown smoke.

Raoul looked back at Barbara and she indicated to go on along the bank. In her mind was the flood channel that led back below the high bank to join One Mile Creek. As she followed him along she could not help looking with horrified fascination down to her right where Sgt Blomburg was stripping the waterbottles and rifles off the dead Dags. One sight of the staring, glazed eyes of the man she had shot at was enough. Sick and guilty to her very core she looked away and hurried on.

For fifty metres they struggled along until they found themselves confronted by a wall of burning grass and weeds. This curved right around to their left as well, blocking the path Barbara had thought to use. The other options were to move along the open, sandy bed of the river, or cross to the far bank and recross further along. While the stretcher party caught up she put this to Raoul. He looked at his watch and muttered, then shook his head.

"We go through the fire I think. It looks not so bad if we run. Safer than going along the open anyway."

Barbara stared at the blazing weeds in dismay. The flames were leaping two or three metres into the air and seemed to be an impenetrable wall. Now they were only ten metres away and she could already feel the heat scorching her. Thick smoke was billowing over them, causing them to cough and sneeze. Where they were, just down on the bank, was below the worst of it but she realized that if they tried to get through the flames they would be enveloped in the stuff. She been told so many times that it was the smoke that kills to have any illusions about this being as deadly a challenge as being shot at!

Can I do it? she wondered, her courage faltering.

She also remembered reading that it was the radiant heat that killed people in bush fires. She gasped, coughed, and rubbed at her stinging eyes, wishing they would water. Now she regretted not having had time to drink so she quickly pulled out a water bottle. Raoul nodded and paused to brief his gasping, coughing men. They crouched and looked at the advancing flames with evident apprehension.

"Go fast," Raoul said. "And shield your faces. The fire is only a few metres wide."

By then Barbara had lifted the waterbottle to her mouth and hesitated. An appalling stench rose to her nostrils, making her gag. Into her mind flashed the images of the scummy water, and its disgusting solids. "Drink!" she ordered herself. She was so hot and dry she knew that she was at serious risk of heat stroke. Using willpower she tilted her head back and drank, letting the vile tasting liquid flow down her gullet in gulps. But even so she gagged. Coughing and feeling like she wanted to vomit she stopped, then splashed a handful of water on her face.

That felt better and she screwed the lid back on her waterbottle and replaced it in its carrier. Raoul nodded with approval and smiled, then said, "Ready? Then let us go. Eh!"

Suddenly he went into a crouch, rifle pointed along to the right front from where rustling and cracking sounds could be heard above the noise of the fire. Barbara tensed, ready to shoot, as did the men behind her.

Suddenly a grey shape bounded out of the thicket into the open. It moved with such speed that she was too surprised to react. The legionnaires and Raoul all raised their rifles, then gaped.

Instead of shooting, they all began pointing and calling to one another: "*Kangourou! Kangourou!*"

Barbara gasped with relief and then smiled at the men's evident pleasure. It was actually a wallaby but she did not feel like trying to explain the difference. The wallaby stopped, turned its head and saw them, its ears swivelling and its nose twitching. Then it took flight and bounded off across the river bed. A second wallaby came out of the thicket: a doe with a joey in its pouch and that caused even more murmurs of interest.

Raoul watched it bound away and then shook his head. "Very interesting," he said, "Now, let us go. Follow me!"

To Barbara it was like a horrible dream: things kept going from bad to worse. She saw Raoul start running and managed to make her own limbs move to follow. Then she was crashing through the weeds and prickles towards the flames, gasping and sobbing with fear. Her eyes tried to detect the best spot but there was so much smoke that all she was able to do was follow Raoul's already hazy form. Several time weeds snagged at her running feet and she almost tripped but luckily Raoul had broken a path and she was able to keep her balance.

Cover your face! her mind cried.

Raoul vanished into the flames. With a sob of anguish Barbara took a deep breath and ran after him, her left arm shielding her face. At the last moment she closed her eyes and jumped. That was a mistake as she almost stumbled. She felt the searing heat lick at her. The sudden flare of another large clump of grass erupting made her cry out in fear and swerve. Through slitted, stinging eyes she saw enough to dodge and avoid a burning bush. Then she was through!

Noting a smouldering, scorched area ahead with only a few small flames Barbara slowed down. Seeing she was safe from the flames she gasped with relief—then was half-choked by wracking coughs as she drew in smoke as well as air. Ahead of her she could dimly see the high bank and the dirt road going up over it. To her relief Raoul was still running but he slowed and looked back, coughing and his eyes streaming.

Barbara slowed as well, then stood bent over and shaken by retching spasms. Through gritty eyes she also looked back, noting with relief that the two with the container were safely through. Then the stretcher party appeared, hurrying, their faces contorted by effort and pain. They struggled on to join them and Raoul waved them past towards the smoking gully to their right front.

Crack!

Barbara jumped in fright. Her mind instantly told her what it was—a bullet. She saw one of the stretcher carriers go down. Raoul yelled at her and pushed her over. She went sprawling in the smouldering ashes, just as more shots cracked past very close.

Even as she landed in the smoking soot Barbara's terrified mind screamed, *Oh no! Out of the frying pan...*

It burnt! It stung! Barbara knew she was lying on hot embers and that sparks were burning through her uniform, but she pressed herself flat regardless. In a nightmarish haze of smoke and pain she noted Raoul roll to one side and his rifle come up. More shots snapped by and she became aware of others firing back.

I should shoot, she thought—but at what? Raising her head with an effort of willpower she looked frantically around, trying to focus and work out what was going on.

Shouts and shots helped her. There was an enemy halfway up the bank beside the road, hiding behind the tree she had sat under during the Leadership Evaluation Exercise. S-Lt de Blainville could be heard calling orders off to her left and she glimpsed a legionnaire—either Tribunga or Cpl Martini—dash across to the smoking slope off to the left of the enemy.

That Dag has the drop on us from there, Barbara thought.

Then she noted the twitching figure lying in the smoking grass beside the stretcher. Even as she looked a bullet struck the ground beside the wounded man, throwing up a shower of ash and dust.

The Dag is shooting at him! Barbara thought in horror.

Stung by both pain and fury Barbara sprang to her feet and raced over to the man. She saw it was the Senior Private, Mendoza. He was gripping his thigh, his face a mask of agony. Blood was staining the leg of his trousers. Through her mind flitted a demonstration Major Conkey had once given the unit on how soldiers moved casualties under fire. He and the staff had demonstrated it but the cadets had not been allowed to practice it. But now Barbara acted on it. Reaching down she grabbed the yoke of Mendoza's webbing behind his head. Then she ran, dragging him behind her across the smouldering ground.

It was much harder than she thought and she was wailing and sobbing with effort as she ran. As she did she looked towards the tree where the Dag was, aware that those puffs of smoke meant he was shooting at her. Dust and ash billowed around the base of the tree as the legionnaires fired back. Close beside her was a small dip with a clean sandy bottom. She jumped into this, hauling Mendoza down after her.

A bullet struck the lip, showering her with sand but she hunched herself down and hoped they were both in dead ground.

If we aren't I'm dead, she thought.

More shots sounded but they were all but drowned out by the uproar of a real battle which erupted away along the road. Satisfied that the others would keep her safe Barbara rolled over and looked at Mendoza. He was using both hands to grip his leg and was shivering in pain. Barbara was appalled at the amount of blood welling out and feared that the bullet had cut an artery.

"Keep a tight grip," she said.

Then she realized she had spoken in English and could tell by the look on his face that he had not understood. While she tried to find the French words she began frantically digging in her webbing for a bandage. This took some digging out, rousing her to a rage of impatience, but she got it out at last and began fastening it firmly around Mendoza's leg. Within seconds blood covered her hands and arms but she ignored this.

Then thudding feet made her look up in alarm. But it was Lamertine, the medic. He jumped down beside her and swung his First Aid kit round to open. Seeing what she was doing he nodded with approval, then reached forward and took over.

Raoul appeared, and gestured. "Get up! Come!"

Barbara did, wondering what had happened to the Dag that it was safe to stand in the open again. As she scrambled out of the gully she saw the reason. The Dag had been shot. His body lay sprawled on the smoking hillside below the tree, right where she had sat. Even as she watched she saw his beard vanish in a puff of flame. That made her sick and she vomited, most of it going down her front.

Men were grouping around the stretcher but Barbara at once saw there were not enough. Brushing off Raoul's hand she hurried over, wiping the sticky mucous off with her sleeve as she did. As she arrived she noted Mendoza's rifle lying in the ash and she bent and quickly scooped it up and placed it on the stretcher. Then she knelt and took a corner, despite the protestations of the men.

"Just bloody lift!" she snapped in English.

So they did. They then hurried across the smoking ground to the deep cleft where One Mile Creek entered the river bed. On the way Barbara saw Cpl Martini and Tribunga climb to the crest of the high bank and then crawl to fire positions looking over the top. Carrying the stretcher even fifty metres was a real strain and Barbara was gasping and in pain by the time they lowered it to the ground in the shelter of the creek bed.

To Barbara's dismay the dead legionnaire was rolled off the stretcher and the men went running back with it. She stood up to follow but S-Lt de Blainville ran down and physically restrained her.

"*Non! Mademoiselle,* the very dangerous it still is. Please stay under cover. You already the *Croix de Guerre* have won."

For a few seconds Barbara struggled angrily to break free of his grip. Then all the fight just drained out of her and she slumped down exhausted, her body stinging and aching. S-Lt de Blainville handed her a waterbottle and only when she sat and took it did he relax. It was more of the foul water from the billabong but she gulped it down anyway. Then she vomited again as her eyes noted the dead Dag sprawled on the bank above her, his clothes smouldering and his skin blackening in the hot ashes. Feeling desperately upset she looked away, forcing herself to drink deeply.

The others arrived very quickly: first Sgt Boucher and Pilsudski with the container, then Raoul, Cpl Fouchet, Tran and Sgt Blomburg carrying the stretcher and Lamertine lugging Mendoza's webbing, and pack.

There followed ten minutes of urgent, exhausting re-organizing. Two entrenching tools came into use and both the dead Dag and the dead legionnaire were hastily buried in the sandy creek bed. Mendoza was made comfortable on the stretcher. Weapons and equipment were redistributed. Barbara insisted on carrying a pack as Raoul did not want to leave any evidence. All the time this was going on the distant battle raged. That sound, more than anything, caused them all to feel anxious and want to be gone.

As Tran shovelled sand over the dead legionnaire all of the others, except the sentries, stood in line. S-Lt de Blainville said a prayer in French, the only bit of which Barbara understood was *'Mort pour la France'*. That moved her to tears and she bit her lip and shuddered.

As S-Lt de Blainville saluted so did Raoul. Barbara did likewise, unsure if she should, but noting that the grim-faced men apparently saw nothing odd in her actions. They presented arms. Then she shivered with goose bumps as the legionnaires all chanted, *"Vive la Legion!"*

That she found so emotional she had to release it. As they set to work tidying up she found tears streaming down her cheeks. Raoul came and put his arms around her and held her, none of the others apparently finding anything unusual in this.

Wiping her eyes, she said, "This creek floods in the Wet Season. His body might be uncovered."

Raoul shook his head. "No matter. Long before then we will recover it and he will get a proper burial."

Then Barbara remembered the man's beret. She eased herself out of Raoul's arms and dug it out of her map pocket. "This is his beret. Do you want to bury it with him?"

Before Raoul could answer S-Lt de Blainville walked over and took the beret. Then he pressed it hard into Barbara's hands, folding her fingers over it.

"Mademoiselle Barbara, we wish you to have it. You are now *un legionnaire honoraire."*

He then leaned forward to kiss her on both cheeks. Emotion surged in Barbara so that she felt almost overwhelmed and also very worried at what the others might think. But one glance at the serious approval on the faces of the other legionnaires, and at their nodding heads, made her aware that she had just been granted a very great honour. All she could do was flame with pride and nod her acceptance.

Raoul nodded, and said, "Very good. Now, let us get away from here before more trouble arrives."

Chapter 37

AT LAST!

The patrol set off back along One Mile Creek. The two scouts moved up on either side, keeping just below the crest and frequently peeking over to check out the flat, open country to east and west. The remainder of the patrol walked along the sandy bed, carrying the cylinder and stretcher. The only one not helping to carry either was Barbara, who walked just ahead of Raoul. She offered to help but they declined and after ten minutes she was glad of that as the weight of the small backpack she found a real burden.

"What's in this pack to make it so heavy?" she whispered to Raoul as they trudged along the creek bed.

"Batteries mostly, the burden of the modern soldier," Raoul explained, "And probably a few items like smoke grenades, flares and so on, and some food and a lightweight sleeping bag and plastic shelter. Not much."

Barbara could only grunt at that and keep walking. Her watch told her it was 1700 but the air was still stifling. It was also filled with the pungent reek of smoke. Mingled with this were various chemical smells, among which she thought she recognized cordite. This particular stench she noted was drifting across from the east, from the Mingela Road area beyond the Triangle. The fighting there had died away and that got her wondering what had happened. Raoul had told her the troops coming from 'Dotswood' were US Marines and she guessed that they had overwhelmed the platoon of Dags.

Being able to now picture exactly what that area must look like she felt sick and depressed. Ghastly images of death floated across her consciousness. That got her morbidly thinking about the bodies they had just buried. Fear of death became physical perspiration and nausea. She also felt very hot and thirsty. It took her an effort to gulp down more of the foul water and already she could feel her stomach gurgling as it became upset.

At least we are in the shade now, she thought, noting that the bed of One Mile Creek was in shadow as the sun slowly sank in the west. She was so sunburnt she was starting to hate the sun. Her whole body seemed to be burning and her face felt like a taut mask of pain.

By the time they approached the place where the Dag troops had crossed the creek she was nearly at the end of her endurance. Stubbornly she struggled grimly on but the weight of the pack was just too much. Finally she was unable to climb over a fallen tree which blocked the creek bed and she had to give up. She stumbled back, gasping and unsteady on her feet.

The stretcher and container were lowered to the creek bed for a rest and Barbara leaned back against the side of the gully to take the weight off her shoulders. Seeing her distress Raoul came forward and quietly took the pack straps. "You have carried that far enough," he murmured.

"I can manage!" Barbara replied, stung by her own weakness. She was ashamed to admit that she felt ready to drop and that tears were close. Her breathing was so laboured that she could hardly speak.

"Nonsense," Raoul murmured. "You must take it off. We will hide it here in this long grass. It was Sorenson's. He doesn't need it any more. We only brought it to help hide the bodies."

"I will help with that container then," Barbara replied.

"No. It may be radioactive and I do not want you harmed," Raoul replied. "I do not want you to risk having deformed babies."

"I might not want to have babies," she snorted.

Raoul grinned. "We will see about that. I think we would make great babies."

Barbara felt a deep glow as her mind took in the implications of that. "Is that a proposal?" she asked, her voice croaking with both thirst and emotion.

Again Raoul grinned. "Maybe. But not yet. I think we should get to know each other much better."

"What do you mean by that?" Barbara asked, guessing from the mischievous glint that had appeared in his eye.

"Per'aps we could practice at the baby making techniques first," Raoul suggested, winking as he did.

Barbara blushed and snorted but realized she wasn't offended. "Men!" she said with a sniff. Then she shrugged off the pack and said, "I will help with the stretcher then."

Raoul gave a soft laugh and took the pack. This opened and a few items passed to others to carry and then it was stuffed up into a large tuft of grass out of sight. Then the march was resumed. Barbara went to the stretcher and saw at once that Pilsudski was looking very drawn and obviously in pain. "I will take over for a while," she offered.

It was a measure of the legionnaire's pain that he reluctantly assented. Barbara took one of the front handles and, on command by S-Lt de Blainville, hoisted it up to her shoulder. The weight and associated aches came as a horrible surprise to Barbara but she bit her lip and summoned up her strength. Even worse was the stinging pain in her hands when the blisters from the fire burst and rubbed on the handles, but she gritted her teeth and kept going. On the other handle was Tran. As they trudged along Tran looked at her and grinned.

While helping lift the stretcher across the log he said, in English with a broad Australian accent, "You are doing very well."

"Thanks," Barbara grunted. Out of curiosity she added, "You sound like an Aussie."

"I am, but I don't look like one, eh?" Tran said with some bitterness.

"Sorry," Barbara muttered. "I didn't mean it like that. Are you of Chinese descent?"

Tran shook his head. "Vietnamese, at least both my parents are. I was born in Australia. Grew up in Cabramatta. But I know all about racism, I can tell you."

That was an uncomfortable subject which made Barbara feel quite guilty. She said, "So why did you join the French Army?"

"Because I took part in a few activities I ain't proud of that made it wiser for me to leave the country, and because my Grandad, he was a paratrooper in the French Army. Back in the First Indochina War."

Barbara felt even more uncomfortable and ignorant. She knew where Vietnam was but her knowledge was almost nil. She had heard of the Vietnam War that some Australian troops had fought in many years before, but that was all. Tran, his first name was actually Ngyen she now learned, gave her a thumbnail history lesson as they sweated along the narrow creek bed. It was all a revelation to her and made her feel quite humble and uneducated. It gave her a sharp lesson into the fact that the world was full of other cultures and countries, all with their own proud traditions and histories.

By the time they reached the depression where the Marlow Road crossed the creek Barbara had reached exhaustion point again. It was with gasping relief that she lowered the stretcher and allowed Pilsudski to take the handle again. Another swig of slimy water was forced down and that at least made her break into a sweat.

The scouts had already cleared the depression so the carrying party did not delay, hurrying on across it as quickly as they could. Then it was on along the creek bed again until they came to the fence line. Raoul allowed another rest for a couple of minutes, during which Barbara finished the first waterbottle. The air still felt very hot but Barbara suspected that part of the problem was her skin being dry from dehydration. She knew she was badly sunburnt and she silently cursed when their travels took them out along a section of the creek where the sun's rays still penetrated.

That was at the point where the creek swung back to run eastwards again towards the Gravel Scrape. Raoul called another halt and S-Lt de Blainville and he went into a huddle over the map. Unbidden Barbara joined them. They made no comment on this and made no attempt to exclude her from their discussion. She saw they were tracing various routes on the map. A quick estimation told her that the New Airfield was only about two kilometres away in a straight line. The intervening ground had only one twenty metre contour shown.

Raoul ran his finger directly to the western end of the airstrip. "That will do us," he said.

"Do we go now?" S-Lt de Blainville asked in French.

"Only a short distance. I think we should get away from this creek line," Raoul replied. "It's too obvious. If there is a search, this must be part of it."

Barbara nodded agreement. "Find a little hollow up in the edge of the burnt-out thicket," she suggested.

Raoul nodded. "Are you able to keep going?"

Barbara licked cracked lips and nodded. She felt light-headed and upset in the stomach and very, very worn out but told herself she could do two kilometres. "I just hope we don't run into any more Dags," she said.

"So do we all," Raoul answered. "Let us hope that *l'Americaines* have wiped them all out."

A niggling thought that had been bothering Barbara she now voiced. Looking at the map had made her think of it. "If there are any Dags left, they might withdraw in this direction," she said.

"Why do you think that?" S-Lt de Blainville asked.

"Because the ones we saw came from the west," Barbara answered. She then pointed to the map. "Yaamba Lagoon. I think that is where their camp is. They must have a local water supply and it would have to come from the creeks. Those men we.... we shot, they knew about the lagoon we went to."

Raoul looked thoughtful and nodded. "I think you may be right, so the sooner we go the better." He turned away to get the group moving.

As he did another horrible, embarrassing thought crossed Barbara's mind. *If we run into Dags I might have to shoot. How many rounds do I have left in my magazine?* she worried.

She tried to remember how many she had fired but wasn't sure. That hurt her juvenile pride as a Cadet Under-Officer, but she decided that this was too important to bluff.

Other people's lives might depend on this, she told herself. Standing beside her was Sgt Blomburg. She looked at him and held up the rifle.

"Excuse me *Mon Sergeant,* help me reload please."

Sgt Blomburg nodded with grave approval. He gently reached across and pointed. "Push that and the magazine falls out. Just make sure you do not pull the trigger."

"Thanks," Barbara replied. She did as she was shown, ignoring the pain in her burnt hands, and removed the magazine, slipping it into her intact basic pouch.

"Do you have another one?" Sgt Blomburg asked.

Barbara shook her head. Sgt Blomburg walked over to the stretcher and bent down to the webbing under Mendoza's head. He extracted a fresh magazine, turning it upside down to check it was full, and making a joke to the wounded soldier about him being nothing but a lazy, malingering, barrack-room lawyer and not needing it. Mendoza managed a weak grin back and said something to the effect that Barbara could use anything he owned, anytime.

As Barbara slipped the fresh magazine into the rifle under Sgt Blomburg's tuition she asked, "How many rounds does this one hold?"

"Twenty-five, so go careful or you run out ver' quick. And next time remember that if you move the safetycatch to here." He indicated a second setting, "It will fire bursts of three, not single shots."

That made clear to Barbara why the weapon had fired the bursts and she bit her lip and nodded. Sgt Blomburg grinned and patted her on the shoulder. "You will be fine. The ver' good soldier you are, worthy of being *un legionnaire*."

At that Barbara blushed with pride. She looked around and saw that all the men were looking at her and smiling and nodding. Through gritty eyes that suddenly misted she saw them as they were—exhausted, sunburnt, uniforms filthy with soot and grime, clothing torn, their tough looking faces grimy and lined, their eyes bloodshot but full of approval. For the first time in her life she emotionally understood the concept of 'Comrades in Arms' and a surge of intense respect and liking for them made her tremble.

I must look like them, she thought.

And she did. She looked down and noted her torn, tattered and filthy uniform, crusted with dried blood and vomit, scorched and pocked with small burn holes. Her bare skin was torn and scratched and the creases in her hands and wrists clotted with soot and sweaty grime. Ruefully she noted her blistered hands and shot-torn webbing.

Heavens! How will I ever explain this to Major Conkey, she thought. But then she smiled. *I have to be alive and able to see him to do that,* she told herself.

By then the scouts were moving and Raoul and Sgt Boucher had hoisted up the container so she smiled her thanks and moved to lead them along the creek bed. The stretcher party followed. The route they took led them east along One Mile Creek for another two hundred metres, then south along a small gully coming in from the side. At the junction Raoul asked her to come last and to try to hide their tracks. This took her a few minutes, during which she felt very isolated and alone. Then, satisfied that no casual search would show they had been that way, she followed the group.

By the time she caught them up they had gone a hundred metres and Raoul had selected a small washout under a clump of scorched thorn trees. One at a time they crossed from the gully to the washout and crawled in under the bushes. By then the sun was low among the trees to the west and the whole scene was bathed in red, made eerie by the amber glow refracted through the clouds of smoke that still drifted away along the now distant line of Keelbottom Creek.

With a sigh of relief Barbara stretched out on the sooty ground, undoing her webbing and trying to make herself as comfortable as she could. She sat with her back to the setting sun, which even now, at 1735, had a bite to it.

I've had more than enough sun for one day! she told herself.

Two sentries were posted and everyone else lay low, except for Raoul , S-Lt de Blainville and Cpl Fouchet. They set up their satellite radio in the centre of the shallow depression and set to work sending and receiving signals. Barbara unclipped her helmet and eased it off, then lay back to watch them. Then reaction set in. She began to tremble and suffer cramps. The pain was agonizing and immediately drew Raoul to her side. She shook her head and pummelled at the offending muscles, then lay back and shivered. Once again she forced herself to drink, almost throwing up just at the smell and uncomfortably aware that her bowels were feeling loose.

Suddenly Cpl Martini hissed and signalled. Barbara rolled over and peered through a bush, her rifle up and ready. The others groaned and sat up, then took up fire positions. Barbara strained her tired eyes and then went stiff as they detected movement. Tiny figures were appearing out of One Mile Creek back near where they had left it.

Dags! she thought, her heart racing with apprehension. She counted them, stopping at eleven. But by then she had deduced they were not heading towards the patrol. Instead they were walking west.

It looks like two of them are helping others, she thought. All she could decide was that they were the survivors of the Dag platoon that had been battling with the US Marines. *Withdrawing towards Yaamba Lagoon?* she told herself.

It became obvious that more than two were wounded. *Going off to lick their wounds,* Barbara thought, then felt sick to the bottom of her heart, knowing now exactly what that meant. It made her glance at the pain-riven form of Mendoza on the stretcher and she shuddered, then prayed.

The Dags vanished amid the haze and bushes into the setting sun. The group relaxed again. Barbara forced herself to drink some more. By then she was feeling weak from lack of food and her stomach was rumbling both from hunger and from the effect of the bad water. Raoul and S-Lt de Blainville finished their radio transmissions and packed up the equipment. The look of quiet satisfaction on Raoul's face told Barbara that they had been successful in their efforts and this was confirmed when he lay down beside her.

"All is well," he explained. "The aircraft will pick us up at twenty one hundred hours."

That raised a very difficult question for Barbara but she made herself ask it. "What should I do?" she asked. "Do I go with you, or do I make my way to the army camp and hand myself over to the Australian Army?"

Raoul looked horrified. "For you to try to make your way through this country alone and at night would be very dangerous. I will not allow it. You might run into le Dags, or even into some nervous and trigger-happy Americaines. The risk is too great. Do not fear. We will look after you and see you safe."

"You just want me to stay with you," said Barbara, trying to deflect deep emotion with banter.

Raoul looked at her very seriously and nodded. "Yes, I think I do. Even before this patrol I thought you were the most interesting and unusual woman—and beautiful too. Now I think you are just amazing and I want even more to get to know you properly."

Barbara was about to melt and kiss him when Tribunga hissed. It was another group moving along One Mile Creek. But these were in the creek line and moving towards the Gravel Scrape. Barbara glimpsed helmets and counted half a dozen. Then several of the men emerged from the cover and walked across the open, weapons ready.

"Americans," Raoul said.

"That camouflage of theirs isn't very effective in this terrain," Barbara commented, noting that the US uniforms were a very pale khaki blotched with brown streaks.

"Their desert uniform," Raoul commented. "I do not think they have anything suitable for savannah country. They were like that in Somalia, very conspicuous."

The US Marines vanished among the burnt-out thicket to the east. The patrol relaxed again and Barbara decided that she had to go to the toilet. She whispered this to Raoul and he nodded and quietly told the others. "Do not go far," he added.

Barbara stood up and hefted her rifle into a comfortable position then walked deeper into the thicket. As instructed she did not go far, only just out of sight of the others. Now fear overcame most of her inhibitions.

Even being only twenty paces away from the patrol made her feel very isolated and alone. After finding a small washout she took off her webbing and helmet and crouched in the small gully to do her business. This included a rather messy liquid release from the bowels and it took her a few minutes to clean herself.

Thank heavens I had toilet paper in my webbing, she thought. Then she worried that the others might be able to smell her as it was quite unpleasant.

She covered the mess with dirt and then stood up and swung her webbing on. As she did she heard bushes crackling and then saw movement. Into view about fifty paces away appeared a US marine. He was scouting, weapon at the ready. Another appeared behind him. The second one kept scanning with a rifle that had a large telescopic sight on it. Barbara froze and lowered herself to a squat, her heart hammering rapidly and her mouth dry with fear.

Suddenly the second man went flat, his weapon aiming at where the legion patrol was hidden. *Oh no! They have been seen!* Barbara thought.

Terrible images of the Americans blasting Raoul and the legionnaires caused her to almost lose control of her bowels again. Searing flashbacks to the effect of the helicopter gunship fire caused her to tremble in terror.

"Oh what can I do?" she muttered, wondering if the legionnaires had seen them and fearful of a battle breaking out.

Even as she said this a third US marine crawled into view over to the left of the others and she suspected there were more back among the burned bushes of the thicket. Then the second marine swung his big telescopic sight and aimed it directly at Barbara. She distinctly saw him speaking into a small radio microphone and a stab of pure terror almost paralysed her.

But then she knew there was only one thing to do to avert the others being killed as well. *I am wearing Australian Army uniform,* she told herself. *Maybe I can bluff them?* she thought.

For an instant she considered picking up the helmet and putting it on but then remembered that it had quite a different camouflage pattern on it from the distinctive Austcam style.

So she stood up with both hands held up, leaving her rifle on the ground. It was one of the most difficult things she had ever done as her whole being was focused on the weapon aimed at her. Through her mind flashed images of bullets striking men and of the damage they did and her flesh crawled in anticipation. She found herself dizzy and gasping for air.

Then she took a deep breath and forced herself to walk towards the Americans. As she did she saw more of them taking up fire positions and she knew that a blood bath could result at any second.

Act cool and calm, she told herself. *These are not the enemy. They are Australia's friends and allies!*

After about thirty paces the third American called to her: "Halt! Keep yer hands up. Who are you?"

"Australian Army," Barbara answered with a voice she hoped sounded normal but to which to her sounded croaky and shaky.

"Come here," the man commanded.

Barbara did so, every step an effort for her trembling legs. She began to fear she would faint or collapse. As she got closer she noted marines with light machine guns and others with sniper rifles or anti-armour weapons. There were at least a dozen marines and she knew they would soon call on massive reinforcements as several radios were in evidence.

Only when Barbara was a few paces away did the marine stand up and he still kept his automatic rifle aimed at Barbara.

AR15, she noted.

She also noted that he wore sergeant stipes, one of the sets that had three chevrons and two curved stripes joining them.

First Sergeant? Master Sergeant—I mean Sargent? she thought. She knew that the Americans had half a dozen grades of sargent but she could not remember the rank diagram she had once studied.

The sargent looked very suspicious and said, "We weren't told there were any Aussies in this area."

"We were trying to avoid some Dags so we made a detour," Barbara replied.

The sargent stared at her hair and was obviously appraising himself of the fact that she was female. "Are you infantry?" he asked.

Barbara was anxiously hoping he couldn't read the words on the blue cadet colour flashes sewn to her upper sleeves. She remembered another ex-cadet who had gone into the army and said, "No. I am an Intelligence officer but my escort patrol are infantry."

The American sergeant was obviously suspicious and he frowned and looked Barbara up and down. "You look a wreck," he commented.

Barbara had to smile at that. "I feel like one!" she replied. "We had to try to outrun a bush fire but couldn't so we had to run through it."

The marine sergeant grunted and then said, "So why were you over there and your patrol over in that gully?"

Barbara's mind raced and then she decided that the simple truth would suffice. "I told them to have a rest in the shade while I went to find somewhere private to go to the toilet," she said.

The American looked slightly embarrassed and again grunted. Before he could ask another question Barbara decided to take the initiative. "If you are after the Dags you had better hurry. We saw a dozen of them in the distance, going that way," she said, pointing to the west.

"When was that?"

"About ten minutes ago," Barbara lied.

The sargent looked that way, squinting into the last of the setting sun. "Have you reported that to your headquarters?" he asked.

Barbara shook her head and felt sick. "No. Our radio isn't working. But another one of your patrols is on their trail. They went past us over there only a few minutes ago."

"Did you report them to our patrol?" the sergeant asked.

Again Barbara shook her head. "No. They didn't see us and we didn't want an accidental clash so we let them go."

At that another marine lying nearby behind a light machine gun said in a sneering tone, "That'll be that dumb-shit Kowalski. We'd better warn him Sarge."

The sargent agreed and Barbara did not wait for more interrogation. Taking the risk she turned her back and began walking away, saying, "Good luck!" as she did.

To her intense relief the sargent did not call her back or ask any more questions. After walking for twenty or so trembling paces she glanced back. Thankfully she saw the marines signalling to each other and getting to their feet. She gave a friendly wave and continued walking. The marines resumed their march. As they did Barbara noted the tiny bumps that were the heads of some of the legionnaires. They were obviously ready to fight but then she saw Raoul stand up and wave. One of the Americans waved back.

Barbara was sweating and shaking by then and had a strong impulse to run to Raoul and throw herself into his arms. But she resisted the urge and instead walked back to where she had left her helmet and rifle. Only after collecting them did she turn and walk towards the others. As she rejoined them she saw that the marine patrol was already a hundred metres further away and rapidly vanishing from view among the bushes and trees.

Back at the patrol Barbara slumped down and had a fit of trembling. She knew she was on the edge of a breakdown and only her pride kept that in check. Raoul and S-Lt de Blainville crouched with her. Raoul kept glancing towards the American patrol.

"What happened?" he asked.

Barbara had to have a drink before she could answer. Her hands shook so much she spilled some of it and had trouble screwing the cap back on her waterbottle. Then she described her actions and the conversation.

Raoul nodded and then smiled. "That was exactly right! You have done ver' well."

S-Lt de Blainville agreed. "*Mademoiselle* is ver' brave. That must 'ave taken the great courage."

Barbara blushed at the praise. To deflect it she said, "I wonder how they spotted us? We were all under cover."

S-Lt de Blainville answered that, gesturing to the rifle held by Cpl Martini. "A thermal imaging scope probably," he said.

That made sense to Barbara but also appalled her. *We can't move anywhere without being spotted,* she thought.

The knowledge that their enemies had such a technical advantage made her feel exposed and helpless. She nodded and then looked around, noting that the Americans were no longer in sight.

There was a simple meal after that. Barbara felt so drained she knew she needed the energy but she was so upset and ill that she did not feel like eating. But she did accept some biscuits and a chocolate. With an effort of willpower she munched the biscuits down and drank some more of the foul smelling water. Then she sat back and nibbled at the chocolate. As she did she noted with satisfaction that the direct rays of the sun no longer shone on her.

At last! she thought, sighing with relief. It had been the longest, hardest day of her life and she felt utterly drained, battered both physically and emotionally.

But it was not over yet! Darkness slowly set in, until by 1900 it was fully dark. During the wait Barbara dozed uncomfortably and became more and more restless and anxious. As well she developed an urgent need to go to the toilet. When she told Raoul this he smiled and said go.

Sgt Blomburg grinned and added, "Yes, it is time for *Mademoiselle* to go out on *la toilette patrol.* Every time you do you save us from the surprise attack."

That made Barbara blush with embarrassment but she still needed to go. After warning Cpl Martini, who was on guard, she walked fifty paces away and crouched among some bushes. It was unpleasant as her bowels really were liquid and she was concerned lest the men could smell the foul odour of what she voided.

By the time she rejoined them the world was dark and very silent. As soon as she was back Raoul got them up and moving. Once again Barbara helped by taking a handle of the stretcher. She was able to keep this up for only a hundred metres before handing back to Pilsudski but she knew her efforts were appreciated. She gave Mendoza a gentle squeeze of the hand and he smiled in gratitude. That helped her to keep going.

The distance was only one thousand, five hundred metres and she knew that in daylight without any gear or battles to fight she could have walked it in twenty minutes. As it was it took an hour, with six short halts to rest. For most of the way Cpl Martini and Tribunga led, using their night vision sights. Because of the strain on the others in moving the stretcher and container the scouts were changed and Cpl Fouchet and Sgt Blomburg became the scouts for the last half-kilometre. There was only one minor obstacle: a barbed wire fence. Barbara knew that this was the one that led to the cattle grid near the Gravel Scrape and it gave her the feeling that they were doomed to walk in circles, even though the Gravel Scrape was now two kilometres away to her left rear.

Just when she thought she could walk no further, when her tired muscles were cramping and giving up and her chafing becoming unbearable, they arrived at the New Airfield. To her it appeared as just a grey ribbon in a clearing, barely visible in the starlight. The patrol halted among a scattering of ironbarks at the edge of the long clearing near its western end. S-Lt de Balinville carefully scanned in all directions with his night vision device. While looking across the airfield he stopped and stared, then muttered something and went on with his search. To Raoul's quiet query he replied in French that he had thought he saw something but was not sure. Apparently satisfied the area was safe he briefed the legionnaires to guard in all-round defence and then signalled to get down.

Oh, at last! Barbara thought, sinking to the ground exhausted.

There was no sound to be heard, not even a bird or the wind. The ground where they were had not been burnt off so had a sparse covering of knee-high dry grass which was a pleasant relief to lie on. Barbara lay back, shivering and sick and prayed for it all to be over soon. Raoul set up the radio and did some more communicating, relaying their position and the wind direction and speed (*Nil!*).

After he had finished he walked quietly over and crouched beside her. "They are not sending an aircraft," he said. "They are sending two helicopters instead. That is much better."

Barbara could only nod. She felt she was now near the extreme limit of her endurance and was very anxious that nothing further should go wrong.

"Will they be long?" she asked.

Raoul shook his head. "*Non*. Twenty minutes. They are on their way now."

Only twenty minutes! Barbara thought.

Now every second seemed to drag. Even though all was quite she felt gripped by tension. Even the sound of one of the men moving away to go to the toilet did not ease her growing sense of apprehension.

Then a gentle vibrating tremor came to her ears from the south. She sat up and groped for her webbing and rifle.

Helicopters, she thought with relief. *At last!*

Chapter 38

FIRE AND FURY

At the sound of the approaching helicopters Barbara heaved a sigh of relief. She half-rose and did up her webbing. As she did Raoul reached out and grabbed her arm. She turned to look and saw he was staring out across the airfield. S-Lt de Blainville was next to him pointing, the faint green glow of his night vision sight lighting up his eyeball.

"What's wrong?" Barbara whispered, catching the tenseness in the Frenchmen's poses.

Raoul pointed. "That man," he whispered back.

Barbara stared hard in the starlight in the direction he was pointing, then gasped in surprise. The black figure of a man could just be seen moving out onto the runway from the bush on the other side. She now saw that the airfield had been constructed along a wide ridge line so the ground curved gently down on all sides. The man had come up from the other side. Even as she watched the man stopped and stood facing west along the strip, both his arms raised.

What on earth is he doing? she wondered. Then curiosity about his nationality came, along with a flood of worry.

By then the helicopters had swung around to the west and were heading towards them. From the sound of their engines they were coming in to land but she could not see even a glimpse of them against the starry sky. Barbara saw that Raoul had called Cpl Fouchet over and that he was now talking urgently on a radio, as quietly as he could.

She could not follow the rapid French so waited in growing apprehension. To get so close, and then to find the enemy waiting at the rendezvous! As soon as Raoul stopped speaking on the radio she could tell things were going badly wrong.

"What is it?" she whispered, her own fear growing by the second.

"Not ours," Raoul replied. Then he added, "The helicopters. There are four of them and they are 'Blackhawks'."

"What will we do?" Barbara asked, peering anxiously to the west where the first of the helicopters had at last emerged from the dark background as it came down across the end of the strip. As Raoul went to answer her rifle and machine gun fire broke out. It was so heavy and so unexpected that it cut him off, mouth open.

Barbara gaped in stunned surprise. This rapidly turned to horror as she understood what she was seeing. From the long grass at the end of the landing strip, on their side, sparkled a cluster of red flashes. From two of these streams of red tracer bullets went up, travelling at amazing, shocking speed. Even with her limited experience Barbara could tell that some of these were striking the first helicopter as several ricocheted. The ricochets twirled and curved off into the night in several directions. Barbara was only dimly aware of the sound of gunfire but a sudden searing flash down among the firers, and then a heart stopping bang, registered themselves in her pulse rate and bloodstream.

The first helicopter was trying to climb. She could tell that by the urgent roar of its engines and the way it veered towards her right. Suddenly it exploded in a fireball. Aghast she gaped up in disbelief as the blazing machine began to simultaneously disintegrate and to plummet downwards. Her shock turned to near panic as it became apparent that the blazing machine was going to crash—and that it could hit her. To escape she rose to her feet, then could only stare in horror as the machine came down like a blazing meteor. As it did pieces flew off in all directions, some of them being flung off in flames.

Barbara's shocked mind raced as it first registered that the helicopter would not hit her, and then that she should dive for cover. By the time she thought of it, it was too late. The burning Blackhawk struck the ground about fifty paces to her right front, just among the trees along the edge of the clearing. To her absolute horror it landed upside down and was instantly engulfed in a fireball as its fuel tanks exploded. Barbara was so appalled at the tragedy she was witnessing that she just stood and stared. Pieces of debris whistled past and several flaming objects flashed by but she ignored them, was barely even aware of them. Nor did she notice Raoul trying to pull her down.

For now her eyes had registered the next act in the terrible drama. The second Blackhawk had also obviously been hit as well. She could now see it, the Perspex windows reflecting the flames from the first one. The second machine began to spiral down, its engine coughing and the whole machine rotating and shuddering. Brief glimpses of firelight reflecting off polished metal and Perspex revealed the other two Blackhawks swerving sharply to Barbara's left as they veered away to the south, their engine noises rising, then dying away as they fled the scene.

And still it wasn't over. By now Barbara was sobbing and weeping as the absolute tragedy and reality of what she was watching swamped her. As it came spiralling down the second Blackhawk was still being shot at!

The second Blackhawk came down in a rapid spiral and crashed with a sickening crumple about fifty paces beyond the end of the runway, landing just among the trees on the far side of the first. As it struck the ground the spinning rotors whipped down and then disintegrated into flying fragments and a cloud of dust. Barbara could see the whole thing as clear as day because the burning Blackhawk near her was lighting up everything for hundreds of metres around.

"At least it landed right way up," she cried, biting her lip and then calling out, "Oh get out! Get out!"

As the dust cleared, she could see figures jumping clear or struggling to get free of the wreckage. There was no fire visible but she knew that the machine could burst into flames at any moment. Then her shock turned to stunned disbelief as she realized that the enemy were still firing. To her horror Barbara saw two of the men who had just jumped clear of the crashed Blackhawk go down as tracer bullets flashed among them.

"They are still shooting!" she shouted angrily.

Clear in the firelight she saw seven or eight men standing up in the grass at the edge of the landing strip, aiming rifles and light machine guns at the wreck. *Dags!* she thought, recognizing the dark brown tunics and funny looking pancake caps. The red flicker of muzzle flashes showed her that. To her dismay Barbara saw another survivor—an Australian soldier by his uniform, knocked down just as he got clear of the wreck. Then her blood ran cold at the shout that went up.

All the Dags flung their arms up in seeming delight and shouted some sort of war cry. Then they resumed firing.

Barbara's blood then ran hot as a pulse of white-hot fury surged through it. "That is murder!" she shouted.

Thinking, *I must stop them killing our men,* she lifted her rifle to her shoulder, aimed and pulled the trigger. Nothing happened, and another spurt of anger swept through her.

Safetycatch, you drongo! she told herself.

She flicked off the safetycatch and aimed again. The Dags were standing targets only a hundred metres away. Without further hesitation she opened fire.

The effect was instantaneous: at least two of the Dags just vanished and the others scattered and threw themselves flat. A feeling of savage exultation surged in Barbara's breast.

Got the bastards! she thought.

Then she spotted what she had been dreading: flames had burst out in the wreckage of the second Blackhawk and in their light she could see figures struggling to extricate themselves.

"We must save them!" she shouted. With that in mind she started running towards the wreck.

But the Dags were firing back! Barbara noted the winking flashes and the flashing red dots but kept firing at them as she ran, till Raoul dragged her down. Some of the shots must have come horribly close as she felt quite stunned and the vicious cracking sounds were very loud. It dawned on her that some of the shots were coming from her left, from across the airfield.

Raoul gripped her firmly and forced her down. "Bravo!" he cried, "But keep your pretty head low. Let us a bit of *le tactique* use."

At that Barbara realized how stupid she had been, and how lucky. *Tactics! Yes,* she thought foolishly. All those lessons by Major Conkey flitted through her mind. While the army cadets were not taught formal infantry minor tactics she had still absorbed quite a bit of tactical knowledge over the years. She also had the huge advantage of having been in those firefights with the Smiley People.

Raoul began shouting orders in French and the legionnaires started firing at the Dags with very controlled, aimed fire, S-Lt de Blainville directing them. But they were forced to keep ducking as shots kept whacking in from their left. S-Lt de Blainville suddenly shouted at Raoul then grabbed at him and pulled him down, just as a shot cracked close by.

Raoul swore in French and then turned to look at him, both puzzled and angry. To her dismay Barbara heard S-Lt de Blainville say, "Infra red sighting. They had a red dot on you."

Oh my God! Barbara thought. She had seen a Night Aiming Device; a 'Nad' in the jargon of the troops, demonstrated on a weekend bivouac.

How can we survive? she wondered. Then she remembered that some of the French rifles were also fitted with the equipment.

Raoul nodded. "Thanks!" he said, then turned and yelled to his men, warning them and urging them to keep down. Barbara glanced towards the other side of the airfield and saw a muzzle flash. The shot tore through the grass near her, making her cringe. There was no sign of the man who had been in the middle of the strip and she assumed he had taken cover.

Luckily the curve of the ground was such that, by keeping low, they were below most of the fire but Barbara knew that it was only a matter of time, if the troops, whoever they were, across the airstrip, hit someone.

Especially if they have night sights, she thought. She decided that the shots from the left were coming from Steyrs. *They might be Australians,* she thought bitterly.

The irony that fellow Australians might be inadvertently preventing the rescue of their own people made her squirm with intense emotion. It was more than she could endure. She could see that the flames on the second Blackhawk were spreading from the engine area at the rear of the fuselage down towards the passenger compartment.

We may have only seconds before it explodes, she thought. What it might be like when it did was being brought fiercely home to her by the scorching heat from the blazing wreck to her right front. *I must do something,* she thought desperately.

With that she sucked a big breath into her gasping, bruised chest and shouted, "Hey! You bloody Aussies! Stop shooting! We are friends over here!"

A bullet fired from there came so close it nicked her helmet, jerking her head back and making her ears ring. That got her really angry. She swore loudly then yelled, "Hey, you stupid drongos! That nearly hit me! Stop shooting at us and shoot at those bloody Dags instead. Give us some covering fire!"

At that the firing stopped. A man yelled back, "Who the hell are you?"

Barbara glanced at Raoul. "Do I tell them?" she asked.

"Yes," he replied, then grinned. "I did not realize that *Mademoiselle* sometimes used rude words," he added.

"Humpf!" snorted Barbara. She drew in another breath, had to cough as smoke got into her lungs, then tried again. "We are a French patrol,

French Foreign Legion," she shouted, adding, *"La Legion Etranger Parachutist. 2 R. E. P."*

"You should not have told them which unit," Raoul chided.

"Too bad," Barbara answered. "Anyway, I didn't say 'Marines'." Aware that she was on the edge of breaking down with emotion she again shouted across the field, "Cover us! We will attack the Dags and rescue the people in the second Blackhawk."

Back across the field came the shouted answer, "Right-o Frogs, but any tricks and we blow you away."

Raoul now gripped Barbara. "You stay here," he hissed fiercely. "Help Mendoza guard the container."

Barbara made no answer. Her mind was made up and she was enraged. As firing began again from the other side of the airstrip, this time directed at the Dags, she tensed ready. As soon as it was obvious that the Australians were indeed providing covering fire Raoul shouted and the attack began.

The French did it by leapfrogging fire and movement. Cpl Martini and Tribunga were out on the right flank of the extended line that had been formed. Then came Sgt Blomburg, and S-Lt de Blainville working as a pair, with Raoul and Cpl Fouchet in the centre and Tran and Sgt Boucher on the left. Lamertine followed them with his First Aid kit. Barbara got to her feet and moved with him, noting that Pilsudski was also moving, even though he was hunched over in pain and could only hold his rifle with one hand.

It was both terrifying and intensely exciting, but her desperate desire to get to the second helicopter over-rode these emotions. Barbara went to ground when Raoul did but it all moved so rapidly it was just a frantic blur and fleeting images. The sheer professional discipline and skill of the Frenchmen was obvious to her even under that stress. At shouted words of command one pair would double forward ten paces, covered by the other groups, Raoul directing the covering fire. This was controlled and very accurate and deadly. She saw Dag heads come up and then vanish. One at least was hit by the covering fire and she distinctly saw his odd pancake cap plucked away in a spray of brains and blood. Another Dag flung his arms in the air and went over backwards to a burst from Tran. As the attack closed to twenty-five paces two Dags stood up and were mown down by a storm of fire from the whole line.

Another Dag jumped up and tried to run. Weapons hammered on automatic and he went tumbling down. At that Raoul sprang up and punched his fist forward several times.

"Attacque! Attacque!" he screamed.

Barbara sprang to her feet, her mind concentrated on that burning helicopter. She still had enough awareness to hold her rifle ready as she forced her legs to work, ignoring the pains in her body. Her mind noted the racing Frenchmen ahead of her firing into the Dags who lay sprawled in the grass. It did not shock her and she pounded on, jumping the body of a Dag who lay flat on his back, eyes open and face covered in blood. An RPG launcher lay in the grass near him.

Then they were past the Dags and still running. Raoul began shouting and Barbara was aware that he was directing some of the groups to go past the burning helicopter to guard them in case of more Dags. He ran to the wreck, Barbara hot on his heels. As she got closer she was appalled at what she saw. The bodies of dead and wounded Australians lay scattered in the grass beside the burning wreck. Others were still inside. At least one of these was already engulfed in flames and it was so ghastly she looked away, only noting that Raoul was pointing and shouting directions to start pulling the sprawled forms towards the airfield and away from the now burning grass. He then went to the passenger compartment and leaned in to try to rescue a wounded man still strapped in his harness.

For a second Barbara paused, her whole being sickened by what she saw. Her eyes noted the flames now flaring up at the rear of the fuselage, and trickles of molten, burning plastic or paint running down to set fire to the grass. Then her gaze locked on the form of the pilot. She saw he was hanging upside down out of the cockpit door. He still had his helmet on and the door was only partly open, resting against him. His visor had slid up and she saw his face in the firelight. His mouth was opening and closing.

He is still alive, Barbara thought. *I must save him!*

Hitching her rifle sling over her right shoulder she ran over and pulled the door open, then saw that the pilot was trapped somehow by his boots. Beyond him the co-pilot was slumped in his seat, not moving. Close up the heat was intense and that, plus fear of an explosion, spurred her to haste. She leaned in and felt along the pilot's legs, noting as she did that both were twisted at odd angles and almost certainly broken.

No time for care, she thought, discarding doubts about moving casualties.

As quickly as she could she unwrapped a tangled safety harness from around one leg. The leg flopped out and she heard the pilot cry out in pain. Ignoring this she groped to find what was holding his other boot. She found it was wedged in under the seat and was unable to free it. It took her two attempts before she realized she had to lift him. In her desperation she grabbed his clothing and lifted with one hand, using the other to drag the boot out from where it was caught. For a few seconds she feared she lacked the strength but a glance over her shoulder showed no-one else able to help. They were all running away, dragging casualties behind them.

At that moment there was a 'whumpf!' near the rear of the wreck and she wet herself in terror. A sudden trickle of blazing liquid flowed down beside her. Flame flared near her hand, burning it and making her cry out in pain.

Oh my God! I must! she told herself.

With all her strength she heaved with one hand and tugged with the other. Suddenly the boot came free and caught her unawares. Lacking the strength she was unable to stop the pilot falling to the ground in a crumpled heap.

By then all she could think of was to get away from the burning wreck so, ignoring the possibility of causing more injuries, she unhooked her webbing from the door handle where it had snagged, and bent to grab at the pilot's collar. As she did she looked at his face and saw he was looking at her while grimacing in pain and shock.

"Sorry," she shouted, then seized a double handful of clothing and began walking backwards, dragging him away from the wreck.

By then she was sobbing from the overexertion and fear. It took her a real effort to pull the man the fifty paces to the gravel. As she reached it the helicopter finally erupted in flames. Luckily it did not explode. Instead the flames just seemed to suddenly engulf it. For a horrible second Barbara saw the body of the co-pilot begin to burn, then she looked away and bent over to vomit.

Someone stopped beside her to lay a wounded Australian soldier next to the pilot. It was Raoul. "Well done *Ma cheri*," he grunted.

That got Barbara's attention. She wiped her face with her sleeve and looked up to see if she needed to move the injured pilot further away. *No,* she decided. Then she glanced down to see how he was. In the firelight she clearly saw his face and received a shock.

Major Hammer, she thought, recognizing him as the pilot of the helicopter that she had flown in during the raid to capture the cattle duffers the previous December.[5] She saw that he was looking at her with a puzzled frown.

"Are you shot?" she asked.

The pilot shook his head and shuddered. "No, broken legs and a few bruises I think," he replied.

At that moment the sound of running boots thudding towards her made Barbara look up. She saw three Australian soldiers racing across the end of the airstrip towards her. They wore Austcams and cloth bush hats and their faces were daubed with camouflage cream. All three had rifles with night sights and these were gripped ready for use. Her initial reaction was relief, and she stood up next to Raoul.

He moved to meet the Australians, his rifle still held ready but not actually threatening. The leader of the three came to a halt facing Raoul, then gestured the other two to go to help beat out the fames that were now spreading from the wreck. After a quick glance at the bodies of the Dags he faced Raoul. "I am Captain Green, Australian Army. Who are you?"

"Lieutenant Raoul de Berg, French Marines," Raoul answered in English.

By then Barbara had stepped up beside Raoul, her mind in ferment. *Captain Green!* she thought. *He was the SAS officer in the HQ building when I saw that disgusting video.*

Captain Green glanced at her and frowned. "The girl with you said you were French Foreign Legion, 2 R. E. P.?"

"Some of us are," Raoul agreed.

Captain Green pointed to the nearby dead Dags. "Who are these people?"

"Dags," Raoul answered. "I hope you have men covering your side of the airfield."

"I have. Why? Are there more of them?"

At that Barbara answered. "We saw a section heading for Yaamba Lagoon just before sunset."

---

[5] Read *Barbara in the Bush* by C.R. Cummings.

Capt Green stared at Barbara. It suddenly dawned on her that he had not recognized her. *Uh oh! I should have stayed out of sight,* she thought, her anxiety level shooting up.

Raoul swung to look at her, then said in French, *"Madem.... Madelaine, go and see how Mendoza's wounds are."*

Barbara did not understand most of what he said but she did get the word Mendoza. Taking the cue she quickly turned and walked away, leaving a puzzled Capt Green staring after her. As she walked back towards the place where they had left the stretcher she realized just how foolish she had been and began to shiver with apprehension.

Oh you fool! she berated herself. *Oh! What will happen to me now?*

Chapter 39

WHAT WILL HAPPEN TO ME NOW?

As she walked slowly away through the grass Barbara heard Raoul say to Capt Green, "Quickly, bring your helicopters back to evacuate these casualties. We have secured this end of the airstrip."

She did not look back until she was well clear and then noted that Raoul was till talking to Capt Green but was signalling Cpl Fouchet to join him. She also noted that Sgt Boucher and Legionnaire Pilsudski were also walking back towards the stretcher. That cheered her as it meant that they had not been hit in the fight. Then, as they reached the stretcher and container, she realized just what a terrible risk her headstrong actions had caused.

I put all these men's lives in danger, she thought guiltily, then realized they had also left the satellite in its container quite unguarded.

Feeling wretched, yet still angry and excited, she sat down beside the stretcher. Mendoza looked at her and said something in French. All she could do was shake her head. Sgt Boucher took up a fire position facing north behind the container and he translated. "He said he was glad you are unhurt."

"I'm sorry. It was foolish of me to open fire, but I was so angry when I saw those men, those Dags, shooting at the men trying to escape from the crashed helicopter," she explained.

Sgt Boucher grunted. "That is how we all felt. But you had the courage to act and provide the lead. Well done."

Pilsudski lay down with a groan and Barbara's attention was taken up for a few minutes with adjusting his bandages. Then she checked Mendoza's. While she was doing this she heard the vibration of rotors and then the deep roar of aero engines. From the south appeared two Blackhawks. They came in low over where the SAS patrol was and settled only fifty paces from her. Australian soldiers began jumping out, weapons ready.

"SAS," Barbara commented, shielding her eyes from the dust and ash being whipped up by the downdraft.

"How can you tell?" Sgt Boucher asked.

"I know their captain, the man back there," Barbara explained, pointing to where Raoul and Capt Green still stood. She then sat and bit her knuckles while her stomach churned with apprehension as she watched the first of the injured Australians being hurried to the closest helicopter. Sgt Blomburg and Tran helped the man aboard, then hurried back to get another one.

As she watched a badly burned man being helped into the helicopter by S-Lt de Blainville and two Australians Barbara began to shake. "What do you think will happen to us now?" she asked.

Sgt Boucher cast her a sympathetic look and shrugged. "Now per'aps we become the prisoners of le Australiens." Then he gestured off into the darkness. "Maybe this is a good time for you to just quietly walk away eh? We make sure you get clear."

Into Barbara's mind came images of what that might entail. *I might have to walk fifty kilometres through the bush till I find a place where I can safely use a telephone,* she thought.

It was a daunting prospect. The previous December she had walked thirty or forty, much of it naked, to escape from the pig hunters who were trying to rape her. Just thinking about that made her shudder.

In this dry heat I will dehydrate and frazzle, she mused.

Thoughts of having to drink from more disgusting waterholes and how it would upset her stomach added to that. Then she watched Raoul talking to Capt Green and all ideas about leaving on her own were thrown out.

A new officer had arrived on the second helicopter and Barbara watched anxiously as Raoul talked to him. By then the first helicopter had been loaded and it lifted off. For a minute or so all she and the others could do was close their eyes and crouch to avoid the stinging grit and dust flung up by its rotor wash. Then it swung away to the south and around to the east.

Heading for Townsville, she decided.

By now the flames from the nearest crashed helicopter were dying down and the burning grass had all been beaten out in the area nearest to where she lay. The second crashed helicopter was still blazing fiercely, the flames lighting up the area like day. From time to time a nauseating stench would waft across to her, a disgusting mixture of burning oil, rubber, paint and worse—burnt hair and roasted flesh smells that made her stomach heave and sent her innermost thoughts into the dark corners of all her fears of death.

By the light of the burning helicopter Barbara was able to clearly see the drama now being played out. She saw Raoul turn away from the two Australian officers to talk on the radio Cpl Fouchet was holding. The Australian officers protested but Raoul ignored them. He then signalled to S-Lt de Blainville who nodded and began walking towards where Barbara and the others lay. By the time he reached them Tribunga and Cpl Martini had appeared from either side of the burning helicopter. They had their rifles at the ready and were looking warily from side to side. Their route led them through the area where the Australians were busy beating out flames and lifting wounded men to carry back.

The lift-off of the second helicopter provided a useful diversion, during which Raoul and Cpl Fouchet walked away from the two Australian officers. They reached the group lying around the container a minute later. By then S-Lt de Blainville had made sure that the legionnaires were deployed in all-round defence. As the second helicopter roared off into the night and the dust settled Barbara could see the two Australian officers looking towards her group as though undecided what to do next. The senior officer must have made some decision as he called over a signaller and began talking on a radio.

Raoul crouched in the grass near Barbara. "Well *Mademoiselle,* what is it that you wish now to do?" he asked.

"What are my options," Barbara asked.

"I think you have several," Raoul replied. "You can just go over to your own people and they can look after you."

"They won't be very pleased when they learn I have helped you," Barbara answered bitterly. "I will probably be arrested for treason or something."

Raoul shook his head. "Do not tell them. Say we forced you, we the terrible Foreign Legion brutes; that you 'ad no choice. And do not say anything about finding the satellite."

Barbara bit her lip. "What if they know you have it? What if they won't let you go?"

"Then the situation becomes very difficult," Raoul answered. "They will 'ave to take it off us by force."

That really hit home. Barbara looked over to where the Australians were and noted that several seemed to be taking up fire positions facing towards her and the French. Feeling even more upset and guilty she shook her head.

There is no way I can shoot at my own people, she thought.

With that she realized her safetycatch was still off. Feeling both embarrassed at her poor soldiering and certain she would not fire at her own people she clicked it on.

"I can't fight them," she answered.

"Nobody expects you to," Raoul answered. "If you like just give me the rifle and walk over to them now. You will be quite safe."

"Is that what you want?" Barbara asked.

Raoul shook his head. "No. But that is my personal desire. I think I 'ave fallen in love you. I want you to come with us."

Barbara glowed for a few seconds at that. "They might have recognized me," she said, again biting her lip.

"Maybe. Why do you say that?" Raoul asked.

Barbara explained about the helicopter pilot and about Capt Green. Raoul looked very thoughtful and nodded, then said, "Even so, it is per'aps best to keep them wondering. They may not be sure and we can build an alibi, or at least confuse the issue. Anyway, the helicopter pilot should be very grateful. After all, you saved his life, at great risk to your own. In fact, you saved many lives by shooting those Dags."

That really hit home. Up till then Barbara had tried not to think about possibly having killed a person, but now the awful doubt almost overwhelmed her. With a sickening insight she knew that it would now cloud her whole life; that the memory would forever haunt her. That hurt. It also made her annoyed.

"I was so angry when I saw the Dags shooting at the men trying to escape from that helicopter," she said.

Raoul placed his hand gently on her sleeve and squeezed. "Do not feel bad about what you did. If you had not shot then you would have been responsible for the deaths of many of your own countrymen. That would have been an even heavier burden to carry on your conscience."

"Weren't you going to fire?" Barbara asked.

Raoul shook his head. "*Non. le Dags* did not know we were here. I was just about to order a withdrawal; to sneak away to some other place to rendezvous with our helicopters when you stood up and began shooting."

That made Barbara even sadder but she still felt in her heart that she had done the right thing. But it hurt! And she was feeling very guilty—and sick. She felt tears trickling down her face and Raoul gently reached across and patted her.

"You can come with us," he said.

"What will happen to me then?" she asked, all sorts of fears flitting across her mind—of spending the remainder of her life in exile.

"If you want we will just arrange for you to be taken to your home," Raoul answered. "Or I'm sure France will provide a home for you." He paused and then added, "And if France will not then I will."

That really moved Barbara but her emotions received another jolt when she saw headlights driving along the airfield towards them.

"Vehicles," she said, pointing. As the headlights got closer she counted them, her dismay increasing with each one. "Three, four, five, six."

"If they are *Americaines* we may the trouble 'ave," Raoul muttered. He turned and gave urgent orders in French to his group, then grabbed the radio handset from Cpl Fouchet and began talking on the radio. After listening to the reply he turned and said, "Our helicopters are only three minutes away. Please Barbara, I do not like to pressure you, but you must decide."

By then the first of the vehicles was driving past: two Australian Land Rovers and a truck, then two ambulances. An American 'Humvee' followed, then one more Land Rover. The vehicles drove right past and were directed by an Australian soldier to stop at the end of the airstrip over on the far side beyond the Australian officers. Armed troops began to climb out and were directed to the Dag casualties. From the American Humvee climbed two American officers and an Australian. Barbara recognized the Australian lieutenant colonel. Firelight glinted on a silver star on the collar of one of the Americans.

She turned to Raoul. "I will go with you," she said.

Raoul smiled. "Good," he said. "Now the tricky bit. I am going to tell them we are leaving. If there is shooting, you just lie down and play dead until it is over please." He then called orders to his men and stood up. Barbara watched him walk towards the gathering of officers and sobbed with apprehension. The knowledge that such a splendid man might be dead in a few minutes almost stunned her into shock.

Cpl Fouchet also stood up and walked out to the edge of the airstrip. There he took two cyalume sticks from his webbing and 'cracked' them. They did not glow so Barbara assumed they must be the infra red type. He then walked out onto the open runway for a few paces and faced east, at the same time holding his arms up. Now Barbara understood what the SAS soldier had been doing.

He was guiding the helicopters in, she told herself.

Meanwhile, Raoul had reached the group of officers. By then Barbara was almost hyperventilating with anxiety. Fear that he would be killed filled her with apprehension. Knowing that Raoul had meant what he said, that the French would not give up the satellite without a fight, made her look around at the faces of the men near her. They were all lying down, bipods on rifles unfolded, hands gripping the weapons ready to fire. One look at their faces made her feel both frightened and proud.

'Composed' was the word that crossed her mind. *These men are facing death and they are doing it without flinching,* she thought. The old expression: 'Over my dead body!' came to her and she shivered, knowing that was exactly what she was seeing.

Then another shiver ran through her as the air began to gently quiver. She knew immediately what was causing it: the French helicopters. Another 'moment of truth' was upon her and she tensed ready.

I must not let them down, she thought, then amended that to 'Raoul', not 'them'.

Sgt Boucher took a firm grip on one of the straps on the container. He looked at Barbara, and said, "Just walk with us *mon petite legionnaire*. And your head you keep turned away so they do not recognize you eh?"

Barbara nodded, then swallowed and tried to calm her fluttering nerves. She also realized that her muscles had all tightened up and that she was in danger of suffering cramps. To prevent this she began to ease her legs out, rubbing at her calf muscles as she did.

And there was the first helicopter!

It arrived with a clatter of rotors and a completely different sounding engine roar. Before the rotor wash caused her to shut her eyes she quite clearly saw it was larger and of a different design to a Blackhawk. A second became visible behind it, also settling into its landing hover.

"Super Puma," Sgt Boucher shouted. He pointed and added, "Marine aircraft you understand? Navy, not *l'armee.*"

Barbara squinted and saw that there was a tricolor roundel painted on the tail of the machine and across this was a black anchor. Then she understood that Sgt Boucher was trying to take her mind off the imminent danger and her heart warmed to him. That got her going. "I will help with the stretcher," she said.

Sgt Boucher nodded and called to Cpl Lamertine. Then he stood up and signalled to the others. Barbara forced herself to get up, overcoming both fear and stiff muscles. She could see Raoul was still with the officers, who were looking agitated. Then her mind was concentrated on bending to grasp one of the stretcher handles, and on following the French words of command. Then she was struggling forward, dismayed by the weight and by her own weakness and hoping she could make it.

Ahead of her she could see a side door was open on the first helicopter and a crewman was facing out. Several armed marines jumped out and went into lying positions facing away from the helicopter. A crew man jumped out and beckoned and another became visible inside. Everything seemed to narrow down to a blurry tunnel to Barbara as she gasped for breath and prayed for strength. Instinctively she hunched as they walked in under the spinning rotor blades and she bit her lip as the strain began to tell.

Then they were there, hands reaching from inside the helicopter to take the stretcher handles from her. As she was pushed from behind she resisted and looked around. The container was close behind.

If there is going to be shooting, it will be now, she thought.

Sgt Boucher was shouting in her ear to get in but now worry about Raoul dominated her thoughts. She shook her head and turned to look for him. To her dismay she saw Australian soldiers with rifles running to spread out in a long line, lying down and aiming towards the helicopters.

Where is Raoul? she wondered anxiously.

Then she saw him. He just stepped back a pace from the group of officers and drew himself up to attention and saluted, then did an about turn as though on the parade ground and began walking towards her.

Will they stop him? she asked herself.

While she stood, staring with gritty eyes at the drama, she was aware that people and equipment were being quickly loaded into the helicopter.

To her enormous relief the Australian soldiers made no move to stop Raoul, just looking up at him as he passed. Now she gave in to Sgt Boucher's urgent tugging and allowed herself to be helped up into the helicopter. A crewman in flying suit and visored helmet took her arm and led her to a bench seat along the far side. She was stopped by Sgt Blomburg, who made gestures indicating she should take off her webbing. He took the rifle off her, checked it was on 'safe', then handed it to a seated soldier on the other side. With a feeling of relief Barbara slumped wearily into the seat, uncomfortably aware she still had her webbing on.

Hands groped around her to pull seat belt straps clear and to buckle up her harness and it was only when she saw the look of surprise on the crewman's face that she realized he had not known she was a girl. By then she could not have cared where his hands were. She was just glad to be in that helicopter. She was even more relieved when Raoul clambered in and sat down beside her. The marines outside began throwing themselves in and even as they did she heard the engine noise rise and that got her all frightened again.

What if we get shot down too? she thought, horrifying images of the roasting bodies in the earlier wrecks filling her terrified mind.

As the last marine scrambled in the helicopter began to lift off. The crewman leaned out to watch and through the open doorway Barbara saw the ground recede, then the glowing red embers of the first helicopter. Seeing that intensified her fears and she gripped her seat belt and Raoul's arm.

Now! If they are going to shoot, it will be now! she thought.

Across the open doorway passed the sight of the second wrecked Blackhawk. It was still burning and the horrific images of it being struck by the rocket propelled grenade and then exploding and spinning down flooded her mind. She tensed in fear. Suddenly the helicopter tilted and she cried out in fright. Raoul put his arm around her and held her tightly.

There was no shattering bang, no sickening lurch. Instead the helicopter levelled out and flew on. Dark bush and treetops showed through the open doorway before the crewman slid it shut. An interior light came on. In its dull red glow Barbara saw two medics or doctors at work on Mendoza. Already they had cut away half his clothing and inserted drips in his arm. Beyond them, being secured by the crewman and Sgt Boucher, was the container.

We made it, she thought.

Suddenly it was all too much for her. She began to sob and shiver. Raoul hugged her and did his best to comfort her but she was now so overwrought that all she could do was shake uncontrollably and weep. There was still just sufficient awareness for her to experience fear when the helicopter went up or down and when it again tilted sharply as it swung to port again. Her tired mind managed to note that they were flying very low, just above the tree tops and well below the tops of the hills.

After half an hour Barbara had wept herself dry and the shaking had reduced to spasms of shuddering from time to time. Tired muscles began to cramp and her whole body seemed to be one huge ache. As she regained self-control Barbara put her arm around Raoul's shoulder and rested her head on it. He kept stroking and holding her, which she found very reassuring.

When the helicopter again swung sharply to port she lifted her head. "Sorry about that," she said. "I'm a bit worn out."

"You 'ave done magnificently," Raoul answered, smiling down at her.

"Where are we going?" Barbara asked.

"To my ship," Raoul answered.

"We are going south," Barbara commented.

Raoul squeezed her and smiled. "Ah! You see? Even when you are in the tears your brain it keeps track of direction. Not quite south. More like southeast. We must avoid the coastal radars and the *Americaine* ships."

Barbara thought about that for a moment, then asked the question that was now bothering her most.

"What will happen to me? How will you get me home?"

Chapter 40

HARD DECISIONS

R aoul smiled and hugged her.

Then he said, "We 'ave our ways. It will mostly depend on you, on what you want."

The options crowded each other in Barbara's mind: go home? Or go with Raoul? Or just go to some French territory? And maybe change her name and have to live with a false identity?

I might have to do that anyway, she thought unhappily, biting her lip. *If the Dags come after me for revenge.*

Then she began to weep as the awful necessity to decide overwhelmed her. Images of all that she would have to give up and leave behind now added to her misery: her father, her friends, the cadets, normal life...

Poor Roger, she thought. *He doesn't even know where I am.*

That got her thinking about Raoul and that made her feel very guilty. It also made her wonder if he was the man for her. She had certainly come to admire and respect him over the last few days.

But even so.... I don't really know him at all, she thought.

But it was very comforting to cling to him in her distress. He gently hugged and, to her great relief, did not press her for a decision. That allowed her to calm down a bit and presently her sobbing eased and sheer exhaustion took over. She fell into a deep sleep.

Barbara came back to consciousness from a long way down, from a dark pit of despair and death full of fire and burning bodies. With an immense effort she opened her eyes and blinked. Bright light hurt, even through sleep-gummed eyelids. For a few moments she did not comprehend what she was seeing, or where she was. Then it all came back to her and she realized she was still in the French helicopter but the motion was different. Bright interior lights were on and a cool wind was blowing in the open door, through which people were climbing in.

Then she saw the stretcher wheeled up to the door and enough of the French being spoken made it through her sleep-fuddled brain for her to understand that it was for her. The fact that people were standing around outside the door, or walking past, told her that the helicopter had landed and then she saw that it was on the flight deck of a ship.

"I'm alright," she muttered as she struggled to sit up.

Raoul was still holding her but was trying to slip his arms under her body to pick her up. "You can relax," he said. "We 'ave arrived."

With that he scooped her up and carried her to the door where hands gently but firmly guided her down onto the stretcher. That confused and upset Barbara. She tried to sit up and take her webbing off but other hands whisked it clear and away. Then she tried to get off the stretcher but was firmly held down. Above her head she noted that the rotors were visible, slowly rotating.

The engines have been turned off, she thought.

She saw Raoul jump down and then the stretcher was wheeled past the side of the helicopter. Anxious that she not be separated from Raoul, she lifted her head, noting a second stretcher being loaded with Mendoza. Behind the helicopter she had just been unloaded from she saw a second one being secured to the flight deck by men wearing bright coloured vests and white helmets. And there was Raoul, walking beside her and smiling down.

Barbara relaxed and lay back, half-blinded by the glare of a row of bright floodlights that shone down from the huge square block of superstructure ahead. A large door was open, leading into a brightly lit, white-painted hangar, the sides of which were festooned with the usual collection of tools, fire fighting equipment, lockers and pipes.

She was wheeled quickly through this and along a companionway. Along the way numerous men, most in blue work overalls, but some in camouflage uniforms, stared curiously at her. By then she was too tired to care. Nor was she too much concerned when she found herself in what could only be the ship's sick bay or hospital. Smiling men in pale green hospital clothing and surgical masks looked down at her.

Raoul took her hand. "I must a report make to the admiral," he explained. "I will leave you here with the doctor so they can look after you. Do not worry, you will be safe and I will see you again soon."

This time Barbara did feel safe. The memory of being in a similar situation on the American ship came to her by contrast. She smiled and nodded.

"Alright. Is this your ship?"

Raoul nodded. "*Oui.* I mean yes. The French Naval Ship *Mistral.* She is the amphibious assault ship; a Landing Ship Dock. Now, I must go." He then said something in French to the medical people and they all laughed and nodded, smiling at Barbara.

She did not want him to leave but knew it had to be so, so she tried to relax. The medics helped her to a seat and the doctor began testing—the usual pulse, heart rate, blood pressure stuff. The doctor was a pleasant, cheerful young man in his twenties and he chatted in quite good English while he did this. He questioned her about her experiences and Barbara assured him she was alright, just thirsty and very tired.

The doctor nodded, apparently satisfied and said, "We have the orders to treat you very well. You are *un heroine.* And my good friend *Lieutenant* de Berg, he say that you are very special—though I think more to him than to France eh?" At that he winked and Barbara blushed with pleasure.

"I would like a bath and change of clothes," she said, by way of changing the conversation.

"Of course, but first a drink." the doctor replied.

Barbara was given a glass of refreshingly cool and sweet cordial, then helped to a shower. After being cautioned about falling over or fainting she was handed soap and towel and some pyjamas. Her webbing was dropped in the corner and the door closed. Very slowly, with seemingly every sore muscle in her battered body stretching in protest, she eased herself onto a bench seat. For a few minutes she could only sit, easing cramps and tight muscles, until she was able to bend down and unlace her boots. Pulling them off was an effort almost beyond her.

Then she stood to undress. As she did a used brass cartridge case fell with a tinkle onto the deck. For a few moments she could only stare at it as the horrible memories flooded back.

Very slowly she bent down and picked it up, then gripped it tightly in her hand. The cordite smell was enough to make her tremble and feel sick. Her eyes searched for a rubbish bin but it was on the others side of the cabin. Unable to explain to herself why she wanted to keep the thing she bent and slid it into the pocket of her trousers.

In the bright light of the cabin she saw that her trousers were absolutely filthy and were torn and pocked with burn marks.

How will I ever explain them to Major Conkey? she wondered. It was that thought that formed her decision. *I want to go home,* she told herself.

Still debating options with herself, but feeling confident that was what she wanted, she continued to undress. Seeing her body shocked her. It seemed to be just one mass of bruises, scratches and welts.

Heavens, I've taken a battering! she thought ruefully.

With a groan she stood up and limped to the shower recess and turned on the taps, all the while clinging to the hand rail there as the ship rolled.

Or is it me going to faint? she wondered.

That hot shower was to stay in Barbara's memory for the rest of her life. Just standing was painful as sore muscles protested and her worn out body shivered with reaction. Several times she felt dizzy and had to hold the railing beside her to stop herself falling over. But it was still bliss and she savoured the easing and cleanliness. The soap stung her chafing and scratches but she ignored that as trivia amid all her other pains and fears.

After the shower she dried her hair and brushed it with a brush she was loaned. Then, dressed in the pyjamas, she hobbled back out to the sick bay. Within seconds she had been whisked into a bed and tucked in. For half an hour she lay there, taking sips of cold cordial and talking to the French medics about France and the ship.

All the while Barbara's anxiety had been growing and despite her extreme tiredness and continual bouts of shivering she remained awake, wondering what would become of her. It was a real relief to see Raoul come back in. Now he was wearing a clean uniform and had obviously also showered and spruced up. On his head was a dark green beret with a gold badge. With him were two senior naval officers and an older marine with a real cluster of gold stripes on his rank badge.

Two stripes, then a gap and then three more, Barbara counted, wondering if her vision was going fuzzy.

Raoul introduced them: an Admiral, the ship's captain and a colonel of marines. Barbara promptly forgot their names but struggled to sit up. The admiral spoke very good English and told her that Raoul had given her glowing praise.

"Not just for guiding him to the satellite," the admiral added, "For he says that without you the patrol would have failed in its mission. He cites a dozen examples where your actions or advice saved them. He says you used a rifle to save his life, and that you rescued a wounded legionnaire under fire. *Mademoiselle,* I am very impressed. France is very grateful to you."

At that Barbara blushed with modesty. She shrugged and smiled and felt tears prickle again.

The admiral then said, "We must now the decision make about your future. You understand your options?"

Barbara nodded and listed them, then said firmly, "I would like to go home please."

Raoul looked concerned. "Are you sure Barbara?" he asked. "You could be in danger."

"I don't care," Barbara replied firmly. "I am going to get on with my life. I would like to be taken back to Australia, and as quickly as possible."

"Why? What is the hurry?" Raoul answered.

"Because school starts on Monday," Barbara replied.

Raoul shook his head, "But surely, a few days of school do not matter."

Barbara pressed her lips together. "Yes they do. I need to start as though nothing has happened. If I am away it will be harder to explain."

The admiral agreed. "*Mademoiselle* is correct," he said. "If she is to build her alibi she must return to her normal life as quickly, and as unobtrusively, as she can."

Raoul still wasn't convinced. "But what if those Australian officers recognized her? She might be punished somehow."

The admiral shook his head. "I doubt it. Australia is not some tin pot dictatorship. It is a civilized democracy ruled by law. And there is already the Class A storm *diplomatique* brewing, but it is more *l'Dags* that are the focus than us. We will do what we can. If she is persecuted by her own people she may appeal to France."

"But the Dags might seek revenge," Raoul persisted.

Once again the admiral disagreed. "I do not think so. They will not know she was involved unless we let it slip, and I think they have many bigger problems anyway." He turned to Barbara. "*Mademoiselle* understands that she must never speak of this to her friends and associates?"

Barbara nodded, but then bit her lip and said, "Sorry, but I must tell my father, and Major Conkey."

"Major Conkey?" the admiral queried.

"The OC of my cadet company."

"Must he know?" the admiral asked. "I advise against it. Can he be trusted."

That settled it for Barbara. "Yes, now please take me home."

The admiral nodded. "Alright. We will arrange it. Be ready to go in half an hour." He gave some orders in French and then left the cabin. Raoul seated himself beside Barbara and asked how she was and then tried to talk her out of her decision. That only made her more stubborn. She was scared and full of fears and doubts but was sure she preferred to face the perils with her friends and family than with strangers in a foreign land.

Preparations went ahead. Barbara was given a set of clothes: jeans and T-shirt and some joggers. A plastic spray jacket was added. There was then a heated argument about what to do with her webbing and uniform.

"I want them," Barbara insisted.

"But how will you explain their condition?" Raoul queried, plainly annoyed at her stubbornness.

"I will. Now give them to me," Barbara insisted. She refused to have them throw away so she was handed a carry bag and a medical orderly stuffed her boots, webbing and soiled uniform and underwear into it. It was then zipped up.

"It is silly!" Raoul cried in exasperation. "It may be the evidence to get you into trouble."

"Too bad! I am taking it home with me," she replied. In her tiredness and emotional state, she was snappy and irritable.

She was aware of that, but could not stop herself. She was now expecting to be parted from Raoul and that added to her distress. Anticipating a tearful farewell she became very tense and weepy.

Instead he stayed with her when she was led back out to the flight deck. In the hangar she found all the other unwounded patrol members lined up, washed and neat in clean uniforms. The legionnaires, she noted wore their green berets with the silver winged badge. Sgt Boucher had a green beret with the same gold anchor badge as Raoul. He smiled at her and she hugged him.

As he released her he said, "You take care *mon petite*. Do not that lieutenant trust. He is *un hom*. You understand?"

Barbara could only cry and laugh at the same time. "After what I've just been through men don't bother me that much anymore. It is you who must take care. Thank you for your help." She leaned forward and kissed him.

At this S-Lt de Blainville muttered, "What about me!"

So Barbara gave them all a kiss on the cheek and found she could hardly see for tears. These threatened to become a flood when Sgt Blomburg added, "You are the great soldier *Mademoiselle.* Do not be tormented by what you had to do. You have saved many lives. We thank you, and we wish you well, and if you ever need help, you call on us eh? Call on *le Legion Etrangere.*"

Sgt Blomburg then drew himself up and saluted her. That really did threaten to bring Barbara undone emotionally but she managed to straighten up and return the salute, only realizing later that she was not in uniform. Obviously none of the others saw anything odd in this as they all grinned and saluted back. Raoul then took her arm and led her on across the hangar.

After wiping her eyes and calming herself with some deep breaths Barbara looked at the other people present. The admiral, captain and colonel were all there and they shook hands and thanked her again. This got her emotions working again so she nodded and deliberately looked around to calm herself. Outside she saw it was still dark, although she had no idea what time it was. The same helicopter was warming up its engines. A second one lifted off as she emerged onto the open flight deck. A third helicopter was just visible by its lights, flying back and forth some way astern of the ship.

Barbara and Raoul were led out to the helicopter and climbed aboard. They were fitted with lifejackets, then strapped in to seats. The helicopter lifted off a minute later. Barbara squirmed to become comfortable, expecting a long flight, so was quite surprised when a crewman signalled for her to undo her seat belt. She noted the helicopter was not climbing but was only moving slowly sideways. She was even more surprised when the crewman held out a safety harness attached to a steel wire cable. Helped by Raoul she was buckled into this.

"What is happening?" she shouted.

"We are being transferred to a submarine," Raoul explained, pointing down.

Barbara was astonished and then deeply anxious. It was so unexpected. "I thought we would go all the way by helicopter," she said, not wanting to go in a submarine at all.

Raoul shook his head and shouted above the engine noise, "Not possible. The Americans, they are now tracking us. They 'ave the radar plane circling and we were escorted back by two of their fighter planes when we returned. They will be still around. If we go by helicopter we will be tracked all the way and you will be arrested when we land. We may as well just go to the airport and hand you over to the police."

That was all worrying news to Barbara, but still did not want to make her risk her life by dangling from a thin wire rope. But she had no time to get worked up as she was at once moved to the door and urged to let go of the door frame. Below her she saw the dark, black shape of the submarine, it hull outlined by the white froth of its wake. The next moment she was dangling on the winch wire, finding that almost more frightening than the parachute jump.

I've had enough thrills to last a lifetime, she told herself as men on the wet deck of the submarine reached up to grab her legs and guide her down.

Within a few seconds they had released the harness and half-carried her to a hatchway. The deck was wet but felt rough and not at all slippery. The cold wind from the helicopter rotors was more of a bother and she began to shiver.

As she was urged down the hatchway Barbara noted with surprise that the submarine was very close alongside the Landing Ship. The Landing Ship towered over them; huge and well lit. Between the two vessels the water surged and boiled and drops of cold spray struck her face, helping her to keep moving.

At the bottom of a shiny steel ladder smiling faces helped her along a well lit but fairly narrow passageway. There were those peculiar oval-shaped watertight doors to climb through before she arrived in a cabin with bench seats and a table. Here she was greeted by a man who introduced himself as the captain of the submarine *Circe*.

A smiling *matelot* in a striped blue and white jersey placed her carry bag on the table and then Raoul arrived, also carrying a small kitbag. There were handshakes all round and Barbara was then invited out to the control room. During all this the relief at safely being winched down was being replaced by another fear. This was swiftly building and now she had to face that as well—the submarine was diving.

Can I face that? she wondered.

A terrible feeling of claustrophobia began to tighten her chest. It gripped her so much she found she was having trouble breathing. But she was unable to tell when they were underwater. It all went so smoothly and quietly she began to relax, although the anxious feeling of being trapped remained.

Raoul kept smiling and seemed to take it all in his stride. The French sailors all just acted calm and efficient. Then the captain came over and introduced another officer as the navigator. "We must the best place to land you decide," he said.

Barbara thought about that and finally selected Ellis Beach. Raoul agreed with this decision and Barbara watched as the navigator began calculating on the chart. With considerable surprise she saw that they were well out to sea; hundreds of kilometres out beyond the Great Barrier Reef, and that they were east of Mackay.

The captain pointed to the area off Townsville on the chart and said, "*Mademoiselle* it was, so I am told, who located the American Task Force for us?"

Barbara nodded and described how she had been taken out to the USS WASP, but again without mentioning being nude. On describing the displays in the control room all the Frenchmen nodded knowingly and smiled. "They all just thought I was a silly little girl," she explained. She then learned that her information had been vital in helping the French to plan their operation, allowing them to fool the Americans into thinking they were sailing away, but then to slip quickly back into helicopter range. It was also explained to her that the reason for the submarine being so close to the Landing Ship, and for the other helicopters being airborne and moving about in close proximity, had been to mask the submarine's radar signature when it surfaced.

"The Americans, they have a maritime surveillance plane, all radar and magnetic anomaly detectors and so on, circling the area. Also they have a sub in the area, a nuclear-powered SSN—a hunter-killer sub you understand. We must dodge them and then it will be easier," the submarine captain explained.

Once the plan was agreed on Barbara was taken back to the wardroom and given a hot coffee. By then she was almost asleep on her feet. After the drink and a visit to the toilet she was shown into a small cabin. Very gingerly she lay down and stretched out her sore limbs. The main light was switched off, leaving only dim floor lighting. With a sigh she lay back. Apart from the hum of motors it was all very quiet.

For a while she had to control rising panic at the thought of being trapped underwater, but she argued sternly with herself.

Don't be silly. We are not at war with America. They won't sink a French submarine.

But then all those movies where such things did happen came to mind and her fears returned as she pictured the two submarines in a deadly game of underwater hide-and-seek. Luckily exhaustion again took over and she slid into a deep, dreamless sleep.

It was ten hours later that she woke. The insistent need to do a pee was what roused her. Very gingerly she eased her cramped and stiff limbs and climbed down to the deck. As she emerged from the cabin a matelot, obviously posted as sentry, helped her to the toilet, then went to inform the captain. He and Raoul were waiting when she re-emerged. They both asked how she was with genuine concern.

Would *Mademoiselle* like some food? she was asked. Yes, *Mademoiselle* would! Barbara was ravenous. She was helped to the wardroom where she met more of the submarine's officers (she was surprised there were so many). A steward then placed a menu card in front of her.

"Oh drat!" she snorted after studying the writing with little result. "It is just like all the fancy restaurants and hotels. They always print the menu in French."

At that the officers all burst out laughing and the captain answered, "But of course! We French are the world's best cooks."

Raoul came to her rescue, translating the menu. And the captain was right—the food was excellent. Barbara ate with real enjoyment and soon felt much better. Drink after drink also went down and she became quite bloated and content.

"Where are we now?" she asked.

They took her to the control room and showed her on an electronic display. To her astonishment she saw the submarine was now close in to the Great Barrier Reef just north of Cairns.

"But... but that is hundreds of kilometres from where we were when I went to bed," she gasped.

The captain smiled. "This submarine, it can go very fast underwater. It is no secret. She does at least fifty kilometres in the hour, and *Mademoiselle* was asleep for ten hours. That is five hundred kilometres."

"Don't you have to come up to get air and recharge batteries and things?" Barbara asked, dimly remembering movies she had seen (but not paid much attention to).

The captain shook his head. "*Non.* This is the nuclear-powered submarine. She can stay underwater for months if need be. We could go all the way back to France if we had to, without once surfacing."

"How do you stand it?" she wondered aloud.

They explained to her how men had to be selected of the right temperament for the conditions, then how they kept themselves fit and sane by exercise, hobbies and so on. While they talked another worrying thought came to Barbara.

"What about the American submarine, is it chasing us?"

Heads shook. "We have not it once detected. We think it is still trailing the surface ships east towards *Caledonie Nouveau.*"

"And the aeroplane?"

"We have not detected it for several hours. We can surface safely."

"How do I get ashore?" Barbara asked.

"By a small rubber boat," the captain answered.

And after dark that is how she did. She was given a diver's wet suit to get into (and felt very self-conscious about how she looked when she put it on, as all her female bulges seemed to be accentuated). A spray jacket and lifejacket were added and she was then led up on deck after the submarine surfaced. Up there all she could see in the darkness was moonlight glittering on wave tops.

On deck were a team of sailors and marines who quickly inflated quite a large inflatable boat made of black rubber or plastic. This had two powerful outboard engines attached to the stern. Barbara noted that there were seats with lockers under them. Three armed sailors, also dressed in diving suits, climbed aboard and then Raoul, also dressed for the trip, helped her to get in. Her kit bag was handed in and placed in a locker.

"How does the boat get into the water?" Barbara asked, looking anxiously at the dark waves surging close alongside.

"The submarine, it goes from under us," Raoul explained.

And it did. Before Barbara had time to get anxious the sailors still on deck vanished down the hatchway and clamped it shut, then compressed air bubbled and spurted from holes along the sides of the deck. The waves quickly washed in and suddenly the boat was afloat and the men were paddling furiously to keep it upright and to get it clear of the turbulence. The black shape of the conning tower slid downwards and, within seconds, was gone.

Suddenly the rubber boat was alone on the vastness of the ocean. Barbara had never in her life been out of sight of land in a small boat, much less one with only a few centimetres of freeboard, so cold fear began to chill her. The fear grew as the waves seemed to tower higher than the boat, which bobbed and rocked alarmingly while the sailors worked on starting the engines.

How on earth will they ever be able to find their way inshore? Barbara wondered. *And what will happen to me when we get there?*

Chapter 41

FAREWELL?

Once the outboard motors were started and engaged the whole motion of the rubber boat changed. It began to dash forward, thumping across the waves at astonishing speed. Spray was punched up at almost every second minute and cold wetness drenched Barbara, making her very glad of the wet suit and jacket. To avoid the spray she hunched low and watched, somewhat less fearfully, as the men balanced the craft to keep its round bow up. After that it became easier and after a time the waves began to appear less threatening.

The navigation, Barbara noted, was being done by GPS. Two of the men scanned ahead with binoculars and night vision equipment. The night was not that dark, nor was the air cold, but being continually wet soon had Barbara shivering. Water sloshed about the bottom of the boat, chilling her feet. From time to time one of the sailors would bail it out. By the time an hour had gone by Barbara was cold and bored.

She sat holding on as the boat continued to bucket across the waves. The experience became wearing and chilling. Bouts of shivering became more frequent and she had to continually change her grip and ease her cramped fingers and arms. Her legs went cold and stiff and, when she tried to ease them, over-worked muscles cramped with agonizing pains.

The boat came in through the Great Barrier Reef via one of the many gaps between two reefs. Progress immediately became smoother in the calmer water. After another hour Raoul pointed to a dim, irregular black line on the horizon. "The coast," he explained.

Seeing that line of mountains caused Barbara very mixed feelings. There were all the horrifying images of the Dags being shot dead by the Americans on the beach, mingled with memories of cadet exercises up in the jungle. Above all it was the nearness of home that dominated and she became more and more anxious as they drew closer to the land. It was the last hour that seemed to drag on the most. By the time they neared the shore Barbara was stiff and shivering. Exhaustion again threatened to overwhelm her.

With amazing abruptness lights began to twinkle along the base of the black mass of mountains. When she realized they were the lights of the coastal suburbs Barbara began to quietly cry. She realized they were now only a few kilometres out. By careful thinking she was able to identify the northern beaches: Machans, Holloways, Yorkeys Knob, Palm, Clifton. To the right of them the coastline became dark, lit only by a tiny cluster that was Ellis Beach, and by the flicker of moving headlights on cars using the Cook Highway.

Now the speed was reduced and they made several detours to avoid small boats and a fishing trawler. That irked Barbara, who became more and more impatient to get ashore.

I just want it to all be over! she thought.

There was also tension building over what to say to Raoul. She knew he was going to ask if he could see her again. Part of her wanted to shout yes, to explore their attraction to see if it was true love. The other part shied away, afraid of becoming seriously involved.

He will always want to be off soldiering in exotic locations, she thought. That got her wondering what being married to a Frenchman might be like. *Could I adapt to living in a foreign country?* she wondered.

For the last half-hour the boat puttered slowly in, making barely any splashing or bow wave. Over the last few hundred metres weapons were taken out of a locker and cocked, then aimed at the shoreline. This was scanned carefully with night vision equipment. Satisfied that all was safe they quietly motored in to the deserted beach. Their landing point was about half a kilometre south of the lights of the Ellis Beach caravan park.

Finally the boat slid to a standstill in the gentle surf. A sailor armed with an automatic weapon sprang out and scurried up the beach to take up a fire position. A second sailor jumped out and held the boat steady in the shallows. The third throttled the motors back, then sat scanning to seaward with binoculars. Raoul stood up and held out his hand. Barbara took it and climbed stiffly to her feet. So frozen up was she that she could hardly move. Groaning softly she clambered awkwardly over the side into knee deep water. The coldness of it woke her up but the feel of sand under her feet lifted her spirits.

Home, she thought. *Or almost.*

Raoul gestured to walk up the beach. "You will need to change," he explained, handing her a bundle of clothing.

"Are you coming with me?" Barbara asked.

Raoul shook his head. "*Non*. I go back to the submarine."

Barbara was both relieved and saddened by that. "I would like my uniform and webbing please," she replied, trying hard to keep the tremor out of her voice.

"I still think you should dispose of it," Raoul answered. "It could cause you great harm."

That nettled Barbara. "I'll take that risk. Please get it for me," she said, adding, "And don't you look at me with those night vision sights while I change!"

"I would not dream of doing such a thing!" Raoul answered with a chuckle.

He made his way back to the boat while Barbara walked slowly up the beach. She went past the armed sailor, who nodded to her but kept scanning the darkness under the trees backing the beach with his night vision sights. After finding a thick tree trunk to hide behind Barbara set about stripping off the wet suit. To her dismay she found she lacked the strength. Her fingers were too stiff and cold and her muscles all seemed to have given up. All she could do was stand there trembling until Raoul returned.

"Help me!" she whispered.

He did, but not without hugging her first. With his help she managed to get the suit off. Then he very tactfully turned his back and waited. Hotly aware of her nakedness and of Raoul's proximity Barbara leaned on a coconut tree to dry herself. Knowing how irritating sand in the pants could be she very carefully dusted her feet before pulling on the jeans. Then an imp seemed to seize her. For a moment she stood holding the shirt.

Then she shook her head. *Not now,* she told herself. *Don't stress yourself too much—or give him the wrong ideas too soon either!* She slipped the T-shirt on and tugged it down, noting how well it displayed her breasts.

Raoul called softly over his shoulder, "Are you ready yet?"

"Almost," Barbara answered, taking several deep breaths to compose herself for a tearful farewell.

"It is not that I personally want to go," Raoul explained, turning and walking back to her. "It is the situation. These men must get safely back to their submarine by daylight. It would not be nice to have yet another diplomatic incident."

"You can go," Barbara said stiffly. "I can phone for someone to pick me up."

Raoul seemed to stiffen in the darkness. "Am I dismissed so soon? I had hoped for a better farewell."

At the tone of his voice Barbara's defences crumbled. She flung herself into his arms and kissed him. "I'm sorry. I don't want you to go at all," she cried.

They kissed again. His hands caressed her back and then her buttocks. Sensations suggesting that liquid fire was flowing through her veins heated her. She trembled. Raoul kissed, hugged and kissed again. Then he held her tight and said, "You are shivering. Are you cold?"

Barbara nodded. "Cold and a bit sick," she replied. "But you are warming me up."

"I would like very much to do that," he said fervently.

That earned him more kisses and hugs. By this time Barbara was crying and clinging to him. Waves of urgent desire flooded through her.

Oh yes! I think he might be the one, she told herself, wishing she could stay with him forever.

Raoul kissed her neck and nibbled her ears, sending waves of shivering through her. He whispered, "May I see you again?"

"I want that," Barbara agreed. But then a horrible thought came to her. "But will you be able to get back into Australia?"

"Legally you mean? Possibly. But if not, then you may come to me. We could have a holiday in Noumea or in Tahiti. I will pay for it," he said.

Images of girls in grass skirts dancing under palm trees on a tropical beach came to Barbara. Then she gave a wry smile.

Cairns is just as tropical—and here we are under a palm tree on a tropical beach already, she thought.

She said, "I would like that—if Daddy will allow it."

Raoul hugged her tightly. "I will on him use all my charm," he joked.

"No, save most of it for me," Barbara answered, trying to make light of the pain now filling her chest.

"May I write, or phone?" Raoul asked.

"Of course," Barbara answered. Then another awful thought came to her. "But what if the security people are still tapping my phone or open my mail?"

"You are becoming paranoid," Raoul answered. "The incident is over. You will soon be forgotten, and, even if you aren't, few governments would have the resources to spend on such a thing without good reason. But you may be right, so, give me the address of a trusted friend to whom I may address your letters."

For a few seconds Barbara's mind raced, deciding who she could trust. Then she named Fiona and gave her address. Raoul mumbled it twice to memorize it, then said, "I must go."

"I know. Kiss me again please," Barbara answered.

They kissed and caressed each other and she clung on, her eyes misted with tears until he firmly but gently disengaged himself. With one last kiss he turned and strode away down the beach, calling in the sentry as he went. Through a blur of tears Barbara stood and watched him help push the rubber boat back through the small waves. A few minutes later it was gone, swallowed up by the blackness. For some time she stood there, shaking and upset. The coconut tree was needed to help her remain standing.

When she had cried herself dry she realized she was trembling with exhaustion and cold. What would have normally been a balmy sea breeze was enough to chill her.

I had better organize a lift home, she thought. *But how, and with whom?*

Picking up her kit bag she began trudging along the beach towards the caravan park, sure there would be a public phone there. Even walking slowly on the beach she found hard going. Several times she hefted her kitbag to the other shoulder or stopped and put it down. As she walked her mind was busy with how to get home.

Someone I can trust not to ever let slip this happened, she decided.

Through her mind she ticked off the list of possible candidates: her father, Willy, Roger, Fiona, Lofty, CSM Sheehan.

Not Dad. The security people will be watching our place and listening to the phone. I've got to sneak back unnoticed and then pretend I have never been away, Barbara reasoned.

For a couple of minutes she paused at the edge of the caravan park and considered dumping her cadet gear and uniform.

Raoul might be right. The police might find it and I will have trouble explaining it, she told herself.

"And how will I ever explain what happened to it to Major Conkey?" she muttered. Then she knew who it must be. It had to be Major Conkey. "I must tell him the truth. I can trust him, and, if he thinks I should, I will tell the authorities and take my medicine."

And there was her answer: Major Conkey. *I might get him into trouble,* she worried, but he seemed like the best option.

Having decided that Barbara walked quickly into the caravan park in search of a phone booth. There was one but she had no money. Nor was there anyone in sight.

It must be after midnight, she decided. That almost made her change her plan, not wanting to get Major Conkey out of bed, or upset his family. *I don't want his wife worrying about me!* she thought, aware that had happened in the past.

Then it came to her: *Dad's mobile phone! Have I still got it?*

With fingers that hardly functioned she struggled to unzip the bag. Her first fumbling attempts failed and left her shaking and in tears. For a couple of minutes she knelt and shivered. But she knew she must act or collapse. With an effort of willpower she dug out items of clothing and searched the pockets. Then she remembered—her webbing.

I put it in my right basic pouch, she told herself.

And there it was. With a gasp of relief her fingers closed on it. Still trembling so much she could hardly work the function buttons, she dialled Major Conkey's number. Then she stood there biting her lip with anxiety as the dial tone rang in her ear. It went on and on and she decided he wasn't home, or wasn't going to answer.

Suddenly, he answered. "Yes, hello. Who is speaking please?"

Barbara sobbed with relief. "Sir! Bar... Barb.... Barbara. Can you (sob)... could you please (sob) come and get me?"

"Barbara! Where are you? Are you in trouble?" Major Conkey asked.

In the background Barbara heard a woman ask, "Who? Oh her! What does she want at this time of night?"

Barbara choked up, and said, "Yes sir. Oh please! I am at the Ellis Beach kiosk. Can you please give me a lift home?"

"Why me? Why not your father?" Major Conkey asked.

"I'm in trouble sir, and I don't want him involved," Barbara answered.

"In trouble? What sort of trouble?" Major Conkey asked.

Barbara felt like slumping to the ground she was so drained. "Please sir, can you pick me up?"

"Yes, but what is going on?" Major Conkey asked.

"It is a long story. I will explain when you get here," Barbara answered. "Please trust me. It is very important."

"Alright. But I will be half an hour or more," Major Conkey answered. He then arranged the location and Barbara heard him talking to his wife as he hung up.

Shaking with fatigue and relief Barbara pocketed the phone and knelt to repack her kitbag. Then she found she could not stand. For several minutes she crouched there, cramped and exhausted until the spasms passed. With an effort she struggled to her feet and picked up her kitbag, then set out to walk to the kiosk. That was only a few hundred metres but was further than she remembered and she feared she might not make it. When she got there she sat down slowly with her back to a tree at the top of the beach and waited.

"Barbara! Oh my God! What has happened? Are you alright?"

Barbara heard this through a fuzz of exhausted sleep. With what seemed like an immense effort of will she roused herself. It was Major Conkey. Relief surged through her and she mumbled, "I'm alright sir. Please just take me home."

"Have you been hurt? Do you need a doctor? An ambulance? Have you been...," Major Conkey asked.

Barbara realized she was lying on the sand. It was still dark and the sound of waves breaking nearby told her she was still at Ellis Beach. She tried to sit up and speak but groaned instead as sore muscles protested.

"No sir. I haven't been. I'm alright. Please take me home. I will explain. No doctors, no... secret, must keep it secret," she babbled.

She tried to stand but felt too weak. Major Conkey grabbed her and then scooped her up. Barbara made feeble protests which he ignored. She could tell he was very concerned and that moved her.

As she was helped into the front seat of his car she said, "Sir, my gear... in a kit bag. Please get it."

She hard him say yes but then slumped down in the seat and relaxed, barely aware that the seat belt was being buckled around her.

Safe! she thought, then passed out.

Barbara came to in bed. It was daylight. *Late afternoon,* she decided from the angle at which the sun's rays were streaming in the window. *My own bed!* she noted, a great feeling of relief welling up. *Pyjamas!* she realized with mild surprise. As she never wore them she had to wonder who had given her a bath and changed her clothes. *Dad I suppose,* she mused.

She lay there for a while, just being glad to be alive and at home. Then the need to go to the toilet drove her to get up. That hurt. Every muscle felt like it had been flailed with a rubber hose and was stiff and sore. She groaned and sat up, then limped to the door. Using the walls for support she made it to the toilet.

As she came out her father appeared, attracted by the sound of the flushing. "Bubs!" he cried, hurrying to hug her. "Are you alright?"

"Yes," she croaked. "What time is it?"

"Twenty past three."

"I mean, what day?"

Her father gave her a very odd look and then said, "Monday."

Barbara nodded and tried to pin all the days together. She found that too hard so asked for a drink. Seated on the sofa with a cold fruit juice she asked, "What happened?"

Again her father gave her an odd look. "I was hoping you might be able to answer that," he said. Then he leaned across and picked up a dusty green beret with a silver winged badge on it. The sight of that was too much for Barbara. The horrible memories flooded back and she began to sob. Her father moved to put his arm around her. For half an hour he just sat and held her while she cried herself out.

At last Barbara wiped her tears and sat up to sip at the drink. "So what happened?" she asked.

"Major Conkey appeared at the back door with you in his arms and muttered about keeping it secret. I gave you a bath—sorry—then put you to bed. Then we unpacked your gear and tried to put two and two together," her father replied. He nodded towards the beret, then picked up the spent cartridge case. "And there was this. Plus your uniform, all filthy and torn and full of scorch marks. You've had a bad time haven't you little Bubs?"

Barbara nodded. She bit her lip and said, "I will tell you all about it but I want to tell Major Conkey too, so could you ask him to come over?"

"He is doing that. We decided that at daybreak this morning when he took himself off home. He said he would be back straight after school. We will wait for him. Would you like a feed while you wait?"

Barbara wanted drinks mostly. She sat there and sipped them all the while turning the brass cartridge case over and over in her fingers. As she did she was assailed by the terrible memories. Major Conkey arrived ten minutes later and was shown in by her father. He asked Barbara how she was and gave her a very quizzical look.

Pointing to the beret he said, "French Foreign Legion Parachute Regiment."

Barbara nodded. Major Conkey seated himself and was served a cup of coffee. He then said, "If you don't think I should know anything then I will go away."

Shaking her head, Barbara replied, "I don't want you to risk getting into trouble sir. But if you are going to keep me in your cadet unit you must know the story. If you then think that you must tell the authorities then do so."

Major Conkey nodded and did not directly reply. Instead he picked up the cartridge case and sniffed it. "Fired recently. Five point five six millimetre, but not Australian or American. You wouldn't know anything about some very strange goings-on at Dotswood over the last few days would you? Like fighting with fanatics from Dagestan, or two Blackhawks being shot down?"

At that Barbara burst into tears, overwhelmed by the horror of it all. The two men comforted her and then gently coaxed the story out of her. After she had calmed down a bit she was able to marshal her thoughts and relate the details in order, only breaking into tears when she mentioned the legionnaire dying, or shooting at the Dags (She could not admit, even to herself, that she might have actually killed someone).

Both men were appalled and amazed. For Barbara it was very revealing when she admitted she had spent the night in a motel room with Raoul. "But we didn't do anything Dad," she added.

Instead of being angry her father just nodded and smiled. "He's a good man that. So what happened next?"

Expecting more drama over that revelation left Barbara a bit flat so she said, "He wants to see me again."

"Good," her father replied. "He is welcome."

"He has asked me to spend a holiday with him in Tahiti," she added, trying to spark a reaction.

Again her father nodded and smiled. "I can imagine that. Do you want to go?"

"If you will let me."

"You must decide Bubs. I am sure you know best. Anyway, in a month's time you will be eighteen. You are an adult then and can do what you like," her father said.

Major Conkey, who had been listening to the conversation with obvious embarrassment, said, "It sounds like she knows how to look after herself." Then he shook his head in disbelief. Ticking points off on his fingers he said, "Shot at; rescued from the Dags by Americans, flown out to an American aircraft carrier, flown back, ran away from the police, hiked over the mountains, picked up by a French aircraft, parachuted into the night, sneaking cross-country with a patrol of the Foreign Legion; finding the satellite, having several battles with the Dags, and shooting at them, saving people from the crashed helicopter, being flown out in a French helicopter to one of their ships, then helicoptered to a nuclear submarine, then snuck ashore in a rubber boat. Heavens above! There are regular soldiers who don't achieve that in twenty years of service—and you have done it all in a week."

Barbara could only nod. Now she was deeply worried. "What should I do sir? Should I tell our security people?"

"Only if they ask and have evidence," Major Conkey replied. "Tell them you did it under duress and leave out most of the details."

"I'm glad I did it!" Barbara wailed, thinking of Raoul and the legionnaires. But then she thought of the bullets striking the Dags and of burying the bodies and she shuddered and sobbed for a few minutes. After she had calmed down again she asked, "Should we go away, change our names and so on in case the Dags come back for revenge?"

Again Major Conkey shook his head. "I don't think so. It said on the radio news as I drove over that there has been a revolution in Dagestan. This business in Australia obviously precipitated some sort of power struggle and they are fighting themselves. I did hear that the Security Ministry had been burnt by a rioting mob. I think you are safe from them."

"Can I stay in Cadets sir?"

At that Major Conkey put back his head and laughed. "Of course! I think you are the best CUO I have ever had. I want you to stay, and we will help you get over the trauma of this as well as we can. We are your friends and you need us now."

That brought the tears and Barbara had to give Major Conkey a hug. Then she changed the subject to ask what had happened to Willy. Major Conkey did not know. She did not find that out until the next day at chool. To her immense relief Willy was alright. He just said the police were annoyed but had not charged him. He and all her other friends all knew that something dramatic had happened but she told them nothing. That was the hardest part—saying nothing. It drove a bit of a wedge between her and Roger, he saying she did not trust him, and she feeling guilty because she had not told him about Raoul. Soon after that she broke off the relationship with Roger, saying she just wanted to be friends.

Perhaps Raoul will forget me as a silly little schoolgirl? she thought.

But he didn't. The letters and then the phone calls began and she was delighted and answered them all. In the Summer holidays, after the Cadet Promotion Course and Christmas, she went to New Caledonia for a two week holiday. But what she and Raoul did during it is their business and very private. Suffice to say that the romance prospered and Barbara began the new year wondering if she would marry him, and what names the children would have.

Also, while she was in New Caledonia, she was the Guest of Honour at a military parade. This came as a quite unexpected surprise, even though she had been a guest at the barracks Officers Mess on several occasions with Raoul. On the day of the parade Raoul had just asked her in an off-hand way if she would join him. Assuming they would just be spectators she had demurred, on the very feminine principle that she had nothing suitable to wear. This objection was brushed aside by a shopping expedition. Raoul, of course, had worn his dress uniform with medals and all, making Barbara very proud to be with him.

Imagine her surprise on reaching the parade ground to see a battalion of the Foreign Legion on parade, resplendent in their dress uniform of khaki, with the bright red epaulets and the famous white kepis. Her surprise was increased when she was led forward and introduced to the general who was the Reviewing Officer. When, after he had bowed low and kissed her hand in true Gallic style, she was requested to walk with him during the inspection of the parade she was dumbfounded.

The inspection got her all weepy and nostalgic because standing among the legionnaires, grinning at her, were her comrades in arms: Tran, Cpl Martini, Cpl Lamertine, Cpl Fouchet, Tribunga and Mendoza, now recovered from his wounds. S-Lt de Blainville stood sword in hand in front of his company and a be-medalled Sgt Blomburg was one of the escorts to the regimental colours.—a post of great honour, the dignity of which he imperilled by winking at her. What really got her embarrassed was the fact that all those male eyes followed her—yet she also realized that they all knew the story.

The battalion then marched past in review and Barbara was astonished by their strange, slow marching pace. Knowing from bitter experience just what good soldiers the legionnaires were really got her emotional. She was mightily impressed and very, very moved. To see all those tough men moving in perfect cadence and rhythm brought her out in goose bumps.

There was then a presentation of honours and awards. To her even greater astonishment and enormous pride she was led out in front of all of them. The general made a speech of thanks for all she had done, stressing the fact that she had done the night parachute jump under combat conditions and without training. The lieutenant colonel commanding the parachute regiment then presented her with a set of parachutist's 'wings', bestowed in the usual French manner with kisses on both cheeks.

Next the general told the assembly how she had guided the patrol, offered important local advice, been the first to spot the enemy on several occasions, then fought bravely beside the others, several times saving the lives of individuals. The fact that she rescued Mendoza under fire was made much of, as was her leading the attack on the Dags to rescue the survivors of the helicopter crash. The word 'heroine' was used half a dozen times, making her squirm with embarrassment and pride.

With that the general pinned on a medal: the *Croix de Guerre*. As the citation read it was for rewarding and distinguishing individual feats of arms; in this case for her courageous rescue of Legionnaire Mendoza while under fire from the enemy. Barbara was almost overcome with emotion but managed to keep a stiff upper lip.

"Unfortunately," the general said, "you may never be able to wear this on your own country's uniform, unless some diplomatic understanding is reached." He also pointed out that Australia owed her a medal for her heroic actions in saving many lives during the Blackhawk crashes. "But as she was not officially there, she will probably never receive one."

The medal presented (and both cheeks again kissed) Barbara had to stand on the dais to receive a 'present arms' by the battalion. That got her all blushing and emotional as well. The CO then marched forward and handed her a brand new kepi and informed her she was now *un legionnaire honoraire.* To her astonishment the battalion then cheered her—and seemed to mean it.

There were other awards as well. All the members of the patrol, including Raoul, received a *Croix de Guerre* as well. Standing with them and feeling their good-wishes, made Barbara feel very proud and affectionate towards them. Later there was a dinner in the Officers Mess and Barbara was made to feel very welcome. She sat between the general and the CO of 2REP and found it all fascinating.

Towards the end of the holiday Raoul hinted at marriage but then Barbara got scared. She said that she thought she was still too young but she would think about it. They agreed to stay in touch and to meet again during her next holiday if they could. With much emotion and many tears and kisses they parted and she flew back to Australia.

And they did meet again—but that is another story.[6] And did she suffer for her actions? Yes, both in her conscience and through nightmares, but also by having her application to become an officer in the Australian Army rejected 'without explanation.'

"Try again next year," she was advised—so she planned to do just that, and in the meantime she stayed on with cadets.

But there were private indications that some people appreciated her efforts. A note from Major Hammer thanked her for saving his life and offered his help if she needed it at any future time. One thing that niggled at her was not answered for some years: why had the Americans not been able to locate the satellite after she had given them the exact Grid Reference? She learnt this seven years later from the then Lt Colonel Green when she met him as an officer of the Army Reserve. It transpired that the map they were using had a different grid system. Hers had been drawn to an old Australian Grid from 1966 while their GPS system had been set on the newer WGS, placing everything a few hundred metres north and on the other side of the Mingela Road.

---

[6] Read *Barbara on the Beach* by C.R. Cummings

FINIS